TO THE DEATH!

Shouting war cries, goblins rushed them in two directions, carrying shields and brandishing long thrusting spears. Good. Their armament of throwing spears seemed used up. Their faces, masked with white warpaint, gleamed in the moonlight. When two of them rushed Feathergrass, he dodged to one side, ducked under and closed in, too close for them to get a good thrust. One swing of his sword struck the head of the one on his right.

Good! That one fell dead. . . .

Ace Books by Carl Miller

DRAGONBOUND
THE WARRIOR AND THE WITCH
THE GOBLIN PLAIN WAR

THE GOBLIN PLAIN WAR

CARL MILLER

ACE BOOKS, NEW YORK

This book is an Ace original edition,
and has never been previously published.

THE GOBLIN PLAIN WAR

An Ace Book / published by arrangement with
the author

PRINTING HISTORY
Ace edition / May 1991

ISBN: 0-441-29430-8

Ace Books are published by The Berkley Publishing Group,
200 Madison Avenue, New York, New York 10016.
The name "ACE" and the "A" logo
are trademarks belonging to Charter Communications, Inc.

PRINTED IN THE UNITED STATES OF AMERICA

10 9 8 7 6 5 4 3 2 1

AUTHOR'S NOTE

These are the books of the history of humans east of the sea. Each one, though part of this history, tells a complete story in itself.

The Warrior and the Witch, previously published, which takes place between the 194th and 199th year, begins the story of the fall of Newport, telling how Rockdream the Warrior and Coral the Witch lead a small group of refugees to safety when the dragon Riversong attacks the city.

This book, *The Goblin Plain War*, which takes place between the 199th and 202nd year, concludes the fall of Newport, telling how General Canticle's army of refugees attempts to conquer Goblin Plain, how the goblins resist, and how Coral the Witch and Drakey the High Shaman help both peoples find a new peace.

Dragonbound, previously published, which takes place mostly in the 203rd year, tells the story of Periwinkle and Bellchime, a warrior and storyteller dragonbound to the young dragon Distance, who plan to battle the dragon Riversong when Distance reaches majesty, but are forced into this battle much sooner.

A fourth book is in preparation.

CONTENTS

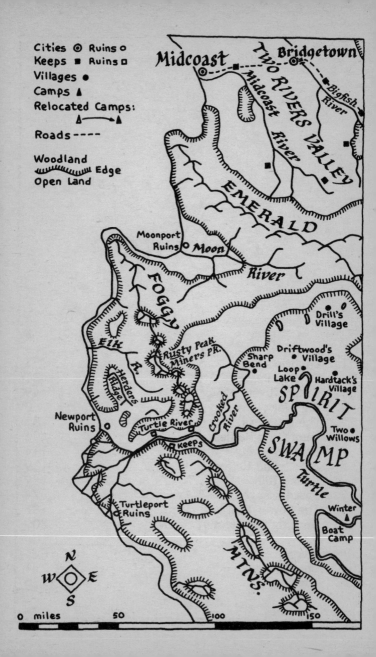

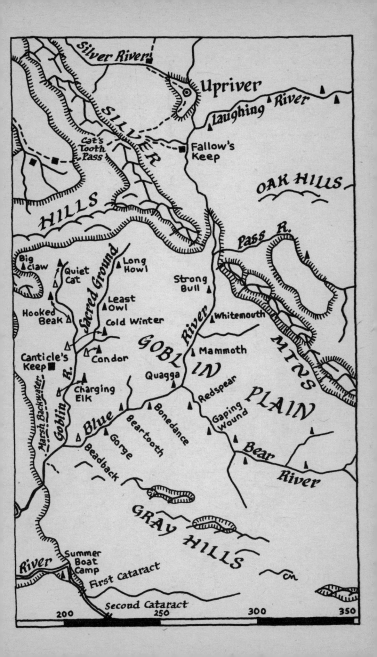

1

CANTICLE'S KEEP

1.

Coral was shaking Rockdream's shoulder.

"What is it?" he mumbled, opening his eyes to darkness. For the first time that night, he heard no sign of rain outside the hut.

"I had a bad dream," she said. Coral was a witch, and often her dreams came true. Indeed, her dreams about the dragon Riversong had saved their lives.

"Can I have a moment to wake up?" Rockdream asked.

She snuggled close to him. "I saw the river," she began, speaking softly so that her voice would not rouse Wedge, their one-and-a-half-year-old son, who was sleeping in his cradle. "It looked very much like the Blue River at Beartooth's Camp, but it was smaller."

"The Goblin River?" Rockdream asked.

"Probably. I am certain I would recognize the place. I dreamed it more clearly than ever before. I was walking through a battlefield, with hundreds of bodies, both human and goblin. The condors and ravens flapped away when I walked close. A few goblin women were also searching there, singing a mourning

1

chant. They saw me, but I began chanting with them, and then they ignored me. When I saw—saw your body, I woke up."

"Why would you be dreaming that?" asked Rockdream. "I remember you having similar dreams years ago, when I was standing dragonwatch in Canticle's Tower, but why now?"

"Please, not so loud," Coral whispered.

"Sorry."

"I think my dream means that Canticle's refugees either are, or soon will be, fighting a war on Goblin Plain, and you are in real danger of becoming involved."

"Canticle's plan of conquest is totally dishonorable," Rockdream said. "I will not join his army no matter what."

"Is that a promise?"

"How many times must I say it?"

"Just hold me. I am sorry. It seemed so real—"

Coral drifted back to sleep soon enough, but Rockdream lay awake wondering. He did not like to be reminded of General Canticle and the main group of Newport refugees. In their opinion he was likely a coward and a deserter. But Rockdream did live in a hidden village on a lake with no outlet in the middle of a vast trackless swamp. Likely no one outside even knew he was still alive. Sometimes Coral was frightened by dreams of no immediate importance. He hoped this dream was one of those.

2.

When Rockdream woke, the hut's translucent parchment windows were dappled with sunlight. He was alone. He dressed hurriedly, for it was cold, and stood outside where the winter sun shone on his platform. About half the people in the village were doing laundry by the main fire. Rockdream jumped to the ground. "Who is hunting today?" he asked Salmon.

"Swanfeather went out with Ironweed and Stonewater," she replied.

"They will not get much."

"Why say that?" asked Salmon. "Why not instead remember the first time you went out with your own archery teacher and brought back something big?"

"Well, just in case they do not—"

Flatfish said, "Bloodroot and I are taking the skiff to do some serious fishing."

"Where is Coral?" Rockdream asked.

"She went out to dig tubers. She said she would be a while," said Birdwade, whose four-year-old daughter, Ripple, was the only child besides Wedge in the village. The children who had fled the city with the other groups of refugees had not survived to reach Loop Lake.

"Did she go out alone with Wedge? I wish she would not do that."

"Stop being so protective," said Salmon. "She has her bow and quiver, and her aim is on the mark often enough."

Birdwade suggested, "You might be able to see them if you walk down to the shore."

Rockdream sighed. "Coral can worry all she wants about *my* life being endangered, but I cannot persuade her to take the simplest precautions herself."

"Did Coral dream something about you?" asked Salmon.

"Oh, she had that dream about finding my body on a battlefield on Goblin Plain, of all unlikely things."

Salmon took a deep breath. "We all know just how many of Coral's bad dreams have come true, or would have, had we not taken action."

Birdwade nodded agreement.

"There is a difference between relevant dreams and dreams of things remote to us," Rockdream said.

"This is true," Salmon admitted.

Flatfish and Bloodroot loaded the skiff with the big net, two small nets, four lidded baskets, and a package of old deer guts for bait.

"This will be easy, now that most of the river lizards have moved to the backwater," Bloodroot said. "There is nothing like catching fish on the lake on a cool sunny day. I love it."

"I might agree if your bait stank less," said Rockdream.

"The more it stinks, the more the fish like it, or so Mom and Dad always told me," Flatfish said. "But you are a hunter. Why you would rather tromp through the muck and mire that passes for land around here—mile after mile, hour after hour—when you could be sitting comfortably on the water, is a mystery to me. But I thank you for doing so. I like the taste of pork and venison just fine, and the guts make good bait." He gave Rockdream a wink.

"Salmon, come, let us give them a good push," Rockdream said.

"We might go all the way to the long end," Bloodroot said. "It would be good to try our nets as far from the village as we can go, while the weather gives us the chance."

Salmon kissed Bloodroot goodbye; he climbed into the skiff behind Flatfish, and she and Rockdream pushed it into the water. Rockdream scanned the shore in both directions, but he could not see Coral and Wedge. Slowly the skiff moved away from shore.

3.

Not long after noon Coral returned, carrying a tired Wedge in one arm, her bow and quiver in the other, and a lidded basket packed full with greens and tubers on her back. "By tomorrow, if it stays clear, the morels and puffballs should start popping up," she told Rockdream, who was sitting by the fire cleaning and oiling his sword and their knives. Salmon and Frond were making bone arrowheads, and Limpet was weaving a basket.

"I wish you would take someone else with you when you leave the village," Rockdream said.

Coral sighed. "I think we were in little danger. We have lived and hunted long enough at Loop Lake for the leopards and drakeys to learn fear of us."

"Even so, how can you dig tubers, keep Wedge away from the itchwort, and watch for leopards and drakeys all at once?"

"I am a mother," she said, as if that explained everything. "We took turns doing what we needed to do. When it was Wedge's turn to explore and play, I gave him full attention. When it was my turn to gather food, he gave me full attention, and tried to help. We do fine with each other."

"I gladly would have gone with you."

"I needed to think about things."

"You mean that dream?"

"I mean *not* that dream. I needed to think about other things—swamp cabbage, and corms, and Wedge's needs."

"That is not Flatfish's skiff!" Salmon said abruptly, and they all turned their heads to watch the small boat beyond the cypresses. No one new had come to the village for several months, and no one but Flatfish and Swanfeather had ever come by water.

"It looks like a goblin canoe," said Rockdream.

"A big one, long enough for five, but I see only two," said Salmon.

Rockdream whistled like a bird, and was answered by a knock like a woodpecker's. Good. Magpie was on guard, ready to shoot to kill if the strangers proved enemies. This precaution had not yet proved necessary, and everyone hoped it never would. Better not to think about it too much. One of those goblins might be a shaman.

"Those are humans," Coral said. "No goblin would paddle that way, and also, the one at the stern is blond."

Both were wearing bulky clothes, so it was not possible to guess their sex until they drew closer. Then, they recognized the tall one with stringy blond hair as the mariner Feathergrass, whose late wife, Loon the Minstrel, had earned herself a place in Lord Herring's court. The stern-faced woman was Fledgeling, a warrior from Canticle's Tower.

"They are bringing a summons from Canticle," Coral said. "I am sure of it."

"I will not join his army," said Rockdream.

"Nor will I," said Salmon.

"Land, hello!" shouted Feathergrass. "We come in peace, with a message from Lord Drill of Newport and General Canticle, for Rockdream the Warrior and Coral the Witch."

"Oh, death," muttered Coral.

"He said message, not summons," said Rockdream.

"It will make little difference."

Wedge pointed at the canoe, saying, "Bo-ya, bo-ya!"

"Boat," Coral corrected.

"Boad. Boat. Boat on bee!" he said.

"Yes, the boat is on the beach."

"Welcome to Loop Lake Village," Rockdream was saying. "Come back with us to the fire. The sun is cold today."

"Not when you are bundled up and paddling," said Feathergrass. "Good to see you again. And Wedge is already talking!"

"Loop Lake?" Fledgeling asked. "This is Hook Lake."

"Hush," Feathergrass whispered.

"I thought no one else knew it was here," said Rockdream. "Someone named it?"

"You live here, so call it what you will," said Feathergrass.

Fledgeling said, "When my grandfather on my mother's side was a young sailor, this was a bend in the river. A flood changed its course, leaving behind this lake. He told me about it when I was a squire. I took my warrior's test right over there, on the peninsula."

From the main fire, four of the village's eight huts were visible. "How many live here?" Feathergrass asked casually.

"Let us come to the real point of your visit," Coral said. "You have been our friend, and Fledgeling has been Rockdream's friend, but you are bringing a message from Canticle, to call us to his service. I will tell you right now, his plan to conquer Goblin Plain is an abomination to me!"

"Your perception of the general's plan is inaccurate," Fledgeling said. "Yes, we have built a settlement on the rise between Goblin Plain and the marsh, but it is well out of their way and even out of their sight. Game is plentiful. High Chief Strong Bull has no real cause to threaten war. We are doing all we can to negotiate peace."

"Has swamp sickness struck your village?" Feathergrass asked Coral.

"No."

"You are very lucky. Nearly eight hundred Newport humans, including five hundred children, died of it last summer. Most people who had objected to building a settlement on Goblin Plain changed their minds after that."

"Strong Bull is threatening war, but each time an incident occurs that might provoke its start, he finds a reason to back down," Fledgeling said. "This suggests he would rather negotiate peace."

"Or else he needs more time to prepare," Rockdream suggested.

"Maybe, but the delay is more to our advantage than his," said Fledgeling. "All the warriors that Strong Bull could muster from all over Goblin Plain would not equal our numbers. The goblins have the advantage only because they are better fighters. Some of the older ones have battle experience from the wars between camps that were fought before Strong Bull became high chief. Many of our people are not skilled warriors yet, but we are training them, and they are quickly getting better."

"I will speak honestly," said Feathergrass. Both sides want to delay the war. For the goblins, waiting till summer means that the animals will crowd closer to the rivers. Easier hunting means more time for fighting. We timed our construction with this in mind, to give ourselves the most time to negotiate peace."

"And to finish construction with minimal interference," said Rockdream.

"We want peace, and High Shaman Drakey also wants peace, even though he has dreamed a goblin victory," said Feathergrass.

"That is interesting," said Coral. "I have also dreamed that the goblins will win the war."

Fledgeling quickly covered her look of alarm with a warrior's scowl. "Is that what you want?" she asked.

"No, of course not," said Coral. "I do not want this war to happen at all."

"Then help us prevent it," said Feathergrass. "You and your husband have a special understanding of goblins from living at Beartooth's Camp. In fact, Drakey says that he chose you both and taught you his people's traditions so that you could help us negotiate an acceptable peace. You see, he dreamed about the dragon, the human settlement, and the coming war, years ago."

"Are you saying that both Canticle and Drakey want us to serve them as impartial diplomats?" Rockdream asked.

"Well, they both want your help," said Feathergrass. "Canticle had no idea where you were or whether you were alive. Drakey told him where to find you. He described this village and this lake, which Fledgeling knew from her warrior's test, so here we are."

Rockdream looked at Coral. "Finding a peace that will satisfy both Canticle and Strong Bull will not be easy."

"It may be impossible," she replied. "I suspect that Canticle has additional reasons of his own for summoning us."

"But I do not see how we can honorably refuse this request."

"We must be very careful about what we agree to do," said Coral. "Canticle must understand that we will not join his settlement. I must heed the warning of my dream. We are impartial diplomats from Loop Lake who have come at the request of both sides."

"Are you denying your Newport citizenship?" asked Fledgeling.

"Yes," said Coral. "We are citizens of Loop Lake Village, and we will return here."

Fledgeling snorted. "Well, so be it. How soon can you leave?"

"As soon as we can pack," said Coral.

"When will you return?" asked Salmon, who had been quietly listening to the whole conversation.

"Strong Bull has given us till spring to settle the issue," said Feathergrass.

"—which likely means the dark moon nearest the equinox," said Rockdream. "Look for us a few days after that at the latest."

4.

Rockdream and Coral took turns holding Wedge and helping Fledgeling and Feathergrass paddle the canoe through the backwater streams. This route was shorter than the river, with no strong current to paddle against, and safer. Some of the Goblin River camps wanted war, and might kill them or take them captive if they recognized them as humans.

Wedge was fussy and restless the whole journey. He did not like sitting still in the canoe, and whenever they had to make a portage or stop for the night, he wanted to investigate everything. By the afternoon of the third day, even Coral was losing patience with him. When they came out of the cypresses and willows onto the reed-choked waters of the marsh, Fledgeling told her, "You must keep him quiet now, and silent when we reach the other side."

"I understand," she said. She had done this three seasons ago when her family fled the city, but now, with Wedge older and more active, it was difficult.

They continued paddling through dusk, toward the rising round moon. Nowhere was it dry enough to camp. "We are too far south," Fledgeling said when they neared the edge. "The rise is the wrong shape, and much too low."

"Keep Wedge quiet," said Feathergrass. "There may be goblins nearby."

"He is asleep," Coral whispered.

"Then help us paddle," said Fledgeling.

They paddled north without talking. Rockdream was not used to thinking of goblins as enemies to be avoided, and did not like the thought. In some places, the reeds and cattails were so tall that they could not see any distance at all, and in other places, they crossed open pools, completely exposed to any watching eyes. The moon was almost overhead when Fledgeling finally whispered, "There it is."

Just below the ridge was a straight pale line, a fortification wall, but Rockdream could not tell how big it was or how far away. They grounded the canoe, climbed out and put on their packs, and began walking; about three miles across flat grassland, up a gentle slope, up a steeper slope, closer and closer to the wall.

"Declare yourselves or be shot!" shouted a voice.

"Lieutenant Fledgeling with Feathergrass, mission for Canticle, and these are Rockdream and Coral!"

"This is a bloody fortress," Coral whispered.

"With walls of dirt-blocks and logs. Hardly secure," said Feathergrass.

"Advance to the wall, and look up, so that we may see your faces clearly."

They did so, and then the two guards atop the wall, which was only twelve feet high but topped with a breastwork of logs, lowered a ladder.

"You have no gate?" Rockdream asked Fledgeling. "If a dragon ever comes here, this keep will be a deathtrap."

"If a dragon comes, we will scatter, but dragons are not our main worry at the moment. Climb the ladder."

Coral went first, carrying Wedge, who was now awake and staring. "Hold still," she said. The top of the wall was about six feet wide. On the inside were crowded many dirt-block buildings, thatched huts, and tents, in more or less regular rows.

"Your name," said one of the guards.

"Coral the Witch, with my son, Wedge, and husband, Rockdream, coming up the ladder."

"Rockdream, what is your occupation?"

"I believe I was brought here as a diplomat. In my own village I am a hunter."

"This is the general's concern," said Fledgeling, coming up the ladder. "We will see him in the morning, unless by chance he is awake at this hour."

"He is off duty. Have you given these people the loyalty oath?" Fledgeling hesitated.

The guard said, "Do you, Rockdream the Hunter and Coral the Witch, swear loyalty to the humans of Newport, to Lord Drill and his family, and to General Canticle?"

"We cannot," said Coral.

"Let me explain," Rockdream said quickly. "Coral and I are free humans of Loop Lake, exiles of Newport, here to serve as impartial diplomats to help negotiate a peace between your people and the people of Goblin Plain. We must be firm about our role here or we have no chance of success. If either Lord Drill or General Canticle judges us unfit for the job, we will return to our home in the swamp."

"I will take responsibility for them," Fledgeling told the guard. "We will report to the general in the morning. Is that understood?"

"Yes, lieutenant."

After they climbed down the inside ladder, Fledgeling led them through the network of narrow streets to the hut that she and

Feathergrass shared with another family. Coral and Rockdream spread their bedding on the floor, lay down with Wedge, and fell into an uncomfortable sleep.

5.

They awoke to the sound of trumpets. The other family was already dressing. "Good to see you back," the older man said to Fledgeling and Feathergrass.

"These are Rockdream and Coral, the general's concern," Fledgeling replied.

"All right, lieutenant. I will not bother you with questions." He looked at the newcomers. "I am Coldrock the Dockhand; my wife is Harmony the Weaver, and our son's name is Forward. Today is our turn to go hunting." They pulled on their boots and coats and went outside.

"We send out at least three hunting groups each day," Fledgeling explained. "We hope to enclose a plot of land big enough to farm, or at least to garden, come spring, which will take the pressure off the wild herds."

"I thought you said game was plentiful," Coral remarked.

"Coldrock and Harmony are old friends of mine," said Feathergrass. "I guess you never met them."

"Shall we go talk to Canticle?" asked Rockdream.

"First we must go to breakfast," Feathergrass said, and when they all were dressed, he passed out bowls. Coral looked at hers dubiously, and wiped it off with her hand-rag.

Outside, the last of the hunters were leading their horses from the stables, up a steep ramp to the top of the wall, and down the outside. At the opposite end of the settlement, hundreds of people, each with a bowl in hand, stood in lines. The breeze shifted, bringing smells of smoke and stew. Feathergrass and his companions took places in one of the lines, and slowly moved toward the serving bench.

The humans of the settlement included people of all ages except small children. But most of them were strong men and women in their twenties and thirties, who may not have been warriors in Newport but were doing their best to be warriors now. Rockdream was surprised at how many Newport people he did not know, even after serving four years as a gate-guard.

"You are new," said the middle-aged woman who ladled stew into Rockdream's bowl. "Who are you?"

Rockdream hesitated after giving his name. "I am a diplomat from Spirit Swamp."

"You look like a warrior to me. More real warriors are what we need most. My name in Endive. Well, move along. Others are waiting. Are you his wife, and with a little one? We do not have many children here. The ones who did not get the sickness are with Lord Drill, or else with the boats. What did you say your name was?"

"Coral, and this is Wedge."

"I will give you a bit extra for the child. Move along. Lieutenant!" she said to Fledgeling. "I was afraid—"

"I am quite alive and well, as is my husband."

"So I see. No one tells me anything, but I know a lot. Is the general really working on a treaty, or just stalling for time? You know what I think? If we attack their camps one at a time, before they have time to group together—"

"Give me my stew and I will move along," Fledgeling said. "Others are waiting."

"All right, all right."

Fledgeling rejoined Rockdream and Coral. "Attack their camps one at a time!" she muttered. "And do what? Kill them all? Take prisoners? Drive them to some other part of the plain, where they will group together? That woman is not the military genius she thinks she is."

Coral was sipping her stew.

"Wanna," said Wedge.

"It is too hot," said Coral. "Let us go back to the hut and get a spoon. Let go of my skirt."

"Wanna," he repeated.

"What do you want?" she asked.

"Wanna mih. Wanna mih."

"Hold this a minute," Coral said, handing Rockdream her bowl of stew. "You want some milk?" she asked, opening the top of her coat and unlacing her bodice. "Say *milk*. Mm-ill-k."

"M-ill-k. Wanna milk," he said.

"Very good. You can tell me just what you want." She picked him up and held him to her breast. "But you are almost too big for me to do this while I am walking."

Back at the hut, Rockdream got spoons from his pack, and they sat on the straw-covered floor, sipping stew. Even though Coral blew on the spoonfuls she offered Wedge, either it was too hot for him or else he just did not like it. "No stew!" he said.

6.

General Canticle's hut was no larger than Fledgeling's, but it had a solid wooden door with bronze hinges, and a table with benches inside, and he had it all to himself. He was seated with a lamp and a map spread out showing all of Goblin Plain, with camps marked by small triangles and the dirt-block fortress by a square. He dismissed Fledgeling and Feathergrass. After they closed the door behind themselves, the hut became warm, for he had a small fire in the hearth. Rockdream and Coral removed their coats and Wedge's, and at first the toddler quietly explored the room while they talked.

"I was told you refused the loyalty oath," Canticle said. "I want to know why. And spare me the nonsense about you being more effective as impartial diplomats. To Strong Bull you are humans of Newport no matter what you say."

"A loyalty oath can mean many things," Rockdream said. "I will serve you as an impartial diplomat. I will not serve you as a warrior. I disagree with your evident belief that might makes right."

"Bah!" said Canticle. "If you do not believe that might makes right, go back to Newport and argue with Riversong about it. Let me know if you win the argument."

"If he is your standard of honor, we have nothing to discuss."

"If he was my standard of honor, I would have sent warriors disguised as messengers to kill Strong Bull and his chiefs, or else I would have massacred their camps one by one before they knew what was happening. No, Riversong is not my standard of honor. He did what he did because he is fierce and Newport was a challenge. Did you know he is guarding both Newport and Moonport now?"

"Really? I have never heard of a dragon doing anything like that."

"My scouts have seen him both places. I was curious. You see, I have been looking for a place to settle and support all these humans. This is the only place. The coast is Riversong's. Spirit Swamp is disease-ridden in the summer, which is why it was unclaimed. Up the Turtle River, the land is desolate or inhabited by goblins whose life is marginal. And other human settlements would each only accept a few of us as bonded servants."

"And here you face war with former friends," said Rockdream.

"I would not quite call them friends. The process of building an alliance with them was hardly begun when Newport was destroyed. But they do know us, and may prove more tolerant of our imposition on them than you suppose." Canticle pointed to the square on his map and said, "If we build a city right where we are, we will not really be in their way. We are a problem to them now only because we are hunting their herds. Once we lay out farms, between this ridge and the backwater, we will hunt much less. Eventually, we can prospect for metals in the Emerald Hills, or even the west front of the Silver Mountains."

Wedge was standing on the opposite bench beside Coral, reaching for the map.

"Watch him!" said the general.

Coral grabbed Wedge's hands gently and pulled them back. "*No*. You must not touch. This is like a book."

"Book?"

"This is a *map*. Do not touch. Play with this instead." She reached into her coat pouch and brought out a soft leather ball.

"Eventually your city will amass enough wealth to attract a dragon," Rockdream was saying. "Then you will be right back where you were last spring."

"I have given that much thought, but before I say more, I must know that I can trust you both to keep a secret."

"I already know what you have in mind," said Coral. "I can hear your thoughts especially well when you want something from me. No, I do not believe that the stormweaving attempted by my mother and her friends can be developed into a practical defense against dragons. I would not want anyone to even try it."

"Had they been allowed to practice their skill—"

"Canticle, lightning is lightning. In sorcery, there is no practice sword."

His eyes met hers for a moment, then he said, "You yourself have practiced some."

"Oh," Coral said, realizing—

"Yes, I can also hear some of *your* thoughts."

"I always thought you had some talent for that," she said.

"You never told me you practiced stormweaving," said Rockdream.

"When I was Treeworm's lover, when I was twelve. He did not teach me lightning, only wind and clouds."

"But you felt with your body how it could be done, and you were frightened," said Canticle.

"That is not your concern!"

"Anything that might kill a dragon is my concern. Perhaps if you can consider this without childish fright or grief for your mother's death, you will understand that this knowledge may someday save many human lives."

"Suppose you had such knowledge now. Would you use it against the goblins?" Coral asked. "Do not bother answering. I perceive your uncertainty. But even if you would not, someone else might. Let us stop playing games with each other. Do you truly want peace with Strong Bull, or are you just stalling for time?"

"Whatever works. I would prefer peace."

"You do not understand what peace is," Coral said. "You think of strength, of defense. You comfort yourself with the knowledge that few human keeps, once established, have ever been destroyed by goblins. This is not peace, but truce. Peace comes only with friendship and understanding."

Rockdream said, "If it comes to war, both Drakey and my wife have dreamed your defeat, and as I see the military situation, they are right. Your warriors may be good enough to defend your walls, but I doubt that they could battle an equal number of goblins in the open. How long can you last against a determined siege? The old keeps were established by warriors who were both professional and ruthless, who saw goblins as vermin to be killed. This fortress is a bluff, and the goblins will see through it."

"The goblins are bluffing also, or they would have attacked with force before we could build this fortress."

"Your best hope is that Strong Bull hesitates to make war not only because his preparations are incomplete, but because he has some understanding and sympathy for your predicament," Rockdream argued.

"Or else because even a goblin victory might be very bloody," Canticle said.

Coral glared at him.

"Anger is what wars are made of," he said quietly.

"How soon can we talk to Strong Bull and Drakey?" Coral asked.

"They have left the area for the time being, most likely to organize their army. I hesitate to send messengers to either Cold Winter's Camp or Charging Elk's Camp until they return. Strong Bull is an honorable opponent, but I am less inclined to trust his chiefs. Human messengers have been known to disappear."

"What if Strong Bull's next contact with us is a siege?" asked Rockdream.

"I do have a navy hidden in the swamp," said Canticle. "The goblins do not have the numbers to both set a siege and guard the river. But I do not think a siege is next. But maybe we can send a message. Coral, can you dreamsend?"

"Certainly not to a powerful shaman like Drakey. If I tried to dreamsend him uninvited, I would face a fierce battle in trance with his spirit beast."

"What do you know about spirit beasts?"

"Not very much. A spirit beast is something like a personal deity in the form of an animal."

"How are they—" Canticle began, then said, "You have one. Yours is the condor."

"So the shamaness Glowfly told me. I do not understand this magic well enough to use it. I fear I would have to set aside the Holy family, and I cannot consider doing that."

Wedge was climbing onto the bench again.

"I should find someone to watch him while we talk to the goblins," Canticle said.

"No," said Coral, pulling the toddler onto her lap. "I want him with me then. He may distract me, but he will remind them that we are people, just as they are."

7.

On the evening of the third day that Coral, Rockdream, and Wedge spent in the keep, one group of hunters did not return, and all that night Coral dreamed of war with goblins.

In the cold mist of dawn, a goblin messenger dressed in red stood on the ridge and spoke to the wall guards. "I am Hot Wolf, of Charging Elk's Camp. My chief, high chief, and high shaman wish to speak with your general. I will wait for his answer."

Within minutes, Canticle, Fledgeling, Rockdream, and Coral, carrying a half-awake Wedge, were climbing a ladder to the wall.

"When and where do your leaders wish to meet with me, and what do they want to discuss?" asked Canticle.

"They will meet with you at the double redbark," said Hot Wolf. "They are building a council fire. They will discuss the war between Charging Elk's Camp and your keep."

"I know of no such war, but I will talk. How many warriors will sit on each side?"

"None. They are dressed in red."

"How many people?"

"However many have something to say. Strong Bull, Drakey, Charging Elk, Enemies Run, Bold, and Hot Wolf will speak for Charging Elk's Camp."

"What did you backstabbers do to Capstone and the others?" a wall guard demanded.

"One more outcry like that and you will be guarding a pick and shovel at the latrine," Canticle told the guard. "We speak politely to messengers here." To Hot Wolf, he said, "We will also choose six, and we will come unarmed."

"I will tell them you are coming," the messenger said.

Canticle spent a short time with his six other lieutenants to order command of the keep. The six humans who would speak at the council were General Canticle, Lieutenant Fledgeling, Rock-dream, Coral, and two others: Whitestone the Storyteller, who had served as a diplomat in Canticle's previous meetings with Strong Bull and Drakey; and Iris, a young warrior from his tower in Newport, whose brother was one of Capstone's hunters.

"I consider it a good omen that the meeting place is near a special redbark tree," Coral told Rockdream. "When I went on that trance journey to the center of the world of my heart, I was sitting under the special redbark near Beartooth's Camp."

"That was a happier time," Rockdream said.

"I do not want the memory spoiled by a war. Our peoples can find a way to live together. Let us think of that, and maybe my dreams last night will not come true."

Coral suggested that the embassy walk to the council site, for goblins found riding horses spiritually offensive. Whitestone agreed that the gesture was a good idea, but Canticle was less sure. "A mounted warrior is a powerful presence," he said.

"Mounted warriors just lost a battle," said Rockdream.

Canticle grunted. "All right, I can walk as far as I can ride, but what about your baby?"

"When he gets tired, we can carry him," said Coral.

She and Rockdream carried Wedge most of the way. About halfway there, the mist quickened to a hard rain with blowing wind, but by the time they reached the council fire, the clouds were parting to reveal patches of blue sky.

Six goblin men wearing red leather vests and fur breeches squatted near the fire. Except for Drakey, whose face was wrinkled with wisdom and whose hair was streaked with white, they looked much alike: swarthy, beardless faces with dark eyes, broad noses, full lips; long dark hair, straight or slightly wavy, hooked behind their pointed ears and tied in back with leather strings. They stood up to greet the humans. They were shorter than the human men but taller than Coral.

"This fire is a blessing," she said.

"Ah! The witch and her husband are here, as I said they would be," Drakey said to the man on his right, who had to be Strong Bull. He was not the largest warrior, though he was stout with powerful muscles, but he was the one with the firmest presence, and his eyes were deep and fierce. When the humans settled themselves near the fire, he stared at Canticle for several moments, then spoke:

"Your people and mine are at war. We have lived in peace with you ever since your city was built. That was almost eighty years ago. But now that your city is destroyed, you want to build a new city on our land. Your hunters come too close to our camps, and kill far too many animals. Yesterday, Charging Elk's warriors fought a battle with your people. This time, no one was killed. We took them captive. But the next time your hunters come so close to a camp, we will kill them."

"Where are these captives?" asked Canticle. "I cannot judge them without hearing their story of the battle. I ordered them to stay well away from your camps, as you requested, and also to hunt no more mammoths, as you requested."

Drakey said, "Even if you hunt no mammoths, the way you hunt other animals is like the way you used to hunt turtles. You kill so many that before long the animals will disappear."

Whitestone said, "Once we have our first harvest, we will need to hunt very little."

Strong Bull said, "You do not understand. If you do not leave Goblin Plain, my people will drive you back across the swamp, over the mountains, and into the dragon's fiery jaws."

Canticle said, "If we do not reach a peace agreement soon, my army will overwhelm your camps one by one."

"We are here to speak of peace," said Drakey. "You are both warriors with hot hearts. If you make war with each other, thousands of people will die, both goblins and humans." The old shaman looked at Coral for a moment, then at Canticle. "A human city would upset the spiritual balance of this land forever. We welcome goblins here. Our ancestors welcomed the Elk Coast goblins and the Moon Valley goblins. You should go to a human place. Go to the Two Rivers Valley. Go to Upriver."

"Upriver could not support our numbers," said Canticle. "As for the Two Rivers Valley, the lords there forced the Moonport refugees to sell themselves into bonded servitude, and would do the same to us."

"What is bonded servitude?" Strong Bull asked.

Whitestone explained, "In the Two Rivers Valley, there are so many humans that there is no open land for free hunting and fishing. If a family lacks work and money, they cannot feed themselves and must sell themselves into bonded servitude. They must work for their bondowner, who must feed, clothe, and house them. The contracts can be for five, eight, or fourteen years, during which time the bonded servants can do very little without permission. The women are seldom allowed to bear children, for example, but are forced to chew freedomwort. To them the root belies its name. It is not exactly slavery but it is close enough."

Strong Bull frowned. "To bind the spirit of an enemy captured in battle—even that is bad. To bind the spirit of a refugee who comes to you for help—I cannot imagine a person so mean-spirited, not even a human." He looked at Canticle. "You are too proud a warrior to submit your people to slavery. It is better to fight to the death."

"But why with us?" asked Enemies Run.

"We have the best land," said Charging Elk.

"May I ask something?" said Coral. "Your feelings are so strong that I cannot hear the thoughts behind them. Exactly how would a human city upset the spiritual balance of Goblin Plain?"

"How can a shamaness not know that?" asked Charging Elk, but Drakey answered her question politely.

"Goblins live with the spirit of the land. Humans bind it. You have been many places. You can sense this."

"Yes, I can," Coral agreed. "But even goblin camps bind the spirit of the land to some extent."

"The difference is like that between a light breeze that rustles the leaves and a howling wind that uproots the tree," said Drakey.

"Of what relevance is this?" Iris demanded. "I want to know about my brother and the others. If you disapprove of enslaving captured warriors, when and under what terms will you release them?"

"We can discuss that after we discuss the big problem," said

Strong Bull. "Your people need land. There is no land for humans on Goblin Plain."

"We are here, and we are not leaving," said Canticle.

"What if you had somewhere else to go where you were welcome?" asked Enemies Run.

"Ah," said Drakey.

"There is no such place," said Canticle.

"You know of no such place," said Drakey. "If you had more time, maybe you could find a good place."

"How much time would you offer us?" Canticle asked Strong Bull.

"I will give you three months."

"Just what I thought," Canticle said. "You want to delay the war till spring, when it will be easier for you to fight."

"Bah! You think I am like you. How much time do you think you need?"

"Given the difficulty of our situation, a year might be more reasonable," said Whitestone.

"No."

"In three months Canticle could send diplomats to all the closer human cities and keeps," Whitestone said. "But suppose they all say they will only accept bonded servants? More distant human cities might offer a better welcome."

"I will give you till the last full moon of spring, which is five months from now. Then we can talk again. But I say that you are not welcome here. Do not try to make your city permanent. Do not build stone walls. Do not plant farms. And you must hunt and fish only west of the rise."

"Do you expect us to feed two thousand humans on swamp pigs and catfish?" Fledgeling asked.

"You can trade with us for grain and meat," said Strong Bull.

"Trade you what? Steel weapons to use against us later?" asked Canticle.

Drakey frowned at the human general. "If we cannot trust each other, we cannot make peace. My people have more cause than yours to expect treachery. Humans break treaties and peace circles with goblins whenever they want to. Your settlement is a perfect example. But even so, we have compassion. We offer you time to solve your problem."

"This is an offer well worth considering," said Whitestone.

"I agree," said Rockdream.

"I say it is a good plan," said Chief Charging Elk. "But other chiefs may not agree. We should have a council of chiefs and strong warriors. If we make a big peace, the peace will be true."

"Make a peace circle," said Bold. "If the humans break the circle, then they will have the bad luck."

"No," said Drakey. "It does not matter who breaks the circle. I will not sit a circle that might be broken."

"My people also need time to consider this offer," Canticle said. "Can we discuss the captives now?"

"We will release them as a sign of good faith," Strong Bull said.

8.

Capstone's hunters showed up at the keep, on foot, at dusk that same day. The tale they told about their capture was about what Canticle had guessed: a sudden attack against the horses by about thirty goblin warriors. The humans surrendered almost at once, and the goblins of several neighboring camps came together to feast on the horses.

At the meeting at Canticle's hut that night, most of his lieutenants except Fledgeling at first opposed the peace proposal.

"There are not enough animals on this side of the rise," said Lieutenant Foam.

"We might be able to get Strong Bull to compromise on that, with time," said Whitestone. "The important thing is that he offers us time. I doubt that we can negotiate anything useful with either Upriver or the Valley cities, but it would not hurt to try."

"And the longer we are here, the more the nearby goblins will get used to us, if we do not continue disrupting their economy," Canticle said. "Our embassy to Midcoast at least should be able to obtain some rice seed, which is not my first choice of grain, but it will grow well in the marsh."

"I am not moving back to the bloody swamp," said Lieutenant Graywall.

"We can live here, and hunt and farm in the marsh," Canticle said. "Once we harvest our first crop of rice—"

"Excuse me," Coral said, "but Strong Bull only gave you till the end of spring."

"And then we will talk again," Whitestone said. "Those were his words. You must appreciate the subtleties of diplomacy. First Strong Bull says we must leave immediately or he will make war; now he says he will give us five months, after which we must

discuss the matter again, though we must remember that we are
not welcome here. Do you see? Strong Bull does not really want
war, and putting it off is a good way to avoid it. Once his chiefs
see that we are no problem—and we do have to stop being a
problem for them—we may well be allowed to stay here."

"I do not think Strong Bull has anything of the sort in mind,"
said Coral. "He is doing you a favor, because Newport and Goblin
Plain have always had peace. But if you do not make an honest
attempt to relocate, he will make war."

"That is what he believes now," said Whitestone. "And we will
try to relocate."

"But not if it means selling a single citizen into bonded
servitude," said Canticle.

"I am not certain I agree with you and Strong Bull about bonded
servitude being worse than death in battle," Coral said. "I think it
is not only the servitude you oppose, but any plan that would
scatter your people. You are now lord of the exiles of Newport in
all but name, and you would lose this power. But if you truly want
a place in history as one of Newport's great leaders—"

"I certainly will not get it by selling people into servitude,"
Canticle snapped. "My father, Drydock, was a bonded servant in
Midcoast, from the time he was orphaned at ten until he was
twenty-eight. He is here at this settlement. You can talk to him
about what it was like."

Coral opened her mouth to speak but saw Rockdream's eyes and
thought better of it. All seven lieutenants were staring at her, and
Fledgeling's scowl was the worst. Coral found herself wishing
that Wedge would distract her, but he was sound asleep on the
general's bed.

"My wife meant no offense," Rockdream said.

"Perhaps she knows a former bonded servant whose experience
was not so bad," Whitestone suggested. "Sometimes the relationship is much like that between master and apprentice."

"Not often," said Canticle.

"True."

They continued talking about possible ways to support the
settlement within the proposed restrictions, and when the meeting
ended, Canticle asked Coral to speak with him in private.

"You may go," he told Rockdream, "and the child is asleep, so
let him be. I will not hurt either of them." After Rockdream put
on his coat and left, the general said, "Coral, I want you to know
that I do value your opinions and perceptions, even the ones that

do not flatter me. You force me to be honest with myself. However, I would appreciate it if you would voice these criticisms to me in private. Is this a fair request?"

Coral sighed. "I am sorry. I did restrain myself while we were with the goblins, but—I am sorry. I do not know how to say this, but I have never quite trusted you. In this matter and in everything else you do, your approach seems manipulative."

"Of course it is," said Canticle. "Which would you rather I do, manipulate Strong Bull and Drakey into a reasonable peace, or kill them in battle?"

"I would rather you reach an honest and honorable agreement."

"Would you sell our people into bonded servitude to do this?"

Coral hesitated. "I do not think your plan to make this settlement permanent will work. I think it will lead to war."

"It might, if we are not very careful," Canticle agreed.

"Do you really think that if you keep the exiles together, you will eventually find a way to kill Riversong and regain the city?"

"Someone must find a way to counter his tactics, or other dragons will copy them and within a few years there will be no more cities. Now this peace agreement gives me reason to send diplomats to every city east of the sea. I think that we would most likely find—but correct me if you know better—skilled witches and wizards in Midcoast, Bridgetown, and Rockport. You could be one of my ambassadors."

"No," said Coral.

"Let me show you something." Canticle got up and pulled a sword from behind his bed. "The scabbard does not look like much, but look at this." He drew the sword and laid it on the table.

"What about it?" Coral asked.

"It looks plain at first sight, but Lord Herring wanted it that way. Go ahead and pick it up. See the way the blade reflects the lantern? This is silversteel of the finest grain."

"It does look kind of different, now that you point it out to me," Coral admitted.

"Band the Weaponmaker made it for Lord Herring when he was heir apparent," said Canticle. "Its worth might be several pounds of gold. Not that it is really that much better than any other good sword, but it is rare. You could sell it quickly and quietly in any marketplace for a pound of gold or more. What you do with the gold I will leave to your own imagination. I will give you and Rockdream this sword if you will help me find people of integrity with knowledge and skill. I am offering them an opportunity. They can decide freely whether they want to help me or not."

"Canticle, I am truly sorry," said Coral. "Something about this plan does not feel right to me. I cannot act against my instincts. May I go now?"

"As you wish," said Canticle.

Coral put on her coat and wrapped the blanket snugly around Wedge, who stirred but did not awaken when she picked him up. Outside, a light snow was falling. She hurried to Fledgeling's hut, but paused at the entrance to listen to the argument going on inside.

"You and Coral had nothing to do with the agreement we reached today," Fledgeling was saying. "Whitestone's description of bonded servitude was what changed Strong Bull's mind."

Pulling aside the hide that served for a door, Coral said, "Quite true, but why did no one think to mention bonded servitude before? Canticle had it in mind because Rockdream and I forced him to justify his choices to us. Also, having us in the circle may have put Drakey in a friendlier mood." Coral crossed the room to put Wedge in his sleeping place.

"In other words, your disrespect for the general and friendship with the high shaman made you valuable today," Fledgeling said.

"I will not say anything, but the witch can hear what I think if she wants," said Coldrock.

"Hush," said Harmony.

"Constructive criticism is valuable to a leader," Coral said.

"But Canticle is not your leader!" Fledgeling replied. "You are not humans of Newport, but impartial citizens of nowhere! You are also living in our midst, and privy to secrets that I cannot share with anyone else in this room. But you know what? A loyalty oath from either of you would not be worth spilled blood. You deserted Newport when Riversong came, and you would desert this settlement if it suited you."

"If I swore loyalty to Canticle and this settlement, I would not desert," Rockdream said. "But I will not join an army whose general plans a war of conquest."

"If it does come to war, we will fight to defend the settlement and that is all," said Fledgeling.

"Building this keep was an act of conquest," said Coral.

"Would you have us die of sickness in the swamp, or starve in the southern wasteland, or sell ourselves into servitude?"

"The peace offer was made to give you time to find a better

choice," said Coral. "I was there. Strong Bull's feelings were clear. He wants you out of here. Am I supposed to let Canticle and Whitestone delude themselves when I know better?"

Fledgeling did not answer.

Feathergrass said, "This has been a long day. Let us get some sleep."

9.

The next morning, after standing in line in the snow for breakfast, Coral and Rockdream were summoned back to General Canticle's hut. "I have given this matter much hard thought," he said. "I am sorry, but I no longer need your services as impartial diplomats. If you wish to take part in future peace talks with the goblins, or to continue living in this settlement, you must swear the loyalty oath."

"I think I am showing the survivors of Newport greater loyalty by refusing this oath," Coral said, bouncing Wedge on her knee.

"Is swearing loyalty to the lord, general, and people of the city you were born in such an unreasonable request for me to make? We are in the middle of a very sensitive negotiation, and I am not sure I can trust either of you not to imperil the agreement with your well-meant ideals."

"You are the one who imperils this agreement," said Coral.

"I am also the one who commands this settlement." The general looked at Rockdream. "You said when you refused the loyalty oath that you would return to the swamp if either Lord Drill or I found your services unsatisfactory. I hope I can trust your word on that. If you intend to go to the goblins, I must arrest you for greater treason."

Coral suppressed a shudder. "That charge is unfair!"

Canticle looked at her impassively. "To be impartial diplomats, you must be accepted as such by both sides. I have told you I cannot continue to do this. Therefore you are legally exiles of Newport. If you talk to the goblins, no matter how discreet you try to be, Drakey will hear my secrets in your thoughts. But with your sympathies as they are, I have no reason to believe you will be discreet."

"Drakey is just as likely to overhear your own thoughts," said Coral.

"I can confuse him, as I confused Riversong."

"You brought us here so that I could teach you sorcery."

"I wanted—indeed, I still want—your loyalty and assistance."

Rockdream sighed and shook his head slightly. "I am sorry. I hope our service has been of some use."

"I am sorry that I cannot provide you transport back to Hook Lake."

"What do you mean?" asked Coral.

"You can walk. The best hunting trail across the marsh goes in your direction. Once you reach the swamp, you can build a raft whenever you need to cross water, or a canoe, if you want to take the time."

"Had I ever imagined you would do this to us—"

"People without loyalties must be able to provide for themselves."

"We can and we will, general," Coral said, pronouncing his title with disgust. Rockdream said nothing, but put on his coat.

Outside the snow was ankle-deep and falling wet. "Wedge, stay near me," Coral said when he began running between buildings. The next moment, he slipped, fell, and started to cry. Rockdream scooped him up. "Whoops! You fell down!" Coral told Wedge. "That did hurt a little bit, yes. Snow is slippery and you can fall. But it will stop hurting soon."

Wedge reached for her, and she took him from Rockdream. The snowflakes on her eyelashes made her look very pretty. "I—I guess we did the best we could do," Rockdream said when Wedge calmed down.

Coral sighed. "Let us discuss it when we are safely out of here."

"Was there anything not said aloud that I should know about?"

"I just want to pack and leave. I know this is poor weather for setting out, but—"

"Let us do it."

Inside the hut, they were packing hurriedly when Lieutenant Swordnotch walked in, saying, "I am ordered to see you out of the settlement and on your way at once. Is that hatchet yours?"

"We are taking nothing away that we did not bring here," Coral said firmly.

"Be polite, traitor."

"I do not think I said anything impolite."

"The proper answer is, 'Yes, my lord lieutenant.' "

"If you say so, my lord lieutenant."

"Swordnotch, we are neither traitors nor squires, so stop passing waste and let us pack," Rockdream said. "You want us out of here and so do we."

"Hurry it up."

Outside, sleet fell heavily, melting the trampled snow to slush. Swordnotch marched them not to the west wall but to the horse ramp. "The woodcutters went out this morning," he said. "Follow their trail to the swamp."

They tramped the slush and mud around the settlement and west toward the marsh. As the ground leveled off, the grass became taller, then changed abruptly to a different kind of grass, then to reeds. Sometimes their steps made puddles in the spongy mat of dead reeds underfoot, but their greased boots kept their feet dry. After about a mile of this, the sleet turned back to snow. Ahead they heard horses and voices.

"I want to hide," Coral whispered. "Squat down over there."

"But why?"

"Do it! We have no time to argue."

"But our footprints—"

"I am a witch, remember? Move!"

They stepped aside into taller and taller reeds, leaving a path that anyone could have seen, but when Coral squatted, holding Wedge on her lap, and began chanting silently, it looked less obvious. Rockdream squatted beside her. Through the reeds, he counted eighteen pack horses loaded with bundles of sticks and wood, each led by a woodcutter. Eventually the voices and tramping faded away, but they waited a few minutes more before returning to the trail.

"I did not know you could hide footprints with a glimmer," Rockdream said.

"I can if I am nearby, and the people I am trying to fool are not looking for footprints."

"We did take a chance. Why did you want to hide from them?"

Coral smiled. "When Canticle asks them if they saw us, they did not, and now their trail obliterates ours. Let him worry and wonder about where we went. He might be more honest the next time he talks to Strong Bull and Drakey."

10.

The snow was again ankle-deep when they reached the edge of the trees, where the woodcutters had done their work. Gusts of wind began to blow. "Making a fire will not be easy tonight, and we must have one," Rockdream said grimly.

"We will find plenty of wood farther along."

"By the time we walk another mile, it will be dark. Is Wedge asleep?"

Coral turned so that Rockdream could see the toddler's face. "Drowsy and quiet. Snow is white, tree trunks are dark, and any flooded ground will also be dark. We will be able to see well enough. On we go."

The snow itself was not so cold, but the wind was sharp, and the leafless alders and willows were no protection. Suddenly they reached the edge of the woodcutters' penetration, and saw dim shapes of brush, and dry dead branches on the bigger alders and pines.

"I want a big fire," Coral said. "If I get comfortable enough, I might be able to do something about this weather. Stopping a storm is more difficult than starting one, but—first thing first." She took off her pack and placed Wedge, who was asleep and wrapped snugly in a blanket, on top of it, then started breaking off dead branches. Rockdream removed the hatchet from his own pack and chopped off larger branches.

Working carefully with her sparker, dry straw, and pitch, Coral worked up a glow that caught fire on the alder twigs. "Get more small stuff," she told Rockdream.

"It looks good," he said a few moments later.

"It may not be so easy to keep it going."

Indeed, the gusts of wind whipped the flame around, and twice almost snuffed it out. It was quite a while before they had a fire hot and steady enough to kindle solid wood.

"It is getting lighter," Rockdream said. "The moon must be up."

"Maybe the clouds are thinning also. I should get to work on that. Keep the fire hot and do not disturb me. My mind must become absolutely peaceful."

Coral sat on Rockdream's pack facing the fire and began chanting the Canticle of Peace:

> The stream flows into the lake.
> The voice falls silent.
> The murmur of thought is suspended.
>
> Nothing is greater than peace.
> All things return to peace.
> Nothing is more blissful than peace.
> All things return to peace.

Nothing is truer than peace.
All things return to peace.
Nothing is more real than peace.
All things return to peace.

Peace is the acceptance, the surrender.
Peace is the end of doing, the dormant.
Peace is the end of thinking, the silent.
Peace is the void.
All things return to peace.

Peace is the void!—beyond life and death, beyond General
Canticle's folly and Coral's own folly, beyond the fire warming
her face and the wind chilling her back, beyond the inspiration that
the Canticle of Peace might serve as a spell to calm the storm. In
the void, Coral was nothing, the storm was nothing, everything
was nothing.
I am nothing.
Nothing is everything.
Everything is divine.
I am Wind the Hunter, first daughter, skin pale as snow, lying
naked on a bed of clouds with brother lover Thunder the King,
swarthy black-haired first son, whose caresses are wild and
passionate, whose words are stern and thoughtful.
I am laughter, playing with goddesses and gods to change the
pattern.
Peace is the end of doing, the dormant. A stream gushes toward
my womb. Peace is the end of thinking, the silent. Gentle kisses.
Nothing is more blissful than peace. I am nothing.
After a timeless time, Coral felt the fire's warmth flare up and
opened her eyes. "Sorry," Rockdream said. "The wood burned
better than I thought it would."
"I think I was asleep," she said, then noticed that the wind and
snow had stopped and the gibbous moon was bright between the
clouds.
"You did it, or it happened anyway," Rockdream said.
"I did it," Coral affirmed. "What disturbs me is how easy it
was."
"You were inspired."
Coral wondered who or what had inspired her, but decided not
to discuss it. As a small boy, Rockdream had wanted to become
a priest, and he might be offended by her spontaneous manipula-

tion of mythic vision. But Salmon would understand, and Coral could talk to her in a few days.

"Shall we make camp?" Coral asked, standing and stretching.

They unpacked and spread the furs and blankets, moved Wedge from Coral's pack to the bed, and undressed. Their first kiss was hesitant. "Might this—um—disturb the magic?" Rockdream asked.

So he had sensed something about the workings of her spell! It must have been potent indeed. "No, my love," she said. "If anything this will strengthen the magic." Saying this made Coral certain it was true.

Rockdream's powerful hands caressed her gently. "It seems so long," he said. "I know we made love once at the settlement."

"Nothing was right there," Coral said, and began a long slow kiss, her lips nibbling his with a light touch of tongue. She rolled onto her back and spread her legs. He was heavy, but she liked that weight, that solidness. Even when he was most excited, he was careful not to hurt her. Tonight his movements mingled smoothness with shudders. She ran her hands up his sides, under his shoulders, down his smooth chest, around to his back, while sensing how he felt each caress.

"Slow down or you will stream too soon," she whispered. He tried to reach down to touch her but it was awkward in this position, so he turned onto his side while she slipped her arm under him.

"The blankets," she said, untangling and adjusting them. Fortunately they had not pulled off of Wedge. The touch of air was cold.

On top now, with rough wool rubbing her back, Coral moved while Rockdream fingered her. Moment after moment she was suspended on the edge of shuddering, then suddenly she did, and when he slid in and out toward his streaming, she shuddered again.

11.

Twice that night they woke from chill and stoked the fire. In the morning, they filled the waterskin with clean snow and discussed whether to hunt from this camp, or continue, and decided to continue.

Walking parallel about a hundred feet apart with Wedge near Coral, they searched for tracks. In the melting snow, a fresh deer trail was obvious. Coral whistled softly, slowing raised one arm, and pointed the direction with the other. "Wedge, you must be quiet, very quiet," she said in a low voice, and put her hand over his mouth for a moment. "Do you understand?"

"Somewhere in the brush over there, I think," Rockdream said quietly. "Make a big circle to get ahead of her, and if you make some noise when you close in, she will bolt toward me—I hope." This technique worked better when there were at least three hunters.

They both strung their bows and notched arrows. Coral and Wedge began circling, taking a few steps, stopping, taking a few more. Rockdream waited.

Suddenly Coral shouted: "Rockdream!"—spun around, and shot her arrow into the scaled belly of the drakey swooping toward Wedge. Its piercing screech bolted the unseen deer. Rockdream's own arrow, from a greater distance, pierced the wing membrane but missed the muscle. Wedge was clinging to Coral's leg. The drakey circled to attack, still agile enough, despite its wounds, to dodge trunks and branches. Coral grabbed Wedge and squirmed under the dense brambles where the deer had bedded; he cried about his scratches. Rockdream's second arrow struck the drakey's wing muscle and it crashed into a tree and fell to the ground.

It was a large drakey, ten feet from snout to tail-tip, wing ribs up to six and a half feet, and curved two-inch claws as sharp as knives. Even so, the attack was puzzling. Drakeys hear thoughts as well as dragons, and almost never risk battle with armed hunters.

"Wedge's fear was louder than our thoughts," Coral said. "He has never before gone hunting, and when I made him be quiet that way, he thought we were in danger. The drakey perceived this and thought we were afraid of it."

"The drakey also may have been hungrier than usual."

"Like us, yes? Come, Wedge, let us break sticks for the fire."

"Fiya? Hot! Hot!"

"Yes, fires are hot," Coral said. "We have to make a fire to cook the drakey. I am hungry enough to eat it all right now!"

Of course, Coral was exaggerating. In fact, added to the roots they dug the next day, the drakey meat was food enough for the entire journey home. Twice they had to make a raft to cross flooded areas, but most of the water was shallow enough to wade or limited enough to detour. The winter clouds did not gather again till the last day of the journey, and it did not begin raining till the moment they reached the village.

2

TWISTED PEACE

12.

"Strong Bull talks with two mouths," said Chief Beartooth, whose camp on the Blue River was forty miles from Canticle's Keep. "One mouth says sit the peace circle. The other says make more shields. This peace agreement must be false. What is false about it?"

Glowfly fed several dry sticks to the fire under the grill, then flipped the flatbread loaves. Her mother, Antelope, was stretching lumps of dough for the next batch. High Shaman Drakey was bringing news of the peace talk to camp. Because of the rain, the men were crowded under the other awning near the big fire, close enough for Glowfly to hear them.

After a silence, Drakey said, "There is no agreement. Canticle thinks that if his people agree to leave, they will be allowed to stay. Strong Bull will keep peace while the human messengers search for another place to go. If they do not find one by the last full moon of spring, he will make war."

"Why does Strong Bull use a peace circle for a truce?" asked Beartooth.

Drakey cleared his throat and spat on the ground. "He wants the humans to think we will not make the first attack. He does not believe a broken peace circle will bring us bad luck. This is his argument: The humans who broke peace circles long ago won the wars they started. They and their people had children. Their cities prospered long after their deaths. What curse is that? Maybe if we do the same, we will win the war we start. Maybe fewer goblins will die than what old Drakey predicts."

"That plan is twisted," said Beartooth. "No good will come of it. What do the other chiefs say?"

"Enough will sit the peace circle to impress Canticle. On the Goblin River, Charging Elk, Cold Winter, Condor, Hooked Beak, Big Claw, and Long Howl have all agreed. Only Least Owl has refused, and Quiet Cat has not decided. On the Blue River, Whitemouth and Mammoth have both agreed. Quagga refuses to sit peace with any humans for any reason, but that is what Canticle would expect him to do."

"That makes nine already."

"Bonedance has refused, and Gorge may refuse also. Who can guess what Beadback will do? And at least two chiefs from the Bear River will sit this false peace. Unless the human messengers find a new place for Canticle's people to go, there will be a broken peace circle, a treacherous first attack, and a long and terrible war. Everything I have done or said to try to prevent this war has been twisted into something that will make it worse."

Antelope hissed at Glowfly, who hurriedly pulled the flatbread loaves off the grill just as they were starting to burn. "You make the loaves and listen," Antelope whispered. "I will bake."

Beartooth asked, "Why has compassion become treachery? Why has ceremony become mockery?"

"When you oppose something, to hunt it or fight it you must become something like it to understand it," Drakey replied.

"Ah," said Beartooth.

"Hunting and war are different," said Screaming Spear, Glowfly's father, who had been chief before Beartooth. "A mammoth is a fierce opponent. He can spear you with his tusks or grab you with his trunk and throw you to the ground. But he is not your enemy. You do not hate him for this. You kill him to feed your camp. A warrior is an enemy."

"With or without the anger of war, it is the same," said Drakey. "To hunt a mammoth, I must fill my mind with his thoughts, to know how he will fight. To oppose a human general, I must do the same, for the same reason. Because his thoughts are twisted, mine become twisted."

"The anger of war prevents this," argued Screaming Spear. "You fill your mind with your enemy's thoughts, but you do not become like him because you hate him."

"No," said Drakey. "When your heart is hateful, you do not notice that you have become like your enemy."

"Check the meat," Antelope said quietly while spreading the last loaves on the grill.

Glowfly went to the smoldering third fire, where the skin-wrapped slabs of mammoth meat were roasting. The smell was just right, but to make sure, she uncovered one bundle with the scoop. The skin was soaked dark with melted fat and starting to turn crisp. "It is done," she said.

Antelope said something to Beartooth. Glowfly watched her take a deep breath, and shouted "Yiyiyi! Yiyiyi!" in unison with her.

Moments later the center of camp was filled with goblins. Men and children formed the circle. Women uncovered the meat, cut portions, and filled serving baskets.

"Before you return to your tents, your chief would speak," the warrior Sees Far shouted, and everyone became quiet.

Beartooth said, "The war with the humans has become twisted even before it starts. Strong Bull wants us to sit the peace circle with Canticle, but he also wants us to make more shields. A peace circle is for peace, not for a truce likely to end in battle. I will not take part in a false ceremony, nor do I want anyone else from this camp to do this. We do not need to fight humans with treachery. That is their weapon. We will use our strength."

Many warriors and some women stomped their feet and howled to applaud this remark, but a few warriors looked displeased. Glowfly was concerned that both her father, Screaming Spear, and her husband, Quick One, were among those who seemed to disagree with Beartooth,.

"But I hope that the human messengers will find a city that will accept the survivors of Newport. That would be best for everyone."

13.

Lord Crossing of Midcoast had many concerns, but the dragon Riversong's conquest of Newport was the one that nagged at his mind and gave him bad dreams. What he actually knew about this, from the hundred or so refugees who had trickled into Midcoast or its vassal keeps and villages, was bad enough. What he guessed, from the fact that no greater number of survivors had turned up anywhere else a year later, was even worse.

Riversong's deadliest innovation was to drop boulders from flight on selected targets. Against ships, the tactic was devastating. He had sunk every ship leaving or bound for Newport. Fortunately, Midcoast, with its vassal keeps and overland trade routes, could not be isolated this way. But the dragon had then bombarded the city of Newport itself, and persisted till it was his.

At the beginning of his attack, he had lured the best warriors onto a wooded island by feigning injury, then set the woods afire to kill most of them. This was such an old dragon trick that Lord Crossing had to wonder why Lord Herring, of all people, had been fooled.

About a week later, Riversong did something similar to a huge sortie of volunteers, most of them not real warriors, but the particulars of this battle were disturbingly vague. Lord Herring died, but his rear general survived, and indeed became more important and powerful as the siege continued.

Lord Crossing was unsure what had happened after this, but he was about to learn. Evidently there had been some evacuation before the end, for two diplomats representing the main group of survivors were now at Midcoast Castle to petition him. He looked at the alcove where Lady Bluestar sat at ease, dressed in a long loose robe, for she was five months pregnant. Though she seemed to be completely engrossed by the leatherbound codex she was reading, she winked to let him know she was ready if he was.

"Bring them in," he said.

A voice outside the door relayed his message, and less than a minute later, Greaseburn brought in two men, both warriors in their late twenties, both wearing travel-stained but professionally made fighting leathers. "These are the warriors Arch and Cold-spray of Newport, serving as diplomats for Lord Pretender Drill," she announced. "They wish to petition you."

"Begging your pardon, my lord, but Lord Drill is no pretender," said Arch.

"I understand your pride, but a ruler without a city is not a lord," said Lord Crossing. "My guard did not mean to imply that Drill is not the true heir of Lord Herring."

"We do have a city, my lord," said Arch.

"Oh?"

"We are building a city on Goblin Plain," amended Coldspray.

"How extraordinary!" said Lord Crossing. "By invitation or invasion? Nothing like this has happened for nearly eighty years. But wait—Before you answer that, tell me everything you know about Riversong's conquest and what followed."

"Everything? That would take quite a while, my lord," said Arch.

"I imagine it will, so be seated," said Lord Crossing, gesturing toward two plain wooden chairs. They waited till he sat in his own upholstered one. Greaseburn remained standing on guard. "And I do suggest that you tell me the entire truth and nothing else, for if I decide to make you repeat your story before a clerical jury, you would not like their response to attempted perjury."

They began their account with the dragon's maritime blockade. Arch's description of the sinking of the *Great Circle* and the death of Baron Oakspear was based on the eyewitness account of the warrior Salmon, sole survivor of this battle. The details were interesting but about what Lord Crossing had expected.

"Could Salmon have been dragonbound?" he asked. "Did anyone think to check?"

"She was examined thoroughly by two midpriests before she was allowed to tell her story," said Arch.

Their account of the battle on the island and the death of Baron Swordfern explained why Lord Herring had been fooled. The skirmish between the herders and the dragon had been the very first time anyone had shot the new steel longbow arrows. The dragon was surprised, and might well have been as seriously wounded as he pretended to be.

"After this defeat, Lord Herring decided to wait out the siege," said Arch.

"Did he have some strategy in mind, or was he just distraught over losing two sons?" Lord Crossing asked, with a thought for his own pregnant wife.

"Dragons are not known for patient and persistent conquest. Waiting might have caused Riversong to chance a less careful attack, or even to give up," said Arch. "Unfortunately, some citizens had less patience than the dragon, and mustered an army of their own."

"Now, the story I heard was that Lord Herring armed the herders and others with these steel longbow arrows because there were not enough real warriors left to make an effective sortie without leaving the city undefended," said Lord Crossing.

"That was what he told the assembled army," said Arch. "I think he was surprised by their resolve, thought they had a fair chance of success, and made their plan his own."

"What was this plan?"

"I should tell this story, for I was in the battle," said Coldspray. "I want you to know, my lord, that I was one of the professional warriors who joined this army when Lord Herring and General Canticle assumed command. Our objective was to drive the cattle, sheep, and goats, which Riversong had scattered, back to the city, and to shoot him when he tried to interfere. With the steady rain that day, we did not fear another firetrap. We marched in a column of eight up the East Road toward Herders Ridge, where the scouts had seen the animals."

"Were these scouts checked for dragonbinding?" asked Lord Crossing.

"No one thought of that. Well—I know the scouts' information was good because we saw hoofprints and scats where the animals were supposed to be. The dragon had more than enough time to drive them farther away. We had no tents, for we dared not burden ourselves with heavy packs, so we made eighty large campfires. Some people disappeared while gathering wood. We hurried because we wanted to be well away from trees or brush before night. Only later were the people missed."

"Perhaps the dragonbound scouts disappeared," suggested Lord Crossing.

"More than fifty were missing. I think it more likely that the dragon cast the fear spell," said Coldspray. "Several times that night we heard sounds that might have been Riversong attacking deserters, but nothing like a roar or a belch of flame that would let us know for certain. Between the noises and the rain, no one slept well.

"In the morning, we saw some cattle about two miles north, on a sloping side-ridge near the edge of the Elk River forest. They moved away when we approached, but this was fine because we saw a bigger herd on the next side-ridge, then a still bigger herd on the ridge after that. No sheep or goats, just cattle. Thus we were lured farther and farther from the road. By the time we had the three herds consolidated and moving toward the top of the main ridge, it was noon, bright and sunny, and we were several hours' march from the road.

"The dragon appeared suddenly, bellowing and belching fire, stampeding the cattle right back into us. Because the grass was wet, people stumbled; hundreds were trampled by cattle charging downhill. Lord Herring and others near him were killed with a big blast of flame. Riversong's blast range and capacity were greater than at the Delta Island Battle, for now he was well fed. The steel longbow arrows lacked the range and penetrating power we needed, and the longbows themselves were easily burned or broken. Many were disarmed. My own crossbow served me no better, for the crank jammed.

"Riversong circled around and roared again to drive the cattle back uphill. We scattered to avoid them. Then the dragon started picking humans up and eating them, or belching flame at isolated warriors who were still armed. At Canticle's command, we drew closer together, spacing ourselves fifteen feet from each other. This put any direct attack in bow range of enough archers to hurt the dragon, but spread us out enough to minimize deaths from burning or trampling. Actually, by this time the cattle were scattered and exhausted."

"I want to know why the dragon did not burn General Canticle," said Lord Crossing.

"Because Canticle is both a good leader and a mighty warrior," said Coldspray. "He did not fire his crossbow even once during that battle, for the dragon dared not come near him. Had he had his chance, the dragon would have been seriously wounded or killed."

"Was Canticle checked for dragonbinding?"

"Everyone who returned to the city was examined," said Arch. "No one was dragonbound."

"How many returned?"

"Four hundred fifty-three," said Arch.

"So the retreat became a rout," said Lord Crossing.

"About a thousand died or disappeared on Herders Ridge, and another five hundred were lost on the way back," said Coldspray. "We divided the army into two companies for the retreat: General Canticle led one through the forest north of the road toward the coast; the warrior Jetty led the other through the forest south of the road toward the river. I was in Jetty's company. Riversong tried to burn the forest around Canticle first, then came our way, but the woods in both places were too green and wet for a serious firetrap. Not that it was easy to have confidence running through hot smoke—but the ones who bolted for the open were the ones who got killed. The trees were tall and stout enough to protect us from direct attack till we reached the River Road. From there on we would be in the open. It was long after dark and we were exhausted, but Jetty urged us on, for the dragon was elsewhere, just possibly sleeping off his own exhaustion. The moon was full, but soon the fog came up the river, thick enough to conceal us. We reached the city after dawn but before the fog thinned. Canticle's company was already there."

"Which company suffered greater losses?" asked Lord Crossing.

"Both about the same, I guess. Canticle was by far the better tactician and leader, but his company was more heavily attacked."

14.

After Lord Herring's death, his three surviving offspring, Barons Pelican and Drill and Baroness Lupine, agreed that none of them would assume the title of ruling lord or lady until the dragon was killed. Lupine assumed command and defense of the castle, Pelican of the inner city, and Drill of the newer section. But Drill was no warrior and assigned his command to General Canticle.

For another two weeks they withstood the siege, though Riversong's boulders struck with increasing effectiveness. Damaged city walls and broken towers made troop movements more difficult. On some foggy nights Riversong dared to land inside the city, and set fires inside buildings. He knew the defenders' thoughts well enough to strike when and where he was least expected. When he destroyed the granaries and polluted the main water supply, the barons put Canticle's evacuation plan into effect.

Each day, sorties would spread out in several directions as if seeking the dragon, while smaller groups of citizens escaped through the forests. Baron Pelican died leading one such sortie. Convoys of riverboats armed with dragon guns sailed up the Turtle River on foggy nights. Whenever Riversong destroyed a boat, he would carry a big piece of wreckage back over the city, set it afire and drop it, while making some remark about the deliciousness of the crew.

The final evacuation began when the last big storm of spring struck Newport. While the heavy winds, rain, and lightning kept the dragon grounded, fifteen more riverboats sailed up the Turtle River, and hundreds of other people, organized in small groups, scattered through the forests.

Baroness Lupine and thirty other warriors stayed behind to defend Newport Castle. She actually believed they had a chance of killing Riversong. No one escaped to tell the story of her failure, but dreams and omens suggested that the castle fell on the night of the 65th, three months after Riversong began the blockade, and a month and a half after Lord Herring's proclamation of war.

General Canticle planned a reunion of forces on the 149th day at a certain location in Spirit Swamp, to be canceled if the dragon attacked or was seen by any boats in the swamp.

Between the evacuation and the reunion, Arch and Coldspray were aboard different boats, but the stories they told were much the same. Both crews suffered great losses from disease in the heat of the summer. Victims experienced high fevers, delusions, and putrid-smelling sweat every day and a half, sometimes passing watery waste so often that their bodies dried out. Most who sickened died within a week, children sooner than that. Recovery was likely once the cycle of fevers stopped, but the patient was weakened for months. Treatments of clerical healers were ineffective.

At the meeting of boats on the 149th, General Canticle outlined a plan to settle on Goblin Plain. His ideal was an arrangement similar to the Dragonstone Mountain Country north of Upriver, where human settlements were surrounded by goblin camps. To establish this, he planned a primitive earthwork fortification to be built in the winter, when the goblins would be unable to provision a large army because the animals would be scattered far from the rivers. Canticle did not have many horses, but he had enough to mount his own hunters. The humans could provision a big army, at least for a while, despite this seasonal scattering.

But meanwhile, the humans needed a place to go, and Lord Drill, who had assumed the title despite Riversong's continued survival, knew just the place. His own boat had sailed all the way up the Turtle River to the first cataract. No goblins lived below the second cataract—for the land was desolate and hunting poor—but the river had fish aplenty, the water was better, and there was no swamp sickness.

There they went. Lord Drill may have hoped that they could settle there permanently, but once the nightjumper salmon run was over, the refugee fleet soon overfished the river, and some of the boats had to return to the swamp.

But the hot weather was over, and no one else caught the sickness. When the steady rains of fall began, Canticle led a force of eighteen hundred to his chosen site, by land—to keep secret the existence of his navy—and immediately began building the fortress. The goblin chiefs soon sent messengers to protest, and High Chief Strong Bull himself threatened Canticle with war, but the humans were too many for the goblins to oppose easily.

Lord Crossing impatiently cut off Coldspray's account of the tedious and twisted truce negotiations by saying, "I believe I understand the recent situation well enough. What is your petition?"

"If I might explain the agreement first, my lord—"

"There is no agreement worth explaining," Lord Crossing snapped. "Present your petition."

Arch said, "First, we would ask you whether you might accept a large number of Newport refugees as citizens of Midcoast, and if so, how many?"

"If you mean to send those who are too sick to work, or anything of the sort, very few. If you mean—but you must keep the most skilled at your settlement. Exactly what do you have in mind?"

"We would abandon our settlement if you offered us a better situation," said Arch. "There are three thousand of us, but among us are the best shipwrights, architects, warriors—"

"Your warriors were defeated," Lord Crossing interrupted. "As a gesture of mercy, I might accept as many as a thousand of you, with eight-year contracts, and I think I can persuade the other Lords of the Valley to accept the rest. We have expected something of the sort. But why, then, did you not come sooner?"

"Because we feared this would be your best offer," said Coldspray. "We do not want bonded servitude."

"I understand and respect your pride, but how else could Midcoast or any other city support such a swelling of population? If you have some wealth, I could shorten the terms proportionately. But bonded servitude in the Two Rivers Valley is not what it was when Moonport was destroyed. Bondholders are now forbidden to cause any servant to run up a debt, and forbidden to renew the bond. So an eight-year bond is exactly that. Women are each allowed to bear one child if they have none already. If religion concerns you, our church does give two services a week in the traditional polytheistic style, in addition to the reformed services."

"My lord, we thank you for your offer," said Arch. "I will repeat it to Lord Drill and General Canticle, but I believe they will choose instead to defend the settlement. So now I would ask you about seed—"

"The harvest this fall was not good," said Lord Crossing. "We have no seed for sale."

"Then we thank you deeply for your time, my lord," Arch said and the two diplomats bowed.

"Would you care for a meal? Greaseburn will see that you find the common room." Lord Crossing's particular phrasing was a signal to his private guard that he wanted these people carefully watched.

15.

After they left, the lord barred the door and walked over to the alcove where his pregnant lady was sitting. "That was very interesting, my lord," she said with a smile. "Let me stand and stretch. I am stiff from being inconspicuous for so long." While doing so, she continued, "Not only was their story interesting and disturbing, but they were both making it quite hard for me to hear their thoughts. Their story is true but incomplete. Something happened during the first week of bombardment, just before the battle of the Citizens' Army. They both relaxed once they got to this."

"I suppose it was something about how that army got put together. Does it matter?"

"I think it was something else. Is the door barred?"

"Yes."

While rummaging through her private trunk, Bluestar said, "I doubt that even the high priest, should we persuade him to sit on a jury, would be able to hear their thoughts very well."

"Are they wizards?"

"Mmm—I do not think so. Their experience with the dragon has taught them how to hide their thoughts, but–Ah, here." She lifted a silken bundle from the trunk. "Perhaps now I can answer both your questions and my own."

"Your cards," he mumbled.

"Hush, my lord." She sat at the table, spread the silk, and began shuffling the cards. Crossing sat opposite her. When one card flew out of the deck and landed face-up on the floor, Bluestar reached awkwardly to retrieve it, looked at it, and showed it to her husband. The picture showed lightning striking a castle tower. "I think we have an answer already," she said. "I can imagine only one reason why anyone would hide thoughts about a storm."

"Black sorcery," Crossing whispered.

"Well, stormweaving," Bluestar whispered back. "I will use this card as significator." She shuffled the deck again, drew a card from the middle of the pile and placed it face down beside the first, cut the deck, shuffled again, drew another card from the middle, and so on, until she had seven more cards.

"The second position is the source," Bluestar explained quietly. "Here we have—" She turned over the card of The Wizard. "This could not be plainer. A wizard or a witch made the storm. The third position is the goal, and here we have the Four of Staves. The picture shows a garden solstice dance, symbolizing peace and prosperity. At least the wizard had a positive image of his goal in mind."

"No goal could justify those means," said Crossing.

Bluestar did not respond to this, but turned over the next card. "The fourth position is the obstacle. Here we have the Ten of Swords, showing bodies on a battlefield, meaning defeat and death. Obviously the wizard failed. The fifth position is the helper. Here we have the Eight of Staves, which suggests to me that this wizard had the help of other wizards or witches. See how the staves are flying toward a common goal. The sixth is the fate, the underlying pattern of events. Here we see The Fool, cheerfully ignorant and about to dance off a cliff. These people were untrained. The seventh is the chance, and here is the Three of Disks, the card of apprenticeship. The wizard who led the stormweaving had some knowledge but not enough. The eighth is the meaning, and here is the Nine of Swords, the card of grief and mourning. Anyone who dares fight a dragon with inadequate training will come to grief."

"But a wizard trained well enough to kill a dragon might be worse than the dragon," said Crossing.

"Might it concern you if General Canticle allows his wizards and witches to have such training?" asked Bluestar. "This wizard and his friends died bravely and honorably, fighting for their city. Even if they had succeeded, they risked severe punishment. This example speaks louder to Canticle than all the abuses of the first century added together. Lightning is one way to strike back at a high-flying dragon dropping rocks. Now that I know of this battle, I realize that Arch and Coldspray have come here partly to recruit witches and wizards."

"Are you sure about this?"

Bluestar took a deep breath. "We cannot let them find any witches. After last year's hard winter, you know how badly Midcoast needs its—practitioners. I have tried to persuade you—"

"You did persuade me, my lady. As far as I am concerned, healing and divination are legal, and I am liberal enough to include love charms as a form of healing, and so forth. But I cannot say so openly."

"Because of the other lords? Except for Lady Agate of Coveport, their attitude is much like yours," said Bluestar. "But as long as witchcraft and wizardry are supposedly crimes like theft and murder, our practitioners could vanish quite suddenly if someone made them a good offer. And to be allowed to study the deeper arts? I may have the good sense to stay away from this, but curiosity is often the ruin of the wise."

"This whole conjecture is based upon—" Crossing gestured toward the cards. "Your reading is clear, but how do I know it is true?"

"I have never had a reading this clear, about events that have already happened, that did not prove true," Bluestar said, putting the cards back into the deck and wrapping it in silk. "If you put Arch or Coldspray before a clerical jury and asked them directly whether they came here looking for witches and why, you would learn what I just told you. But please, please do not do this."

"I will not," said Crossing, "but I will let *them* think otherwise. I will have a messenger offer them a guest room in the castle, but let it slip that I was somewhat skeptical of certain parts of their story and wanted to see them again. If you are right about their intentions, they will leave the castle and city immediately, and we will not be bothered with them."

"My lord, that is almost as twisted as their truce negotiations," Lady Bluestar said, but she smiled.

16.

Aboard the *Great Stag*, anchored in a backwater pool near the Turtle River not many miles upstream from the Blue River, Lieutenant Fledgeling and the mariner Feathergrass were discussing the peace circle arrangements with Lord Drill, Lieutenant Conch, and Captain Frogsong.

"If this peace is as solid as you say, then why not just sail the

Stag up the Goblin River?" asked Lord Drill. "Why does Canticle want me to sneak in?"

"Because the peace is only solid for three months after the ceremony, and we are not sure what will happen after that," said Fledgeling. "We want the fleet kept secret for now."

"Yes, yes, I know the strategy quite well. I helped Canticle develop it," said Lord Drill. "One small fishing boat will not give away the fleet."

"Better not to remind them of boats at all," argued Fledgeling. "Let them suppose that all the boats went elsewhere, or got destroyed by the dragon."

"The eastern marsh is flooded deep," said Feathergrass. "We could sail that way as easily as the river. More easily, for the current is less."

"I need at least three feet of water to sail the *Great Stag*," said Frogsong. "And how do you plan to get it over the levee?"

"Much of the levee is underwater," said Feathergrass. "Our trouble was finding dry ground to camp on."

"If the levee is broken, the backwater could drain quickly," said Frogsong. "The peace circle is more than a week from now, and it could be a week with little rain."

"I will not spend six days each way paddling that canoe of yours," Lord Drill told Fledgeling and Feathergrass. "I will come to the peace circle aboard the *Great Stag* by whatever route my captain favors. I trust my general will understand the need for this."

Frogsong's sailors helped Feathergrass secure the canoe to the starboard side of the *Great Stag*, above the oars. This looked awkward but worked well enough. The canoe was as long as the boat but no heavier than a skiff.

Rain swelled the rivers the day they left. Sailing down the Turtle to the Blue was easy, but making progress up the Blue was hard even with the wind behind them. When it shifted, they had to furl the sails and row with all eight oars. Though the wide river was everywhere swollen over its banks and joined to backwater pools, tacking was impossible because the forward component of their motion would then be less than the current.

Feathergrass's arms ached. Had they used the canoe, they would instead be paddling through these quiet pools. Hour after hour Captain Frogsong beat the drum. It seemed as though the crew had to row with all their strength just to stay in one place. Had they ground to walk on, that would have been quicker.

Finally the captain ordered them to steer for a pool and quit for the day.

Because they had not been able to troll for fish and the pools were too murky for chumming and netting, they had to eat some of the stores. Rations were scant for humans who had worked so hard.

"The only time I ever rowed like this before was when the *Sea Flute* ran into a storm near the reefs of Cape Horn, coming into Prosperity Bay," Feathergrass said.

Fledgeling squeezed the aching muscles in her arms and shoulders. "I think tomorrow the captain and lord will choose the backwater route."

The next day was cold but clear, there was less current, and they made better time. Beyond the edge of the swamp, the eastern marsh was all one big lake, and the captain and lord did agree that this route was better. On this broad, quiet water almost any breeze was usable. It was too shallow for trolling, but this was no concern, for they knew now that they would reach Canticle's Keep that evening.

"If we dug a canal," Feathergrass told his wife, "we could use boats here in the summer, and the land would drain well enough to become healthy."

"A canal forty miles long, and how big and deep? That would take years of work."

"Digging out Newport Harbor was a big job."

"Not compared to this," said Fledgeling.

"It can be done. In southern Godsfavor I have seen canals much longer, and built for the same reason," Feathergrass said. "Dragons were troublesome on the coast, and the inland was much too swampy before they changed it."

"And how many million humans live in Godsfavor to do whatever work the Queen commands?" asked Lord Drill, who had been listening quietly.

"There is that," Feathergrass admitted. "It was just an idea. You know, my lord, there is much to be said for a large population. If Newport had numbered thirty thousand or a hundred thousand instead of ten, Riversong could not have done this to us. We were using only a small part of our land. Had we built keeps and farms north of the Elk River, or south of the delta, we could have retreated to these."

Lord Drill said, "Windsong the Mariner and her followers came east of the sea because they did not want to live like that. My great-grandparents, Wentletrap and Pip the Elf, made Newport the way they did because that was the best way for it to be. Even then the Two Rivers Valley was crowded enough to have no free hunting and debt servitude. The Valley Lords had enough wisdom to keep their cities small, but they allowed too many keeps and villages to be built. A city must both be small and surrounded by wild land for humans to have freedom. Our merchants said proudly that Newport was the biggest city east of the sea, because that was good business, but I am glad it was no bigger than it was."

Near Canticle's Keep where they anchored, the lake was still a mile wide but only marginally deep enough for the boat. North of this, the path that Rockdream, Coral, and Wedge had used to return home was now a knee-deep ford. Captain Frogsong and some of the crew stayed behind to guard the *Great Stag*, and to move it if the water level dropped. Lord Drill and his escort could ride horses from the settlement to any new anchorage. Feather-grass offered to hurry ahead now to fetch horses, but Lord Drill said, "I can walk that far. It will be worth it to give my general a surprise inspection."

Lieutenant Fledgling said, "He may have been surprised by the report of a sailboat in the marsh, but now he knows you are coming." Indeed, less than a third of the way to the walls they were met by Lieutenant Foam and four other mounted warriors leading horses for them to ride.

17.

At noon on the day of the last full moon of winter, the 353rd day of the 199th year, the shaman Sees Patterns of Strong Bull's Camp, who led the ceremony in High Shaman Drakey's absence, drew a large circle with chalk dust on the cleared ground, just inside the circle of standing humans and goblins. Nearby to the north, where its evergreen canopy would not shade and chill them, was the large lone redbark that stood midway between the Goblin River and the low rise that hid the human settlement.

"Step inside the circle," said Sees Patterns, and now they stood closer together.

Around the western half of the circle, with Lord Drill and General Canticle in the center, stood the humans: Lieutenants Conch, Graywall, Foam, Fledgeling, Strike, and Swordnotch; the diplomat Whitestone; sixteen hunting group leaders; and eighteen other warriors, including a few capable nonprofessionals like Feathergrass the Mariner. No priests or priestesses were present, for by human custom political agreements were not the concern of the Church.

Around the eastern half of the circle, with High Chief Strong Bull in the center, stood the goblins: Chiefs Charging Elk, Cold Winter, Hooked Beak, Quiet Cat, Big Claw, Condor, and Long Howl of the Goblin River; Chiefs Beadback, Mammoth, and Whitemouth of the Blue River; Chiefs Redspear and Gaping Wound of the Bear River; many warriors; five shamans, including Sees Patterns; and two shamanesses who were the only goblin women present. By goblin custom peace agreements were not the concern of ordinary women.

Though Feathergrass knew all the chiefs' names from hearing Fledgeling memorize them, he could match only a few with their faces.

"This is better than anything I had hoped for," said Lord Drill. "Not since the reign of my grandfather Stock has any Lord of Newport sat the peace circle with the High Chief of Goblin Plain. May this circle long endure!"

"Ah."

"Yes."

"So be it."

"I am a fierce man, but I am a fair man," said Strong Bull. "I could have made war and won. Instead I chose to talk and listen and understand. We reached an agreement. Sitting this peace circle means we will keep our agreement and have peace. The spirits and gods will make sure we do this."

Again, voices around the circle murmured agreement.

"I am known for my ambition," said General Canticle. "When I want something, I work as hard as I can for it. My greatest ambition is to find peace and prosperity for all of us."

Chief Charging Elk spoke next, then Lieutenant Conch, and so on, alternating human and goblin, each making a brief remark about desiring peace. Fledgeling said, "May this peace prove stronger than any misunderstanding."

Feathergrass was still trying to think of the best way to say what he really felt when Fledgeling nudged him. "I want peace," he said. "May the circle strengthen this desire we all share." When several goblin chiefs facing him murmured assent, he felt awkward, for he was standing closer to Lord Drill than others of higher rank, and spoke sooner. Fledgeling was a lieutenant, and twelve years his senior, but as his wife she was also his equal. Asking him to stand beside her at this ceremony was her way of showing him this. He felt shamed to think of how, late last summer when they had first become lovers, he had considered her merely a moment of passion and no substitute for his first wife, Loon the Minstrel.

After the last person's remark and a long moment of silence, Sees Patterns said, "Sit down, clasp hands, and close your eyes. Feel the strong rope of peace bind us together, one hand to the next."

When Feathergrass closed his eyes he felt nothing. The seating arrangement was wrong, he realized. If the humans and goblins were all mixed in together, rather than arranged by race and rank, the energy would flow freely. He had the sudden thought that Loon's spirit was telling him this.

"Yes, yes, it is me," she said, with the soft accent of the Four Lakes Kingdom he remembered so well. "No, I am not jealous of your new wife. She is very strong, and her body is warm for you, and you have love, yes? But you do not need to hold her hand right now. You need to hold a goblin's hand."

Feathergrass tried to find the voice to repeat his dead wife's suggestion, but he could not summon the will. His mind and body were filled with a warm sleepy mist, like the time he and Loon had drunk sleepflower tea together in that sailors' bar in Lizard River. He felt peaceful—yes, the peace circle was working. This was a powerful magic. Now he was seeing the tame dappled unicorn they had seen together in the bestiary gardens of Prosperity.

Fledgeling squeezed his hand and released it, and Lieutenant Strike released his other hand. Feathergrass opened his eyes and blinked, blinded momentarily by the sunlit plain.

"The circle is completed," said Sees Patterns. "Now we stand, step out of the circle, and scatter the chalk." The ground was damp, and their kicks sent clods of dirt flying in all directions.

3

GRASS, RIVER, WIND

18.

"Wake up," Fledgeling whispered.

Feathergrass opened his eyes to the hearthfire's dim glow.
Fledgeling was already dressed and heating a bowl of stew for
their breakfast. He quickly pulled on his undershirt and tunic and
looked for his pants, for the fire was too small to break the chill.
His breath made puffs of mist.

It was just a few days past the spring equinox that began the
200th year of humans east of the sea, but there had been no grand
celebration here, just a day off from work and a small feast.

"Is it almost dawn or are we leaving early?" Feathergrass
asked.

"Keep your voice soft. We have something private to discuss."
This had to be something difficult, for Coldrock, Harmony, and
Forward, who were asleep in the two other beds, were as discreet
as roommates could be. "Nothing bad," Fledgeling said, smiling
at her husband's look of concern. "In fact, an honor for you, but
still a hard decision. Canticle wants to promote you to hunting
group leader."

"But I am not even a real warrior," Feathergrass objected.

"You can do the job, and Canticle knows it."

"You are the one who has formed his opinion of me. I suppose I am a good hunter, but how could I command a group with real warriors in it? Suppose some warrior was disgusted enough with the hunting to want to go east of the rise. Do you really think I could handle a mutiny?"

"You know the difference between good leadership and bad," said Fledgeling.

"I suppose I could manage, but—" He hesitated. "I am not sure how to say what I mean. When we married, you said you would always put duty first and I should do the same; but it goes against all custom to separate husband from wife by assigning them separate commands."

"This would not be like becoming lieutenants of separate towers or captains of separate ships, for we would still live together," said Fledgeling. "We need more hunting groups."

"We need farms and a river full of fish," Feathergrass countered. "No matter how many hunting groups we send out, we cannot continue feeding people this way much longer."

"If you want to make policy your concern, I suggest you accept the promotion. Finish the stew. We have a long day ahead of us."

The stew tasted like sour mud. Feathergrass forced it down his dry throat. "I—I do not want the promotion. For me, the best part of our marriage is working together to do something important. With my first wife, I was just a young mariner sharing adventures. I did not appreciate how carefully she considered her art and the meaning of her life until just before she died. Her ballad about Baron Oakspear's death was her masterpiece. I am the only one who ever heard it, and I cannot remember it well enough to reproduce it. Hunting with you is like hearing that song, or maybe like being someone in that song." Feathergrass sighed and drank the last swallow of stew. "I am sorry. Did that make any sense at all?"

"As your lieutenant I am somewhat disappointed, but as your wife I am deeply honored. There are others Canticle can promote. Shall we go?"

In the moonless mist before dawn they walked the settlement's narrow streets to the three stables, each a large dirt-block building with twenty-two stalls and a hayloft, but only eighteen horses. Fledgeling opened the door to the center stable and lit the lantern.

Some of the younger horses snorted and stamped. "Good. We are first," Fledgeling said.

"I know which horses you and I want, but who else is in our group today?" Some hunters did not like certain horses that others might particularly want.

"Keg and Henna, Poach, Gill, Scoff and Hemstitch, and Jib's family," Fledgeling replied.

The stable door creaked open again. "Ho, ho, my lady lieutenant," boomed the warrior Bloodstorm, another hunting group leader. With him stood Nettle and Splash, who were often in his group.

"My group is going north," Fledgeling said. "We have first choice of horses from this stable."

"Then we will go south. Let the latercomers hunt the swamp and run the traps. But since there are four groups today, and three stables—"

"Choose from one of the others," Fledgeling said firmly. "Let the traprunners have the old workhorses."

"The next time your group and mine get scheduled the same day, I am sleeping in this stable," Bloodstorm said as he closed the door on his way out.

Fledgeling and Feathergrass began feeding the horses and checking their feet. "We should wait till the embassies return with more horses before we make more groups," Feathergrass said. "Already most of these go out three days out of four, and it shows."

"The groups will be smaller," Fledgeling replied.

When Scoff and Hemstitch arrived, they helped prepare the horses, while Fledgeling went out to tell the wall guards her group's plan. One, two, three at a time, the other hunters came to the stable and joined the work. The sky was just beginning to brighten toward a gray dawn when they led their horses up the ramp, over the wall, and out.

They rode north slightly below the crest of the rise, looking always ahead and down toward the marsh for shapes of distant herds or lone bulls. To the west the marsh waters had receded since the peace circle three weeks before. An hour's ride farther north, much of the land was dry. Now it was full daylight. The grass was so green and lush that it was hard to believe they had still seen nothing.

"If there were days when nobody rode this way, the herds might come back," said Jib.

"No matter how we do it, we kill more than the goblins, so the beasts prefer their side," said Keg.

"Enough talk," said Fledgeling. "The time for conversation is after the kill. We may see nothing, but our voices could alert a beast just over the rise who would otherwise come our way."

At midmorning the hunters spotted a small group of antelope a few miles ahead and a mile east of the rise. They spread out to form an arc, but the antelope bolted ahead when the first horse got within half a mile. "No sense chasing them, but stay spread," Fledgeling shouted. Antelope were delicious but small and very hard to shoot; they wanted larger, slower game.

Toward noon they stopped to let the horses graze. They thought the afternoon westerlies would improve their luck, but at first the only animals west of the rise were the elusive antelope.

Then Poach, who had the best eyesight, made the hunter's point, a subtle gesture. Feathergrass, Fledgeling, and Henna saw it then, most likely a lone auroch bull. The hunters spread their arc and did not move toward the auroch till they were directly between him and the rise. The bull continued to graze, even at half a mile, two thousand feet, fifteen hundred feet.

He snorted, then bellowed. This bull was dark brown, with horns almost as long as a great elk's antlers and a body bigger than any great elk. He was not about to back off or let himself be encircled. The bows were bent, the arrows notched, the hunters ready—but even so, his sudden charge, a crazed weaving lunge to disrupt their whole formation, took them by surprise.

Feathergrass's first arrow, aimed for the bull's flank, hit his shoulder; then the horse was too jumpy for him to aim again. Another arrow, Poach's, grazed the bull's thigh, but the two wounds did not slow him at all. He was furious.

Henna and Gill were unhorsed but rolled to their feet. The other horses were bucking or trying to run, frightened by those long but still unblooded horns. Henna took aim but her arrow only grazed him. She ran to dodge while Gil shot. Then the bull charged the horses again before the mounted hunters could reorganize.

Fledgeling drew her sword and urged her stallion behind the bull. Her mount was almost fearless; in Newport he had been Baron Swordfern's own hunting mount. Now he was the best horse in the settlement, for those who knew how to ride him. He galloped the outside of the bull's turn, just behind those deadly horns. Fledgeling leaned quickly, lunged deep, and let go of her sword, trusting the stallion's ability to dodge. The bull screamed but before he could strike back, several arrows pierced his other flank and he fell with a mighty crash.

Once the lieutenant knew that the horses were all unhurt and the fallen hunters only bruised, she offered a prayer of deep thanks to Wind the Hunter, for this hunt had been exceptionally dangerous.

"Let us thank Fire the Warrior as well," said Feathergrass. "This hunt was a battle."

"This was a lone bull," said Henna. "I do not ever want to meet the bull who drove him from the herd."

Quickly the hunters skinned, dismembered, and quartered the carcass for the return trip.

19.

When the first full moon of spring rose in the east, all the goblins of Beartooth's Camp gathered around the fire to feast and dance the Wolf Dance. For the third year, the young shamaness Glowfly was the one who told the traditional tale of the long, long winter, when snow did not melt but piled thicker every year until vast sheets of ice spread over the world. But Great Mother Wolf, who was a mighty shamaness, and her husband, the high chief of wolves, and all his warriors drove the ice spirits back to the far north and high into the mountains. "Every year since then, Mother Wolf makes certain that the ice spirits leave in the spring, and we do this dance to help her," Glowfly concluded.

The shamaness Cicada, who was Chief Beartooth's wife, beat the big drum; Glowfly's mother, Antelope, beat the smaller drum; and several other women played hoop drums or shook rattles. Beartooth, the warriors, High Shaman Drakey, Glowfly, many other women, and all of the older children made two circles around the fire, one inside the other, and began to dance.

The first time Glowfly had told the wolf story, the humans Rockdream and Coral had been guests of the camp. She became for those two weeks a close friend of Coral, who was about her own age and a witch, or human shamaness. The Wolf Dance reminded her of this. But Glowfly could also see that the spread of humans over the continent was very like the spread of winter long, long ago. And now the humans were living on Goblin Plain.

Round and round they danced. Glowfly's nose became moist and sensitive; her jaw lengthened; her skin sprouted fur; her hands and feet became paws. In the spirit world she was a wolf trotting the scent of quagga flesh, closer and closer, when suddenly the ground fell beneath her and a long fang bit her through.

Rolling in pain on the ground inside the circles, Glowfly saw flashes of fire and smelled burnt leather. People slapped her, pulled her to her feet. She struggled and barked and spat. The drums faltered, then continued.

"Keep dancing," growled a man's voice.

She felt a chill. Somehow the double circle no longer included the fire. While she danced, the deep vision returned. Again her nose lengthened, her skin sprouted fur. This time she trotted the scent more carefully. Something was under that brush. Something grabbed her neck and flung her into the air, violently, like the toss of an auroch's horns. Choking, she hung from a sapling.

Glowfly coughed, growled, and tumbled to the ground. The drums beat the slow rhythm of a heartbeat. This helped Glowfly return to herself. Great Mother Wolf was not Glowfly's totem, but a spirit from outside, and the possession was fierce. The drums stopped with a loud slap.

"This dance has a new meaning," said High Shaman Drakey. "Mother Wolf has a new battle to fight, and we must help her. The humans are killing her warriors with traps, and also the other warrior beasts. Glowfly, speak your vision."

Now she was conscious of her singed and torn dress, her scratched and exposed skin. "I was a wolf stabbed by a spike in a hidden pit. I was a wolf strangled by a rope tied to a bent tree."

Drakey said, "The humans are the new ice spirits. Their hearts are cold. This coldness makes them twisted, as trees in the high mountains are twisted. This coldness spreads over our land, chilling our own hearts. Let the Wolf Dance become a War Dance."

"May I speak? It was my vision," said Glowfly. "Before we make war with the humans, we must talk to them about the traps. They do many cold and twisted things without understanding because their lives are not whole."

"Talk is useless," Drakey said bitterly. "No matter what we explain to them, always we must explain more."

"Goblins and humans cannot be friends," said Screaming Spear, former chief and Glowfly's father. "We have learned enough about them to know this."

Chief Beartooth said, "I say we cannot dance war until we can make war. This camp is strong, but fifty warriors cannot battle two thousand. The truce that Strong Bull made will last two more months."

"Dance, and Mother Wolf's purpose will become clear," said Drakey.

"I have been dancing."

"The Wolf Dance is a shaman's dance. Mother Wolf possessed Glowfly and spoke to me. Dance a warrior's dance this night and Mother Wolf will speak to all of you."

"I say we can try this," said Screaming Spear.

"If the war we dance is a spirit war, the dance is true," said Beartooth.

The women and children made a sitting circle outside two circles of standing men. "You should play the small drum," Antelope told Glowfly.

"Mother, I have no heart for this."

"You are the one who was the wolf," Cicada said. "You can drum the truth better than I can. You play the big drum and I will play the small drum."

This command and honor Glowfly could not refuse. She had never before played the big drum in ceremony. She prayed to her totem, Father Otter, for endurance.

Glowfly took a deep breath and howled with all her might while playing a deep rumbling roll that suddenly broke into an emphatic variation of the rhythm of the trotting wolf. The startled men drew their knives and began pacing the dance. Cicada played leaps and gallops on the small drum. Other women shook rattles and played hoop drums. The ground shook with drumming and dancing.

The ripped top of Glowfly's dress kept sliding off her right shoulder, chafing the scratches and burns on her back, more so the more she sweated. "Take it off if it bothers you," Cicada said into her ear. While Cicada briefly played both drums, Glowfly pulled down the top of her dress, hesitated, then took it off completely, and resumed drumming, naked but for her soft shoes. After a few moments she kicked these off as well so that her bare feet could feel the ground.

At some time Glowfly felt overwhelmed by deep sadness; tears flowed from her eyes against her will. She tried to summon determination, anger, any feeling that would make her keep drumming. She was surprised to see Cicada now also naked, her arms and breasts glistening with sweat in the bright moonlight. Cicada howled, Glowfly howled louder, and the dancing warriors howled together, stabbing and slashing at the air with their knives. In the distance a wolf pack howled in response.

Finally Glowfly's arms ached so much and her hands were so numb that she had to stop playing that rhythm, so she played a slow beat for a chant. When the other women stopped playing, Glowfly chanted,

> Grass, river, wind, I run.
> Sparsely scattered trees, I run.
> Skin stretched by my ribs, I run.
> Panting with my breath, I run.
> My teeth are sharp, my jaws are long.

> Grass, river, wind, I smell.
> Sparsely scattered trees I smell.
> Something good to eat I smell.
> Skin stretched by my ribs, I run.
> Panting with my strength, I run.
> Drooling with my joy, I run.
> My teeth are sharp, my jaws are long.

> Grass, river, wind, I see.
> Sparsely scattered trees I see.
> Something good to eat I see.
> I hear, I smell, I slowly step.
> Skin stretched by my ribs, I leap.
> Drooling with my joy, I snap.
> My jaws are long, my teeth are sharp.

"Ah. Ha! Hey, yo. Ha!" said one of the warriors. Walking slowly with knives held high, they changed Glowfly's chant to this:

> Grass, river, wind, we run.
> Sparsely scattered trees, we run.
> Our knives are sharp, our spears are long.
> A host of enemies we fight.
> Skin stretched by our ribs, we fight.
> Panting with out strength, we fight.
> Shouting with our joy, we fight.
> Yiyiyi! Our spears are sharp.
> Yiyiyi! Our aim is true.
> Yiyiyi! Our enemies fall.

Each beat that Glowfly played while the warriors made chants like this made a pain in her heart. She told herself that she was no common woman but a shamaness fierce enough to become a wolf in the spirit world. She could ignore the hot tears rolling from her eyes even as she ignored the scratches and burns on her skin and the deadness in her hands.

"Coral, Coral," Glowfly thought bitterly, "why did this have to happen to your people, and to mine?"

20.

By the second month of spring, warm sunny days were plentiful, the river lizards were returning to Loop Lake, and the villagers were doing more hunting than fishing. One misty morning, while Rockdream, Salmon, and Bloodroot were trailing a wild pig farther west of the lake than usual, they encountered a human woman wearing a mud-spattered dress, with no boots, no pack, and no weapon but a short knife in her belt.

"Stay away. I am lost." Her voice was slow, slurred, and loud like someone drunk, and she staggered.

"You have nothing to fear," said Rockdream. "Come closer so we do not have to shout."

"No. You do not understand. I am sick."

"She is not drunk. Her wits are addled by a fever," said Salmon, who could hear the woman's thoughts.

"Maybe she has swamp sickness," Bloodroot muttered.

"Yes. Stay away. You might get my sickness. I could not find the food. I think I went to the right place." She took a raspy breath and crumpled to her knees. "No! Stay back!" She told Salmon.

"Did your people exile you because you were sick?" Salmon asked incredulously.

"They leave me food every day but I got lost," she said, trying to stand but ending up seated on the damp ground.

"Probably a raccoon or a raven got to it first," said Salmon, squatting beside her. "Are there no healers in your village?"

"They died. They died. There is no cure for this. You live or you die. If I get well, I can go back. I thought I was well last night, but the fever came back. Do your priests know a cure? Do people die in your village?"

"I am a witch. I think I can help you," Salmon said.

"I thought my fever was gone. I just thought I was cold when I got out of bed."

"Do you have bedding? A pack?"

"Oh, blood. I forgot them. I had them last night."

"Then I can find them," said Rockdream.

"You might catch the sickness from them. I am dying. You know this and I know this. You should just go away."

"No," said Salmon. "You need someone to take care of you. I think it is unspeakable cruelty to exile someone in your condition. We will bring you back to our village, and give you medicines and keep you warm, and you will recover." She emphasized the words, "you will recover."

Rockdream backtracked the woman's trail for half a mile before losing it on the hard ground of a long, low hummock. Here in a thicket of bronzeberry bushes he found her campsite, just two tattered, smelly wool blankets and a small pack, and no remains of a fire. By the time he returned, Salmon and Bloodroot had cut poles, assembled the litter, and the woman was lying on this, eyes closed, breathing unevenly.

"She is more relaxed now," Salmon said. "She should not have been walking. Let us tuck these blankets around her." The woman had the same foul odor as her bedding. "We can take turns carrying her. She likely weighs less than the pig we were hunting."

"Did you learn anything more about her?" Rockdream asked.

"Right now, she does not even remember her name. Maybe when her fever breaks, she will be more coherent. She said it comes and goes."

While Rockdream carried their bows and quivers, Salmon and Bloodroot carefully lifted the litter and began walking. The woman groaned, opened her eyes, then closed them again. They stopped twice to rest. On the third march, when Salmon and Rockdream were carrying the litter, Salmon said, "Put her down."

She kneeled beside the woman, felt for her pulse, and shook her head, saying, "She is dead."

Bloodroot went back to the village for shovels, and they spent most of that afternoon burying the body.

Coral called a village meeting at dusk around the main fire. "I am deeply concerned about this woman's death," she said. "Almost certainly she had the swamp sickness that afflicted Canticle's people last summer. This woman's exile proves to me, even more than Feathergrass's death count, just how much this illness is feared by those familiar with it."

"My guess is that she comes from Sharp Bend, for we were far in that direction," Salmon said. "If so, we cannot offer them our help, not with their attitude toward witches. But even if she came from somewhere else, any humans who have become twisted and ugly enough to exile their sick are no people I want to go near."

"If someone comes here to ask for help, I will do what I can, but my first concern is for our own village," said Coral. "If we build a large hut, maybe half a mile from here, we can use it to isolate and care for anyone who catches this disease."

"Good idea," said Magpie.

"The hut should be as well-made as any of our homes, and kept in good repair," Coral added.

"I say let us do it," said Swanfeather. "We can build it in two days if we work together."

Flatfish said, "One agreement we should make is not to bring back any strangers who are dying of this plague."

"Now, what else could I have done, without being as cruel as the people who exiled her?" demanded Salmon.

"In the future, we can bring such people to the isolation hut," said Coral.

"Being cautious need not mean being cowardly," said Rockdream. "I would avoid going near anyone with swamp sickness, but not if that person needed my help, as this woman did."

They spent some time discussing the design of the isolation hut, and the village's sanitary practices.

4

BIG WAR

21.

"You come too," Beartooth said, and that was that. Cicada and Glowfly would both march with the warriors to serve as healers. They packed their salves and herbs, their stones and bowls, their leather bandages.

Glowfly's husband, Quick One, was displeased. "You are too soft and gentle for a war camp," he said.

"I have enough fierceness and strength to do this work. Do not worry about me," she replied.

"Your softness makes me soft when I must be fierce."

Glowfly sighed and made the goblin gesture of negation.

"What I say is true," Quick One replied.

"I do not mean to weaken you in any way. I am a healer. I bind wounds and strengthen hearts."

"Do not speak of wounds! I do not march to war to be wounded, but to fight and kill. I am fierce. Remember that."

"Fierceness is for your enemies, not for me," Glowfly said.

"Fierce is fierce!" Quick One snapped, then took a deep breath and spoke more evenly. "At the war camp, you should stay with Cicada. When the fighting ends, I can be gentle with you."

Glowfly bowed her head in resignation and held back her tears. Her throat and heart were filled with stones.

In a moment of privacy with Cicada, she complained, "Why must my husband be a man who reacts to war like this?"

Cicada's brown eyes widened with concern. "Quick One is young and lacks confidence. He has never known war even between camps. When the last battle happened, I was a young girl. This will be a big war. He needs you to understand and accept him. He will not ask you to do this, because he thinks he should not have to. Be careful what you say to him, or your marriage will be hurt."

"That is just my problem. What kind of marriage do I have if my husband and I cannot talk?"

"If he lives, better times will come. If he dies in battle, you will wish you had spoken more carefully."

Tears escaped from Glowfly's stinging eyes. Cicada frowned for a moment, then embraced her.

"Keeping balance is hard both for him and for you. It is hard for everyone. Even Beartooth is sometimes sullen."

Glowfly made a half-smile.

Late in the afternoon, everyone gathered in the center of camp. At Beartooth's command, five warriors would stay behind with the old men and larger boys to defend the women and children. "Watch the river, the west, and the north, but do not neglect the east," said Beartooth. "Always be ready to hide. Do not fight unless you are sure you will win. Respect the red of messengers."

They began their march when the almost round moon was rising, just before sunset. Each goblin warrior bore a shield, a spearthrower, two short spears, a sleeping fur, and a store of food, all bound together into one backload. This was much to carry but scant supply for a big war. The camps up the branches of the Goblin River would bring the bulk of the weapons and supplies on big reed rafts. The plan was to muster quickly by night, to give the humans as little warning as possible.

To cover thirty miles in one night they had to march briskly and steadily. With such loads, this was much easier by moonlight than in the heat of the day. To Glowfly the plain seemed vast enough to swallow Strong Bull's whole army. The high chief's camp was a hundred miles from the human settlement, and some of the Bear River camps were even farther. Would the camps all send warriors? Would there be enough to attack the settlement? Maybe it was better to walk without thinking. Walk the thoughts away.

Grass, river, wind, we march, step, step, step, beneath the bright opal moon and the faint stars.

22.

The east wall of Canticle's Keep was just far enough back from the crest of the rise that no part of it could be seen from the east, but anyone standing atop the breastwork could see all the way to the Goblin River. The guards who stood watch while the sky brightened toward sunrise expected to see something, for this was the day the humans had agreed to leave Goblin Plain. But even by full daylight, Condor's Camp, where the goblin army was mustering, was no more than a vague something almost on the horizon, sometimes marked by a tiny puff of smoke.

The day passed, and no messenger came. The goblins crossed the river where tall willows on the west bank hid their rafts from human view. Not until the pink haze of sunset embraced the moonrise did the wall guards recognize the approaching army. General Canticle stood atop the breastwork with Lieutenants Fledgeling and Wolfkiller, while the wall guard and Feathergrass stood nearby.

"Strong Bull's intent is plain enough," said Fledgeling.

"Yes, but our needs are not," said Canticle. "If that army numbers six hundred or less, we can win the battle tonight and make a good peace tomorrow without the help of the boats. If we do need them, I want to make certain they have the best possible information."

Considering the shortage of competent warriors aboard the boats, this was prudent. "I have one worry, lord general," Fledgeling said. "What if the army is so large that you cannot contrive our escape?"

"If there are more than a thousand, many must be boys and old men. I can bulk out our own army to match. Wolfkiller!"

"Yes, lord general."

"I want the entire settlement—warriors, regulars, and auxiliary—lined up and ready to go over the wall by the time that army gets here. You command a platoon of archers to guard the wall. Use my authority to pull any archers you want from other platoons, but no good swordfighters. I will want concentrated cover around the horse ramp, but do not neglect any part of the wall."

"Ho, ho!" he said, and jumped down from the breastwork to the wall top and gave orders to various warriors.

"Fledgeling and Feathergrass!" said Canticle.

"Yes, lord general," they both said.

"First plan, if the army is small enough to defeat tonight: You stay with the lines and fight. Second plan, if we are not doing so well but the army is small enough that the camps are well guarded: You go to Lord Drill, and the boats attack a couple of camps with dragon guns and burning spears, then come this way. Third plan, if the army is big enough that the camps are poorly guarded: The boats raid the camps. Kill any warriors and whoever else resists, but let some escape. Raid the stores. Take the tents themselves if you can. Try to avoid setting fires. Remember that our objective is to make them use more of their force to guard their camps, to reduce the size of their army. We do not want to anger them so much that they fight us to the death of their last warrior."

"Understood, lord general," said Fledgeling.

"I hope we can defeat them tonight," Canticle said. "We do have experience fighting as a large unit, and they do not. Still, I must admit that Strong Bull mustered his army very quickly and they do move more like a disciplined human force than a raid of goblin berserkers." Indeed, Canticle soon saw that the goblins carried round shields much like his own. "Whether theirs are good enough to stop or deflect longbow arrows remains to be seen, but they will not stop crossbow bolts. Maybe I will have a chance to shoot down Strong Bull myself. War paint or no, I will recognize him. Feathergrass!"

"Yes, lord general."

"Find Wolfkiller and tell him I want the best archers of his platoon armed with crossbows. And bring me my own."

"Right away, my lord." Feathergrass ran down the inside ramp, asked a few questions, found Lieutenant Wolfkiller, and relayed the general's orders.

"I have already done so," Wolfkiller replied. "Crossbows as far as they go, longbows for the rest, pikes for close combat. We should be starting up the ramp in two minutes, in our places in seven."

Feathergrass then hurried to Canticle's hut for the general's own crossbow and quiver. By the time he returned to the ramp, it was filled with Wolfkiller's platoon mounting the wall.

"Your crossbow, general," said Feathergrass.

"Where are they?" Canticle asked Fledgeling, who was still perched atop the breastwork.

"Not coming closer, but spreading out, about a thousand of them. Look out!" She jumped back off the breastwork into a squat just as a single short spear pierced the air where she had stood.

"What was the range of that?" Canticle asked.

"Three hundred fifty feet. They are just out of sight from this level."

"Wolfkiller!" the general shouted.

"Ho!"

"I want your crossbow archers to hop onto the breastwork, shoot once, and take cover."

"Crossbows to the breastwork; count of three, aim, shoot, and down," said Wolfkiller. "One! Two! Three!"

Thirty warriors and regulars did so. In response, a volley of spears flew overhead or struck the breastwork. On the north and south walls, Wolfkiller's sergeants gave orders to shoot. Their goblins were visible from the wall.

"They have enough to circle us with a column of one, but that is useless," said Canticle. "Strong Bull must plan to swarm over some other part of the wall. Wolfkiller! Strengthen the west wall with auxiliaries from other platoons. Bring them up on ladders. Hardtack! Graywall! Foam! Strike! Swordnotch! When I give the order, I want all your regulars to run up and down the ramp and rush the goblin line."

Wolf howls and war cries came from the west, not from goblins, who were still keeping quiet, but from the human wall guard signaling goblin attack.

"Fledgeling and Feathergrass, you go with Hardtack," Canticle said quietly, then shouted, "Up and over!"

With that, Feathergrass and Fledgeling were running down the ramp, which had its own breastwork, but at the bottom they had to dodge flying spears. One struck Feathergrass's shield. Arrows from the wall flew overhead in reply. Feathergrass drew his sword and ran with the others.

Shouting war cries, goblins rushed them from two directions, carrying shields and brandishing long thrusting spears. Good. Their armament of throwing spears seemed used up. Their faces, masked with white warpaint, gleamed in the moonlight. When two of them rushed Feathergrass, he dodged to one side, ducked under and closed in, too close for them to get a good thrust. One swing of his sword struck the head of the one on his right. Ugh!

That one fell dead. And Feathergrass swung back and cut the spear arm of the one who was pressing Fledgeling.

"Get back in the bloody formation, mariner!" she shouted. "You cannot drive them overboard here!"

Indeed, he was already in trouble, for the goblin line was doubled and tripled. "Clear behind!" someone shouted, and Feathergrass and Fledgeling both stepped back. "Pikes forward!" shouted Lieutenant Hardtack. While the swordfighters held their ground, the pikefighters advanced between them.

Now the swordfighters ran south, behind and beyond the pike line. Suddenly spears flew toward them. Feathergrass swung his shield to knock one aside, an awkward maneuver that worked. Fledgeling brandished her sword and shouted, "Run them down!" This time most of the line tried Feathergrass's tactic of closing in fast. Some swordfighters killed or disabled their goblins, but others were killed or wounded. More goblins came around the south wall to try to surround the squad of swordfighters, but a new squad of human pikefighters came to even out the line.

"The main column is coming around the north wall," Fledgeling told Feathergrass in a moment of relative quiet. "We should break before they reach the main battlefield."

"Do we have enough to cut through this group?"

"We can try. Run them down!" she shouted.

The goblins couched their thrusting spears. One of them, possibly a chief, changed position to oppose Fledgeling, who was clearly the swordfighters' leader. Feathergrass struck his opponent's spear with the flat of his sword and jumped forward, sliding his sword along the spear's shaft to cut the hand that held it, then swung up to slice the goblin's throat. Fledgeling's goblin also fell dead.

"Now!" she said and jumped into a run. Feathergrass slung his shield over his back and ran after her. As soon as they were well away from the battle, they flung their shields aside. Now running was easier, but after ten minutes of hard running, Feathergrass's heart beat an ache inside his ribs and his breath was forced. When they slowed to a walk to sheathe their swords, his legs burned. Fledgeling gestured silence and began jogging. He followed.

They continued this easier pace for several miles, keeping close to the rise, where the hard ground and shorter grass would reveal less of their trail. Finally Fledgeling slowed to a walk. "Are you all right?" she asked quietly.

After catching his breath, Feathergrass replied, "I will live."

"How much farther can you go?"

"What I think I can do does not matter. We must either go well beyond Charging Elk's Camp or else across the marsh."

Fledgeling said, "If we cross the marsh, we will be delayed. Speed is vital. But there may be scouts near Charging Elk's Camp, where the river and the marsh are only seven miles apart. If they saw us, we would not dare stop."

"I see what you mean. We might be safest waiting somewhere around here until tomorrow night." He stood still and looked around.

"Forget what seems reasonable for a moment," Fledgeling said. "What does your intuition say?"

After a moment the words flowed out. "Charging Elk's warriors are our worst enemies. Likely none missed the battle, so the camp will not be well-guarded tonight. Tomorrow that may change."

"Yes. We should walk as far as we can tonight," Fledgeling agreed.

23.

They walked southwest, away from the rise toward the darker grass and reeds of the marsh. When the grass became knee-high, they began following whichever trail went the way they wanted, avoiding any ground soft enough to show a bootprint. They also watched for manure, which if stepped on would give them away just as certainly. But in the moonlight they did not notice that the horse or quagga droppings were not quite right for either animal.

When they detoured around the finger of reeds, they did not see the three-toed hoofprints. What they finally did see was a white animal bedded down on the grass in the shadow of a lone willow.

"It must be Snowflake, and with a dappled colt!" Fledgeling said, guessing that the animal was a pregnant white mare lost five months before when Charging Elk had captured Capstone's hunting group. "This is our lucky night. Snowflake! You remember me, Fledgeling, yes, you do."

But the mare raising her head had never borne a human rider and never would, for on that head was a foot-and-a-half-long horn. She stood quickly, as did the mottled, hornless colt, and pawed the ground and snorted.

"We are backing off. We mean no harm. We are not hunting," Fledgeling said in what she hoped was a more soothing voice. "Whatever you do, do not run," she muttered to Feathergrass.

"Stoop down and pretend to eat some grass," he said, and did so. "That is the quickest way to calm a jittery unicorn."

Fledgeling picked some seeds and made a show of eating them. "These actually are not bad."

"Goblin wheat, I guess," Feathergrass said. "Now stand up, walk a few feet, and eat some more."

They did this several times before looking toward the willow. The unicorn and her colt were gone. Both humans plucked a good handful of seeds before resuming their walk.

"Where did you learn that one?" Fledgeling asked.

"From the old herder of the Prosperity Bestiary Garden. They had several unicorns there, including one so tame that Loon and I got to pet her. Those were dappled unicorns of course. Only over here do they grow up solid white or silver. I never saw a wild one before."

"Nor have I," said Fledgeling, "but I have heard stories enough. I was expecting trouble like we had with that auroch bull. Remember him? Who would think to find a unicorn here, surrounded by grassland and marsh? We must be at least sixty miles from the Emerald Hills, where the unicorns are supposed to live."

"Very strange," Feathergrass said, and thought of Loon. If she were here, she would say that a unicorn mare and colt bedded down in such a place was so strange that it had to be an omen.

"They do not belong here and neither do you," said Loon's voice. "You both should go over the Emerald Hills to Midcoast. Forget the bonded servitude. Just go down to the harbor and sign on. You stopped sailing because of that pirate battle. What you face here is much, much worse."

For a moment, Feathergrass allowed himself to feel the horror of knowing that he had killed two goblins—two *people*—and disabled a third. But they were trying to kill him, or else his wife. But only because he and his wife were on Goblin Plain. But he could not desert. He could not even suggest such a thing to Fledgeling.

"Feathergrass, are you all right?" she asked.

"Very tired, possibly battle-shocked. I was thinking of Loon and that brought it on somehow."

Fledgeling was standing in front of him, holding his arms with her very strong hands while looking into his eyes. Hers were wide and black in the moonlight. "I know," she said earnestly. "I never killed anybody before tonight, and he was an old man, no match for me at all. War is not much like fencing. But you and I are warriors, and sometimes warriors find themselves at war."

"So do mariners. You know about the pirates."

"See those willows about a quarter-mile ahead?" Fledgeling asked. "You and I are going to lie down inside that screen of branches and celebrate our victory and successful escape."

Feathergrass did not remember some of that walk, did not remember undressing. Fledgeling's nude body, so familiar after three seasons of being first lovers, then married, seemed strange. Even her breasts felt like solid, flexed muscles. She was kissing him, pulling him inside. The next thing he remembered was sleeping fitfully through the morning and the heat of the day, fully dressed. Fledgeling was dressed also, and slept with her right hand on her sword hilt.

24.

Who won the battle? Strong Bull's army drove the humans back inside the walls, but the human archers drove the goblins out of bow range. More humans died than goblins, but few good fighters, and the human army had been bigger to begin with. It was a standoff, a siege. The goblins made a new camp on the rise, far enough north of the walls to be out of bow range, but close enough to quickly intercept any human sorties or messengers.

Glowfly was one of seventeen shamanic healers who came to this new camp late that morning. The work was at first overwhelming, for nearly two hundred goblins had wounds serious enough to require attention. Her husband, Quick One, had a pike wound in his right side just under the shoulder, which might put him out of battle for half a month. But many warriors who had fought swordfighters or been pierced by one of those solid steel dragon arrows would never fight another battle at all, if they even survived.

Strong Bull's father, Gray Wolf, was one of these. In a skirmish well away from the main battle, a woman warrior had stabbed his chest with her sword and left him for dead when he fell. Sees Patterns, a shaman from Strong Bull's Camp, was treating him but had little hope that he would recover. Though the sword had missed his heart, his lung was pierced. He was drifting in and out of awareness and coughing up blood, too much blood.

When Strong Bull spoke with his father, Glowfly could sense how disturbed the high chief was and how firmly he suppressed this feeling. She realized she was doing the same thing herself when she talked to her husband. If this was strength, if this was the best way to respond to the shock of war, she did not like it. But if she let herself feel, if she let herself cry, she would be unable to work. These warriors needed her.

She would pray for a vision. She would sleep, as soon as she had time. She would dream. Father Otter could swim any river, even this one.

25.

Fledgeling and Feathergrass left the willows two hours before sunset and walked south along the marsh's edge through the night. By the time they reached the Blue River, they were famished and lead-footed, but the human fleet was in sight. After eating thick slabs of grilled sturgeon aboard the *Great Stag*, they gave their report to Lord Drill and Lieutenant Conch, with Drill's son Marten also listening.

"A siege is about what we expected," said Conch, "but Canticle's priorities are amiss. No peace or truce the goblins make will mean anything at all unless they know that we can and will kill them all if they break it."

"The general does not want a massacre. He made that quite clear to me," said Fledgeling. "We are only supposed to raid the camps for stores, and to battle warriors."

"I outrank the general," said Lord Drill. "In this case I must overrule him. We are fighting for our survival and we must win. Canticle warned Strong Bull that if his people did not make peace with us, we would destroy their camps, one by one. Strong Bull's response was to muster an army big enough to leave the camps all but unguarded. We must follow through on our threat."

"Yes, but not by killing noncombatants. That was never the plan," Fledgeling protested. "We do not want to make the goblins hate us so much that they fight to the death of their last warrior."

"We want a decisive victory," said Conch. "We are through making threats and haggling over peace agreements."

"My lord, excuse me," said Feathergrass. "But look at your ten-year-old son for a moment. Those camps are filled with children his age and younger. Think about it."

"I have thought about it," said Lord Drill. "I regret that anyone at all has to die, for all life is precious. But the goblins began the fighting. We were willing to coexist. This is war, and we must fight to win, or our own children—what few we have left—will die. This was a hard decision for me. I do not wish to discuss it any more."

Fledgeling and Feathergrass looked at each other, then back at the lord.

"Do you want the assistance of me and my people or not?" he asked.

"We meant no offense, my lord," Fledgeling said.

"Good. We will split the navy into two fleets. I would assign you command of the Goblin River fleet."

"I accept, my lord," Fledgeling said.

"You will work with Captains Wetrock, Shiver, Seabrand, Terrapin, Scuppie, Reedflower, and—I guess those are all. You will have about fifty professional warriors and maybe five times that many competent archers, plus full crews for each boat, and six clerical healers."

26.

At Feathergrass's suggestion, Fledgeling made Captain Terrapin's *Golden Turtle* her command ship. It was not the biggest but it was well-armed, sturdy, and maneuverable, and Terrapin was experienced, and dependable in a crisis.

"Commander, I will tell you this right now," Terrapin said. "You will not like this advice any more than I like giving it, but we must do more than win a decisive victory. We must destroy the goblin army as a fighting unit. If we do not, then no matter what kind of truce they agree to, they will regroup sometime this summer and wipe us out. You may have noticed that the Blue River is much lower than it was last year at this time. The Goblin River is also much lower. By midsummer, even if the boats do not get stranded, they will be very vulnerable to attack from shore. Of course, a rainy summer would prove me wrong, but if the goblin shamans can affect the weather the way some say they can, well—"

"This is war, captain," said Fledgeling. "We must fight to win."

Feathergrass felt a queasiness in his stomach, knowing that he had already killed in battle, and would do so again and again and again before this was ended, or else be killed himself.

27.

The ships set sail before dawn the next morning, to reach the Goblin River well after sunrise but still early. The two fleets, each with six large riverboats and a number of fishing boats, sailed in tandem with a good breeze from the south-southwest.

When the *Golden Turtle* entered the mouth of the Goblin River, the forward dragon-gunner, a sharp-eyed sailor who proudly called himself Dead Center, shot a pike at a squatting goblin scout who no one else had seen. The impaled goblin staggered to his feet and screamed with all his might for a few seconds before falling dead.

"Blood! I meant to silence him," Dead Center grumbled.

"There must be others," Terrapin said. "Beadback's Camp is too far for anyone to hear even that."

"But how many others, and was he telling them to flee or to fight?" Fledgeling wondered. "Never mind. Stay the course. Beadback's Camp is Lord Drill's concern."

If there were any other scouts, no one in Fledgeling's fleet saw them. About an hour later, when they were halfway to Charging Elk's Camp, they saw clouds of smoke astern, from the direction of Beadback's Camp. "That took them a while," Fledgeling said.

"I hope it is Beadback's Camp and not the boats that are burning," said Captain Terrapin.

"Maybe Lord Drill and Conch found a real battle," said Feathergrass. "Beadback's Camp might have been well-guarded."

"Charging Elk's Camp may also be well-guarded," said Fledgeling. "Captain, is there any way we can rig up something like a pelican's roost on the mainmast?"

"I know just the one for the job," Terrapin replied. "Packtail!"

"Aye sir!" A boy no older than Drill's son Marten made his way around the crowded deck.

"The commander wants a lookout atop the mainmast. Maybe you can climb up and rig a pelican's roost with something."

"Aye, sir. Am I the lookout?"

"Your eyes are sharp but you cannot shoot worth a curse, and you climb like a squirrel. Who else?" The captain turned to his skeptical commander and said, "The boy is good. Just tell him what you want him to look for and he will describe it for you sooner than you could see it yourself."

"Terrapin knows his crew," Feathergrass said.

Fledgeling looked at the boy. "I want you to watch both sides of the river. Point out any nearby scouts to Dead Center and Greenwave. Let me know when and where you see Charging Elk's Camp, Strong Bull's army, or any other goblin groups. I want a full description, how many and what they are doing. Also note any signs of recent activity such as wide trails, skid marks, or canoes. And alert me to any mammoths, aurochs, fangcats, or other dangerous animals."

"Aye, my lady," he said. In moments, he had climbed up the mast with a coil of rope and rigged himself a seat. Terrapin was giving instructions to the dragon gunners and other sailors. Soon Packtail saw Charging Elk's Camp, which was moved to a new site, two miles west of the river.

"No cookfire smoke," Packtail said. "Too far to see goblins. Maybe I see a few. None near the river, unless they are hiding in the trees."

There were willows ahead, scattered along the west bank in clumps, and single trees on the east bank. The *Golden Turtle* tacked toward the more open shore, and the other boats did the same. Packtail said that there was little but open grassland between the river and Charging Elk's Camp. Then the tall willows blocked Packtail's view.

"What do you think?" Fledgeling asked Feathergrass. "There they are in plain sight, tempting a raid. What could go wrong?"

"They might have both moved their camp and set a strong guard. They will certainly retreat from a large force. We would be delayed. Something tells me to hurry north. Maybe the main army is retreating toward the river, pressed hard by a sortie from the keep. Ten more miles, and Packtail can tell us."

When the *Golden Turtle* was about a mile north of Charging Elk's Camp, Packtail saw a signal fire about two miles ahead and two miles east of the river. As the fleet moved north, he saw two goblins covering and uncovering the fire with a large skin, after throwing something onto it to make it smoke.

"This code is obvious," said Fledgeling. "The big puffs are riverboats and the small ones fishing boats."

Terrapin looked astern at the rest of the fleet. "If they prepared a special code, we know they are ready for us."

"I wonder what they plan to do. No matter, I guess. Whether they try to fight us or flee, we will cut them down. Hear me!" Fledgeling raised her voice to a shout. "To war! We sail to war! The goblin army will fall, struck by our arrows, stabbed by our pikes, slashed by our swords!"

The warriors and crew cheered their commander's show of enthusiasm. As yet no goblin army was in sight.

28.

Twelve miles north of the fleet, Glowfly was sometimes marching, sometimes running in the center of the retreating goblin army beside her bandaged husband, Quick One. Most of the other wounded warriors had been evacuated the night before last, and Strong Bull's father, Gray Wolf, had been carried with the other dead to the Sacred Ground.

In the first skirmish of the day, Strong Bull's warriors had found the newly devised handguards on their thrusting spears a most effective defense against certain swordfighter moves. The humans had not risked close combat for a while after that. But now that the goblins were nearing the river, the humans found a new way to harry them. Forty archers on horseback, galloping out of spear range, circled ahead, while the foot soldiers closed in from behind.

Strong Bull gave a shout and now the goblins were running again, toward the horses and the river. From the sound of it, at least two horses were hit by throwing spears. But in a battle of missiles, arrows had the greater range, and flew among the goblins from all directions. Quick One raised his shield overhead, as did many others. They slowed to a walk to avoid stumbling. The humans held their fire till the goblins lowered their guard to try to run again. Several times they ran suddenly, shielded themselves and marched, then ran again. Glowfly was careful to stay near her husband's shield.

After half an hour of this, the mounted humans galloped ahead, leaving the goblins free to run. In a few more minutes smoke rose from the river, where the riders were shooting burning arrows at the reed rafts and battling the raft guards. And downstream was more smoke, where goblin scouts were hurling burning spears at the humans' sails.

29.

"Do *not* furl them! Soak the sails!" Commander Fledgeling shouted. "This is not dragon fire!"

"Pass the commander's bloody command and hoist those buckets!" shouted Captain Terrapin.

Similar orders were being shouted aboard the other boats of the fleet, many of which were targets of burning spears from other small groups of goblins. Some of the boats' crews in the rear of the fleet were furling their sails, just as the goblins likely wanted, so that fewer humans would be free to fight a boarding party. Signals and orders relayed from boat to boat caused at least two captains to change their orders, but three others did not. Evidently the discipline enforced at the settlement did not exist in Spirit Swamp. Well, Fledgeling would remember which captains obeyed promptly and which did not.

"I will climb back up for another look," Packtail said to the captain and commander, quietly enough that they might not hear him.

"What? No!" said Fledgeling, but by this time Packtail was already halfway up the mainmast. "Get down!"

"One moment—The goblins are soaking the fires on the rafts and the riders are leaving because the goblin army is coming too close but the humans are right behind them."

"Get down right now!" said Fledgeling. "We can see well enough from the bow. This is war. Obey your commander."

"All right," he said reluctantly and scuttled down the mast.

"Do not climb up there again unless either I or the captain tells you to do so," Fledgeling said firmly. "Now go astern and relay my command to those three fools to set their sails immediately. We cannot afford delay and the other boats are passing them."

Packtail did so. One of the three crews was already setting sails, and soon the other two did the same.

30.

The rafts were now secured to make a floating bridge across the river. Wet, slippery, bobbing, braided reeds made a treacherous surface, but Glowfly was running, in a group of warriors who might trample her if she fell. Twice she slipped or staggered, but Quick One yanked her to her feet. They splashed through the shallow, ran up the bank, regrouped. More goblins ran across the bridge, shields slung over their backs. Some fell, their shields and bodies pierced by those deadly dragon arrows. Several hundred warriors still stood on the far shore trying to hold back the human army. Downstream, the ships were less than a mile away.

"Run to Condor's Camp," Quick One told Glowfly.

"You come too. You are not well enough to fight."

"You go now," he said firmly.

Now most of the goblins were running across the bridge. The rearguard, including Strong Bull and Chief Beartooth, fought fiercely while retreating from shore to the first raft. The humans followed.

"Run!" Quick One said, pushing her angrily.

Glowfly ran.

31.

"Where is the lord?" shouted Lieutenant Foam, leader of the mounted warriors who paced the *Golden Turtle*.

"Burning camps on the Blue River, or trying to," shouted Fledgeling. "He burned something. The goblins set watch and moved Charging Elk's Camp two miles inland. We let it be and hurried here. But it looks like you beat them without us. What is the plan?"

"We only beat them because they feared you. Some bold demonstration of power would be best. But watch out for those rafts if the goblins cut them loose! They are much more massive than they look."

"Those hay bales?" scoffed Captain Terrapin. "If we must, we will board and steer them. As for our attack, get one of your warriors on board who can spot Strong Bull quickly and Dead Center will spit him with the dragon gun and end the war."

At Foam's command, one of the riders, a woman named Sonnet, urged her horse into a gallop, stopped and dismounted ahead, and was treading water in the river when the *Golden Turtle* reached her and a sailor threw down a knotted line.

"Find me dry leathers to wear and I will be grateful," she said. "I presume the front gunner is Dead Center?"

"The rafts are moving!" shouted Feathergrass. "The goblins are splashing to shore."

At that moment, as if by the enemy's will, the breeze that had blown steady from the south or southwest all morning suddenly failed. "To oars!" shouted Captain Terrapin, and every other captain of the fleet.

While the human crews furled their sails and took oars, several groups of goblins ashore suddenly shouted war cries and ran after the drifting rafts, dropped their shields, and swam.

"They are not boarding the rafts but clinging to them," said Packtail.

"A good way to shield themselves from the dragon guns," remarked Sonnet.

"Pikes and archers to the rails!" shouted Fledgeling.

"Two rafts closing in!" shouted Packtail.

Captain Terrapin ordered his rowers to steer for the west shore to avoid being caught between them. When the nearer raft bumped the hull, the rowers tried to push it away with their oars. But the goblins bobbed up between raft and boat to chop at these oars, and at the pikes thrust toward them, with their big axes. Some also took a few chops at the hull. The planking of the *Golden Turtle* was too thick to penetrate with a few blows, but the smaller fishing boats might be hulled this way.

Fledgeling tried to seize the offensive by ordering twenty warriors with pikes and shields to jump onto the raft. Ten jumped, but the ten who were to follow did not, for the goblins had all but severed the raft's binding, and when the first ten hit the raft they were enmeshed in a tangle of loose reeds and water. In the moment's confusion the goblins managed to kill or disable most of the humans in the water, then quickly swam away from the blood toward another raft.

But Dead Center aimed his dragon gun low and spitted one of them, and Fledgeling got another with her crossbow. Then they were safely behind or below the other raft, and somewhat astern from the *Golden Turtle*.

Meanwhile, the *Golden Turtle's* crew was busy shifting and replacing oars while trying to hold their own against the current. Two survivors of the skirmish were pulled back aboard with lines; a third swam to shore and was met by Lieutenant Foam's people.

The three fishing boats between the *Golden Turtle* and the second riverboat, the *Bold Sturgeon*, at first rowed to avoid the attack-raft but then circled back to surround it. At a signal from the *Bold Sturgeon*, warriors aboard all four boats loosed arrows and bolts at all the edges of the raft. At least two goblins were hit. The others swam away underwater, but three of these were killed by human archers when they surfaced. The rest came ashore near a line of old willows, but two more were killed before they could dodge behind them.

And that was the last blow struck by either side that day. By the time the fleet reached the site of the crossing, the goblin army was well out of range, and Canticle's army was too battle-weary to risk pursuit across the river, even augmented by Fledgeling's eager force.

"I think that we have achieved our goal," said the general. "Tomorrow there may be no goblin army for us to pursue. They must disperse to defend their camps. Instead we will move against the camps of Charging Elk and Cold Winter. From now on, the land on this side of the Goblin River is ours!"

"It is the Human River now!" said Lieutenant Foam.

"For now it is," said Commander Fledgeling, "but in a dry year like this it can drop to less than six feet deep after midsummer."

"Which is deep enough for fishing boats," said Canticle. "And riverboats on the Blue River are threat enough."

32.

"I do not believe this!" said Glowfly. "Where is my husband? Surely even he would not try to swim with that wound in his side." But she knew from the way he had handled his spear and shield during the retreat that his wound was not painful enough to stop him.

"He was brave and bold and fierce," said Cicada.

"Yes," said Glowfly, but she wished from the center of her heart that Quick One had possessed other qualities as well.

Cicada embraced her while she wept hot tears.

Strong Bull held council that night at Condor's Camp. Not only the shamanesses but many of the other women sat council, for news of the massacre of Beadback's Camp had reached Strong Bull. If women were being killed in battle, they had the right to speak about the war in council.

Tusk, a messenger from Gorge's Camp, described the battle. "When scouts first saw the boats, they gave shouts and signals. The women and children kept quiet and hidden. The warriors prepared an ambush. A force of humans came, equal in number to Beadback's augmented force. Humans fight only when they outnumber goblins, because we fight better. When Beadback's people attacked, the humans ran. But this was their plan. A second group of humans had stayed hidden on the boats until the first group killed the scouts. This human force was bigger. Beadback was surprised. The battle was fierce. Only a few wounded goblins left for dead survived. But a greater number of humans were killed, nearly two hundred.

"Of course, few humans were left to guard the boats. Hungry Snake and I and six others from Gorge's Camp set fire to some of them. We filled canoes with straw and mammoth grease. We paddled them until we were just around the bend from the boats. Then we set the canoes afire and swam across the river. The current took them right into the human fleet. Two big boats and three small ones caught fire. We hid ourselves to watch.

"A large group of humans hurried back, but they could not put out the fires. They went into the other boats and sailed down the river. These were all the survivors, but we did not know this yet. When we went to the battlefield, two goblins who had been left for dead told us the story. We searched for Beadback's Camp. What we found is hard to believe. These humans were determined to destroy this camp, even after losing more than half their number in the battle. They killed at least forty women. Even children of two and three years were pierced by their arrows."

Warriors and women both made cries of disbelief and rage.

"They did this to make us break up the army," said Strong Bull. "This we will do tonight. But we will continue the war. We will fight as goblins fight best. We will attack them with small groups where they are weak. We will destroy the boats. These boats are hard for humans to make. The wood must dry for a long time. The seams must be sealed. When the boats are gone, we will attack their hunting groups. This war will be slower and longer than the big war, but we will win. These two humans we will seek out and kill first: The man who led the assault on Beadback's Camp. The woman who killed my father, Gray Wolf, and fled the battle to bring the message to the boats."

"I will dream their names," said High Shaman Drakey.

"I will dream their deaths," said Sees Patterns, the shaman of Strong Bull's Camp.

Glowfly's heart was an aching emptiness. It was bad that her husband was killed, and worse that all the people of Beadback's Camp were massacred, but worst of all was the inner ice and fire of spirit death. Both humans and goblins were dying spirit death, and there was no way to stop or change this now.

33.

"Are you certain you want your son to witness this?" Mother Mallow's voice was both stern and kind. Though not a midpriestess, she had learned many things in her long years, and Lord Herring had often consulted her at the castle.

"Marten will one day become Lord of Newport," said Lord Drill.

The priestess looked impassively at the boy, then turned back to the father. They were alone aboard the *River Lizard*, a fishing boat anchored in a backwater pool near the confluence of the Blue and Turtle Rivers.

"I invoke the Lord of Light and Darkness, who is embodied in the Mother, the Father, the Three Daughters, and the Three Sons. I pray that you accept this boat cabin as a room in your Church suitable for the purification ceremony. I pray that you embody yourself in me to purify this supplicant. I invoke especially that part of you who is embodied in Fire, goddess of war. So be it, so it is." She rang a small bell and muttered, "At least this is the proper bell." She rang it again and asked Lord Drill, "Have you done any act that was unquestionably wrong that you wish to renounce and atone?"

"I—I am not certain."

Mother Mallow rang the bell again.

"What I did was wrong, more wrong than anything else I have done in this life, but—but I did have a reason," said Lord Drill.

She rang the bell again.

"It was unquestionably wrong," he said.

"You know this."

"Yes."

"Then you know that your reason is unimportant," said the priestess.

"I know this now," said the lord.

Mother Mallow rang the bell, took a deep breath, and sighed. "What have you done?"

"I commanded my warriors to fight and kill some goblins who were not armed to fight, and they did so."

The bell rang. "Why was this unquestionably wrong?"

"It—it just was."

The bell rang. "Think," said the priestess. "Why was this unquestionably wrong?"

"It was massacre, which is abhorrent to the goddess of war. It was murder, which is abhorrent to the goddess of love. It was spiritual pollution, which is abhorrent to the god of piety. It was wrathful command, which is abhorrent to the god of leadership."

The bell rang. After a long hesitation the priestess said, "It is hard to be lord of a people at war, especially for one who is not a warrior at heart. You were given a test, the hardest of tests, and you failed. What penance can you do for such a failure?"

Lord Drill was silent.

"Speak through me," Mother Mallow whispered, ringing the bell four times. She closed her eyes and rocked back and forth in her seat while speaking in a monotone. "For your merciless deed you are accursed. In life and in death the true spirits of this world will torment you with visions of blood and terror. For penance you must yield yourself—yield yourself to Strong Bull? No! I cannot believe this!"

She jolted out of trance and opened her eyes.

"Vile spirits who shape yourselves as beasts, I fence you out. I call upon Wind the Hunter to drive you from my fence. I call upon Thunder the King to make my fence a strong wall. You cannot use my voice. I am a priestess of the Holy Church, pledged to celibate service of the Lord of Light and Darkness—" The old woman lost her voice in a hoarse cough and slumped in her chair, panting for breath.

"Goblin sorcery!" said Lord Drill.

The priestess drank some water. "You are cursed indeed. What you did must indeed by abhorrent to the Holy Ones, if they let your enemies' totem beasts speak through me. This is what you must do. You must form clearly in your mind the image of Fire the Warrior with all her attributes, and pray to her for forgiveness. You must do this once each day. You must also do this with Lake the Lover, Thunder the King, and Mountain the Priest. Keep each image conscious in your mind and do not lapse into trance. Be conscious of all the implications of everything you decide to do." The priestess almost rang her bell but decided against it.

"I will do what you say," said Lord Drill.

34.

When Canticle's scouts brought back word that Charging Elk's Camp and Cold Winter's Camp had moved across the river, he said, "Good. They have yielded us the land."

But the humans no longer had complete control of the rivers. The dispersal of Strong Bull's army meant that now, many more goblin warriors could be lurking anywhere. They could and did take advantage of every opportunity to attack a boat. Most often the last boat of a fleet moving downstream was singled out; by the time the other boats turned back to help, the attackers had disappeared. But few boats were damaged and only one boat was lost this way.

More of a worry to Canticle was the fleet's failure to find any sign of Lord Drill and the other boats. Not until the sixth day after the massacre did a messenger sent by the lord deliver a sealed note to the general. Canticle did not reveal the note's message, but the wording of his reply made it evident that Lord Drill had abandoned the war. After describing the present military situation, Canticle added, "I will dutifully continue to defend my lord's city and people."

5

THE PRIESTESS

35.

"Salmon, Coral, Rockdream, look!"

Stonewater was coming back to the village from a hunting trip, hurrying ahead of her husband Ironweed and Magpie, proudly carrying the drakey she had shot and killed, her first. It was not the usual dark gray or brown, either, but a silvery blue.

"I never saw one that color before," said Rockdream. "Where did you get it?"

"We were down at the far end of the lake," said Magpie. "It was eating a river lizard larva."

"Let me tell the story. It was my kill," said Stonewater. "We were following a pig trail from the portage through the cattails when it sensed us and jumped into flight, with the larva's tail still dangling from its mouth. I saw it, aimed ahead, and shot. Look!" She lifted the drakey's left wing. "I was aiming for the wing muscle. I hit that and the heart. Splash! Dead and floating on the surface. I was already swimming after it."

"And we both jumped in after her," said Ironweed.

"I almost had it back to shore by the time either of you did so," said Stonewater.

"The grown river lizard that was following you turned tail," said Magpie.

"They all turned tail the moment I jumped in myself," said Stonewater. "Not that any of them were very close."

Magpie sighed. "You are becoming a good hunter, but you still cannot tell a good hunter's tale."

"With two witches hearing my thoughts while I speak, what good is hunter's exaggeration?" Stonewater said laughing. "It is not a big one, but it is a beauty. Will the skin keep its color if I tan it?"

"Only one way to find out," said Rockdream. "What do you want to make from it? Consider that before you start cutting."

"There is enough wing skin to make a tunic, I think. The scales are the prettiest part, but there is less of that."

"About an equal amount of each, if you skin it right," said Coral. "We made two pairs of boots and several bags and belts from the scaled skin of the one we killed last winter. That one was bigger, but the proportions of yours look about the same."

After showing her kill to everyone in the village who was at all interested in seeing it, Stonewater and Ironweed began skinning it. She cut the connective tissue with a sharp knife while he pulled the skin away from the muscle. Suddenly she screamed. The knife had slipped and made a deep stab on her right thigh.

Coral was there with her medicine bag before anyone had time to call for her. "Somebody! Get me some boiling water and two clean cups, quickly!" she said. "Stonewater, stay still. Ironweed, help me pull off her pants." Coral kept her fingers away from the wound when she pressed it together. Salmon had the water and cups. "Good," Coral said. "See how I am holding her? Put your hands in the same place." Coral took out the small jar of sleepflower gum and rolled a pellet about half the size of a grain of wheat, dropped this into an empty cup, and filled the cup with steaming water from the pot. After the gum dissolved, she poured the tea again and again from one cup to another until it was just slightly cooler than scalding hot.

"Stonewater, listen. I am going to wash out the wound with hot tea. For a few seconds it will feel like fire but then it will go numb. Ironweed, help Salmon hold her still."

Coral spread the wound and poured the tea quickly, washing away all the blood for a moment. Stonewater shuddered and tried to thrash. She could not help it. Now Salmon pressed the wound closed, and Coral washed the new blood off the skin with plain boiled water.

"Oh, god. Oh, death. Oh, blood," Stonewater said over and over, taking deep breaths. "That felt like—that felt like—like nothing I have ever felt. It feels a little better now."

Coral spread goldroot powder on a large bandage of thin, supple leather, then applied this to the wound and tied it on. "This is thin enough for your skin to breathe, and cleaner and less likely to irritate you than any cloth we have left. I do not want to take any risk."

"What happened to Daffodil, exactly?" Stonewater asked.

Coral stiffened, but relaxed as she spoke. "Captain Daffodil was skinning a deer and her knife slipped, much as yours did. Her wound killed her only because the two priests who were her healers did everything wrong. They washed her wound with unboiled water and used no herbs to prevent festering. Her wound festered and she became feverish. But I have successfully treated people in that condition as well. One thing you do not do is break the fever. It might make the patient feel better briefly, but greatly increases the danger of death. Well, they broke the fever. I might have been able to save her even then, but I was not allowed to try. In fact, after Daffodil's death, I was accused of wanting to poison her."

"Will I be all right?" Stonewater asked.

"You have little to fear. In a few days you will be walking around again. But lie still for today."

Salmon and Rockdream put Stonewater on a litter and carried her to her hut and put her to bed.

"Could one of you please help Ironweed skin and butcher my drakey?" Stonewater asked. "I felt so proud, and now I feel so incompetent. I could have been more careful."

That evening, Coral changed the bandage and dressing, and the next morning, she changed it again. She was more relieved than she let show that the wound had formed a clean scab, with no swelling or festering. Stonewater was able to walk a few steps around the hut and platform, but for several days after, she seldom wanted to go farther. Her wound healed well, but she was still limping and needed help climbing on and off her platform a week and a half later when the priestess and her huntswoman came to the village.

36.

"I am Mother Cedar, and my companion is Thornbush," the priestess told Magpie and Swanfeather, who were standing guard. "May I speak with the master of your village?"

The guards introduced themselves. "What do you want to discuss?" asked Magpie.

"Whether we might be made welcome here," replied Mother Cedar.

"This village has no master," said Magpie. "Whenever someone new wants to join us, we have a meeting, as we do whenever we have anything else important to discuss."

"Are you both in good health?" asked Swanfeather.

"Would you turn us away if we were not?" asked Mother Cedar.

"No, but we would ask to stay in the isolation hut, and allow our healers to care for you."

"You have witches here," said Mother Cedar. "You are fortunate. I will meet them and talk with them, and if I am not welcome here, Thornbush and I will go somewhere else. I offer my service to you. I have some experience working with the disease you most fear. But I do not impose myself."

"You sound all right," said Magpie. "Our witches had a bad experience with two priests in another village, but I would welcome the presence of the Church."

"If my presence proves divisive, I will leave," said Mother Cedar.

"We can disagree with each other here and still live together," said Magpie. "Come with us to the main fire and have some stew."

"Do you have your own bowls?" asked Swanfeather.

At the fire, Coral and Salmon introduced themselves.

"I understand you had a bad experience with the priests of another village," said Mother Cedar.

Coral's mouth momentarily went dry. "Those two accused me of black sorcery. When Captain Daffodil accidentally wounded herself, she yelled, 'Keep that witch away from me!' She had always been cordial to me before. I felt a flash of anger, but at the same moment I felt fear for Daffodil's life, for her wound was deep and could fester. The priests overheard these thoughts and feelings, misinterpreted them as a curse, and spread rumors without examining me.

"They washed the wound with unboiled water and used no goldroot, so it is no surprise that it festered and gave Daffodil a high fever. They broke the fever much too soon, then came to me for stimulants, exactly the wrong thing to give her. She had no strength left to stimulate. Only a massive dose of goldroot, more than I had, or a minute dose of fairlady, which was plentiful and in bloom nearby, might have saved her then.

"Daffodil died, and the younger priest all but accused me of wanting to poison her. The captain had been master of the village; most of the villagers had been her crew and passengers. She had gotten them out of doomed Newport alive, and rightfully they respected her. I had reason not to like her, for Rockdream and I had found the site and built the first huts, and they had taken over. Even though the priests publicly examined and exonerated me, people remained suspicious. So we came here and started over. I do not want to repeat that experience."

"I would prefer you settle somewhere else," said Salmon.

"And I would welcome you, Mother Cedar," said Stonewater. "I am living proof that Coral is a good healer, but I miss the chant and prayer. I think such misunderstandings can be avoided."

Mother Cedar looked at Coral. "I understand your reservations about my presence here, but look—" She pulled back the hood of her red robe to reveal her short curly hair. She looked less like a priestess, more like a woman. "I am a woman of the spirit and so are you. We can share our knowledge with each other. I know what swamp sickness is like, and which treatments have no effect or make the patient get worse. You know the dosages and uses of the proscribed herbs. We can work together when the sickness comes here, as sooner or later it will."

"Are you saying you would actually use proscribed herbs?" asked Salmon.

"Against this disease, I would. In the troubled year and season since the city fell, I have learned to listen to what the Holy Ones tell me, even if this seems at variance with the teaching of the Church. We are each and all being tested. Everything we took for granted—a good lord, a beautiful church, a secure and prosperous city—all this was taken from us. But maybe some of us will find new wisdom that will make this world a better place to live. Those who have died bitter deaths in battle or sickness will appreciate this, when they are reborn. This is what the Holy Ones tell me."

Coral smiled at the priestess.

"Tell us how you escaped from the city, and what you know

about other survivors," Rockdream asked Thornbush, who looked like enough of a warrior to appreciate his concern.

Thornbush looked at him, sighed, and stared at the fire. "We escaped the city aboard one of the boats the night of the storm," she said. "Our boat suffered more than some of the others. A month after we left the city, more than half the crew and passengers had the fever. The captain died, the first mate died, the second mate became captain. He thought the disease came from the foul pools of the backwater, and argued that it was better to chance discovery by the dragon on the river than to die this way. From time to time we encountered other riverboats. From one of these we caught the sickness afresh. Fewer of us got the fever, but almost all who did so died."

Mother Cedar said, "A person may survive swamp sickness once with good care and good luck, but a person who sickens a second time will die. I know of no exceptions. Fortunately, a person who has had it once is less likely to catch it again."

"My husband died quickly," Thornbush continued. "My daughter went through two weeks of fever that came and went before she jumped overboard in a moment of muddled wits."

"We had a long discussion about whether to go to the meeting of boats," said Mother Cedar. "On one hand, we might get exposed to the sickness again. On the other hand, the lord and the general had plans, and it seemed better to learn about these than to wander aimlessly through the swamp. We went to the meeting. Lord Drill had sailed up the Turtle River as far as the first cataract and recommended we all go there. 'Though the land is barren and hunting is poor, fishing is good, and if we dig a short irrigation canal we can farm,' he said, but Canticle had doubts. He wanted to build a settlement on Goblin Plain, 'where we know the climate, hunting, and soil are good.' But this could not be done till winter, so we all went to Lord Drill's site."

"The first cataract offered no solution to our problem," said Thornbush. "Fishing was fine only till the spawning run ended, then we fished out the river. The canal proved much harder to dig than Lord Drill had guessed. The heat was relentless and the ground was rocky. The boats sailed farther and farther downstream to fish. By the first rains of fall, most of the boats, including ours, were back in the swamp. We spent the winter in the backwater near the joining of the two rivers, while Canticle took the bulk of our people, including most of the warriors, to Goblin Plain to establish a settlement. The plan was for us to join him later, but some of us refused to take part in any war of conquest, even if it meant staying in the swamp."

Mother Cedar said, "When spring came, and Lord Drill and Canticle sat the peace circle with Strong Bull and his chiefs, I prayed that the agreement would work, but in my heart I knew it would not. I was not surprised when the call came for armed riverboats. I was quite surprised when Lord Drill took command of the fleet."

"I was one of the few warriors who stayed behind with the noncombatants," said Thornbush.

"When Lord Drill returned two days later, he and most of those who went with him were so spiritually polluted that—" Mother Cedar stopped herself. "I am sorry. I should not be talking about this."

"If Lord Drill has done something terrible it is indeed our concern," said Salmon.

"I already know what happened," Coral said, trying to keep herself from shuddering or breaking into tears. "I have dreamed this battle many times. My husband otherwise might have gone with those warriors. But which camp was destroyed? I must know."

"Beadback's Camp," said Thornbush.

"I would not battle noncombatants no matter what," Rockdream said at the same time.

"Beadback's Camp!" Coral exclaimed, and now the hot tears swelled from her eyes.

"At least it was not Beartooth's Camp," Rockdream said. "But this—this—"

"This is horrible!" said Coral.

"I prayed for guidance," said Mother Cedar. "I felt ashamed to be a human of Newport, ashamed to be a priestess of the Church of Newport. That Church has failed. I have failed. A woman I married, enraged by her husband's death, killed two noncombatant goblin women. A man I once purified shot a toddler to death. Can I purify him now and believe it will do any good? Lord Drill was given the confession and purification by the strictest, harshest priestess of us all, but I could see with my trance-eye that whatever she did made no real difference.

"I prayed for guidance. The Holy Ones reminded me that I am being tested. What I do is my choice, but I must take responsibility for that choice. If I am ashamed of what I am, I can become something else. I decided to leave."

"I made the same decision," said Thornbush. "I talked to Mother Cedar because she had tried to heal my husband and daughter, and had comforted me in my grief. I said, 'Drill is not my lord. Newport is not my city. I must pack what is mine and go away.' I expected her to try to talk me out of it. I hoped she would give me some reason to stay. But she said, 'Good. We will go together. You can hunt, and I can dream, and together we will find the place where we should go.' We set off on foot about a month ago."

"Will you welcome us?" asked Mother Cedar, looking around the fire at the villagers.

"Yes," said Coral, and all the others, even Salmon, also said yes or made gestures of affirmation.

37.

The next day, Rockdream, Salmon, Bloodroot, Ironweed, and Magpie offered to help Mother Cedar and Thornbush build a hut.

"I would like a small hut of my own," said the huntswoman, "but let us build Mother Cedar's church hut first."

"We might not have to put the whole meeting room on a platform," said the priestess.

"Yes we do, if we want to be able to use it," said Magpie. "In the winter, the ground turns to muck even when it is not flooded. In the summer, the mosquitos are thicker near the ground, not to mention the crawling bugs. I would hate to have a big thirty-legger crawl up my leg and bite me in the middle of a meditation."

"The building you have in mind is too big," said Salmon. "It must be completely hidden from the air."

"Do you seriously think you can hide from a dragon this way?" asked Mother Cedar.

"Yes, we do," said Salmon.

"Oh, that is right! Salmon! You—are you?—you are the warrior who survived that sea battle with Riversong."

"Yes, I am. I did," she replied. "What is more, when we fled the city, we passed practically under the dragon's nose and he did not notice us. So we do have experience at hiding from dragons."

"Let me explain our defense," said Rockdream. "First, we do not stand dragonwatch, for thinking obsessively about dragons tends to attract their notice. Second, except in the most bitter weather, our only fire is the community cookfire. If any dragon sees this smoke, it is outside on the ground like a campfire. With the huts all concealed, the site does not look like much. Third, if a dragon does attack, we scatter."

"I suppose I could hold multiple services," said Mother Cedar. "A church seating twelve would be no bigger than the largest hut you have already."

And that was what they built—a platform supported by nine stout poles each charred and soaked in grease at the buried end to resist rot. The floor beams were three six-inch logs, each fourteen feet long. Raising these to the notched pole tops, above shoulder height, was the hardest single task. The ten joists, notched four-inch logs, were much lighter. The deck was made of saplings lashed with willow wands. In fact, the rest of the construction was more like basketwork than carpentry. The walls and roof of the hut itself were woven of willow and thatched with reeds. The two small windows were left open; in winter they would be sealed with river-lizard parchment.

The church hut took five days to build; different people worked on different days. On the third day of construction, Mother Cedar, who had worn her red velvet robe all through her travels, at last put on a leather tunic and pants.

"When I first wore the robe of the Church, I felt like a new and different person, and rightly so, for the robe was given to me with ceremony. I feared that wearing ordinary clothes would make me feel like a lay person again. None of the other clergy at the boat camp did this. They believe they will die or have access to more velvet before their robes wear out. But here I am in hunter's clothes, doing carpentry of a sort, and I am still a priestess." After this, Cedar only wore her robe while leading the chant and prayer or doing a healing.

Birdwade and Ripple attended the very first chant and prayer service, which Birdwade afterwards described for Coral and Salmon. "It felt different, for I am used to a huge stone church with a thousand voices chanting, but there is also power in intimacy. The last big services in Newport were distorted, at least the ones I attended. But Mother Cedar knows how to do it right. When we left the meeting room, we felt empowered by the Holy Ones."

Coral said, "I know most of the Church's rituals and chants, and the theory behind them, but I have never actually attended a chant and prayer service."

"You have not missed much," said Salmon.

"I think you both might like it," said Birdwade. " I do not know why two witches and a priestess who serve the same goddesses and gods cannot chant together."

"Mother Cedar is a good person," said Salmon, "but she represents a body of opinion that over the centuries has become dry and cracked in the skin and rotten at the heart."

"If we with this village are trying a new and more appropriate way of life, perhaps our priestess can lead a new and more appropriate chant and prayer," said Birdwade.

"I dislike the very idea of a church and a clergy," said Salmon.

"You and I do not need them for our spiritual lives, but Birdwade obviously feels differently," said Coral.

"Yes," Birdwade agreed. "I need someone like Mother Cedar to open my heart and spirit to the Holy Ones, because I am not a priestess or witch who can do this for herself. But even though you do not need the chant and prayer as I do, you might enjoy it."

"I doubt that," said Salmon.

"I am considering it," said Coral.

When she discussed attending church with her husband, Rockdream, he said, "I know you would not have liked the chant and prayer services done in Newport, and those are the services she knows."

"Cedar is trying to befriend me and learn from me. It would not hurt me to experience her way. Will you come with me?"

Rockdream hesitated, not knowing how to express what he felt.

"Oh, husband, if you like it and I do not, you can go back by yourself. I never meant to make you choose between me and your own spiritual way."

"The Church holds marriage sacred," Rockdream explained. "I did continue going to church for a while after we married—not often, maybe once a month. The fourth time, a priest pulled me aside as I was leaving, and asked where my wife was. Of course, he immediately perceived that you are a witch. He said it would be better for me to stay home with you than for the Church to separate us in any way."

"So it was their decision."

"I think it was best."

Coral took his hand. "Maybe so, back then. But now you have no fear that our marriage is fragile. We have a child together, and we both helped create this village—"

"Just go to the chant and prayer and tell me what you think. Then we can decide."

"All right."

And a few days later at dawn, Coral was climbing the platform of the village church behind Birdwade and Ripple, going inside, and sitting beside them on the front bench, feeling slightly embarrassed. She let this feeling go and stared at the altar, just a hewn table with eight candles.

Mother Cedar emerged from her private room, stood in front of the altar, and began chanting the long tones. Coral let these tones guide her into trance as she joined her voice to the harmony. For a moment Coral was seeing the white radiance of the face of the Nameless Mother, but then the chanting subsided.

Mother Cedar spoke, startling Coral out of her vision, coincidentally to invoke and praise the Nameless Mother. The priestess continued. Praise Father Sky. Praise the daughters: Wind the Hunter, Fire the Warrior, and Lake the Lover. Praise the sons: Thunder the King, Cloud the Messenger—who should be called Cloud the Wizard in Coral's opinion—and Mountain the Priest.

Now they were chanting the Canticle of Mercy.

Now Mother Cedar was speaking about new beginnings, new hope, new wisdom—it sounded almost like a rephrasing of Coral's own ideas about the village. A year of this way of life had made it seem less new, but it was still unproven. No woman had yet chosen to risk having a baby. Swamp sickness was a feared unknown. This summer, the unusually dry weather might be preventing the disease; the backwater was all but dried up. Next year might be different. Mother Cedar offered prayers that the healers might find a cure, and other prayers about the welfare of the village.

Coral wondered, Could this possibly be effective? The whole hierarchy of high clergy, midclergy, and plain clergy had offered similar prayers for the welfare of Newport, its warriors, and its citizens. Yet Newport was now a dragon's lair, and its rightful lord had ordered his warriors to massacre innocent people. Cedar was right about the failure of Newport's Church, but was Cedar's own Church doing anything more?

In the minutes of silent meditation and prayer, Coral recognized her doubts as doubts, and prayed for guidance. She was just settling into a deep enough trance to hear a clear response, when Mother Cedar began the chant of the sixty-four names.

This monotheists' ritual was nonsense as far as Coral was concerned. Why should the Lord of Light and Darkness have so many names, and what was the point to chanting them?

After the service, Coral told Birdwade, "The service frustrated me because Mother Cedar went from one thing to another so suddenly. Each time a chant or prayer brought me close to a divine experience, she started something else. I am used to taking more time and going deeper."

38.

Mother Cedar understood and respected Coral's reasons for choosing nonattendance, but as the priestess learned more about the witch's methods of healing, she did not like her attitude toward the Holy Family. Cedar told Coral, "I praise and worship them. You use them as your tools."

"It would be better to say I work with them, as people might work with each other," the witch replied. "Sometimes I know exactly what to do, and guide the threads of existence a certain way even if I feel some opposition. But if this persists, I will try to talk to whatever is opposing the healing. At other times, I pray for guidance and follow that guidance."

"I always let myself be guided."

"You seem to be guided less by vision than by tradition: For this symptom, use this herb. When you use light, you surrender completely to the divine will. It might be more accurate to say the light uses you. My approach makes the most use of both my own and the divine creativity. Sometimes the light uses me, sometimes I use it, but most of the time we work together. Usually I do prepare the traditional remedy, but sometimes I try an alternate remedy, or even a new one—whatever feels best under the circumstances."

"That is letting yourself be guided," said Mother Cedar.

"Yes, but the guidance must feel right to me before I will follow it," replied Coral.

"This feeling of rightness is your awareness of the divine will."

Coral sighed. "I suppose so. The important question is, Does the treatment work? Does what feels right yield results? Some witches need many years of apprenticeship to attune their feelings. For others, and I am one of these, it comes naturally. I was working cures on my own when I was thirteen, and I have never lost a patient I felt certain I could save."

When they discussed which herbs proved helpful or harmful for swamp sickness, the priestess was precise. Breaking the fever was always a mistake. Any but the mildest pain reliever would cause a deep sleep ending in death. But Mother Cedar could not describe the light patterns of a person with swamp sickness in any detail, even when Coral drew diagrams on a river-lizard parchment.

"My consciousness is gone and there is only light," said Mother Cedar.

"Yes, but what does the light look like? How does it feel? There are so many things I can determine from the patterns." As an example, Coral explained how certain patterns could be used to distinguish different types of stomach pain.

"That is amazing," said Mother Cedar. "But you consciously alter these patterns when you heal. Is that not dangerous?"

"Black witchcraft cannot be done unintentionally," Coral said. "The pattern can be pushed toward health much more easily than toward greater sickness. I can immediately feel the effect of what I do."

"Then changing this pattern for the worse is how black witchcraft is done."

"It is one way for a black witch to create illness," admitted Coral. "But creating an illness with no physical cause requires constant attention, which creates a strong rope between the black witch and her victim, a kind of rope that I know you have been trained to recognize and trace."

"But what if the victim dies?"

"It would take several days of concentration for even a dragonbound witch to kill someone this way, and by that time the victim's healer would detect and cut the rope, and identify the black witch."

"Unless the healer was the black witch."

For a moment, Coral's thoughts wandered to the memory of her father's death.

"You have done something like this, from mercy," Cedar said.

"I am not a black witch," Coral said firmly. "A warrior who kills a fatally wounded companion after battle is not a murderer, and a witch who helps guide a dying patient into the spirit world—at the patient's conscious request, I might add—is not a black witch. And if you are going to rummage through my memories looking for wrong actions or thoughts, I will have to close my mind to you and end our friendship. I do not want to do this. We have so much to offer each other."

The priestess looked into the witch's concerned eyes, then bowed her head and folded her hands. "I am sorry. I meant no judgment against you. You are a lay person, and I was treating you as I would treat another priestess."

"Can I trust you?" Coral asked. "Can I trust you not to spread rumors about what I think or what I have done? Can I trust you not to turn other people against me?"

"You can trust me," said Cedar. "It may be hard, to consider yourself a good woman, an honorable woman, yet be forced to keep secrets even from your husband lest you be misunderstood and unloved. I would not want to be a witch for anything, yet here I am, at the will of the Holy Ones, learning witchcraft."

6

HUNTS AND BATTLES

39.

Feathergrass opened his eyes to sunlight streaming through the hut's one window, and Fledgeling still snuggled against him. "Wake up," he whispered.

She made a guttural mumble and blinked her eyes open. "Time to get up and kill those goblins, or mammoths, or whatever," she said. "Where did I throw my pants and tunic?"

Feathergrass was pulling on his own pants. "I hope this hunt does not become another battle."

"I do agree, but we are at war and therefore just might encounter battle. In this weather, animals, goblins, and humans all seem to crowd the river. I cannot imagine why."

"I dreamed about the river," said Feathergrass. "It was reduced to scattered pools and trickles. I hope it rains soon. I remember when the backwater was almost as deep as the river is now."

"Ah, this is the work of those powerful black shamans," Fledgeling said, making a face that a children's storyteller might use to represent a lurking goblin. "No rain. Never again shall it rain until all the humans pack up and sail back across the sea where they belong. I learned about this plot from Endive the Cook. No one tells her anything, but she knows a lot."

Feathergrass laughed.

"My lady lieutenant, are you going to keep us waiting all day?" asked Henna, peering through the leather curtain covering the doorway. "We are all saddled and ready to ride."

"We must ride and hunt while the sun is most blistering," said Fledgeling, "and, incidently, when the local mammoth herd comes to the river."

Outside, the morning was already warm.

"No cloud, not even the slightest dampness," said Feathergrass.

"If you ask me, I say let us build a stronghold right beside the bloody river rather than ten miles away from it," Henna said. "We do have a good pressure-well here and plenty of wild grain, but face it, our real source of life is the river."

"If we win the war, yes," said Fledgeling. "If the goblins make a real and reasonable peace, yes. But otherwise, this ten-mile inconvenience is our best defense against a siege. It saved us the first time, and it will be even more important if the river level drops to where we cannot safely use the boats."

"This ten-mile inconvenience makes the horses too bloody important," Henna said. "Those quagga colts, even if they can be broken, will not be much use this year, and do you seriously still expect the diplomats to bring back a good number of horses?"

"I have learned to expect nothing from diplomats," Fledgeling said.

The mounted hunters were waiting at the foot of the ramp, with saddled horses for the others. They mounted, and Fledgeling led the group over the wall and southeast toward the river. They rode slowly and stopped from time to time to let the horses graze.

To the northeast they saw four carts pulled by teams of auroch steers and guarded by a platoon of warriors, moving a load of either smoked fish or mammoth from the Blue River up the road toward the settlement. Capturing the eight yearling bulls alive had not been easy, but once gelded they were docile enough. Next year, the wild calves would be grown, and maybe, just maybe, they could be bred and herded, and the settlement would have milk, butter, and cheese. Most of the cattle east of the sea had some auroch blood, but pure aurochs, even raised from calves, were hard to manage.

"We should turn north," said Scoff. "The mammoth herd is

nowhere in sight, and no wonder, with all the bustle at the landing and downstream. They will be north of the fork, coming from that place where the goblins do not hunt."

"We do not hunt there, either," Fledgeling said. "Humans hunting on the ceremonial ground would be just what Strong Bull needs to stir the embers of his holy war against us back into flame."

"If there is a place where nobody hunts, it stands to reason that the animals eventually will all go there," said Jib.

"There is nothing wrong with hunting up north on our side of the river," said Scoff.

"You are not thinking this through," said Fledgeling. "If mammoths were that easily disturbed by boats, the sailors on the Blue River would not be spitting them with dragon guns. The mammoths will be following the same route they have used the past two weeks, likely as not. If we reach the ford when they do, we will get one."

When they were about two miles from the river, Fledgeling noticed vague puffs of smoke far to the north, probably from Condor's Camp, though the direction did not seem quite right.

"Blood!" said Scoff, pointing to the smoke message now rising from Charging Elk's new camp across the river. "Just when we are butchering our kill, every goblin warrior in twenty miles will set upon us."

"No," said Fledgeling. "That was a response to a message from Condor's Camp."

"There are the mammoths," said Feathergrass, pointing to some gray lumps near the river.

"They came earlier today; no wonder we did not see them before," said Fledgeling. "Well, ride slowly straight toward them, but veer aside at about half a mile, as though we wanted to approach the river but avoid mammoths. Crank up your crossbows now and set the safety catch. Stay together for this hunt. You never want to surround mammoths. Some may charge anyway, but leave them a clear direction of escape. At need, we can outrun them. But first we must water the horses."

Fledgeling led them toward an open place on the bank. About half the riverbed was now dry sand and gravel. While the horses drank, the hunters watched the mammoths a quarter mile downstream, sucking up water into their trunks and curling them into their mouths, making a cacophony of deep grunts and rumbles. One large female flapped her ears, took a few steps toward the hunters, and trumpeted. The horses twitched their tails and stared at her. She was huge—more than twice as high at the shoulders as any horse; her tusks were long, and her naked gray hide was deeply creased with wrinkles.

"Ugly beast," muttered Henna.

"Let her come in range before aiming," said Fledgeling.

Several smaller mammoths, likely grown offspring and calves of this matriarch, faced the riders and also stepped forward.

"Come here," Fledgling said quietly. "Do not make us chase you."

Suddenly from behind the mammoths came goblin war cries, yips and yelps and howls of thirty or forty warriors, and now the entire mammoth herd thundered toward the humans. The horses panicked and galloped upstream; some even tried to buck off their riders. Fledgeling urged her horse toward the bank, hoping the others would follow, for no command could be heard over this clamor. Two horses stumbled; they and their riders, Poach and Gill, were trampled to death.

But the riders whose horses scrambled up the bank were met by spears flying from two directions. Henna screamed. A spear had pierced her thigh and pinned her to her horse, and when they fell the pain was unimaginable. Four other horses were struck down but the dismounted riders staggered to their feet and loosed crossbow bolts at the goblins. Fledgeling, still mounted, took aim at the leader. Unbelievably, he struck aside her missile with his thrusting spear. Despite his warpaint, she knew him now. This was High Chief Strong Bull himself.

"She is mine!" he bellowed.

"You wish single combat? Let my hunters go!" she shouted back.

But his answer, whatever it was, was lost in thunder. The mammoths, finding themselves penned between the goblins who had stampeded them, the river, and the humans and goblins beginning to do battle, charged up the bank, led by a huge enraged bull with a broken left tusk. Feathergrass grabbed Hemstitch, one of the dismounted riders, and pulled her up onto his horse. Jib similarly managed to rescue Drymoss, but Scoff was heavy and slipped from Hawthorn's grip. Now the mammoths were close and the horses bucking and galloping in panic.

"Who is here, who is dead, who is missing?" Fledgeling shouted as soon as they had ridden far enough from the tumult to be out of immediate danger.

They shouted out their names; Feathergrass and Hemstitch, Jib and Drymoss, Hawthorn, and Comfrey. "That is Keg's horse," Comfrey said. "He must have tried to save Henna."

"Someone should have killed her. She would not have survived that wound. As it was, she was probably trampled," said Fledgeling. "Blood of the earth, they have regrouped already!"

"They are used to coping with charging mammoths," said Feathergrass.

"So Keg is missing at the battle site, and Scoff, and Henna was mortally wounded—" Fledgeling said.

"The mammoths got Poach and Gill down by the river," said Jib.

"The goblins have Scoff and Keg!" Hemstitch shouted. They could see the warriors yanking Scoff (who was Hemstitch's husband) and Keg to their feet. She gasped when Strong Bull stabbed each one to death with his thrusting spear.

"Nothing we can do with sixty of them and seven of us," Fledgeling said. "Let us get Keg's horse." They did so by fanning out to surround him, then Drymoss mounted his saddle.

"I am very sorry about the dead," Fledgeling said. "The general may ask any or all of you for a report. Do not spare me any criticism."

Hemstitch fought her tears; the time for grief would come when they were safely home. "You did well, lieutenant," she said quietly.

40.

This human woman was a warrior who would never fight again. If she survived, she would be crippled, and a slave wife to Lizard Toes, who had saved her life by claiming her. His wife and daughter had died in the massacre. In the old stories such captives sometimes came to love their captors, but the women in the old stories were not human warriors.

"Keg?" the woman mumbled. "Keg?"

"He lives only in your dreams," Glowfly said.

The woman opened her eyes. "You are a goblin," she said, and tried to sit up but gasped in pain.

"You lie still!" Glowfly said sharply. "Yes, I am a goblin—a goblin healer. Drink this." She gave her a sip of sleepflower tea, just enough to calm her and dull the pain. "You have a deep wound and a broken bone. I think I can save your leg, but only if you do not try to move. Can you remember that? Good. Now what is your name?"

"Henna. What will—What will happen to me?"

"Henna, you worry too much. You are alive and you are being treated."

"P-p-prisoner—Am I—?"

"Not prisoner," said Glowfly. "Unlike your people we have no dungeons or mines. You will breathe the open sky. But you are a captive, yes. Not that you could go anywhere, anyway, in your condition."

"Oh. But I thought—I thought goblins were not taking—um—captives."

"Henna, stop forcing yourself to think. Your spirit needs to drift. I gave you sleepflower to calm your pain. I do not want to have to give you more. How do you feel?"

The human's face became more placid. "Numb . . . drifting," was all she managed to say.

"Good."

Once Henna was sound asleep, Glowfly called for Little Ant, the twelfth-summer girl who wanted to be her apprentice. "How are the warriors?" she asked.

"All asleep except for Hunting Star, who was talking to me."

"I will look at them. You watch the human woman. Her name is Henna. Call for me if she starts to wake up."

Little Ant sighed. "She is pretty, even though her hair is a funny color. Do you think she will like Lizard Toes?"

"Hush, hush," Glowfly said, then whispered, "She does not know about that yet. I will know when and how to tell her."

Outside the moon was round and bright. Elsewhere goblins must be gathering to feast and dance the midsummer moon, but not anywhere on Goblin Plain. Glowfly entered the first hospital tent, which was dark, and asked quietly, "Are you all asleep?" When no one answered or groaned, she went to the other tent, where a light was burning and Hunting Star was holding a bloodstained wooden crossbow bolt.

"Give me that," Glowfly said, taking it from him. "You should not be moving your arms. How did you get this?"

"I asked the girl to show it to me."

Glowfly made a clucking noise and sighed. So many things to tell that girl!

"We almost killed them all," said Hunting Star, "the hunters, the horses, their leader, but the mammoths—the mammoths—"

"Strong Bull and Charging Elk are angry with each other over that," said Glowfly. "Strong Bull says Charging Elk should have controlled them. Charging Elk says that there was nothing more his group could do with Big One Tusk leading the herd."

"Ah. No wonder. We do not hunt that herd when he joins it. But sometimes he is there and we do not see him. Mammoths are big. The near ones hide the far ones."

41.

Fledgeling woke in a cold sweat. "No matter where I go, he will be waiting."

"What?" asked Feathergrass, stirring from sleep. "Who? Strong Bull? Are you feverish? You feel hot."

"I—I do not think so. Hold me close. My dream—I have not been frightened by any dream since I was a small girl."

"What did you dream?"

The way Fledgeling responded by kissing him so intensely reminded him of his first wife, Loon. "I would rather do this first," Fledgeling said, holding him with a strength that made her fear seem absurd. Loon had never been afraid of death, not even while the dragon Riversong was dreamsending.

"Dreamsending," Feathergrass whispered.

Fledgeling stopped moving for a moment. "You are right. Oh, Feathergrass, this—Do not make me think, not now, not now—" She trembled while sliding faster and faster, then suddenly jerked five times like a fish flopping on deck. "Oh, oh," she said, finding her breath. "That was a big one. Did you—? Go ahead, my love. Fill me, fill me now."

While he moved toward his streaming she trembled again, then stopped to feel the fluid. They were both surprised when she jerked again after lying still for several moments.

"Good, good, excellent," she said. "I feel more like myself. I think my dream means we will hunt goblins today. Let us talk to the general before we meet our group."

They dressed hurriedly and walked through the settlement's narrow streets to the general's hut, where the warrior Iris was seated outside the door, sipping a bowl of hot stew.

"Lieutenant," she said, standing up. "The general is conferring with Lieutenants Swordnotch and Foam about boat and caravan security, I think. How urgent is your concern?"

"One moment. This is unfortunate," Fledgeling mumbled to

Feathergrass. "Of all the staff, Foam and Swordnotch scoff the most at fears of goblin sorcery."

"As did you, until recently."

"My lord general!" Fledgeling called out. "Lieutenant Fledgeling here! I need to see you in private for just a few minutes before I leave with my hunters."

"All right, come in," he replied. Iris frowned, but opened the door for Fledgeling and Feathergrass. "Now, what is it?" Canticle demanded.

"Can we speak in private?" Fledgeling asked.

"Will you excuse us for a few moments?" the general asked the others, then muttered, "I hope this is important." He and Fledgeling sat together on his bed and whispered.

"Strong Bull had a shaman dreamsend to me last night," she told him. "In my dream Strong Bull again surprised my group with a superior force. The shaman standing beside him was the one who led the peace circle ceremony. Strong Bull said, 'I know you now. No matter where you go, I will be waiting.' And then he threw a spear at me so that I would wake up, remember, and know that what he said is true. I am not one to shudder at dreams of defeat. I do not think this shaman can hear my waking thoughts right now, but once I am out riding, and thinking about the hunt and possible battle, he can learn what he needs to know."

"Cross the marsh and hunt pigs," Canticle whispered. "Do not worry about swamp sickness. The drought this year has lessened that danger."

"I was hoping to use the opportunity to hunt goblins. If we kill Strong Bull, their resistance might collapse."

"Yes, especially if we kill him on our side of the river. But the terrain does not make surprise easy. Let us see what Foam and Swordnotch think. If we can quickly come up with workable tactics, we will try it."

They moved back to the table and Feathergrass joined them. "Just repeat what you told me," Canticle said, and Fledgeling did.

Swordnotch said, "All right, suppose Strong Bull does consider Fledgeling a special enemy. Suppose his battle with her last week gave the shaman Sees Patterns enough of a sense of who she is to send her a dream. Unlikely, I would say, but possible. But this dreamsending might be a lie, a distraction. While we are busy thinking about how to shadow Fledgeling's group with a platoon to surprise Strong Bull, he could be preparing an attack on something else."

"When speaking directly mind to mind, as in a dreamsending, an outright lie is impossible," Canticle said. "If Strong Bull told Fledgeling, 'No matter where you go, I will be waiting,' and these were his exact words, were they not?"

"Yes," said Fledgeling.

"Then we know that at least a few hours ago Strong Bull had this intention."

"—if we accept the dream as a sending," said Foam. "It may well just be fear."

"I think I would know the difference," said Fledgeling.

"But even though I do not believe your dream was a sending, I think occasionally shadowing a hunting group with a guard platoon is a good idea. We could have the platoon take the road to the river, as if to meet a boat, while your hunters locate the nearest game. Then we move to meet you, maybe just in time to skewer some goblins."

"Excellent!" said Canticle. "Other opinions?"

"Sounds workable," said Swordnotch.

42.

"Do you not remember how quickly Strong Bull began battle the last time?" Hemstitch said. "By the time Foam arrives with reinforcements, we will all be speared."

"We were surprised last time," said Fledgeling. "This time we have our shields, and we know what to expect."

"I would think you would welcome this chance to avenge your husband," said Feathergrass.

"Killing Strong Bull might end the war, but it will not bring Scoff back to me," Hemstitch said.

Bloodstorm said, "But now the group has me, and Crevice, and Bottom, all of us quite good at fighting goblins, and I am also an experienced leader. We are going to kill a mammoth, bring back the meat, and if Strong Bull tries to interfere, we will kill him and bring him back."

"Yes, my lord lieutenant," Fledgeling said, sarcastically—for Bloodstorm had no such title. "Shall we get on with it?"

They led their horses out of the stable to the bottom of the ramp and mounted. From the top of the wall they could see Foam's platoon, a hundred good warriors, already a mile ahead down the road. "We will ride slowly, circling to the north but never out of sight," said Fledgeling.

The grass was yellow and dead. Usually in the summer Goblin Plain had rain at least once every week or two, but this year there had not been even a drizzle for more than two months, not since the war began, in fact. But if this was the will of the shamans, they were destroying their own land. Except for the scattered winter oak and redbark trees, it looked as barren as the dry uplands of the Turtle River cataracts.

Despite the easy pace of the ride, the horses were hot and tired by the time they were halfway to the river. Several large redbarks, branching wide with dense crowns, offered welcome shade. The guard was now several miles away on the road, but no one expected an attack here, at one small grove much like many others the hunters might have passed near, and far from any game.

The split-second sound of spears flying gave Fledgeling time to duck, and the spear that was aimed true at her heart only grazed her left shoulder. Feathergrass, who was farther from the trees, was able to grab his shield in time to deflect the spear aimed at him. Others were less quick, or less lucky. Bloodstorm, Crevice, and Bottom, all quite good at fighting goblins, were all spitted to death, as were Jib, Drymoss, and Comfrey from the original group. Only the spears aimed at Hemstitch and Hawthorn missed completely.

The second volley of spears was aimed at the four horses still bearing riders, but these were now galloping and dodging, and only Fledgeling's horse, the closest, took a direct hit. But this horse, once Baron Swordfern's mount and the best at the settlement, gave his all and galloped out of range before he fell. Fledgeling was ready, sprang off, and rolled to her feet. The cut was worse than she had thought; her left arm was wet with blood.

"Help me up," she said, stretching her right arm toward Feathergrass, who had circled back for her.

"Slow down!" he shouted to Hemstitch and Hawthorn, while helping Fledgeling mount in front of him. "We are already out of range."

"I need to bind this," said Fledgeling.

"Trot about a mile toward Foam, then wait!" Feathergrass shouted, then told his wife, "Just hold it closed till we reach a safer place. I can hold you and the reins both. How frustrating! There cannot be many more than ten of them, yet we cannot fight."

"More like twenty is my guess," said Fledgeling. "But only ten of them had a clear throw at us."

"If so, why did they not wait a few moments more? I was thinking they threw too soon because they feared we would see them first."

"They threw too soon because Strong Bull hates me and could not hesitate when he thought he had me."

Feathergrass looked back. "Two riderless horses are following us; a third is circling toward Hemstitch and Hawthorn."

They all stopped in a place far from any brush or trees.

"We must be cursed," Hawthorn said.

"I do not understand it," said Fledgeling. "Even if the shaman can hear my every thought, how could he know in advance we would stop there? I had no such plan in mind."

Feathergrass dismounted, then he and Hawthorn together lifted Fledgeling off the horse. When her hand slipped from the wound for a moment, more blood gushed out. "Get me a water pouch," Feathergrass told Hemstitch. "Let me unlace you," he told Fledgeling. When he did so, he was alarmed at how bloody her undershirt was. He held the wound closed while Hawthorn pulled off both right sleeves and then, very carefully, the left ones.

Hemstitch was also nude to the waist and tearing her own undershirt into strips for the compress and binding. "Are you ready for the water?" she asked.

First they wiped the blood from Fledgeling's arm, back, and breast with her own undershirt; then they carefully washed the wound itself. It was deep, and Fledgeling's fall and tumble had gotten some dirt onto the area. Quickly, lest she lose more blood, they tied on the compress with strips over her shoulder, across her chest, and under her other arm.

"The pressure eases the pain some," Fledgeling said. "At least this bloody heat is good for one thing—I am not cramping up."

"You will in about an hour, if not sooner," said Hawthorn. "We must get you back to the settlement."

"I should have ducked just a bit more to my right. Ah, well, this happens. I will fight again."

"Blood! There they go, running fast for the river!" said Feathergrass. As Fledgeling had guessed, there were about twenty goblins. "Hawthorn, Hemstitch, you take care of Fledgeling. Get her back to the settlement and report to Canticle. I am riding to Foam. It is a race, but we might just catch those backstabbers!" He jumped on his horse. "Can you gallop two miles after all we have done already? Can you try? Hey, yah!" he shouted. "Let us go!"

The horse was wild-eyed, sweating, foaming at the mouth, but showing his speed. Ahead, Lieutenant Foam's platoon was already responding, turning off the road toward the northeast and marching briskly.

"We see them! We will get them!" Foam cried out. "What happened?"

"Somehow they knew we would choose the shade of those particular trees to rest our horses, and they were hiding up in the branches." Feathergrass exhaled heavily. "They killed six of us, including Bloodstorm, and wounded Fledgeling."

"We will get them," Foam repeated. "Platoon!" he shouted. "Count of four, start jogging. One, two, three, go!"

Feathergrass rode beside the column, hoping this horse would weather the effort. But a hard jog for humans was an easy trot for even a tired horse, and from the look of it they would intercept the fleeing goblins before long.

As the slight breeze fell calm, the sun shone hotter and hotter, baking the ground until the air shimmered with heat. The yellow grass was so brilliant it hurt the eyes. Sweat-soaked leathers of a hundred humans running made a powerful stench.

No one was completely alert, but even so, the more than two hundred goblin warriors appeared with unlikely suddenness, popping up from behind or beneath every bit of brush at once and charging the column. This was too many to fight and Foam knew it, but they had no clear direction in which to retreat, and hardly time to exchange one volley of arrows for throwing spears before combat was hand-to-hand.

Feathergrass grabbed his shield and jumped off his horse immediately. Mounted, he was too conspicuous a target. He reached for his sword but noticed a throwing spear and picked that up instead. It was long enough to serve as a pike. Better not to let them close in too soon. He had no chance to notice what became of his horse, for he was parrying two goblins who rushed him, and occasionally jabbing at others who were fighting the humans next to him.

Then the woman on his right cried out and fell, her leg pierced from behind by a spear. The circle had collapsed! Feathergrass raised his spear and spun around to get a quick view, then lowered it just in time to skewer the shield of an opponent. His spear's head came off when he tried to pull it out.

Drawing his sword and swinging quickly, he knocked aside one spear with the flat and lunged for the warrior, who did not move quickly enough to avoid being stabbed. Feathergrass withdrew his sword and spun around slashing. Now he was surrounded. Even as he lunged for another warrior, he felt the inevitable spear strike his back, the hot blood throbbing out as he fell.

For the moment, the goblins turned their attention to other humans still fighting. Maybe, just maybe, if Feathergrass lay still enough, they would leave him for dead. The clamor of battle dwindled to nothing. Then someone kicked Feathergrass in the side and yanked him to his feet.

"Stand if you can. You are no use to me otherwise and I will kill you." The goblin who spoke was Strong Bull. The bloody point of his thrusting spear was inches from Feathergrass's heart.

"Hui! Kill that one! He fights too well," Chief Charging Elk said.

"Of course he does. This is Lieutenant Woman's husband. Lucky for him, he is just the one to deliver our message." Strong Bull deepened his voice and spoke slowly; Feathergrass trembled at the hate in his eyes. "Your wife stabbed my father and left him for dead, but he took two days to die. You and she ran from battle to fetch Lord Coward and the boats. His people killed almost all the goblins of Beadback's Camp—warriors, wives, old women, children. Even toddlers and babies were pierced by arrows and swords."

Feathergrass's voice was hoarse and thin. "My wife and I both argued long and hard against—"

"You keep still until I am finished speaking," Strong Bull said, pricking him with his spear for emphasis. "Your arguments with Lord Coward were ineffective. You cannot argue with me. Can you argue with General Canticle? Your wife should die. You should die. If I spare you now, I do so because I think you have influence. I have an argument for your general. My people will win this war. Soon your boats will be too big for the Goblin River. Soon your people must abandon your settlement. I know this. I have dreamed this. I have shown you today how I will win. I dreamed where my warriors would have to wait today. But your people have another choice. The war could end with this battle. Lord Blackwood of Upriver will welcome all your people."

"What do you mean?" asked Feathergrass. "Our embassy to Upriver returned before the war began. Lord Blackwood refused to accept more than three hundred, and only as bonded servants."

"He has reconsidered," said Strong Bull. "The diplomats Arch and Coldspray told me so."

"Where are Arch and Coldspray?"

"They will return with you. Bind him." The goblins who held Feathergrass's arms twisted them behind his back and bound them with leather. "This one I want. Kill any others," the high chief said. Feathergrass tried to stifle any reaction, any thought, while goblin warriors stabbed three other human captives to death.

43.

"You are not a captive of war," Glowfly told Henna, firmly but gently. "High Chief Strong Bull was about to execute you. You are alive only because you were claimed by Lizard Toes. Even if your people go to Upriver and the war ends, you will stay with him."

"What do you mean? Just what kind of captive am I?" Henna was still unable to get out of bed and go outside to void her wastes without assistance, but despite the constant dull pain in her leg, her mind was clear. She knew that if she kept her voice and thoughts as calm as she could, the goblin woman would answer.

Glowfly took a deep breath and released it. "Lizard Toes has claimed you for his wife."

"His wife? His slave wife?"

"The better a wife you become for him, the less it will be like slavery. His wife and daughter were killed in the massacre of Beadback's Camp, while he was here in the big army. I think his spirit beast moved him to claim you, to spare your life and become your husband, to lessen the hate in his heart."

"The idea has the opposite effect on me. I am a citizen of Newport, where no one was even a bonded servant, much less a slave. I am a herder and a hunter. How can I be a slave wife?"

"You want life," said Glowfly. "You want a child to replace the one you lost in Spirit Swamp."

Against her will, Henna trembled and tears swelled in her eyes. "When did I tell you that?"

"You have said much that you do not remember. His name was Bramble. His hair was not reddish like yours, but brown and curly. He was in his fourth summer."

"Stop, please stop."

Glowfly wiped the tears from Henna's eyes and rubbed her shoulders, the way Henna's mother had done years before when she was a child who did not understand things. "I know things about you that you have not told me."

"You hear thoughts like a priestess or a witch."

"I do not know how a priestess or a witch hears thoughts. I talk with your spirit beast. I dream. I learn what I need to know to help you heal."

"My spirit beast?" Henna asked.

"You are a child of Great Mother Wolf," said Glowfly. "Chief Beadback, who died trying to defend his camp, was another of her children."

"I had nothing to do with that. Why must you—But Strong Bull's attack on our hunters was almost as shameful—sixty of them against twelve of us, and we were not really armed to fight."

"Little children, like your Bramble, and babies—*babies*—were slashed by sword and pierced by arrow. Henna, there is no comparison. I might understand your people, whose women fight, considering grown goblin women enemies, but children?"

"I had nothing, nothing to do with that. I would never follow such an order. No one, no one could fault me for refusing to obey." Henna was crying and pounding the bed with her fists.

"Calm down, calm down," Glowfly said gently, again rubbing the human woman's shoulders and wiping her tears. "I believe you. In fact I know what you say is true. I have talked to your Mother Wolf. I have dreamed. Remember? But some night, some night when you and Lizard Toes are feeling very close, he may say something to you about the massacre. You must be very careful about what you say in reply. He is strong in the spirit, but he is not a shaman. He may not understand the way I do."

"What are you doing to me?" Henna asked.

"Helping you heal," Glowfly replied.

"This is not just healing. You are trying to change me. What are you doing to my mind? For a moment I actually envisioned—I am Keg's wife. I am a human of Newport. I am a herder and hunter."

"You were once all those things," Glowfly said. "But Keg is dead, Newport is destroyed, and your leg will never be as strong as it was."

"I am still Henna of Newport."

"No," said Glowfly. "Henna of Newport was killed by Strong Bull. You are Henna of Grass, River, Wind. You are Henna of Many True Dreams. You are Henna of Best Hunting. You are Henna of Ha! Hey, yo. Ha! In our old language this land had many names. Those are some of them. When our people began speaking your language, we gave this land a new name, Goblin Plain, so that all humans would know this land is ours. You came here to live, and now you will live here. Ha! Hey, yo. Ha! This is our land. This is your land. Let me show you something. Close your eyes."

This also reminded Henna of childhood and Mother. What was the surprise?

"Keep your eyes closed. What I want to show you is inside your eyelids, on the edge of dreams, but you will be awake. You will continue to hear my voice." Glowfly changed her voice, making it softer, deeper, slower. She unwrapped a scent twist and moved it in circles to purify the inside of the tent while she spoke.

"When I was in my twelfth summer I searched for my spirit. I had to go somewhere I had never gone before. For a girl, this was not hard. All my life I had been told to stay close to camp. Now I had to go somewhere else and stay there for four days, or until I had a clear vision. I knew where I wanted to go. There was a big redbark tree I had seen a few times from a distance. Maybe with your eyes closed you can see the green grass, the open miles with herds of antelope and auroch, the one tree all by itself. Can you describe it to me, or should we walk a little closer?"

"All right. I see a tree, far away, but I cannot walk."

"In the spirit world you can walk. You can come closer to the tree. I walked closer and closer to the tree. I kept thinking I must be almost there, but the tree kept looking bigger, and there was still more ground to walk. Grasshoppers sprang up. Flies buzzed past. Finally I got there. Its trunk was as big around as a tent. Its branches were four feet across. Its shade was deep. Are you with me?"

Henna's voice was almost a whisper. "This looks unreal. This redbark is too beautiful, too perfect. The four big branches split into smaller branches the size of an ordinary redbark's trunk. The ground is covered with yellow leaves, but all the leaves on the tree are green."

"I sat down on the north side of the trunk, so that I was looking away from camp," Glowfly continued. "I had no blanket, no tools, only a small water pouch. I drank a sip and stared at the horizon. I prayed for a vision."

"I see someone coming," Henna whispered.

"You see Keg and Bramble," said Glowfly.

"Yes. I wish I could be with them."

"But you are with them, all together under the tree. Do they have something to tell you? Do you want to say something to them?"

Henna's tears flowed freely. "I love you so much. Why are you gone? Why am I still here?"

Glowfly hesitated for a moment, then lay down beside the human woman and hugged her. "Did they answer you?" she whispered. "What did you hear them say?"

"Just—private things."

"But you know that they are well in the spirit world. You know you can talk with them in your dreams."

"There is a black cloud," Henna whispered. "Fear—rage—death in battle—endless sorrow. The battle creates that cloud. But you can leave the struggle behind and go somewhere else. Everything has changed. Keg, Bramble, and I are sitting at a campsite on Herders Ridge, surrounded by our sheep. The fog is rising. Brush wolves are yelping in the distance. I cannot see anything except near the fire. Now I cannot see anything at all. Something is coming. It is a wolf, a female wolf, but not like any I have ever seen. She is outlined in glowing colors—rust, ochre, turquoise. Her fur is so shiny that I cannot say what color it is. Silver, maybe." Henna chuckled—not much of a laugh, but the first Glowfly had heard her make. "She is wagging her tail and sniffing my hands. Her fur is soft, like nothing I have ever felt—" Henna's voice fell to a whisper. Her breathing became very slow.

Glowfly sat up and moved off the bed. Touching the totem had put Henna into deep trance. Whatever lesson she was getting now was hers alone. Maybe Henna would tell Glowfly about it afterwards, but this would be her choice.

"Glowfly? Glowfly!" someone called with a voiced whisper—Little Ant, of course, peering through the tent flaps.

"Talk quietly, please. What is it?"

"The warriors are back from battle with the wounded. They will be here in a few minutes."

"What battle? What warriors?" Glowfly asked, moving to the entrance.

"Mostly Charging Elk's and Beartooth's people, I guess. They were—"

"Beartooth's people?" Glowfly asked sharply.

"The warriors made a trap for a human force across the river. They won. They killed all the humans. Well, that was what they said. It was a big battle, too. I do not think any goblins died, or maybe just a few. Ten were badly wounded. We have to get things ready."

"All right," Glowfly said, looking at Henna for a moment, then back at Little Ant. "Are Picks Herbs and Heavy Dew getting ready?"

"I came to you first."

"Well, go to them. And find out how much good water we have in camp."

"At least a load," said Little Ant.

"We may need three of four loads. Of course, right now we cannot send women to the river, and of course, warriors will not want to carry water. Someone should have told us in advance that Strong Bull planned battle. He should surprise his enemies, not his healers."

"We might have three loads," said Little Ant.

"Tell Picks Herbs to tell the chief to arrange something if we do not have enough. Tell her if she does not, I will."

"I will tell her," Little Ant said, and left.

In the deepening blue twilight, Glowfly could easily see the light patterns around Henna's face. She was in deep trance, and would probably sleep till dawn. Glowfly gathered up her wrapped herbs, her pot of salve, her special stones, her water bowls. This would be a long night.

7

SPIRIT WARNING

44.

Feathergrass was cold, wet, tired, and frightened. Being wounded and captured had changed him. While he walked the miles between river and settlement with Arch and Coldspray, he thought he heard goblins each time a small animal rustled through the dry grass, and thought he saw them where nothing at all was moving.

Strong Bull had told the truth about Lord Blackwood's offer. It did involve bonded servitude, but not the usual kind. All Newport refugees would be bonded to the lord himself, and for only four years. Their work would be to enlarge the city and farmland to make space for themselves, after which they would become full citizens of Upriver.

"But what is the situation here?" Arch asked. "If the goblins really are winning, why have they retreated so far?"

Feathergrass feared to answer. He did not want to think of anything but Lord Blackwood's offer and the long cold walk, lest the goblins hear his thoughts.

"He is battle-shocked," said Coldspray. "He needs to see a priest."

Feathergrass began imagining Fledgeling's solid breasts, her strong arms, the joy of kissing her while sliding slowly inside. "Watch what you say and think. They listen like Riversong. That is how they got us," he said quietly and quickly while continuing to imagine lovemaking.

But the woman in his arms was small, soft, and spoke with a Four Lakes accent:

"Give up the war," said Loon. "You do not want to die in the black cloud. Your death time will be troubled. You are not innocent. Argue for going to Upriver. I helped save you for that. Please, please. You are loyal and that is good, but you are loyal to a bad war and that is bad."

"Stand where you are and raise your arms slowly!" a man's voice boomed, so suddenly that Feathergrass almost passed waste in his pants. He tried to comply but was stopped by sharp pain in his back.

"I cannot. I am wounded. We are unarmed," Feathergrass said, trying to find his voice.

"Who are you?" asked the man.

They were surrounded by warriors—human warriors. A large force was moving through the shadows.

"Arch, Coldspray, and Feathergrass," said Arch.

"Arch and Coldspray? Huh. Well, first thing first. Feathergrass! Lieutenant Wolfkiller here. Glad you are alive. What happened to Foam's platoon?"

"All dead, except for me. We were surprised by about two hundred goblins."

"Where?"

"In the brush, about two miles northwest of the boat landing. I was struck down by a spear in the back and taken captive to Charging Elk's Camp, where Arch and Coldspray were being held. Their news is that Lord Blackwood of Upriver has improved his relocation offer: He will take all of us for four years' bondage."

"Bah!" said Wolfkiller.

"What this actually means—" Arch began, but let his voice fall to a mumble when he realized it was irrelevant. His people had just lost a battle, but were determined to win the war.

"Charging Elk's Camp is the military center," Feathergrass continued. "A hundred sixty warriors are there now. The others went toward Condor's Camp with the wounded. Strong Bull, Charging Elk, Beartooth, Long Howl, and Gaping Wound are all at Charging Elk's Camp. Drakey and Sees Patterns are there, and probably other shamans as well. I must warn you about them. They are master sorcerers. Our movements were unplanned, or so we thought, but they knew just where to wait for us. They claim that their dreams tell them what to do."

"Their exact method does not matter," said Wolfkiller. "We have taken precautions, but I cannot discuss them with you. Go back to the settlement. Your wife is in the care of the acting high priest."

"What?" Feathergrass asked. "Who is that?"

"I have said all I will say."

Wolfkiller and the warriors who had stayed with him hurried off to join the others moving toward the river, and Feathergrass, Arch, and Coldspray resumed walking toward the settlement.

45.

Glowfly and Heavy Dew kneeled on either side of the warrior with the sword-slashed arm. "You will feel sudden pain when we pour the hot water and pull on the wound, but you must not move."

"I do not think I could move," he said slowly. The limpwort had taken effect. Two months ago, Glowfly would have given sleepflower, but that made the mind too foggy. With the patient on limpwort, the subtle currents were clear. Glowfly could perceive them and press the muscle back together exactly right. But the man was awake and would feel pain.

"Heavy Dew will hold you," said Glowfly. "Little Ant, be ready."

"Yes." She was holding the bowl.

"Pour," Glowfly said, and pulled the wound open. The man trembled slightly, but did not otherwise move. With her trance-eye Glowfly saw exactly how to press the wound together. "More. Get the blood off my hands so they do not slip." Glowfly lapsed into trance for a moment to make certain she had done it right. Yes—but something else nagged at her, something important.

First, bind this wound. Herbal compress, soft leather, splint. "You can do the rest," Glowfly told Heavy Dew and Little Ant. "I must—I must go into deep trance for a few minutes. I must."

"You and your deep trances," Heavy Dew muttered. "You have the touch. I cannot deny it. But I say leave the deep visions for the shaman."

The shaman of Condor's Camp, Star Bear, was not even a competent healer, let alone one who swam with the spirits. Occasionally he dreamed true, but occasionally was not often enough for a people at war.

Glowfly sat cross-legged, closed her eyes, and relaxed into trance. Wolves were trotting in the starlit vastness—bright wolves, shimmering wolves, dark wolves fierce with power. Glowfly felt her wrists lengthening, her fingers shortening to paws, her nails thickening into blunt claws, her nose and jaw stretching into a muzzle.

"Where are we? Where are we going?" she asked.

"Ha! Hey, yo. Ha! The humans have crossed the river," said a male wolf, a fierce warrior. "Hoaff! Hoaff! A thousand warriors come to Charging Elk's Camp. Ro! Ro! They come to Condor's Camp. You must run, Otter's daughter. Tell the chief to throw down his tents and smother the fire. Tell the chief to flee with his people."

Glowfly was falling through the stars, falling through the clouds. She fell awake.

Either I believe in my vision, or I do not.

I believe.

Glowfly got up, stooped through the tent flap, and ran toward the central fires. "Yiyiyi! Yiyiyi!" she shouted. "Hear me! Hear me! I give a voice to Great Mother Wolf. I give a voice to her bright warriors and her dark warriors. Hear me! A human army has crossed the river. A thousand warriors attack Charging Elk's Camp. They will win the battle. They will come here. We must throw down our tents and smother the fire. We must carry the wounded and flee."

Not many goblins had been at the fire. Not many had even been awake inside their tents. But now a crowd of warriors gathered around the fire where she stood, and stared at her with grim faces.

Chief Condor spoke: "Shamaness, how can we know that your vision is true?"

Glowfly answered, "If we had time to dance, I would take you to the spirit plain with drums and chants, and Mother Wolf's warriors would dance with you. If we had time to dream, I would take you there with soft words, and Mother Wolf's warriors would speak to you. But we do not have the time. We must throw down the tents and smother the fire. We must carry the wounded and flee. We must do this now."

Star Bear said, "Glowfly is the best healer at this camp. She is best not because she has the most knowledge or experience, but because she has the most power. The spirits work with her. Cicada, Chief Beartooth's wife, has told me about her. When that camp danced the wolf dance, Glowfly became a wolf. She was caught by a human snare. She fell into a human pit trap. Cold Winter's people and Charging Elk's people have found and destroyed such traps. Glowfly's vision was true. Great Mother Wolf spoke to Glowfly."

"Ah," said Chief Condor, and other warriors made similar sounds of assent. "We have no time for council. Throw down the tents. Smother the fire. Put the wounded back onto their litters."

The warriors and women began this work. Glowfly hurried to her own tent, where Little Ant was gathering up some trivial possessions. "Forget those things," Glowfly said. "Help me put Henna on the litter. We must carry her outside and throw down the tent. Henna, are you awake?"

"Oh, the insides of my head are swirling," she groaned.

"The humans are coming to massacre this camp and Charging Elk's Camp," Glowfly said. "If you do not want one of this camp's warriors to kill you, you must be one of us. Your totem, Mother Wolf, gave me a dream warning of this attack. We do have time to get away. We will carry you."

"The wolf—Mother Wolf—gave me a dream about humans— humans killing women, children, babies," Henna said hoarsely. "I thought it was the massacre of Beadback's Camp until I recognized some of the people here. If my people, I mean Canticle's humans, do this, I would—I would rather be—"

"You are a daughter of Great Mother Wolf," said Glowfly. "We have no time to talk. We must put you on the litter."

Carefully Glowfly and Little Ant carried Henna outside. With a whoosh of leather and a clatter of poles, a tent collapsed, then another, then several others. Glowfly reached for the binding rope of her own tent.

"I will unwrap that, shamaness," said a man's voice.

When all the tents were down and the fire was dark, the goblins walked east across the starlit plain. Two warriors, one the man who had helped throw down Glowfly's tent, carried Henna's litter. When the moon rose, the goblins scattered, crouched in the brush, and waited. Walking Toad, a young warrior with sharp eyes, climbed a large lone oak to keep watch. Glowfly offered a silent prayer to Great Mother Wolf and her warriors, thanking them for the vision. Somewhere in the distance, wolves of the solid world were howling.

46.

On the settlement wall, Feathergrass, Arch, and Coldspray were questioned by the guards, then placed under clerical arrest. "It would be better if you did not try to guess what is going on," said Iris, the guard who led them. "The more you know, the more our enemies might learn."

"Will you tell my wife that I am alive?" Feathergrass asked.

"That request is reasonable," said Iris. "But save any others for the acting high priest."

The three men entered the dirt-block room where the midpriest Father Petrel, who just hours ago had begun acting as the settlement's first high priest, was talking to two other priests and three priestesses. "Feathergrass, lie down on the pallet," he said. "Arch and Coldspray, you will find an unoccupied hut four doors toward the south wall. Go there. There is food and bedding. We will examine you when we are done with Feathergrass. This is a clerical jury, and you are under arrest, but not because we accuse you of any spiritual crime—rather, because you may be victims of such a crime. We will not hurt or punish you. We want to help you. Do you understand?"

"I neither understand nor accept this arrest," said Coldspray.

"Nor do I," said Arch. "What Newport law gives you such authority?"

"Today we have discovered goblinbinding," said Father Petrel. "I think the analogy with the dragonbinding laws is clear. Now, will you two do as I asked or must I shout the alarm?"

After Arch and Coldspray left, the priests and priestesses kneeled on opposite sides of Feathergrass's pallet. "The goblins bandaged your wound," said Father Petrel. "We must replace this before we proceed. Take off your tunic."

Feathergrass sat up to do so.

Mother Jasmine, a healer, loosened the knots of the soft leather bandage the shaman had made. She poured a small amount of water on it where it was stuck to the wound, and pulled it away. Then she washed the wound and applied some cream that felt cool at first, then burned. She tied on a pad of soft cloth with a strip of clean rag. Feathergrass put on his tunic and lay back down.

Father Petrel said, "In the name of the Father, the Mother, the

Three Sons, and the Three Daughters, may we see what must be seen, hear what must be heard, and do what must be done." He held his left hand a few inches above Feathergrass's stomach, and moved his right hand to a place over his knees. "Keep your eyes open. Stare up at the rafters. You may have sudden feelings or thoughts. Just let them pass."

Feathergrass sensed the priest's hands moving through the subtle light around his body. He had thoughts. He was making love with Fledgeling. He was making love with Loon. He felt a sudden fear. He thought about his duty. He felt a different fear. He made a difficult decision. He remembered the face of a pirate he had killed in battle. He was surrounded by goblins and fighting. He was a young boy, aroused by his older sister. He was staring up at the stars, trying to understand what he was. Many of these thoughts he did not want exposed, but there were too many coming too quickly. He could not hide them.

"You need not fear us," a priestess said gently.

Loon was singing something in a language Feathergrass did not understand. He began drifting into grayness.

"Keep your eyes open," said a priest.

For a few moments Feathergrass stared at the shadowy rafters, but then heard Loon singing again, this time the last verse of her last work, the *Ballad of Baron Oakspear*:

> From the bright morning
> to the gray twilight
> brave Oakspear has gone.
> His life was cut short
> by fire and teeth.
> He has found peace.
> The dragon who killed him
> besieges our city.
> > What do we fear,
> > what do we fear?

Now she spoke: "I sing you this song to remind you what it is like to be the city. Now the goblins are the city and you are the dragon. You have choice. Do you want to be the dragon?"

"Does she talk to you often?" asked Father Petrel.

"That is not your concern," Feathergrass said defensively.

"Both you and your dead wife would do well to end this relationship," said Father Petrel. "Being here for you keeps her tied to the solid world, when she could be singing in the gardens of Heaven. She is just a human spirit. She may understand a few things now that confused her when she was alive, but she does not know very much. Pray to the gods and goddesses, who know much more. With your sensitive ear, you can hear them speak."

"All right, I will pray to them," said Feathergrass.

"Do so now," said Father Petrel.

"I call upon Cloud the Wizard, who knows how things are connected, and on his younger brother, Mountain the Priest, who knows the peace beyond deeds and thought. I am afraid and confused. I think I am goblinbound, as Father Petrel calls it. My enemies in war know where I will go before I do, and wait for me there. They also do this to my wife, Fledgeling. Can you help your priests and priestesses find and remove this binding from my spirit?"

After a silence, Father Petrel said, "Did you hear their reply?"

"No," said Feathergrass.

"Your dead wife, Loon, presumes to guide your spirit. She has come between you and the Holy Ones. But I hear them speaking to you. Cloud the Messenger says that your spirit and Fledgeling's are too well-known to your enemies. Their dreams about you are prophetic, detailed, and clear."

Feathergrass felt a knot of fear in his stomach. "What can I do about this? How can I change who I am in spirit?"

"A simple image prescribed by Mountain the Priest should suffice to protect you," said Father Petrel. "You imagine a shield of silver light completely surrounding you like an egg. This shield will hide and protect your spirit from your enemies. They will have to search for you the hard way in the solid world. This shield will also stop Loon from whispering things to you unbidden and half noticed. She will have to get your full attention if she wants to say something. You will know which thoughts are your own and which are hers."

"That would be better," said Feathergrass.

"Imagine this shield of light right now," said Mother Jasmine. "We will help you get a feel for it."

Feathergrass found himself imagining the silver fog, waves, and sand of a distant shore he had once walked with Loon. With effort he managed to swirl the silver light into an egg, but Loon was with him inside this egg.

"Listen to me, please," she said. "Gods and goddesses know more things, but I know you more, how you are strong and how you are weak. I see the pattern of things. Canticle tonight wins the big battle, but Strong Bull escapes away. No one will want to go to Upriver. The goblins do not fight for a few weeks or months, but they never give up—not till they are all dead or else the humans are all dead or all go away. Were I alive, we would not stay in this war. You would be persuaded by my talk."

"Feathergrass, do you want to follow this spirit's advice?" asked Mother Jasmine. Her voice was a shock. "Do you want to abandon your wife and your people? Speak back to this spirit out loud."

"Loon, I have sworn loyalty to General Canticle. I am married to Lieutenant Fledgeling."

"Both Canticle and Strong Bull are almost as lost in the black smoke as Lord Drill," said Loon. "Sometimes desertion is better than duty. You never try to talk to your wife. After this day's experience she may feel differently. The goblins will stop fighting for a while, but when they start again, they will surprise. They will be waiting where you go."

"This shield of light will protect you," said Father Petrel.

"Loon, I will not listen to these temptations. Even if Fledgeling were willing to go away with me, I have my duty here. This is my shield and you are unwelcome."

The moment Feathergrass spoke these last words, Loon was gone. At first he felt relief. No more whispers, no more confusion. But then he felt isolated, vulnerable, frightened. The emptiness seemed infinite.

"Pray to the Holy Ones!" said a priest.

"Pray quickly!" said a priestess.

"Pray!" said Father Petrel.

"I call upon Mountain the Priest, who knows the emptiness. I call upon Lake the Lover, who—who—" Feathergrass felt flowing tears. "I need help. I fear—I fear that I love my dead wife more than I love my living wife. I feel so empty. What if Loon is right, and my weaknesses cause me to become evil in war?"

A sudden flash of light and a long roll of thunder startled Feathergrass into opening his eyes. "Was that real?" he asked the red-robed figures.

"Close your eyes and hear the voice of Thunder the King," said Father Petrel.

In the egg with Feathergrass was a swarthy man in his prime, whose features were much like General Canticle's, but he wore robes of embroidered silk and a golden crown. "I can answer your prayer best," the king said. "I am known for my anger, my passion, my passion, my power, and my wisdom. You also have these qualities. In war, your anger and passion may cause you to misuse your power. Your wisdom may prevent this. The choice is always yours."

After a moment of silence, Feathergrass offered a silent prayer of thanks. What the god said was true. He opened his eyes and saw another lightning flash, heard another boom of thunder, followed by a slowly increasing patter of rain.

47.

A darkness hid the stars near the northern horizon. When it spread over a third of the sky, lightning flashed and thunder boomed. Glowfly, surrounded by warriors while she crouched in the brush near the human Henna, was not afraid when she heard someone approach.

"Shamaness!" whispered Chief Condor.

Glowfly knew he wanted her to follow him. They went just far enough to talk quietly in private.

"What does this storm mean?" he asked.

"If the drought was caused by our shamans' power, a storm on this night of battle does suggest the power has failed. But I say let us make this storm our own! Let us dance rain, hard and heavy. We can stop the lightning fires. We can feel our own strength. We are safe here for now, if we dance. Ha! Hey, yo. Ha! This land is ours. This sky is ours. Let it rain. Dance around the tree."

While Glowfly spoke, she realized that her words came from Great Mother Wolf as easily as they would from her own totem. Ah! Father Otter was her totem, but Mother Wolf was also her totem. No one had told Glowfly this was possible, but she thought it must be true.

"Call it out, shamaness," said Chief Condor.

"Yiyiyi! Yiyiyi!" Glowfly shouted. "Circle the oak and dance the rain!"

"Ha! Hey, yo. Ha!" Condor shouted. "Dance the rain!"

On her way to the tree, Glowfly told Little Ant, "You watch Henna. Be certain she stays warm and safe. Lie beside her and hold her if she shivers in the rain."

A lightning flash momentarily illuminated the warriors and women pacing the dance. The shaman Star Bear began chanting:

Ha! Hey, yo, Huh! Hum.
Ha! Hey, yo, Huh! Hum.

All the men chanted this in their deepest voices. Glowfly began the women's part:

Yiya! Ho. Yiyiyi!
Yiya! Ho. Yiyiyi!

They paced the dance around the oak in one direction. Each time lightning flashed and boomed, they reversed direction. Glowfly was not surprised when her hands and feet became paws and her mouth became a muzzle. She was a wolf trotting across the star plain. The other goblins were also wolves. The circle of the solid world was a straight line in the spirit world. They were trotting toward the mountains, where the clouds were dark, the thunder was loud, the rain was heavy. She felt the first drops of water on her muzzle. She smelled the wolves' wet fur. What a delightful musk!

"Ro! Ro!" said a strong black warrior wolf. When the lightning flashed, the raindrops on his fur looked like stars in the sky. "Run to the clouds, to the heart of the storm. This night on the solid world plain must be dark as night in the thickest forest."

The rain fell hard and cold. Glowfly was a woman pacing the dance. A searing, tingling, blinding flash struck the trunk of the oak with a deafening boom. Orange flames leapt high from the wood, but the ground and foliage were too wet to burn.

Walking Toad had jumped down from his branch to join the dance some time ago, when the clouds came close. The chanting had stopped. All the other goblins had run from the tree. Glowfly still stared at the flicker of red flame smothered in thick smoke.

She turned and walked away. Her unbound hair and clothes clung to her wet skin. She stumbled in the darkness, huddled in a squat, and shivered. She could not see anything, not even the burning tree. "Is anyone near me?" she asked. The rain muffled her voice. "I am chilled."

A warrior's strong arms embraced her. Maybe she should have asked for a woman. "You were right about the rain," he said, and she knew he was Chief Condor. "It put out the lightning fire. It makes the darkness complete. Maybe Strong Bull and the other chiefs and warriors can escape."

"Yes."

"I saw the wolf spirits," said Condor. "They are beautiful and strong."

The thought behind this was *You are beautiful and strong*.

Ever since Cicada had gone, leaving Glowfly in charge of the healers at Condor's Camp, the young shamaness had approached the stern chief through his wife, Picks Herbs, whenever she needed anything from him. Glowfly soon noticed that their marriage was troubled. Now, in the cold darkness and pouring rain, Condor held Glowfly in his arms.

She wanted to become the wolf spirit again, wanted Condor to be the strong black wolf with stars on his fur, and wanted him to bite her neck ruff, mount, and penetrate her.

But Glowfly was a woman, not a wolf. She had to think about things before allowing such passion. Condor was married, but maybe to the wrong woman. Condor was chief; Glowfly was a strong shamaness; this could be a good match. He was attentive and gentle, as Quick One had not been. He was no youth but a man in his prime. He was thinking these thoughts, knowing that she was hearing them. He resented—ah!—he resented the way Picks Herbs listened to his thoughts and used what she learned against him in petty ways. He could not hear Glowfly's thoughts but he knew there was nothing petty about her.

Could this passion become love, or would it just make trouble? Would the opportunity still be hers if she hesitated?

His breath warmed the side of her neck. His lips touched her skin. When he licked off the rainwater, she giggled and turned her head to meet his lips with her own. They lost their balance and tumbled to the ground, luckily not on any thistles. She found his mouth again and sucked his lower lip; he licked her upper lip; their tongues touched and twisted.

"My other mouth is hungry for something," she whispered after a time. Something was hard and aching and hot. After a brief maneuvering of breeches and skirt, it slid wonderfully inside. For timeless time, she squeezed a rhythm, made small movements, trembled. He made each thrust a surprise. Rain dripped off his face onto hers. Now their movements quickened toward her shudder and his stream. Afterwards, they lay linked together till they saw each other as vague dark shapes, then pulled apart, rearranged their clothing, and stood.

Dawn revealed dark clouds blurred by heavy rain, but the clouds coming from the north were lighter gray. Condor and

Glowfly were closer to the oak than anyone else. The fire was out but the trunk's charred hollow was large.

"Should we wait here a while, to give the humans time to retreat?" asked Condor.

"You might want to send out a scout," Glowfly suggested, facing just east of south. "Send him that way."

48.

Walking Toad, Condor's scout, found a group of goblins about four miles away in the direction the shamaness had indicated. With the blur of mist and rain, and his caution and theirs, they did not discover each other till they were quite close. Strong Bull, Beartooth, and Drakey led a group of twenty-six other warriors, including Lizard Toes, and seven women, and a boy of thirteen summers. The grim story they told of the night's battle suggested that few if any other goblins from Charging Elk's Camp survived.

That camp received no spirit warning. Their first notice of the advancing humans was the death scream of a scout near the river, maybe two miles away. Drakey was sure that the human force was big, that they knew about Foam's platoon and were coming to retaliate.

Strong Bull was shocked. He had dreamed the day's successes, as had Sees Patterns. Both the human hunting group and the platoon had passed exactly where the dream predicted. Except for Strong Bull's spear missing Lieutenant Woman's heart and instead glancing off her shoulder, all had gone exactly right. But that made the difference. Lieutenant Woman went back to the settlement and told Canticle, who sent out an army. Maybe he was even leading the army. Canticle had spiritual power. He might be able to block the spirit warning.

The hundred and sixty goblin warriors surrounded the twenty some women and few older children when they ran east from camp. They thought the humans were all behind them, but they were wrong. The humans had crossed the river miles to the south, then spread to circle the camp before killing the scout who screamed.

They closed in on the goblins like the fingers and thumb of a hand grabbing a lizard. Arrows flew, many more than the goblins could shield against. Warriors fell; women fell. The rising moon made it easier for the human archers.

Then Charging Elk and twenty other warriors stopped short to fight. Their throwing spears struck down several humans, slowing the vanguard momentarily, but all too soon the goblins were surrounded and overwhelmed.

A human platoon threw down their shields for speed and ran ahead of the goblins, cutting off their clear retreat. Even by moonlight and several hundred feet away, Strong Bull knew the man in the center of the line. This was General Canticle himself. As he notched an arrow into his longbow, lightning flashed behind him and thunder boomed. The humans have a god named Thunder who is a fierce warrior king. At this moment, Canticle seemed to be this god.

The goblins couched their thrusting spears, ducked their heads under their shields, and rushed the human line. Canticle was not the only excellent archer in his platoon. Maybe a third of the goblins fell wounded, or stumbled, and now the shielded humans from behind surrounded them for what promised to be a brief and terrible thrusting-spear battle.

But the humans now outnumbered the goblins more than ten to one, and fought more cautiously, confident they would kill them all in the end. Lightning flashed again, rain began falling, and clouds covered the moon. Then there was no more lightning. The sky became so dark that the goblins could not even see their own shields. The rain fell so hard that the clamor of battle was muted.

"Ha! Hey, yo. Ha!" Drakey shouted.

When the goblins somehow rushed the weakest part of the human circle, they were also wolves trotting on the spirit plain. The humans could not see, could not hear, and injured each other in the confusion. The goblins confused them more by throwing their shields. Many goblins were killed but some fought free.

> Grass, river, wind, we run.
> Skin stretched by our ribs, we run.
> Panting with our strength, we run.

They were able to run together through the dark, furious storm because they were also spirit wolves on the star plain.

49.

The rain was little more than a mist by that afternoon, when Canticle's army returned to the settlement, bearing the tents and goods of Charging Elk's Camp, the dead warriors of Foam's platoon, and some few of their own who were dead or wounded. The main goblin force was destroyed, though Strong Bull, Drakey, and a few others escaped in the sorcerous storm. Chiefs Charging Elk, Long Howl, and Gaping Wound were dead, as was the shaman Sees Patterns.

"From now on, if the goblins attack any humans, the camps concerned will face the might of the human army," Canticle said. "And if they try to muster an army of matching size, their camps will again be defenseless against our boats. The Church has agreed to help us oppose their unholy sorcery. Maybe the goblins will learn to leave us alone. Then we will leave them alone. We may yet, in years to come, reach real peace with them."

8

ATTACK AND RETREAT

50.

In the second month of fall, on a cold clear day after many days of rain, Bloodroot, Salmon, and Swanfeather returned from a hunt with a memorably fat pig, and two men from a neighboring village, whom they had invited to join the feast. One of them was Holdfast the Herder, whose family had built the second hut at Sharp Bend.

"I was actually looking for you when I found the village I am living in now," he told Coral and Rockdream. "When you decided to leave Sharp Bend, I tried to talk my wife and her mother into going with you, but they wanted to stay there, in a good hut in a prospering village. But I had a bad feeling about those priests." The herder took a deep breath. "I was right. When the swamp sickness came, neither one had any idea what to do. Wren and Wave both died of it. So did both priests, but by that time I was long gone. I had to leave the goats and their kids behind. I looked for you and found Driftwood's Village."

"Driftwood the Merchant?" asked Coral.

"The same. He had a good government organized, one that

cannot be disrupted by the arrival of a mere boat captain like Daffodil. I decided to stay there. We have a very good healer, a young priest named Father Brine, and an older priest who helps him. They figured out that swamp sickness comes from mosquito bites."

"Mosquito bites? That is nonsense!" said Salmon. "If mosquito bites caused swamp sickness, we would all be dead many times over, but the sickness has not even come here."

"You are lucky," said Holdfast. "Well, there must be something to the notion, for the precautions work. In the summer, we stay indoors at dawn and dusk when the mosquitos are worst, and cover our windows and doors with a fine netting like cheesecloth to keep them out. We seldom have big feasts like this. Each hut has its own clay hearth. We get bitten even so, of course, but not as much. The first summer, fifteen people in our village caught swamp sickness, and once one person had it, it spread rapidly. This summer, with the precautions, only two people got sick, and neither gave it to anyone else."

"I would attribute that difference to the weather," Mother Cedar argued. "I have been everywhere, from Newport to the first cataract, and this much is evident: Swamp sickness grows in the body like a mold, whenever you have both hot weather and sodden ground. This summer there was less sickness because it did not rain at all until that big storm, and not much afterwards, so the backwater became relatively dry."

"—which can minimize mosquitos," said Holdfast. "But Sharp Bend had more mosquitos than last year, even though it was drier, and they had more sickness."

"So much that they exiled the sick," muttered Rockdream.

"What?" asked Holdfast.

Rockdream and Salmon told him about the feverish, witless woman they found and tried to save that spring.

"That must have happened while they had no healers," said Holdfast. "They have one now, a midpriestess named Mother Stepstone, who came on a fishing boat early this summer. I met her last month when I went back there to try to trade one of Driftwood's pack horses for one of my own nanny goats. Not that I thought they had much use for a pack horse."

"Let us get back to the mosquitos," said Coral. "Might it be that only a certain kind of mosquito causes the sickness, and this kind is relatively rare? Here we have three common kinds: big ones, small brown ones, and small ones with striped legs that hum in your ears. But once in a while I notice one that looks different from these in one way or another."

Salmon looked at Coral thoughtfully. "I never thought to look carefully at what I was swatting."

"The bad mosquitos may be a kind that does not live here, or comes here but seldom," Coral continued. "This would not mean we are safe, for the disease does strike people not many miles from us, and if it is caused by bad mosquitos, a chance wind might blow a swarm of them our way. But there might be another reason why we have so far been spared. How do the people of Driftwood's Village treat their drinking water and dishwater?"

"We decant it and boil it, but not because of swamp sickness," Holdfast said. "Drinking only boiled water does not prevent that. It does prevent stomach cramps and loose waste."

Conversation then moved to hunting stories, speculations about the war, and anecdotes of village life. Birdwade afterwards could not remember exactly how she and Holdfast got into a conversation with just each other, or exactly what they discussed, but all too soon most of the others had gone to their huts, and Ripple was done playing with Wedge and wanted to go to bed.

"You know where the bed is," said Birdwade.

"Mom, it is too cold tonight without you."

Birdwade sighed and looked at Holdfast. "Well, I much enjoyed talking with you. I am sorry, but——"

"Maybe Ripple would like to hear a story before Greensword and I make our camp," Holdfast suggested.

Birdwade hesitated, but her daughter said, "Please, Mom?"

"I guess that would be nice," Birdwade said.

She made Holdfast wait outside on the platform while she and her daughter undressed and snuggled into their bed.

"Tell me a story I never heard," said Ripple.

"You might not know this one," Holdfast said, and told the story of the Two Princes of Great Rock. The older prince married a foreign princess, as was the custom of the time, but she caused him and his country much grief. His brother married a woman who was but a common herder, and worse, a widow with a young child, but she was clever and strong and loving, and was an excellent wife and queen. After her time, the heirs apparent often married commoners of merit.

"Ripple is asleep," Birdwade said quietly. "I was starting to drift off. I think you want her asleep and me awake, do you not?"

"Well—"

Birdwade giggled, and said, "Come here."

51.

In the last month of fall, when rains had swollen the rivers of Goblin Plain enough to make navigation difficult, goblin warriors from Quagga's Camp attacked and sank the *Slow and Steady*, a well-armed riverboat. A companion boat, called the *Piece of Waste* because it stank and was hard to maneuver, managed to escape. As its captain said, "The *Waste* had a mind of its own. It did not go where we were trying to make it go, or where the goblins expected it to go, so we got away. We were lucky." Now there was no doubt about what had happened to the *Golden Turtle*.

In response, Canticle ferried an army across the Goblin River and led it overland toward Quagga's Camp. Smoke messages relayed the warnings of goblin scouts, but the fires used for this were far from any camps. Canticle's own scouts reported groups of goblin warriors shadowing the army. Because Canticle assumed these groups were bait for one of Strong Bull's traps, he either moved his whole army toward them or ignored them. By the time he reached the land of Quagga's Camp, the goblins had assembled an army of their own, but still kept their distance. Canticle tried to surprise a detached group with Lieutenant Wolfkiller's platoon, then tried to bait the main army with a false retreat, but could not get close enough to do battle.

Lieutenant Hardtack prepared an analysis of goblin movements that suggested they were using several campsites, each with a store of folded tents, smoked meat, waterskins, and the like. So the army moved against one of these theoretical sites that night, hoping to surprise the goblins, but they found none, and despite a thorough search the next morning, they found no store. Because the human army's own supplies were running low, and because gathering clouds threatened a long, cold rain, Canticle ordered a retreat.

52.

Meanwhile, west of the Goblin River, Chiefs Hooked Beak, Quiet Cat and Big Claw led raids against human hunting groups. Once, they even made a bold attack against Lieutenant Strike's platoon, to interfere with the unloading of a cargo of fish. Strike and Fledgeling, who shared temporary command of the keep, decided to move a platoon in diffuse formation on the goblins' trail, and flipped a coin to decide which one would go.

Fledgeling was privately terrified that the goblins would predict her platoon's movements and set a trap, as was Feathergrass, but either their protective visualization worked, or else these goblins lacked such ability, for they were the ones who were surprised. In the dark of the moon, Fledgeling's vanguard found two groups of goblin warriors asleep in traveler's tents, concealed in the brush from all but chance discovery or the most thorough sweep. Killing them before they could wriggle out of these low tents was almost as easy as crashing a snail in its shell. Chief Hooked Beak was one of the dead.

But one goblin managed a death scream, which sounded the alarm. Other goblins somewhere ahead were already out of their own traveler's tents and running away, yelping like brush wolves.

Despite the unknown risk, Fledgeling ordered the sweep to continue, and so her platoon gathered many abandoned tents and stores before returning to the keep.

53.

Glowfly woke from her dream with a shudder. She was alone, very alone, now that Condor and most of the warriors were off shadowing the human army. Something could have gone wrong. Her dream might be a spirit warning, but if so it was unclear. She needed to talk to someone. Star Bear was her only choice.

Pulling on her dress and soft shoes and wrapping herself in a fur robe, Glowfly opened the tent flap and stepped outside. Picks Herbs, just the person Glowfly had hoped to avoid, was one of the women making flatbread. Picks Herbs would wonder, and guess, and know why Glowfly wanted to consult with Star Bear.

Four days after the night of the storm when Chief Condor and Glowfly had become lovers, he divorced Picks Herbs. He could have humiliated her by saying his reason was the disharmony of their tent, which was well known in camp. Instead he said his reason was that he wanted to marry Glowfly, a shamaness of far greater vision and power. Since he and Picks Herbs had no children, this should not cause any problem.

Glowfly and Condor were married four days after the divorce, which was also the day of a new moon, a good time to begin something. Outwardly, Picks Herbs was polite. She had, after all, been spared the blame. But in reality she was just waiting for Glowfly to make a mistake.

"Is your father awake?" Glowfly asked Star Bear's daughter.

"He is expecting you," she replied. This was promising. Maybe Star Bear had his own vision. Glowfly walked across camp to his tent; he invited her inside.

"This time my vision is not clear," the young shamaness began. "I think we must move camp again, but I am not sure where. I fear something may happen, or may had already happened, to the warriors. In my dream a human platoon lay in wait while the bulk of the army moved on. It felt more like fear than a clear warning. I should remember more than I do. If I entered trance now, I do not think I could have a clear vision."

"Every shaman has limitations," replied Star Bear. "I know mine. You are learning yours. I will not say that marrying Condor was foolish. Your love for each other has become clear and deep. But the woman he divorced for you is angry and bitter. She has many friends here. You will seem stronger if you admit your limitations. Call for a spirit dance."

Glowfly went to Skyrock, who was acting chief. He was Charging Elk's younger brother, one of the few warriors from that camp who survived the big defeat. Glowfly did not like him much, for his personality reminded her too much of Quick One, but he did have real reason to appreciate her.

She said, "I dreamed of a platoon of humans detached from the army, waiting for Condor and the warriors. I do not know when or where. I also have a strong feeling that we must move camp soon but I do not know in which direction. This vision is not much use. It may be only my fear shaped into a dream. So I call for a dance. Perhaps Great Mother Wolf or another spirit will tell someone else in camp what we need to know."

Five women took turns playing the two big drums while Star Bear led the dance. When Glowfly and Picks Herbs began playing the drums together, the rhythm became much like the rhythm of war. Each strove to surprise and outdo the other. Both somehow realized that this was right, this was the best way to drum in the vision.

The human Henna, who was two and a half months pregnant by her goblin husband, Lizard Toes, did not pace the dance, for she was lame. Bundled in her robe, she sat near Glowfly, watching the dancers. These were mostly women, but Lizard Toes was one of the nine men.

Glowfly was nothing but the battling rhythm, the flexing of elbows and wrists, the boom and slap of palms and fingertips. She closed her eyes and saw nothing. She opened her eyes and saw a circle of dancers, a dance fire, and miles of grass with scattered trees beneath a pale gray sky. No one was jumping or howling or rolling on the ground. There was no vision. Glowfly and Picks Herbs looked at each other, and with a shout of "Ha! Hey, yo. Ha!" they stopped drumming.

"Will anyone speak?" asked Star Bear.

"We have drummed and danced Glowfly's dream. It was a false warning," said Picks Herbs.

But even if the dream was dramatized fear rather than a warning, it did prove true. When Chief Condor and the warriors returned two days later, he described a platoon just like the one in the dream. "Did the humans really think that our scouts could not count the difference between an army of nearly a thousand and an army of about nine hundred?" Condor asked scornfully.

At this time it was raining steadily. The humans, discouraged and short of supplies, retreated the same way they had come, and so Condor's Camp did not have to move again.

54.

After Canticle's army returned, most of the Newport riverboats retreated to the swamp, where flooding made the rivers broader rather than swifter. But on the night of the next new moon, just before the beginning of winter, a large force of goblins in canoes, led by Strong Bull, made a devastating surprise attack against the winter boat camp. Fifteen riverboats were burned to the waterline or sunk.

The boat camp had made no large watchfires, lest the light attract either goblins or the dragon, but this was their undoing, for a force of goblins who already knew where to go could approach unseen in the cloudy moonless night. But the first burning boats gave light to the human archers, who forced the goblins back into the gloom.

In the morning, the surviving captains held debate with Commander Conch and Lord Drill. Most of them wanted to pursue the goblins up the Blue River. Drill thought this was too risky and Conch thought it was futile, so they tried to forbid it, but most of the captains openly refused to obey. Drill said that he would rather be a bonded servant in a real city than lord of a rabble of so-called warriors who refused to obey a reasonable command.

The disobedient captains' sailboats came close to overtaking the canoes but lost them in the reed-choked shallows south of the river. Probably the goblins then returned home on foot over the Gray Hills. The humans might have lost one boat in the marsh, but this was uncertain. Some captains believed that the missing boat, Frogsong's *Great Stag*, was spying for Lord Drill. It could have returned to the river by another channel and hurried downstream with news of the goblin escape. However this was, when the fleet returned to the swamp, Drill, Conch, and the relatively few captains, warriors, and citizens who had chosen to obey them were gone.

General Canticle knew that he needed the loyalty and respect of the boat captains much more than he needed Lord Drill, so he told Captain Laurel to tell them to choose a suitable commander from their own number, to do whatever seemed best for their own defense, and to fell suitable wood for the eventual construction of more boats.

Shortly after Captain Laurel's departure, Endive the Cook was saying that Lord Drill had taken his foolish followers to Midcoast, where they would all become bonded servants.

55.

Loop Lake Village now had two rafts, fitted with square sails and centerboards, for local fishing, which freed Flatfish's skiff for hunting and fishing trips to the far end of the lake. Rigged with a mast, triangular mainsail, and jib, the skiff made a small but swift sailboat, able to make the trip in less than an hour with a good breeze.

On the morning of the first day of winter, Rockdream, Salmon, and Bloodroot sailed the skiff to the western shore near the far end, where Flatfish and Swanfeather had seen a large group of pigs a few days before. After hiding the skiff, they found the pig trail and followed it west and south.

"Look," Rockdream said quietly, pointing toward a sudden column of smoke. "That does not look like a campfire."

"It might be closer and smaller than it looks," said Bloodroot.

Cautiously, they paced a distance to triangulate its location, but instead discovered that the fire was moving.

"A burning boat," Bloodroot said.

"Maybe the dragon has come," said Rockdream, "or the boat is doing battle with goblins."

"Or maybe that boat has suffered a terrible accident," said Bloodroot. "Such things do happen. But battle seems likely."

"Hush your voices and quiet your minds, both of you," Salmon said. "Let me weave a glimmer around us, a good one, so that we may spy out the situation in relative safety."

Rockdream wondered whether they were near enough to the river to hear the clamor of battle. Probably they were close enough to hear Riversong's bellow, if he were bellowing. Rockdream looked down at the mud, trying not to think about dragons, especially not that one. But he kept peering up through the bare branches at the sky, and worrying about how exposed he and his companions were.

But were they truly easy to see? Their weather-stained leathers matched the browns of trees and mud. They were the best hunters of the village, skilled at moving quietly. Surely they could spy out the situation safely and return with the news in plenty of time.

"The glimmer is starting to work," Salmon said quietly. "We are nothing of interest. We are not easy to notice."

They approached the river through stands of swamp pine wherever possible, for here was better cover and drier ground. The levee itself was dry, but too exposed, and the stand of willows between it and the hummock where they stood was flooded two feet deep. But the view they had was good enough to show them that no dragon was pursuing the burning boat or circling above a second fire that erupted suddenly somewhere upstream. Gradually this fire drifted closer into clear view, a full-sized riverboat feeding tall orange flames that were just beginning to billow black smoke.

"It was set ablaze by its own crew," Salmon said abruptly. "At the base of the flames you can see glowing embers from the kindling that was spread over the deck."

"But why would they do this?" asked Bloodroot.

"I do not know. To hide the boat? But the smoke must be visible for miles. To make a signal? But of what, and to whom? Rockdream, what do you think?"

"I think the crews and passengers of these boats are likely walking toward our lake. We must spy out the portage."

Quickly and quietly as possible, the three hunters traced a route through the maze of hummocks and hard flats toward the end of the lake. After a year and a half of living here, they knew well how to distinguish the silt of a hard flat from the mud of a mire, even when both were flooded. But no such special knowledge was needed to reach the lake from the river farther upstream. You could simply walk along either of the old levees made by the river years and years before when Loop Lake was one of its bends.

They came to the western levee farther from the lake and closer to the river than they had intended, and so approached it cautiously. It was marked more by the change from bare willows to green pines than by any noticeable rise. This pine stand was two miles long but no more than a few trees wide. Beyond it was a bank thick with berry brush, dropping to the open reedflat that stretched to the line of pines marking the other levee. And in those distant trees was movement, marked by chance flashes of sunlight off weapons.

"I was hoping we could get close enough to see who they are without being seen, but it does not look easy," said Rockdream.

"We can count them from here, and likely see something to verify that they are human," said Bloodroot.

"Ah, we will have to get a good look at them sooner or later. Better sooner," said Salmon.

So the three hunters hurried ahead on their own levee, to increase their distance from the others; then made their way down the bank and across the reedflat, choosing a route that kept them near but not in the tall reeds and cattails. About midway across, they startled a heron they had not noticed, which fortunately flew overhead and landed somewhere behind them where they would not disturb it again.

"The glimmer is holding," said Salmon. "We got quite close before the heron saw us, and its flight did not reveal us."

About a quarter mile from the pines, they walked hesitantly, like deer, watching for any movement, listening for any sound. Then they stooped low and darted for the cover of a thorn tangle just six hundred feet from the eastern levee, crawled under it, and waited.

It seemed to take forever for the column of people to come into sight. Yes, they were humans—men, women, and a small number of children. Some used pikes for walking sticks. Most had heavy packs.

"The fifth one from the front looks like Lord Drill," Salmon mumbled.

"Yes," Rockdream agreed. "I think I see Conch, and the woman from Moonport who won the tournament. Canticle should be at the rear, if he is part of this."

They recognized some of the other warriors and sailors, but Canticle was not among them. When the end of the column passed a half mile ahead, the three hunters sneaked back across the reedflat and hurried through the trees toward their skiff.

Lord Drill's humans were already walking on the opposite shore, about a mile away. Rockdream felt certain that neither the distance, nor the glimmer, nor the small wisps of cold stream dancing on the water's surface would serve to hide their sails once they were under way. Nonetheless, they pushed the skiff out of the brush into the water, climbed aboard, raised the mast and sails, found their breeze, and moved north near the western shore.

"Just as I expected, someone is waving," Rockdream said. "They see us."

Salmon touched his free arm. "Do not wave back. They may be unsure of what they see. A return wave would break the glimmer."

"But Salmon—"

"Do what my wife says," said Bloodroot. "She is the one here who knows things."

"Look, no one else is waving or pointing," said Salmon.

"Likely they think we are unfriendly and are pointing with small gestures," said Rockdream. "What else could we be but a little sailboat?"

"We could be a drakey, soaring low on ribbed wings, sensing the armed hunters across the lake and hoping that the thin mist will obscure their view."

"Are you serious?" asked Rockdream.

"The red-robes in the procession think they are hearing a drakey's thoughts. I am not using words, of course, but images and emotions. I have played enough thought games with drakeys while hunting them to do a likely imitation."

In response to a chance slackening of the breeze, the sails snapped twice, then filled out smooth again.

"I just flapped my wings," said Salmon.

Gradually Lord Drill's column dwindled and became obscure; the mist now blurred the trees on that shore. The ten-mile journey seemed to take a long time only because the three hunters were so anxious to reach the village.

"Where is our pig?" asked Flatfish even before they beached his skiff. Coral and Wedge were with him.

"We got distracted by two burning riverboats," said Rockdream. "Lord Drill and Commander Conch are heading this way with about a hundred and ten Newport people. Fortunately they were heavily burdened and moving slow. They were ten miles away when we last saw them, probably no more than a mile or two closer now, and it will be dark soon. We have time for a council."

"We are not sure whether they saw us or not," Bloodroot added as he climbed out of the skiff.

"Drill must know about this village from Canticle and Fledgeling," Coral said. "Like them, he will call us traitors. And I despise Drill and Conch, for their wrathful command that caused the massacre of Beadback's Camp. Loop Lake might support us all, but we cannot share it with them. I do not know what to do."

"Hi, Daddy, hi, hi!" said Wedge. Rockdream scooped the little boy up into his arms.

"I do not think they mean to stay here," said Bloodroot. "If they did, they would have hidden the riverboats for future salvage instead of burning them."

"You are assuming that Drill thinks like a warrior or a merchant, when in fact he thinks more like a priest," said Salmon. "He and his command may be doing some penance to cleanse their spiritual pollution. They may believe that those riverboats were accursed."

"Did you overhear such thoughts or are you guessing?" Coral asked sharply.

"I am guessing," Salmon admitted. "Most of my attention was on my glimmer. They saw the skiff, but might have been confused about what it was."

"Maybe so. You are good at glimmers," Coral said, then brightened her voice. "I just got an idea. Mother Cedar will not like it unless we find the right way to explain it, but—well, suppose that just before dawn tomorrow I make a dreamsending to Drill. I know he must be afraid of goblins. If I weave some of his own images of fear into a dream of a goblin surprise attack on his people here at the lake, and make it frightening enough to wake him up, he may think the dream is prophetic. Now, suppose when he wakes he sees a goblin smoke message coming from the river. I know how smoke messages are put together. The code changes with the circumstances, likely often in war. I can tell you how to make something that will look like the real thing."

"That is luscious, Coral," Salmon said appreciatively. "No matter what Drill plans now, tomorrow morning he will lead his retinue away from here so fast— But wait, do you know Drill well enough to dreamsend him?"

Coral just smiled smugly.

"That is marginally black sorcery," said Rockdream.

"How so?" Coral asked. "I do not mean Drill any harm. I just want him to go away."

"But to give him a bad dream—"

"This is a valid military bluff," said Salmon.

"If you can think of a better way to make Drill leave, let us hear it," said Coral.

"Well, the smoke message alone might be enough," Rockdream said hesitantly.

"I like a sure thing much better," said Flatfish. "But let us propose just the smoke message ploy to the whole village, and let Coral do whatever she can to increase its effectiveness."

"Excellent," said Coral, again smiling smugly.

"I cannot make myself like this plan, but I will accept it, unless someone else thinks of a better one," said Rockdream.

All the villagers were present for the council, except Birdwade, her daughter Ripple, and the other two widows, Magpie and Thornbush, who had gone together to Driftwood's Village to visit the three men they had befriended. Naturally, once Birdwade and Thornbush began seeing Holdfast and Greensword, Magpie had to go to Driftwood's Village to see what other men were available. She found one. Now the women and men were taking turns visiting each other. Birdwade and Holdfast seemed to be contemplating marriage; the other two couples seemed less certain.

Rockdream, Salmon, and Bloodroot began the council by describing the burning riverboats and Lord Drill's retinue crossing the portage to the eastern shore. Mother Cedar immediately offered to talk to the lord to find out what was happening.

"There are some in that group who are decent enough, but there are others each of us would do well to avoid," Salmon said. "Even you, good mother. I think you said that Mother Mallow did Lord Drill's purification, so you know her. I remember her from the castle. She is with the lord now, and might well accuse you of treason to the Church for your work here with us."

"I can defend myself," said Mother Cedar. "My soul is clean. But yours and Coral's and some others here are stained with hate."

"We want Lord Drill and his people to go away," said Rockdream. "We cannot force them to leave, but we might trick them into doing so, if none of us talk to them first. Tell me, how many of you want to live here in a much larger village under the rule of Lord Drill? Nobody? How many want to have to move away to avoid this?"

"We are with you, Rockdream," said Ironweed, and others nodded agreement. "What must we do?"

56.

Coral sat on her bed, staring at the flames of eight tallow candles. In deep slow trance she searched for Lord Drill's face. Dawn was still hours away. Could Drill be awake, or was he somehow protected? Yes, there was an egg of silver light, as hot to the touch as a cauldron over a fire. Coral jerked out of trance, breathing hard. That shield was done well. Were it not for her own egg of blue light, she now would have a splitting headache.

This dreamsending might not be so easy, after all. Someone who knew things had made this protection for the lord, and might sense anything but the most subtle intrusion. Who? Maybe that priestess Salmon had mentioned, Mother Mallow. Why? Drill must have either suffered some sorcerous attack or have real reason to fear such attack. From whom? Goblin shamans!

Breathing slowly and deeply, Coral let her body return to relaxation and peace. She had eight candles lit, for the Mother, the Father, the Three Daughters, and the Three Sons. Which light offered an entrance? Lake the Lover, youngest daughter. Coral could get inside the egg as the woman of Lord Drill's dreams, whoever this woman might be.

"What am I thinking of?" Coral whispered to herself. "That would be dark sorcery indeed, to pretend to be his lover when I am his enemy. Lake, I cannot— Lake!" she repeated. The name gave the witch a better idea.

Coral felt herself expanding, dissolving. She was wide and long, motionless and covered with thinning mist. Reeds grew through her edges. Catfish and carp wriggled through her. There was Drill, standing with several others who were but vague forms to Coral. They had heard something, and were trying to see what it was.

Coral felt the tickle of hundreds of paddles, the smooth movement of many leather-covered keels. "Lord Coward, I have found you!" said the voice of High Chief Strong Bull. Coral could feel the image's strong muscles, his rough leather vest and breeches, his keen and righteous anger. Drill had escaped Strong

Bull's surprise attack on the boat camp, but would not escape now.

Drill's shadowy retinue fired their crossbows. Coral had enough control over the dream to make all the arrows miss but the one aimed at Strong Bull. This one he deflected with his throwing spear. Now the goblin warriors were splashing through the shallow, hurling spears. One struck Drill in the back. He fell awake, and Coral shuddered out of trance through a veil of spirit fire.

The room was dark, and now she did have a splitting headache. That dreamsending had been powerful indeed for the candles to be extinguished by Drill's awakening. Coral wondered whether she was the only power responsible. Strong Bull's image had seemed so real. What if he really was leading a force to attack Drill at Loop Lake? What if these goblins found Rockdream and Flatfish making a false smoke message?

Coral climbed out of bed and opened the door to her hut. The air outside was chill and damp, but less stuffy. There was just a trace of light; sunrise would come in about an hour, and Wedge would awaken. "Maybe I can get some sleep," she said, and closed the door and lay down in her bed.

57.

At dawn, on the western levee midway between the lake and the river, Rockdream and Flatfish kindled a fire. As soon as the mist was thin enough for them to see the trees of the other levee, they added green boughs to make thick gray smoke. Rockdream then covered this with a wet hide, and uncovered it to make four series of puffs, which was the form of a who, what, where, and when message, such as, "Lord Drill's force, camped, north, now." Then they kicked the fire apart and trampled out the embers.

By the time Rockdream and Flatfish returned to the skiff's hiding place, the slight breeze from the south had cleared the mists from the southern half of the lake, and they could see clearly that Lord Drill's camp was gone.

"But where did they go, and what are they doing now?" asked Flatfish. "It all depends on the success of Coral's dream message."

"She would not discuss her plans with me, but wanted to follow her intuition," said Rockdream.

"We can guess how it has to work. Lord Drill had a prophetic dream about a large goblin force coming around the north end of the lake."

"Or else across the lake," suggested Rockdream.

"Yes. What worries me is Lord Drill. Surely any lord would take strong precautions against a witch tampering with his mind."

"Coral knows those things well enough," Rockdream said, "but do not say so to anyone else."

"I hear you."

"I do not think I want to risk using the sail," said Rockdream.

"All right. We will row."

This delayed their return to the village long enough to worry Coral, who feared that Strong Bull might have really followed Lord Drill to Loop Lake. In fact, the high chief and his warriors were nowhere near. As for Lord Drill, Salmon spied out his force about two miles east of the lake, moving north. Maybe they were going to try climbing over the Emerald Hills.

58.

Captain Laurel's boat had been the first that winter to use the backwater west of the rise to reach the settlement, but no human boats would use the Goblin River again till the floods of winter and spring subsided. After Laurel's departure, another long rain, sometimes turning to sleet, forced Canticle's scouts to return to the settlement. The general hoped that the goblins were similarly afflicted with colds and winter fevers, but thought it more likely that Strong Bull was using the time to muster an army big enough for siege or decisive battle.

On the first day after the rain stopped, Canticle sent two platoons under Lieutenants Hardtack and Wolfkiller to patrol the Goblin River. With them went two groups of mounted hunters to pursue any startled game. The hunters killed two auroch bulls and a lone mammoth, and the lieutenants reported no signs of goblins closer than two plumes of smoke at least five miles east of the river.

Late in the afternoon two days after this, Fledgeling and Feathergrass were called to the west wall to identify the fishing boat coming up the backwater.

"The *Great Stag*, Captain Frogsong's boat," Fledgeling told Hawthorn and the other guards. "Supposedly that boat went with Lord Drill. Maybe Frogsong is bringing him here. The attack on the boat camp might have convinced him that this is the safest place to be."

"Well, either Frogsong's sailors have forgotten how to come about, or something is wrong with the rudder," said Feathergrass. "It could be fouled by reeds."

Hawthorn muttered, "The last thing we need just when the goblins are heating up the war is Lord Drill."

"I should rebuke you for that remark, but in truth I agree with you," said Fledgeling.

"Who are you fooling? Who gave the gossips their information?" asked Hawthorn. "The general ought to be our lord. He is our lord in all but name. I took the gossip as a sign that he was getting ready to say so. But for Lord Drill to show up now, that is a touchy situation."

"Better to let Lord Drill keep his bloody title, as long as he does not interfere with the government," said another guard.

"You know he will," said Hawthorn, and the third guard nodded agreement to that.

"I cannot say that this is not your concern, for it does indeed concern all of us," said Fledgeling. "But if Canticle is competent to be lord of this settlement, surely he is competent to deal with the likes of Lord Drill. Stand watch till I return or send a message."

Feathergrass knew then that Canticle really did plan to become lord. Possibly Frogsong, who after all had lived for many years in Canticle's Tower, owed the general her first loyalty. Her apparent obedience to Lord Drill might be Canticle's plan. Feathergrass guessed that the party sent to meet the boat would be small and carefully selected.

"What do you think?" asked Hawthorn.

Speaking aloud changed the flow of Feathergrass's thought. "I think we will have a beautiful sunset and a dark night before anyone reaches that boat. There will be ample time before moonrise for a goblin surprise attack. I hope Canticle considers this danger and sends out a full platoon. I feel uneasy."

The slowly moving fishing boat was now silhouetted by the water reflecting the golden sun.

"Guard, hello!" called a voice from below and behind. "Feathergrass and Hawthorn, Lieutenant Fledgeling wants you both to report to the middle stable."

"Oh, blood," Feathergrass muttered, and climbed down the ladder. The messenger, the warrior Iris, was already running off to summon the next chosen ones. After Hawthorn climbed down, they both hurried across the settlement to the stables.

"Fledgeling, I fear a goblin attack before moonrise," Feathergrass said. "To go out like this—"

"Take a moment," she said slowly and firmly. "Take a deep breath, strengthen your egg of silver light, and tell me if you are still so uneasy."

Feathergrass did so. "My hesitation remains. The reeds are tall. The night will be dark, perhaps misty."

"We will ride in a diffuse formation. Most of us will be out of range of any goblin ambush. Even a force of several hundred could be eluded."

"Maybe so. But what about when we reach the boat?"

"I would rather wait and give those instructions when we are all here. Prepare your horses."

When all twenty of the selected ones were there, Fledgeling explained the plan. Only she and Hawthorn would actually meet the boat; the others would stay spread out. This precaution would be explained to Lord Drill. They would bring no extra horses. Depending on how many companions Drill brought with him, they could either ride double, or walk with the riders, or wait till morning. On the way back, the riders would close ranks. If it did prove necessary to arrest Lord Drill, or to compel him to swear an oath, this would be done then.

The faces of the other riders were grim. Feathergrass sensed no hesitation. Lord Drill would be forced to submit to Canticle's authority.

As Feathergrass led his horse from the stall and followed the others outside, he forced doubt from his own mind. The tactics against possible goblin attack were excellent.

The mildness of afternoon was cooling quickly to the chill of night; except for the ramparts of the east wall, the settlement was in shadow. They rode over the ramp, around the south wall, and west, spreading out into a block five wide and four deep, a hundred feet between riders, with Fledgeling in the middle of the front row and Feathergrass in the middle of the rear.

The *Great Stag*'s crew had already furled the sails and dropped anchor. Now someone lit a lantern, which showed the boat's direction clearly but obscured the movements of the crew. The rich blue twilight darkened to starry night. Even the water's edge was hard to see.

"Ship, hello! Lieutenant Fledgeling here!" she shouted.

"Land, hello! Give us a bloody minute to load up the skiff!" a man's voice shouted.

"Wait a bloody moment yourself, sailor! I need to talk to the captain before you go piling up goods on shore. Frogsong!"

After a moment's hesitation, the man said, "The captain—the captain cannot shout. Have a bit of patience!"

Something seemed wrong, but Feathergrass did not know just what. He urged his horse forward to the second row.

"Who are you, sailor?" Fledgeling called to the man.

"He is a pirate!" Feathergrass shouted. "Any name he gives will be false. Retreat!"

"Oh, right!" the man called back. "I am bloody Chief Beartooth of Goblin Plain, my captain is Strong Bull, and we have come here to kill you! I am coming ashore to talk before I get as hoarse as the rest of the crew!"

Now Feathergrass thought he recognized the voice as Crabclaw, a sailor of Frogsong's crew who often made wisecracks. Feathergrass heard the oars stroking the water, the keel running aground in the shallow, the two sailors climbing out. He could just barely see them. In this darkness even Fledgeling, who was closest, must not have seen exactly what they were doing. But from their viewpoint, Fledgeling, on a tall horse silhouetted against the sky, was a good enough target for the spear that killed her.

The spear struck. Fledgeling fell without a cry. Her horse reared up, turned, and panicked. Hawthorn, Feathergrass, and a third rider shot arrows toward the skiff. "Surround them! Strong Bull and Beartooth!" Feathergrass shouted and splashed his horse through the shallow on the far side of the skiff.

But before most of the other riders could react, goblin war cries came from north and south. In the moment that Feathergrass was distracted, Strong Bull and Beartooth splashed toward the deep. Now a spear thrown from the *Great Stag* just missed Feathergrass's horse. The boat's lantern was extinguished.

"Retreat!" a woman, probably Iris, was shouting, and most of the riders were doing so.

Feathergrass urged his horse back to land, stopped at Fledgeling's body, and dismounted. As soon as he touched her, he knew she was dead. He pulled out the spear, slung her body over his horse's back, mounted, and urged the horse to a fast trot. Another thrown spear just missed. Feathergrass galloped his horse away from the twenty or so goblin warriors rushing him from the north, then rode toward the other riders.

How many goblins were there? This group, and the crew of the boat, and others coming from the south. At least sixty, maybe many more. Without better light, the riders had no choice but to retreat.

Returning to the settlement seemed to take forever.

Feathergrass, Hawthorn, and Iris made a brief report to Lieutenant Hardtack, then repeated it for General Canticle.

"Maybe the whole force that attacked the winter boat camp was closing in," said Feathergrass. "I do not know. They expected a platoon on foot, somewhat later. They were not quite ready for us."

Canticle's appropriate remarks did nothing to ease the pain Feathergrass was just beginning to feel. He excused himself, walked back to his own hut, pulled off his boots, climbed into bed, and tried to fall asleep.

"What happened?" asked Forward's voice, after a while.

"They killed her," Feathergrass replied. "I do not—"

"Oh, I am sorry. I am so sorry," said the young man.

"I wish we had a bloody witch at this settlement. I need some sleepflower, or something. I want to sleep and sleep and forget everything, but I cannot sleep and cannot stop thinking."

"Maybe you should talk to a priestess," Forward suggested.

"Bah! I got enough bloody platitudes from the general. Just let me be and go to sleep. I do not want to talk."

9

WOLF'S KILL

59.

At the main fire, Glowfly was listening to Strong Bull telling how his warriors paddled a canoe fleet to the human boat camp on the new moon night, eighteen days before. They burned fifteen boats and killed or wounded at least a hundred humans, but Strong Bull did not know whether Lord Drill and Commander Conch were alive or dead.

"The humans' sailboats chased us the next day, even into the backwater shallows of the southern marsh," Strong Bull was saying. "One smaller boat followed us too far and ran aground. We came back around through the reeds and killed the crew and captain while they were trying to push the boat off the bottom. We were going to burn the boat, but then I said, 'Maybe we can use it.'

"Just before we mustered this force, I had several dreams about boats, as did Drakey and some others. But one of my dreams was funny. I dreamed I was captain of a human boat. My sailors were goblins wearing human clothes. I spoke about this dream now.

"We could send the wounded to Gorge's Camp and Beartooth's

Camp and still have enough warriors to battle a human platoon. We could make up a crew for the sailboat and sail up the marsh behind the human keep. In the afternoon the wind would be behind us. The rest of the warriors would paddle canoes through the swamp. The humans would see our boat from their wall and send a platoon. By the time they reached us, it would be dark and our surprise would be ready. If anything went too wrong, we could retreat to the swamp.

"We waited for a couple of days, to make sure the swamp people had given up looking for us. Then that big storm delayed us half the month. Two days ago we left the southern marsh. Sailing was harder than I expected, but we managed. We came near Canticle's Keep just before yesterday's sunset.

"But Canticle knows things and countered my tactics. He sent horse riders to meet the boat. They arrived before we were ready. They were spaced far apart so we could not kill more than one or two by surprise. Their leader was Lieutenant Woman. She and her husband were suspicious. They knew the real crew of our boat.

"But Beartooth spoke just like a human sailor. He said, 'I am bloody Chief Beartooth of Goblin Plain, my captain is Strong Bull, and we have come here to kill you.' This fooled them."

The warriors at the fire yowled and laughed and stamped their feet. Glowfly thought bitterly of Chief Beartooth lying wounded in the hospital tent, his pain and awareness both obliterated by a strong brew of sleepflower.

Now Strong Bull was telling how his spear pierced Fledgeling's heart, how he and Beartooth tried to elude the mounted archers in the dark, how Beartooth was wounded, how the riders fled the main goblin force led by Chief Redspear, how Strong Bull left behind one scout to burn the boat later so that the humans would not recover it and would be fooled about where the goblins might be, how the whole force hurried north to the brush and east over the rise toward the river, how the human riders searching for them by moonlight failed to find them, and how they swam across the river to safety. The warriors who were wounded in the boat camp battle had a much easier journey to Gorge's Camp than poor Beartooth had to this one.

When Strong Bull and the chiefs and warriors present began discussing how to attack the humans next, Glowfly left the fire. After checking on Little Ant and Beartooth, she went to her husband's tent, undressed, went to bed, and prayed for a vision.

When Condor came to bed, much later, he asked her about her new song.

"What song?" she asked.

"I thought you left the fire to make a chant about burning the boats," he replied.

"That is a good idea. But I left because I feel troubled in my heart. The humans' long reach is cut short, but their short reach will grab for this camp. Strong Bull should not harass hunting groups. The time has come for a siege."

"Not now, not yet," said Condor. "The humans are much better fighters than they were three seasons ago. They expect a siege. We want to annoy them, to make them come out. Maybe they will try something reckless."

"When they came last month my dreams were vague," said Glowfly.

"Our scouts were good. That time a spirit warning did not matter. When it matters, you will dream a clear warning."

"After last time, the camp may not heed me."

"When you are sure of something, you are very convincing," said Condor. "But even that vague dream, though no warning, was much like what actually happened. That impressed everyone."

"I still feel uneasy," Glowfly said. "But tomorrow I will make a chant about the victory."

"I know another way to make fear go away," Condor said, and put his arms around her and rubbed his lips on hers. "Even the most timid boy is a brave chief in his lover's arms."

"Mmm," said Glowfly. "Even the most timid girl is a powerful shamaness."

Hands danced over skin. She reached for something, guided it in, and melted with the joy of each surprising thrust. He loved her, he honored her, he understood her fear and her strength. She shuddered and fell and shuddered again before he streamed.

"I love you," Glowfly whispered, and Condor said the same.

But in the middle of the night she woke from fear: a dream of wolves running on the star plain, of danger to both Condor and his camp. "Condor?" she said, reaching to touch him, but he was not in bed. People were moving and talking quietly outside. Glowfly hurriedly pulled on her dress, wrapped herself in a robe, and went out.

Nearly a hundred warriors were already crowded around the fire, and others were pulling apart their traveler's tents. "Strong

Bull! Condor!" Glowfly said, for they were standing together. "I do not know what plan or dream caused you to muster now, but I am concerned. This camp will be in great danger. The human army is coming."

"We are going to meet them," said Strong Bull. "They will be ferrying across the river farther south."

Glowfly took a deep breath and released it quickly, making a sound like a choked back sob. "I give a voice to Mother Wolf. Condor lies bleeding near the river, his body pierced by a flying spear. A smaller human force unseen by goblin scouts surprises this camp. We run. Many die. This is no time to muster. We must throw down our tents, smother the fire, and flee."

"My plan is good," Strong Bull said firmly. "Each other time when the human army crossed the river, they had sailboats with dragon guns. This time they are making a reed raft. Their crossing will be slow. This is their most vulnerable time."

"Where is the force that endangers this camp?" Condor asked.

Glowfly hesitated, then again gave a voice to Mother Wolf. "In the brush. They moved there before moonrise. When the warriors leave camp they will come here."

"This is too vague," said Strong Bull. "How far away are they? In which direction? How many?"

"I am sorry. Their leader knows things. He can hide from my eyes and nose like a deer posed motionless upwind."

"Who dreams true?" asked Strong Bull. "I dream a human army crosses the river and moves south toward Beartooth's Camp. Scouts see this beginning to happen. You dream a smaller force attacks this camp. If so, then the army will expect my force. I dream victory. Do you dream defeat?"

Glowfly tried to speak, but could not find words.

"She dreams my death," said Condor. "This could happen no matter how the battle goes. But how could she dream clearly about other warriors once I was dead? If she is right about everything she says, the humans have a good plan. We could not know about it without a spirit warning."

"But there is another interpretation," said Split Hoof. He was an older shaman from Mammoth's Camp who had replaced Sees Patterns as Strong Bull's substitute advisor, when Drakey was either elsewhere or uncooperative. "Glowfly dreamed a true warning once, before she was closely connected to this camp. Now she is the chief's wife. Her fear of Condor's death has already made her give one false warning."

"I had doubts about that dream. I am sure about this one," Glowfly said, but there was doubt in her voice.

Condor said, "I will go with Strong Bull. I will be careful, for I accept your warning. Sundance will be acting chief."

"If you accepted my warning, you would do what I suggested," Glowfly said, choking back her tears, for the warriors were all looking at her. "I hope that you are right and I am wrong."

60.

Glowfly went to the hospital tent.

"What is happening?" asked Little Ant.

"The warriors are mustering. The human army is crossing the river somewhere to the south. I dreamed that Condor will die in this battle."

"Condor is going anyway?" asked Little Ant. "How could they expect to win? Even without a warning, defeat is obvious."

"Strong Bull thinks the humans will have a slow and troublesome crossing. Maybe they want him to think this. But that is not the worst of it. There is a smaller human force somewhere else. They will attack this camp after the warriors leave."

"And no one believes you," said Little Ant.

"I should not have mentioned Condor's death. I should have just warned him about the second human force. But I do not know where it is. Their leader knows things. He is hiding from me."

"They cannot be too far away. Maybe they are in the gully."

"We have scouts watching that," said Glowfly. "I think the place they are hiding is brushy and flat. They went there in the dark of the moon."

"So, likely they are somewhere between us and the river," said Little Ant, "unless you think they could hide from the warriors going to fight the army."

"I do not know," Glowfly said. "Maybe they could have even circled around to surprise us from the east. But I do not think the dark of tonight's moon gave them that much time."

"So have Sundance send out scouts to look for the humans."

"They would not find them in time."

"You could find them," said Little Ant.

"But I—Do you mean actually leave camp and be a scout myself?"

"Go into a really really deep trance and become Mother Wolf," said Little Ant. "She will protect you. You can see, hear, smell, and run much better as a wolf."

"But I do not actually become—" Glowfly stopped herself. If she was in deep enough trance to dream the night eyes, the long nose, the moving ears, the claws and pads, maybe in some sense she really was a wolf. Maybe if she went even deeper, anyone who looked at her would see a wolf. Maybe that was what the shamans did in the old stories. But some of them could become birds. How did they fly?

"Sit like a wolf," said Little Ant.

Glowfly squatted with her arms between her knees, her fingers on the ground, her wrists raised.

"Close your eyes and let the position become comfortable." Little Ant's voice sounded less like a girl's, more like a wise old woman's.

Glowfly let this voice guide her deeper and deeper into her own spirit. She became a wolf more vividly than ever before. She wriggled her skin to fluff out her fur for a cold night. She twisted an ear and noticed how sounds changed. She sniffed and sorted out the subtle swirl of scents inside her nose.

Still Little Ant's wise old woman voice took her deeper.

The wolf listened and sniffed. Cautiously she crawled out the tent door, wrinkling her nose in disgust at the stench of the smoldering fire. Quietly she walked around to the back of the tent, trotted straight away from camp, then circled toward the west, stopping for a moment to sniff the fresh trail of Strong Bull's force. She recognized Condor's musk among all the other men.

The air was cold and clear and fresh. She made a wolf's prayer for a breeze from the west. A moment's twinkling of the stars brought this breeze. Was that the musk of men? Was that the musk of women? Humans! How many and where? The wolf trotted the scent several miles.

Now she heard things. A stick snapped. Leather trousers creaked. Humans were fools to wear clothes that made such noise. In the distance she saw a chance glint of moonlight off a weapon. The humans were crouched in the shadows, moving and stopping, moving and stopping.

Mother Wolf felt the dark cloud in the human leader's mind. She knew this cloud. When warriors who were her children died in battle, she would pull them free of its hate and turmoil. This living human warrior was trapped there by grief and rage. He was her enemy. She would not help him.

She carefully edged away through the shadows, then trotted, then ran south as fast as she could until fatigue slowed her again to a steady trot. There was time, just enough time. She made a wolf's prayer for a breeze from the south, and a twinkling of stars brought a breeze with the faint scent of Condor, Strong Bull, and all the other goblin men.

Finally she found them, barked four times to get their attention, and circled toward Strong Bull.

"Stop! Stop!" she cried. "I give a voice to Mother Wolf! Lieutenant Woman's husband leads a platoon less than five miles west of camp. He lusts for bloody massacre. Come back and give it to him. He will be surprised. Come back now!"

Strong Bull stared at her without speaking. More than two hundred other warriors did the same thing.

"I trailed their scent. I heard them. I saw them. Come, come back now," she said.

"Glowfly, is that you?" Condor asked.

"I give my voice and body to Mother Wolf."

"We will do what the wolf woman says," said Strong Bull. "Condor, you take your own warriors and enough others and return to camp as fast as you can. I will take the others north to head off a retreat. Is this good?" he asked the wolf woman.

"It is good," she replied.

61.

This was the human plan: General Canticle would contrive a river crossing clumsy enough to make his army look vulnerable, in hopes of luring Strong Bull into battle. Meanwhile, Feathergrass, newly promoted to lieutenant, would lead a platoon across both forks of the Goblin River and the Sacred Ground by the dark of the moon and take cover within striking distance of Condor's Camp.

So far, so good—maybe, Feathergrass thought. His scout had reported that Strong Bull, Condor, and most of the warriors had left camp to fight the army. But then that wolf came. Feathergrass was unsure why he noticed it, for its gray fur blended well with the moonlit brush and it did not come close. But it came from the direction of Condor's Camp and ran off in the direction of Strong Bull's force as if it were a scout. Goblin Plain people did not tame and train animals, but what if the shamans could speak to wild animals and gain their cooperation the way some elves were said to do?

While Feathergrass was moving from shadow to shadow, he watched his troops to see who was most skilled at being unseen. He wanted to send out another scout to verify that Strong Bull's force was not returning to Condor's Camp. He intercepted his chosen scout, gave her instructions, cautioned her to watch out for the lone wolf, then melted back into the movement of his troops.

62.

Glowfly was so deep in trance that she had lost awareness of herself as Glowfly. She could not say whether she was a shamaness in a thin leather dress, chilled by the sweat of her exertions, or a wolf in thick fur, panting while she trotted. Except when she had to speak, being a wolf was more comfortable, so she was a wolf, trotting near but not in the column of goblin warriors hurrying back to Condor's Camp.

The wolf moved stealthily from shadow to shadow, looking ahead and toward her left and wondering. She caught the scent of a human woman's sweat. A scout! Now the wolf heard the woman retreating. Now the wolf was bounding a great circle to intercept her.

The human woman heard something, notched an arrow into her bow, and stood facing the sound. The wolf moved silently now, melting through the moonlight between shadow and shadow just when the human's attention was elsewhere.

What am I doing?

What I must do!

Three bounds from cover, the wolf knocked the woman down. Her arrow missed. Her knife stuck in its sheath just long enough for the wolf's jaws to tear open her throat.

What have I done?

What I had to do!

The wolf was trotting toward Condor's Camp, but the landscape she crossed became ever more vague and dreamlike.

63.

Lieutenant Feathergrass was starting to worry about his scout. Maybe she had gotten captured or killed. Maybe she had just gotten lost. This landscape could fool you. A tree that seemed unusual enough to serve as a landmark would turn out to have a close copy somewhere else, and the pattern of brush and open grass was hopelessly random. The moon and stars were a sure guide only if you knew your direction and remembered to allow for passing time.

Suddenly something bolted through the brush. Several archers shot at the sound. Something fell. They found a goblin scout lying on his stomach. He was not quite dead, but the arrow piercing his throat from behind had prevented a death scream. Feathergrass stabbed him in the back to make the mercy killing.

Now the platoon hurried toward Condor's Camp.

Feathergrass hoped Strong Bull would die in battle with Canticle's army, but thought he more likely would escape. The two goblin camps destroyed last summer had not been reestablished. Without this one, Strong Bull would have no effective base. Whenever Feathergrass felt hesitant about commanding a massacre, he remembered Fledgeling, and if this was not enough to harden his heart, he remembered surviving the massacre of Foam's platoon.

Without war cries, goblin warriors rushed the human vanguard, hurling spears. Feathergrass knocked aside the one aimed at him with his shield rim, slung his longbow over his quiver since he had no time for a shot, and drew his sword. This one was shorter than the sword he had lost in Foam's last battle, but otherwise as good or better.

Feathergrass parried the goblin's thrusting spear. What was this? The goblin jerked back his spear to try to hook the sword. A new move, and a good one. Feathergrass lunged forward and twisted to keep grip on his sword, but the goblin knocked him down with a sideswipe of the spear. Feathergrass rolled aside and jumped to his feet just fast enough to avoid being spitted. A few arrows fell from his quiver; the goblin trampled these while they circled each other.

This goblin was his match, and leader of the defense. Both he and Feathergrass were taking measure of the battle even while they feinted at each other. As far as the lieutenant could see, his humans were holding their own, but all were engaged in battle. The advantage of the diffuse foot platoon was secret movement and sudden attack. In open battle with equal or greater numbers, it was weak, for the slightest advantage won by either side could be quickly compounded.

"Condor! Where is Strong Bull?" Feathergrass said, but instead of hearing Condor's unvoiced thoughts about this, he heard an angry growl. For a moment Condor seemed to be a huge bear about to charge, but Feathergrass saw through this image in time to parry Condor's real spear thrust.

Now the human backed off a pace. Could that spirit bear distract him for a fatal moment? As an experiment, Feathergrass tried to hear whatever the chief was thinking about his next move, and felt the bear only as a flash of pain in his head. Good.

An instant before Condor did so, Feathergrass knew he was going to throw his shield. It just missed. Rather than being surprised or stunned, Feathergrass lunged forward. His sword pierced Condor's gut. At the same moment, Condor cracked his spear shaft, clubbing Feathergrass's head. Then the chief fell, and the lieutenant stabbed him through the heart.

Feathergrass's head was throbbing with pain but he dared not stagger. What was happening? Battle clamor farther west, no one fighting nearby. On the ground, four humans and no goblins but Condor. This was not promising. The humans all proved to be dead. Ooh. The landscape was starting to wobble. Feathergrass was staggering. Any goblin who saw him would kill him quick.

He dashed for cover, crawled under the damp, prickly brush. A few minutes' rest should make the ground stop spinning. He carefully touched the growing lump on his skull. He took a deep breath—yes, that helped—and another.

But the next thing Feathergrass remembered was waking to brightening daylight. He tried to lie still but could not stop shivering. This was no good. Even though he was less than a mile from Condor's Camp, he had to break cover and run. Better to die from a goblin's spear than from chill. He checked his gear, crawled out from under the brush, stood up, looked around, and began walking.

64.

The wolf splashed across the gully and climbed up the crumbling muddy bank. Sometimes she could see the women and old men carrying goods and tents. Sometimes she was tired and distracted, nuzzling at wet fur with clacking teeth to pull out stickers, licking grit from the creases of her paws.

Now she was trotting home across the open plain. Home was a certain smell, sometimes weak, sometimes strong, always swirling in the chambers of her sensitive nose.

In her dreams the den was soft. Sometimes she voiced sounds she did not understand. The one who lay with her made similar sounds. This one was also female, but smaller and younger.

"Glowfly! What are you saying? Must we move again?"

She struggled to find her voice and the words. "I—I do not know." It was daylight. She was bundled in a traveler's tent with Little Ant. "I feel weak and confused. I do not remember where I am or how I got here."

"Tell me what you do remember."

"I remember you helping me become a wolf. I remember finding the human platoon and running to warn Strong Bull and Condor. They called me Wolf Woman. I remember—" Glowfly remembered stalking and killing the human scout, but did not want to speak about this. But Little Ant knew. The girl had to know. "I remember running across the gully and seeing the women and old men carrying the camp."

"Well, I remember helping carry you across the gully," said Little Ant.

"Maybe I dreamed that part. Maybe I dreamed it all. But I feel more like a wolf who is dreaming that she is Glowfly."

Little Ant spoke softly. "I did not know what I was saying last night. The words just came to me. When you left the tent, it was too dark for me to see you clearly. I thought I heard an animal outside. It went away before I could see what it was. Strong Bull said he saw a wolf who became a woman to warn him about the human platoon. Some of the warriors saw this, but others just saw a lone wolf."

"Maybe I was dreaming. Maybe my dream gave them a vision."

"You left camp strong but returned exhausted and feverish. From your sleep you spoke, warning us to move camp, for the whole human army was coming there. This was after Strong Bull and the warriors defeated the platoon."

"Where is Condor?"

Little Ant sighed. "He is dead. He was killed by the human lieutenant."

Glowfly shuddered and cried hot tears. "My husband is dead. I killed—I killed—"

"You do not have to talk about it," said Little Ant. "But I think you did a brave thing."

"Brave? It was horrible!" Glowfly protested. "I can still taste her blood. I am a woman, a *woman*, not a warrior or a wolf."

"I understand. Believe me, I understand." The girl embraced the woman with strength. "You became Mother Wolf, and now you are yourself again."

"I do not know who or what I am," said Glowfly. "I might feel better if I had something to eat."

"You need a tea or a warm broth, but all I have is dry meat and crisp flatbread."

"We do have water. Let me try the flatbread."

After some fumbling, Little Ant handed her a pouch filled with crumbs. Despite herself, Glowfly laughed.

"Sorry," said Little Ant. "I packed in a hurry. The meat is on the bottom if you want any."

While Glowfly chewed the crumbled bread, several men and a woman outside were saying something, then the woman shouted, "Yiyiyi! Yiyiyi!" Little Ant and Glowfly crawled out of the low tent.

"Can you stand?" Little Ant asked.

"I think so. I feel just a bit unsteady," Glowfly mumbled.

Walking Toad spoke as Strong Bull's messenger: "The human army has decamped. They are retreating from the Sacred Ground across the river's west branch. Unless Wolf Woman has foresight against this, we can go back to our own hunting ground and set up camp. Strong Bull has sent the smoke message to muster the army. By tomorrow evening we will set the siege."

"My name is Glowfly, daughter of Great Father Otter. I do not accept the name of Wolf Woman. I wish we could have found a good way to share this land with the humans. I have lost two husbands to this war. Last night I killed a human scout. I made myself fierce and strong. Now my heart is filled with stones and ice. I think we as a people have made the wrong choices. But I do not know what we should do now. I am too sick at heart to seek a new vision."

The warriors did not speak yet. Last night's victory would have been a terrible defeat if not for Glowfly's warning and her exertions. Her despair might be personal, but it might be more than that.

Little Ant spoke quickly: "Glowfly had visions in her fever that she may not remember now. She gave two warnings: Strong Bull will die by Canticle's sword. Strong Bull will be killed by warriors from Upriver."

"Both cannot be true," said Sundance, who was acting chief.

"A spirit warning may tell of more than one possible danger," said the shaman Star Bear. "This might be why she said both things: If Strong Bull attacks the keep too boldly, he may die by Canticle's sword. He must be cautious. But if he is too cautious, this will prolong the war. Then Upriver's warriors may come. Upriver began as a keep like the one we are fighting. They won their war with the help of humans from other cities. Maybe Upriver's lord offered Canticle's people asylum as short-term slaves to test their resolve. Now that he knows they are determined, maybe his people will make an alliance."

"Glowfly! Can you remember anything about the visions that went with what you said?" asked Sundance.

Glowfly made the gesture of negation.

"Maybe Mother Wolf will find another voice," said Picks Herbs. The thought behind this was, *I know how you are weak and I will do all I can to hurt you.*

65.

Sundance organized the portage of the camp. It was easier than it might have been, for they had hidden their stores and big tent poles before moving camp last night. Also, a cold, sunny day was best for moving heavy loads. But it was eight miles, and the gully crossing was slippery and difficult. By the time they had reassembled the camp and kindled the cookfire, it was nearly dusk.

Now there was debate, for the warriors and women originally from Charging Elk's Camp wanted his brother Skyrock to be chief. Some of Condor's people agreed to this, but others wanted Sundance. Because Skyrock was with Strong Bull, those who favored him wanted to delay the choosing till his return.

Glowfly spent this time in the hospital tent talking privately with Beartooth. "I would like to come home to your camp," she said.

"You have made a bitter enemy who has many friends here," said the chief, who had been cared for by both Glowfly and Picks Herbs. "Your marriage to Condor was foolish."

"She did not love Condor. I did. Our love was deep. Had I lived with Condor longer, his people would have become my people. They respect me as a shamaness but do not really know me, not enough to help me through my grief."

"I understand," said Beartooth. "What about your apprentice? Have you discussed this with her yet?"

"No, but I will give her free choice."

At that moment, Little Ant rushed into the tent. "Glowfly! You should come back—"

"Hush!" Glowfly said. "Beartooth does not need to be startled, and the others need their sleep. Speak softly."

"Sorry," Little Ant said, lowering her voice to a whisper. "You should come back to the fire. It does not look good for Sundance, and Skyrock is not even here. Maybe if you said something, it would help Sundance. Some of the warriors even want to split the camp."

"That might be best," said Glowfly.

"You think so? I like it better the way it is."

"It would be much easier for the hunters if we had two camps, and harder for the humans to find us."

"But Charging Elk's Camp was destroyed because they did not have you," protested Little Ant.

"This is nonsense," said Glowfly. "Charging Elk's Camp was attacked because the humans knew Strong Bull was there. It was not destroyed. The survivors joined this camp because Condor was a great chief. Sundance and Skyrock both have less experience. It is natural for the camp to split now."

"What are you thinking about that you do not know how to tell me?" asked Little Ant. "You want to leave. You want to go home to Beartooth's Camp."

"Is that so terrible? You can either come with me or stay here."

"Can I come with you?" The girl's voice brightened; then she remembered to be quiet. "I wish we could both stay here, but I know how you feel. You must take me with you. It would be awful here without you. When are we going?"

"Maybe when Beartooth is well enough to walk forty miles. Maybe when messengers go that way. I am not sure."

"I suggest you go as soon as you can, before Strong Bull or some other chief tries to order you to stay," said Beartooth.

"By ourselves! We can do it," said Little Ant.

"Hush!" Glowfly whispered in the girl's ear, then stepped quickly around a wounded warrior's bed to the tent floor. To her relief, the person listening was the human Henna, leaning on her walking stick.

"Glowfly, I must talk to you," she said quietly.

"Then come in," the shamaness replied. "I should look at your leg, anyway. That was a long walk for you last night and today."

Henna was crying hot tears for Lizard Toes, who had died in the battle, whose child was growing in her belly. "Hidden Pool says my tears are false, that I am glad to be free of her brother, who I was forced to marry. Glowfly, I *love* Lizard Toes. He gave me new life. I certainly would not spy for the man whose platoon came here to massacre us."

"I thought Hidden Pool was your friend," said Glowfly.

Little Ant frowned.

"Maybe while Lizard Toes was alive, but not now," said Henna. "And she is all the family I have. If she rejects me and my child, I am an enemy to be killed unless another warrior claims my life."

"I will not let that happen," said Glowfly.

"But you are going away," said Henna.

"I think Picks Herbs is calling Henna an enemy for some reason," said Little Ant.

Glowfly considered this possibility. "Whether Picks Herbs started the talk or not, she will encourage it. People say Henna is my friend. If she were an enemy of this people—well, no one could call me a traitor, but I would look foolish. I should talk to Hidden Pool."

"Hidden Pool wants to believe Henna is bad," Little Ant insisted.

The human woman shuddered.

"Henna, come here," said Beartooth. "Look at my eyes." By the smelly flame of the mammoth-fat lamp, his eyes were deep, black, inscrutable. Henna's fox-colored hair rippled to her shoulders; her face and eyes were pale. Though the chief was bandaged and lying in bed, he frightened her. "Who do you want to win the war?" he asked gruffly.

Henna looked down and hesitated.

"Look at my eyes and tell me."

"I do not want there to be a war," Henna said, raising her eyes to his, and trying to make her voice firm.

"Who are your people?"

"I—I really do not know. Maybe I have no people. I cannot go back to living the human way. In spirit I am a goblin woman. But now that my husband is—is dead, his sister rejects me. Women who laughed with me yesterday fear to speak with me today." Tears trickled down Henna's cheeks but still she looked at Beartooth's eyes.

"Glowfly! Is this woman your friend?" he asked. The way he said the word, he clearly meant what a human would call a good friend or a close friend.

"Yes, she is," Glowfly said quietly.
"Then take her with you to my camp."

66.

Feathergrass was lying in bed, in one of the settlement's small thatch-roofed huts. It was too dark to see much. His headache and bad dreams had roused him; now memories and thoughts were chasing each other around the hold of his battered skull like hungry rats. Awake or asleep he could find no peace.

Canticle's army had found Feathergrass and about twenty other human survivors of the battle—less than a quarter of his platoon. The general had a simple, devastating explanation for Strong Bull's unexpected return: The goblins must have seen Feathergrass's second scout, the woman he had sent when he was worried about the wolf. Canticle was furious. Feathergrass fully expected his next duty would be digging latrines.

A woman's voice said something to someone outside the hut, making Feathergrass realize that he was confined under guard. Was he under clerical arrest again, or military arrest?

She entered the hut and asked, "How do you feel?"

Probably she was a healing priestess. "Is it after midnight?" he asked. That was usually when priests retired and priestesses took over.

"Dawn comes soon. How do you feel?" she repeated.

"Then the moon should be bright—but I cannot even see the window."

"It is blocked, remember?" said the priestess. "The light made your headache worse."

"Ugh," said Feathergrass. "I wish I remembered less than I do. I wish I had a pipe full of sleepflower and a jug of rum." This was rude, to imply that no Church-sanctioned remedy was strong enough to help.

The priestess took no offense, but helped him drink a cup of fresh water. "You want oblivion," she said quietly.

"Any way I can get it," said Feathergrass.

"If you want oblivion, you need purification." When she struck the small bell, the high pure sound rippled through his body and spirit, making him all the more aware of the filth he had accumulated. "Do you deny it?" she asked.

"Maybe it would help," he said sullenly.

She rang the bell again.

"All right, all right, go ahead," said Feathergrass.

"Does the bell make your headache worse?" the priestess asked.

"Not exactly, but the sound goes on and on, and each time you ring it, it goes on longer."

She struck the bell again. "How does this sound frighten you?"

"I feel like a rat," he replied, "despised, wounded, waiting to be killed."

She struck the bell. "And who is the cat who toys with you?"

"You. Canticle. Strong Bull. The monstrous gods who made this wretched world."

The priestess struck the bell and prayed, "Lord of Light and Darkness, who is embodied in the Mother, the Father, the Three Daughters, and the Three Sons, I pray that you help me free this man's spirit from sin and despair." She rang the bell again. "Feathergrass, have you done any act that was unquestionably wrong that you wish to renounce and atone?"

"Yes," Feathergrass said. "I helped plan the massacre of Condor's Camp, and led the platoon that attempted it."

"Why was this unquestionably wrong?"

"Why do you ask me that? Massacre is forbidden by Fire the Warrior. I knew that, yet in my rage and grief over Fledgeling's death, and my desire to win the war, I tried to do it. That was wrathful command, forbidden by Thunder the King."

"You are not guilty of wrathful command," said the priestess. "Your warriors were volunteers. They knew the plan, and chose to attempt to carry it out."

"Are you defending me?"

"I am examining you. If you were defensive about your sin, I would examine your rationalizations. But you are filled with self-loathing." After a pause, the priestess struck the bell sharply. "Two nights ago, you led a platoon against Condor's Camp. But now you think that the whole war is dishonorable and wrong, indeed that this keep itself is dishonorable and wrong. I must examine you for treason."

Now there was enough light for Feathergrass to see the priestess seated on the edge of the bed. He could not yet see her face, but he recognized her voice.

"Mother Jasmine, I did everything I could to win that back-stabbing battle, and you bloody well know it."

The priestess was silent.

After a long moment, Feathergrass said, "At the start of the war, I was shocked and disgusted when Lord Drill and Conch commanded the massacre of Beadback's Camp. Yet I became so tainted that two days ago I was able to rationalize the massacre of Condor's Camp. This war is wrong. The longer it lasts, the more corrupt each one of us becomes. Loon's spirit foresaw this, and forsook the joy of Heaven's gardens again and again to try to warn me, so much did she love me in life."

Mother Jasmine tapped her bell very softly but said nothing for a long time. Feathergrass listened to people outside, hunters walking to the stables or guards walking to the walls. He tried to make out bits of conversation.

"I am sorry," the priestess said quietly. "I have begun a ceremony for you that I am not fit to perform. It is better for me to stop than to give you the form without the substance. I helped estrange you from your dead wife Loon. I taught you things that you have used to kill in battle. If my mistakes have helped you become corrupt, how can I purify you?"

"We have all become corrupt," Feathergrass said.

She looked away from him while she spoke. "I thought the darkness in the futures of so many Newport humans was death, but for some it is worse than death. It might have been better if the dragon had killed us all. That shows my taint, for how can a healer doubt the value of life?"

"We have all become corrupt," Feathergrass repeated.

67.

Glowfly woke again to the smell and warmth of Little Ant and Henna crowded beside her in a hidden traveler's tent. Again she made herself relax into trance and prayed to her totem, Father Otter, for a dreamless sleep.

At dusk, when they woke and pulled the greased robes off the tent's makeshift framework, a light mist was falling.

"We should have eaten first," Henna grumbled.

Glowfly stood up to look around.

"Do you know where we are?" Henna asked. "I admit I am lost. How far east did we go last night? I am worried we will end up on the wrong side of the gully you and Beartooth discussed. Quagga's Camp has never welcomed people like me."

Glowfly pointed to a certain place between two distant trees. "If the sunset were visible, it would be about there." She then pointed toward Beartooth's Camp and Quagga's Camp. "I may not have done much traveling between camps, but the directions are very different."

After chewing a few bites of crisp flatbread and smoked auroch, they strapped on their packs and set off across the misty plain. Soon their lower legs were chafed and chilled by the wet grass. Glowfly could not see her feet stepping on the dark ground, but with her trance eye she saw a spirit path—the strand of light that marked the safest, surest way to Beartooth's Camp. Sometimes this spirit path would move, perhaps to avoid goblin warriors or scouts who would be awkward about three women traveling alone, or perhaps to avoid real dangers like human scouts or fierce animals.

Henna was skeptical about these sudden shifts of direction. When they stopped to rest for a few minutes in a sheltered thicket, she asked Glowfly how she knew about these supposed hazards.

"I am walking a spirit path," the shamaness replied. "If you stay near me, you are also on this path and we all should be safe or as safe as we can be."

"Sometimes I think I see it, but sometimes I do not," said Little Ant. "Glowfly is very good. She knows as many things as the great shamanesses in the old stories."

While they walked, the overcast sky brightened with moonrise. The mist increased to a drizzle, then stopped completely. Toward dawn, a light snow began falling.

"There is the gully, and we are indeed on the side of Beartooth's Camp," said Glowfly.

"Even my good leg is numb," said Henna. "How much farther is the camp?"

"I am not sure. If I were alone, I would keep going till I got there. But I think we should find a good place to make the tent again."

"You want to bed down in the snow without a fire?" asked Henna.

"Snuggling together kept us warm yesterday," said Glowfly. "Today will not be that much colder."

68.

The morning of the second day after Feathergrass's battle and head injury, he had the confrontation with General Canticle that he had been dreading.

"What have you said to stir up the bloody clergy?" the general demanded. "The way they are talking now, you would think I mean to kill every goblin and conquer the whole country, like Lord Whitethorn of Moonport. You know better than that."

"What you intend and what will happen need not be the same," said Feathergrass.

"We gave those backstabbing goblins fair chance to coexist with us. Our attack two nights ago was defensive. If you want to be a lieutenant or even a warrior, you must know yourself better. No one ordered you to massacre Condor's Camp. You offered to make the attempt. You agreed with me that it was necessary."

"I was wrong."

The general sighed. "I understand."

"No, you do not," said Feathergrass. "If you did, you would agree with me, and we would all go to Upriver."

"And be bonded servants to the great-grandson of Stark-weather, the lord who exiled Wentletrap?"

"Your pride is absurd," said Feathergrass. "It is not worth the lives of all those who have died already, much less the many more who will die before you change your mind."

"You swore loyalty to me. Do you forswear that loyalty?"

"We have both changed since then."

"Then I must accuse you of greater treason," Canticle said sternly.

"I do not fear your anger," said Feathergrass. "I have served ship's captains with worse. What can you do to me, anyway? If you execute me, I will make a speech exposing your folly. Kill me privately and people will talk all the more. Keep me prisoner and I will corrupt my guards."

"That speech only proves that your head injury has lessened your ability to think," Canticle replied.

After the general left, Feathergrass lay in bed repeating their dialogue over and over in his mind, trying to find the words he should have used, and worrying about what would happen next.

He woke in late afternoon to shouts of alarm and sounds of people running outside. Staggering to his feet and taking deep breaths to lessen his headache, he pulled on his outer pants and tunic, and tried the door to his hut. It was unblocked, the guard was gone, and the air smelled of smoke.

"We are under attack!" someone shouted. "Get your weapons and come to the wall!"

Feathergrass realized that he must have slept through the first alarm—not that it made much difference, for he had no weapons and was hardly in shape to fight. Was the smoke a dragon attack, or were the goblins close enough to hurl burning spears over the walls? Feathergrass put on his coat and walked the narrow streets as fast as he could.

"Lieutenant!" said a man's voice—Hawthorn from his old hunting group. "I have been looking for you."

"What the bloody death is happening?"

"I think they are shooting burning spears at us with a dragon gun. As wet as the roofs are from the melt of last night's snow, this is not harming much, but when I think of next summer—" Hawthorn dropped his voice. "I understand you have come to regret that cursed fool attempt to massacre Condor's Camp."

"It was wrong," Feathergrass mumbled.

"This is what we get. We have no future here. Lord Drill might as well be in command, the way Canticle is thinking. I am ready to run. Are you with me?"

"What is your plan?"

"Are you with me?" Hawthorn repeated.

"Yes."

"Then just follow me and do what I do. I think we still have time." They walked to a ladder on the west wall, which was thinly guarded. Evidently the goblin army was grouped to the east, where a large sortie was moving over the ramp.

"They will not get near those dragon guns," said Hemstitch, who stood near the ladder. "There are more goblins and fewer humans than the first siege. Canticle will be forced to retreat, if he is not killed. They spitted Swordnotch already. I am with you." She was holding two pikes, and gave one to Feathergrass.

Even while he was about to desert, Feathergrass wondered just how many dragon guns the goblins had, which boats they might have salvaged them from, and how they had managed to carry them. It did not matter.

At the count of three, he jumped from the rampart, holding his pike near the head. Its butt end struck the ground after a minimal fall and he vaulted to a safe landing. So did Hawthorn and Hemstitch beside him, and four others. No one atop the wall made any outcry. Even those who were not yet ready to desert had sympathy for the deserters.

They ran. The throbbing of Feathergrass's heart made the throbbing of his head unbearable, but still he ran. To his left, the reddened sun sank momentarily between the clouds and the dark line of distant trees edging the swamp. In a song, Loon would have used this sunset to symbolize the end of Canticle's Keep, the end of the people of Newport, and the end of Feathergrass's honor, strength, and life. He slipped on the frosted ground and fell.

Strong hands rubbed his legs and arms.

"Can you stand?" Hawthorn asked, after he and one of the other men pulled Feathergrass to his feet.

"You—you may as well leave me. I cannot keep running. Lucky that I did not twist my leg."

"We are not leaving you," said Hemstitch. "You are the one who knows the way to Loop Lake."

69.

Glowfly and her two companions took apart the traveler's tent at dusk and came to Beartooth's Camp before midnight. All Little Ant and Henna wanted to do was sit close to the main fire and rub the aches from their legs.

There were few warriors in camp. Long Flood, an old man, was acting chief. Glowfly expected her father, Screaming Spear, to be with Strong Bull's army, but was surprised to find her young brother Brown Fox also gone. Only her mother, Antelope, and her youngest brother, Big Toad, were there to greet her. They made room in their tent for Glowfly and her companions.

But the next morning, Antelope questioned Glowfly sharply about why she had left Condor's Camp in the company of a twelve-year-old girl and a pregnant human woman. Glowfly's evasive answers did not satisfy her.

Then Beartooth's wife, Cicada, questioned Glowfly even more sharply about her marriage to Chief Condor, about her prophetic trance visions and dreams, about the magic that made her become a wolf, about her killing the human scout, about her grief over Condor's death, about her opposition to the war, about her raw fear and confusion. She could not hide anything from Cicada.

"Your heart is too open," Cicada said. "If you are a chief's wife in wartime, you must be able to accept his death. If you are a scout, you must be able to kill an enemy scout."

"I am neither of those things now," Glowfly said sullenly.

Not long after noon, High Shaman Drakey returned to camp from the direction of the river. Glowfly had thought he was with Strong Bull's army.

"Not yet," said Drakey. "I was seeking a big vision. I am

concerned about Strong Bull. We need his strength and determination, maybe even his tricks, to win the war. But once we win, Strong Bull will be a problem. He will get no satisfaction from the victory. He will continue fighting in his mind. He will seek new enemies to kill." Drakey made a gesture of negation. "How is Beartooth?" he asked.

"He should return soon," Glowfly replied. "He is recovering, but he was badly wounded. He will be out of the war for some time."

"Cicada will be glad."

"That is not the impression she gave me," said Glowfly.

Drakey glared at the young shamaness. "If Beartooth dies, Cicada will cry many more tears than you are crying over Condor. If she wants to pretend otherwise, that is her concern."

70.

Feathergrass, Hawthorn, and the others had hoped to find some abandoned goblin canoes for their journey through the swamp, but they dared not linger near the marsh long enough to make a thorough search, and so were forced to find their way to Loop Lake on foot. Traveling with scant provisions, they lived mostly on small carp and catfish netted in the channels. Hunting was hard. The deer that got away on the fourth day was a topic of grumbling for the rest of the journey.

Finally they saw open water ahead, made for it, and found themselves at the northern end of Loop Lake, less than a mile from the village. One of the guards who intercepted them was Rockdream, who was inclined to welcome the others but not Feathergrass.

"You are no friend of mine after what you did to me and my family a year ago," Rockdream said. "I guess this time you came here by the same sort of route we were forced to use then. Can you imagine such a journey with snow and a one-and-a-half-year-old baby? What can you say for yourself?"

"It was not my choice, but I am sorry," Feathergrass replied. "Look. You were right and we were wrong. The keep was wrong, the war was wrong, and we should have accepted the Upriver resettlement offer. But the offer was belated. By then we thought we were winning the war. Our army controlled most of the land between the marsh and the Goblin River; our fleet controlled both rivers. Then we started losing. I do not know whether Drakey and the other shamans heard thoughts or dreamed prophecy or what, but they anticipated us almost as well as Riversong did. Battle by battle, they built up their advantage. Now their army besieges the keep, and this siege will be a long one. My friends and I escaped while they were fighting Canticle's first sortie."

"What made you change your minds and desert?" asked Rockdream.

"Canticle màde massacres of noncombatants part of his strategy," Hawthorn said, and Hemstitch and two others nodded their heads in agreement.

"The war is dishonorable, defeat is inevitable, and I wonder why there are only seven of us here now," said another man.

"There will be more," said Hemstitch.

"Where is Fledgeling?" Rockdream asked.

"Strong Bull killed her," said Hawthorn.

"He hated her," said Feathergrass. "In the first battle, she killed his father in close combat."

"I am sorry," said Rockdream. "I am sorry. Come to the village and we will discuss things."

The arrival of seven newcomers and the likelihood of more to come soon caused Salmon to speak strongly in favor of choosing a governing council. "Some of these people may choose to stay, but others will want to cross the Emerald Hills come spring or summer. We could easily be outnumbered by transients."

After a long discussion, Rockdream was chosen village master, with the council to consist of all villagers who had lived there for at least one full year and who were concerned with the issues being discussed.

Of the people who would be excluded by this rule, Mother Cedar said her place was in the church not the council; Thornbush disliked giving up her voice until next summer but understood the need; Holdfast did not care, for he considered himself just a visitor—he and Birdwade planned to move to Driftwood's Village after their marriage; and Feathergrass and the other newcomers thought it was reasonable.

Feathergrass asked Mother Cedar for a purification ceremony, and in the privacy of this he confessed his role in the attempted massacre of Condor's Camp.

She said, "You have lived in a keep where too much was kept secret, because too much was required or forbidden. You could not share your true feelings with either your wife or your friends. Even the Church there was corrupt. No wonder the spirit of your dead wife, Loon, concerned herself with you! Being open is a strong cure for corruption. The more you can discuss your thoughts, feelings, and deeds, the better. The confession of the purification ceremony is secret so that you will feel safe to speak. But once you have spoken, it is easier to speak again."

"But if Rockdream learns that less than two weeks ago I was lieutenant of a platoon attempting a camp massacre, he will despise me even more than he does, and he is now the village master. I need to stay here at least until the snow melts in the Emerald Hills."

The priestess sighed and rang her bell. "Would it not be better for him to learn this from you than in some other way? I think he would welcome honest communication. He will think that your command was twisted and wrong, but that is now your own opinion. I do not think he will despise you. He may even begin to respect you."

10

SAFE PASSAGE

71.

The second siege of Canticle's Keep lasted more than two months. Had the goblins been able to maintain the siege one more month, they would have starved the humans out. But by this time, their own stores were long exhausted, and hunting and fishing anywhere near the keep had become poor. Also, the rivers were beginning to fall, and Strong Bull was concerned about what the remaining human boats might do to the unguarded camps. So for now the warriors returned home.

Only then did Glowfly learn that her father, Screaming Spear, and her young brother Brown Fox had been killed in a skirmish nearly a month before. Her tears were no longer hot, but slow and bitter.

Then, just a few days before the spring equinox that began the humans' 201st year, Canticle's people, all of them, abandoned their settlement and began moving down the west bank of the Goblin River. Strong Bull, who was at Skyrock's Camp, the new camp replacing Charging Elk's, summoned all the warriors from all the camps farther up both branches of the Goblin River, and put the rest of Goblin Plain on alert.

For the first time since the war began, two months less than a year ago, the humans and goblins sent messengers to each other. Lieutenant Hardtack was now in command of the humans, for General Canticle had a festering wound in his sword arm, from a spear shot from one of the goblins' dragon guns, just before the end of the siege.

The humans were meeting the boats at the joining of the rivers and going back to the swamp for now, but later in the spring when the Blue would become readily navigable, they wanted to sail to Upriver. They did not want any trouble, but were still willing and able to fight if the goblins opposed them.

Strong Bull let them go back to the swamp, but then wanted to make a massive surprise attack to finish them off, a proposal spoken against by all the other chiefs.

"We defeated them," said Chief Sundance, Condor's successor. "If they want to leave, we should let them go."

72.

Birdwade and Holdfast were married by Mother Cedar, on a sunny day about a week after Midwinter's Day. The celebration was a slightly sad occasion for many at Loop Lake, for it meant that Birdwade was moving away.

Meanwhile, Feathergrass and the other six newcomers were building huts and making friends. By the time their planned journey through the backwater and over the hills became possible, they had come to feel at home at Loop Lake, the journey seemed difficult, and life as bonded servants in Midcoast seemed undesirable. Even Feathergrass, who could avoid servitude by signing on for an overseas voyage, stayed where he was.

Two of the newcomers were Splash and his wife, Nettle, who had often hunted with Bloodstorm's group in the early months of the keep. In the first week of spring, Splash woke before dawn with a fever. Nettle went to get Mother Cedar, who thought it must be a bad cold or other winter illness, for she had never seen swamp sickness strike anyone so early in the spring. But Coral could tell from Splash's light patterns that his illness was something that she had not seen before, and wanted to move him to the isolation hut.

"I do not have swamp sickness, and I am staying in my home," said Splash.

"His fever would be hotter if it were that," Mother Cedar said, and she and Coral gave him willow bark tea, and garlic from

Coral's planter baskets, and by that evening he seemed his usual self. Nettle felt fine about leaving him alone the next day while she went fishing with Swanfeather and Flatfish. But at noon his fever returned, hotter than before.

Mother Cedar found Coral and Wedge on the bank of the lake, pulling corms. "You were right," she said.

"Oh, blood," Coral said. "So much for the mosquitoes. I have yet to see one this year. And Splash was eating with everyone else last night and this morning. The disease might be spread that way. We should move him to the isolation hut at once."

"If we try to move him before the fever breaks, it would kill him." The priestess sighed. "Nettle might have made love with him last night, and she is handling today's catch. I should have listened to you."

"I might be able to tell if Nettle has the sickness from her light patterns," said Coral.

"We are lucky that the willow bark did not kill him," said Cedar.

Wedge pulled on Coral's skirt to get her attention and asked, "Is he swamp sick?"

"I fear so," Coral replied.

"Will he die?"

"Cedar and I will do all we can to save him, and so will Salmon when she comes back."

"How?" asked Wedge.

"We will give him herbs and magic," said Coral.

"Oh. What if I die?" asked the child.

"What gave you that idea?"

"What if I die?" he repeated. "Tell me."

Coral sighed, and realized she was trembling. "You stop breathing, your heart stops beating, and you cannot move. Then you float above your body, and go away to the spirit world, which is like a long, long dream. Then your daddy and I are very sad because we miss you."

"No," said Wedge. "I will never die. I will stay with you always."

Coral picked him up and hugged him. "You promise?" she asked.

"I promise."

Coral left Wedge with Stonewater and went with the priestess to see Splash, who was asleep and bundled up tight in his bedding as if he was very cold, though the afternoon was warm. His head and hands felt very hot. He stirred at Coral's touch but did not waken. With her trance-eye, Coral saw that his light patterns were thin and disrupted, especially around his head, chest, and stomach.

"The best thing we can do for him now is let him sleep," said Cedar.

"Let me try something before we go," said Coral.

The witch closed her eyes and imagined her roots growing through the platform of the hut, deep into the Nameless Mother, and surrounded herself with a strong egg of white light. Gently, very gently, she tried to reconnect Splash's pattern of light. The first thread seemed to brighten and become stronger, but the second was too fragile and broke into a shower of tiny crystals. Coral let herself relax more deeply, to let her energy become more subtle. Carefully, carefully, she spun a new thread, but as soon as this thread became stronger than any of the others, it began to damage other threads.

Coral sighed. This would not be easy, but there was one more technique she could try. She made a bath of blue light to strengthen all of the threads at once, but this immediately felt wrong, and she stopped. She tried other colors. Red felt the best, but she had to control the strength of this very carefully or the threads would melt into globules. She took a deep breath. She was not sure what she was doing or what she was seeing. She checked the strength of her own egg of light, then examined Splash's pattern. Maybe it was stronger, but she was not sure.

"Maybe he will feel better when he wakes," Coral said, giving emphasis to the words "feel better."

The witch and the priestess went outside and sat together on the platform. "Magic alone will not do much, not even the most subtle and delicate magic, but I did get an idea," Coral said. "If breaking the fever is always a mistake, what would happen if I gave him something to raise his fever?"

Mother Cedar shook her head. "People usually die when their fever is hottest. He has at least one chance in two of surviving this if we do nothing but keep him warm and quiet."

Coral frowned. "Let me review what you know. His fever will return every day and a half, and in between, he may have cramps and pains, or he may feel so good that he thinks the sickness is over, but in either case he must be kept quiet. What happens when a person really does recover?"

"The fever becomes less each time, and then does not return. A person who has no fever at all for a week has probably recovered."

"What about the smell? I did not notice any."

"That comes with the sweat, when the fever breaks."

"Might washing off this sweat be helpful?" Coral asked.

"Certainly it makes the patient, and anyone else who has to be in the room, feel better, but you might catch the disease from the sweat."

That afternoon, Salmon and Bloodroot returned from Driftwood's Village. Birdwade, Ripple, and Holdfast were doing well and sent their love. Thornbush and Magpie had decided to stay a few days more, with the two men they liked but did not care for deeply enough to marry.

Salmon went with Coral to look at Splash, and said that though the disruption of his light patterns was less extreme than that of the woman who died last year, it was similar. When Nettle returned with Swanfeather and Flatfish, both witches examined her thoroughly. She seemed healthy, but as a precaution she moved to the isolation hut that night and ate alone. The next day, when Splash's fever broke, he was carried on a litter to the isolation hut. The healers tried to persuade Nettle to come back to the village, but she said she was already exposed to the sickness and wanted to stay with her husband.

Toward the end of the second week of Splash's sickness, his fevers became milder, and then did not return. No one else caught the sickness that time, which Coral credited to their precautions, and Cedar to good luck.

73.

Meanwhile, other humans came from Goblin Plain to Loop Lake—a group of five, a group of eight, and two lone individuals. From these people, the villagers learned about the long siege and Canticle's wound (which festered because the healers had run out of herbs), the abandonment of the keep, the safe passage agreement, and Strong Bull's treacherous attack against the Winter Boat Camp. The humans won that battle decisively but Strong Bull escaped.

Now most of the humans were back on Goblin Plain. Some wished to sail for Upriver as quickly as possible, but others wanted revenge. The goblins also seemed divided. Some were willing to let the boats go through, but others attacked them. Some of the battles and skirmishes most fiercely fought had little if any strategic purpose for either side.

Some of the newcomers to Loop Lake Village were spiritually tainted by their deeds in these battles, and had much to confess to Mother Cedar.

To Coral, in private, Salmon expressed her worry that all the purification ceremonies given by Mother Cedar were making her too popular and powerful. She could turn the community against the witches if she and Coral ever had a serious disagreement. But Coral reaffirmed her trust in the priestess, and refused to consider this.

"I hope you are right," said Salmon.

74.

The war that might have ended was continuing, and many chiefs and warriors blamed Strong Bull. Some chiefs punished or even refused to welcome the survivors of his force. The unwelcomed warriors went with Strong Bull to his own camp.

At Beartooth's Camp, Glowfly woke after moonset one night to distant war cries, fumbled hurriedly with her dress, and opened her tent flap, but a warrior told her, "This is nothing. A few humans from a small boat thought they could surprise us."

At Condor's Camp, Glowfly would have dreamed a spirit warning. Here, she slept through the muster. "Might there be wounded for me to see to?" she asked.

"I doubt it," said the warrior. "It sounded like the humans passed waste in their pants and ran for the river."

The attack that came six days later was much more serious. Three riverboats and two fishing boats came sailing before a strong, steady breeze as if going to Upriver. Suddenly the crews furled their sails, dropped their anchors, and put ashore a force of two hundred forty.

Beartooth's Camp was then three miles from the river, so his people did have time to pack some of their goods before retreating.

Little Ant asked Glowfly, "Why did you not dream a spirit warning?"

"Hush! Keep packing!" she replied. "If I think about that, I will forget something important."

Beartooth's goblins left the tents standing when they left. Hopefully the humans would be drawn first to the camp, and would not discover Gray Lizard, Sees Far, and the twelve other warriors who had gone toward the river that morning to stalk a lone mammoth.

After a long retreat with an awkward load, Glowfly pulled off her pack and tunneled into the brush. Crouched beside her was Henna, whose knees were spread wide to leave room for her swollen belly, whose fox-red hair and pale blue eyes were human, but whose thoughts were those of a she-wolf peering from the den.

Despite the risk, Beartooth had a smoke message sent, and saw replies from the camps of Sundance, Gorge, and Bonedance, all saying they would send warriors. Of course this was just a bluff, for they dared not leave their own camps unguarded. But it worked. The humans fled Beartooth's Camp with minimal spoils, and continued upstream.

That evening, Little Ant repeated her question about spirit warnings.

"I do not know," said Glowfly.

"You have some idea," Little Ant insisted.

Glowfly lowered her voice. "It is too easy for me to think a wolf's thoughts, or dream a wolf's dreams. If I did the deep meditations that might again open my mind to spirit warnings, I might find myself becoming a wolf again. There are stories of shamans who became trapped in their other shapes."

"So what?" said Little Ant. "There are other stories of shapeshifters who succeeded."

"The dangers are great. I have no guidance. Even Drakey has no personal experience with this magic."

Before dawn the next day, the same five boats of human raiders were attacked by a fleet of canoes from Quagga's Camp. The goblins won, but at the cost of ten killed and twenty-seven wounded. Three boats were sunk. The other two, now overloaded with survivors, retreated downstream. Beartooth's people saw them pass that afternoon. At dusk a messenger from Bonedance's Camp relayed the full story of the battle.

Beartooth said, "That victory was foolish. Those humans would have sailed to Upriver and been gone from Goblin Plain forever. Now they cannot leave so easily, and are even angrier than before. Quagga and Strong Bull say that the Newport humans might bring back an army from Upriver to help General Canticle. That fear is foolish."

In private, Henna told Glowfly, "I keep my mind and heart alive by thinking small. I think of just today, and those who are close to me now. But sometimes I remember that some of the humans on those boats are people I know, people who were once my friends. I wish the safe passage truce had worked."

"So do I," Glowfly said, then hesitantly added, "I may be partly responsible for its failure."

"What do you mean?" asked Henna.

"I mean the prophecy I spoke from the dream I do not remember, that terrible night our husbands died. It seemed to warn Strong Bull of two dangers—death by Canticle's sword, death by warriors from Upriver. Now that Canticle's sword arm is permanently crippled, Strong Bull fears the Upriver invasion. He thinks if he fights as fiercely as he can, Upriver's lord will not want to get involved."

"Glowfly, Strong Bull's cause is righteous. His people's land was invaded. He came to hate the invaders, and now this hate blinds him to his own victory. Even if you had never spoken those words, he would find a reason to keep fighting as fiercely as he can."

"Drakey said something like that to me the day after we came here," said Glowfly.

"Do you think your prophecy is real?" asked Henna. Do you think there could be war with Upriver?"

"If those words are real, they could mean something other than what they seem to mean," Glowfly replied. "Maybe some Newport warriors who go to Upriver will return for some reason. Maybe there are not enough boats to move all the humans in one trip. Maybe one of these warriors, wielding Canticle's sword, will kill Strong Bull in battle. That seems possible. By his present actions, Strong Bull makes it more likely. We call this kind of prophecy a spirit trick. Strong Bull is accursed by all the totems of the land for planning to break the peace circle before he sat it, and for pressuring other chiefs to do the same. Do you know that most of the chiefs who sat that circle have died in battle? As far as I know, all the chiefs who did not are still alive."

75.

In the last month of spring, a large number of humans under the joint command of Lieutenants Strike and Wolfkiller made camp on the south shore of the Blue River opposite the mouth of the Goblin River. Concerned messengers from Gorge's Camp and Beartooth's Camp counted more than six hundred humans. Lieutenant Strike told these messengers that the humans were still on their way to Upriver, but because Strong Bull and certain other chiefs were still at war with them, they had to move defensively. General Canticle was not with this force, and they did not know where he was.

Sees Far, the messenger from Beartooth's Camp, recognized some of Strike's people as the raiders from the month before.

"Such raids will not happen again unless your camp attacks the boats," Strike promised.

But after several weeks, Beartooth began to wonder whether the humans would ever move. They were indeed repairing their boats, but they were also digging a trench and mounding a crude wall.

Then they did move, all at once. About a third of the humans, including most of the noncombatants but some of the best archers, sailed aboard the boats under the command of Lieutenant Wolf-killer. The rest marched upstream along the south shore under Lieutenant Strike. They passed Gorge's Camp without incident, and stopped right across the river from Beartooth.

High Shaman Drakey stayed inside his tent while the humans were near. He did not want to be seen by any of their messengers, should any come to camp. "Some of those humans consider me a more dangerous enemy than Strong Bull," he said. "What I did in the war, what Sees Patterns did, what Split Hoof and certain others do now—the humans blame me for all of it. They might attack this camp if they knew I was here. They do not know and would not believe that Strong Bull and I have refused to speak to each other since he broke the safe passage truce."

Henna also stayed hidden. What she feared was her own desire to rejoin the humans. She did not want to be offered that choice. In her swollen belly, a baby goblin waited to be born. Despite her appearance, she herself was a goblin.

After a few days, the humans moved again, this time by night. At dawn, just upstream from Bonedance's Camp, the small boats ferried the foot force across the river. Two considerations dictated this move: First, to continue upstream the foot force would have to cross either the Blue or Bear River, and it was better to cross where attack was less likely; and second, the breeze and current tended to push boats toward the north shore near Quagga's Camp, where attack was likely, and it was better to have the foot force on the same shore. The humans camped at the crossing that day and night and moved again at dawn the day after.

Quagga's Camp was concealed as though these goblins anticipated battle, but the humans passed the vicinity with no trouble.
Farther upstream, the river flowed more from the north than the
east, so the foot force's shore was now the west shore. The
humans camped opposite the mouth of the stream between
Mammoth's Camp and Whitemouth's Camp.

Strong Bull's first move was a massive night attack from the
east shore. But Strike and Wolfkiller outguessed him, and even as
his canoes came out of the starlit reeds, Strike's platoon was
nearing Quagga's Camp. It was still where the human scouts had
spotted it, and poorly guarded. The few warriors there were killed,
or fled. Most of the noncombatants escaped, but some were killed,
and twenty-three women and their children were captured.

In the main battle at the boats, Chief Mammoth was killed by
a longbow arrow, Chief Whitemouth was mortally wounded by a
pike while trying to board a riverboat, and other great warriors
were lost. The humans also suffered losses, but their boats all
remained fit to sail.

At dawn, Strike and Wolfkiller used Strike's captives, and the
implied threat against any other camp aiding Strong Bull, to negotiate a new safe passage truce with Chief Quagga and warriors
representing Mammoth's Camp and Whitemouth's Camp. Strong
Bull and his own camp's warriors left while the others were
talking.

The human boat captains knew that ten miles upstream from
Strong Bull's Camp high cliffs on either side of the river valley
marked the end of the plain. Here the river became swift enough
that the boats might have to wait a few days for a strong south
wind. The foot force would not be able to walk very far up the
valley before a bend in the river swept against the cliffs, and
climbing these cliffs would be difficult and dangerous. And of
course, if the humans made two or three boat trips from there to
Upriver or even to Fallow's Keep, those left behind would be
vulnerable to attack.

Under these conditions, Strong Bull was no trivial threat, even
without the help of warriors from other camps. And if the humans
were delayed by one thing or another, Strong Bull might have time
to muster warriors from the Goblin River Camps, which had
suffered most from the war and now were least exposed to
counterattack.

76.

Two days later, on the afternoon of the summer solstice, Cicada and Glowfly relayed two smoke messages from Bonedance's Camp toward Gorge and Skyrock: Whitemouth was dead, and Spincloud was now chief of that camp; and the human foot force and fleet passed that camp just before noon.

In Henna's dreams that night humans and goblins fought close combat by starlight at the foot of a dark cliff near a river. Each blow was a sudden pain that made her cry out. A boat was burning. The heat made her whole body sweat. Aboard other boats, humans struggled pulling the long oars to move against the current. Each pull was a contraction of her womb.

Glowfly lit mammoth-fat candles. Little Ant filled large bowls with hot and cool water. Cicada was chanting and twirling a stick of smoldering sage. Other women entered the tent to help with the birthing.

"Give voice to your breath," Glowfly said. "Tell us your rhythm."

Henna wanted to say something about the dream, but not in front of all these women. The sound she made was like a hoarse snore. The other women made this sound in unison with her. Whenever she cried out in pain from a contraction, the women shouted, "Yiyiyi! Yiyiyi!"

When Henna's first child, Bramble, had been born, her midwife, the priestess Mother Fernbank, had brought her back to awareness each time she had lapsed into trance. But this goblin ceremony encouraged trance. Each sound Henna made became a chant. She could think words, but was unable to speak them. The chanting took her deep inside each wave of contraction. From the deep place she heard herself scream the pain of stretching open.

Push. Breathe. Push. There it goes. Breathe. Relax. Push harder.

The baby came out much faster than Bramble had done. One more push, and the afterbirth came out. The baby cried.

Henna tried to say, "Let me see the baby."

"You have a girl," Glowfly said, and handed her to Henna after washing off the blood.

Her skin was tan, her eyes were deep brown, and the fuzz atop her head was black, but her nose was narrow and turned up, and her ears were round. Henna held her close while Little Ant washed the blood from Henna's own legs.

"She looks human," Cicada said, "but so do you, and you are a true woman of Ha! Hey, yo. Ha! What will you name her?"

Henna found her voice. "I will name her Jay."

Cicada offered a prayer: "I give a voice to the north, to the night, to the stars, to the spirit of the wolf in Jay's mother. I give a voice to the east, to the sun that will rise on the first day of Jay's life. I give a voice to the south, to summer, to the fullness of life. I give a voice to the west, where black-headed jays nest in the marsh. Ha! Hey, yo. Ha! Let us welcome this new girl, Jay, to our people. May she grow to be a strong, gentle, wise, and loving woman of Grass, River, Wind."

Henna was crying. Thinking of the east reminded her of the battle she had just dreamed. Thinking of the west reminded her of Newport and Herders Ridge and the life she had lost forever, and of Spirit Swamp where her son Bramble had died. She thought of more recent griefs—Keg's death, Lizard Toes' death. Whatever happened to the humans moving with Strike and Wolfkiller, there were others still alive somewhere else. General Canticle might still be alive. There could be more battles, more griefs.

"Think small," Glowfly said gently. "Right here, right now, there is joy for you."

"Thank you," Henna whispered.

The next day when a smoke message told Beartooth's people about Strong Bull's new victory over the humans, Henna knew from her dream that many or most of them had escaped and were now on their way to Upriver. Some part of her love went with them. But then she released this feeling and nursed baby Jay.

77.

For two months after Splash's recovery, no one at Loop Lake caught swamp sickness. But one morning in the first month of summer, Magpie woke with a fever, and despite the isolation hut and all the other precautions, by Midsummer's Day it had spread to seven others. One of these was Splash, who this time died within a few hours of his first symptoms.

"People who catch the sickness a second time usually die quickly," said Mother Cedar.

"The next time someone gets sick a second time, I want to know immediately," said Coral. "Maybe I can learn something."

"I watched his light pattern," said the priestess. "It was much like those of the others, but it came apart more quickly."

Coral was so busy at that time she seldom saw Wedge while he was awake. One day her breasts dried up, and that was that. Wedge was weaned. Coral felt sad, and he was angry for a few days, but she was also glad that he was growing up.

Twelve people, almost half the village, caught swamp sickness sometime that summer. Seven died, including Magpie, Splash, Thornbush, Hawthorn, and Hemstitch. Of the five who recovered, only the last, Ironweed, seemed to benefit from treatment. Coral gave him massive doses of goldroot, most of what she had. Unfortunately, she could not easily get more, for goldroot grew wild only in the highlands. She had not been able to get it to grow in her planter baskets. She tried to get the same effect with fairlady, which was common enough near the lake, but one person she treated this way did not get quite enough to stop the disease, and another got too much and died of poisoning.

That fall, Salmon and Bloodroot made a journey back to the Foggy Mountains to gather goldroot. Even though they carried enough provisions and seldom had to hunt, the round trip took more than three weeks, much longer than they had expected. But they returned with many pounds of goldroot, and also freedom-wort—which did grow well enough in Coral's baskets. As Salmon explained, "It was plentiful, and every woman in the village but Cedar needs the stuff, or might need it, so I brought back a few pounds."

It was good that she did so, for less than a week after their return, Holdfast came to Loop Lake, with a message from Master Driftwood, who wanted to talk to Coral the Witch about trading for goldroot and freedomwort, should she have a source for these.

"He wants to talk about trading for freedomwort?" Coral asked with disbelief. "Freedomwort is free, everywhere and always, a gift from any woman to any other woman who needs it. We do have a good supply, which we will share with the women of your village, and I will teach them how to plant the tubers to grow more."

"How do you get it to grow?" asked Holdfast. "We tried using baskets like yours, but the tubers just rotted."

"Maybe you watered them too much, or your soil was too dense, or too rich. I will show you. As for the goldroot, even I cannot get that to grow. It needs cooler weather, both summer and winter. We might trade, but it would be better if you gathered it yourself. Salmon found a good amount in the Foggy Mountains."

"But the dragon is there," said Holdfast.

"We stayed on this side of the Foggies, and we did not see him, or any sign of him," said Salmon. "It seemed a lesser risk than trying to live through next summer without the stuff."

Coral and Salmon took Wedge with them when they went to Driftwood's Village, so that he could see Ripple again. A few weeks after this visit, Birdwade, Ripple, and Holdfast moved back to Loop Lake. They considered many things before deciding to do this, including the luck of each village's healers, but their most important reason was Birdwade's love for Coral, Rock-dream, Wedge, Salmon, and Bloodroot. Most of Holdfast's close friends at Driftwood's Village had died.

That winter, four people came to Loop Lake in a skiff, and from them, the villagers learned about the deaths of General Canticle and Lieutenant Graywall when three riverboats were attacked near Quagga's Camp.

"Graywall was our actual commander," one of the skiff people said. "Canticle was unfit to fight. Graywall kept him hidden in the hold of one of the two other boats. Even the chiefs who usually let boats go through would bother us if they knew we had him along. But Drakey dreams everything. The goblins knew. Strong Bull and Quagga put together a big force just for the occasion.

"The afternoon breeze was good enough to sail upstream, but not very quickly. Our boat lagged behind the others. That was what saved us. The goblins set their trap thinking we would be closer together. They came yelping out of the brush on both banks and ran to the water carrying canoes, which they quickly climbed into and paddled. Suddenly the first boat started rocking crazily, then the middle boat, then something ripped through the top of our own mainsail. A goblin on shore was shooting blunt poles at our sails with a dragon gun, to rock the boats and spoil our aim. The canoes surrounded the two other boats, and were coming after us. Our captain ordered us to furl the sails and start rowing downstream like we never rowed before. We just barely got away."

The skiff people stayed at Loop Lake until the first warm days of spring—this was the start of the 202nd year—then left, to try their luck at crossing the Emerald Hills. Six villagers, including Splash's widow, Nettle, went with them.

11

THE POWER THAT WILL HELP

78.

One morning in the second month of summer, Rockdream woke to Wedge fussing, crying, and thrashing his arms and legs like an angry baby. "What is wrong?" he asked. Ordinarily, he would have told the child to calm down if he wanted comforting, but this time Rockdream just picked him up and held him. Wedge's whole body was hot.

"My head hurts. My stomach hurts. I am cold. I—" he hesitated. "I wet the bed."

"You cannot help that if you are sick. Can you wait here a few minutes while I look for Mommy? Will you stay in bed? Do you need to pass waste?"

"No," Wedge said.

Rockdream felt the straw and blankets for wet places, and wrapped the boy snugly. He then pulled on his own pants, laced his tunic, and opened the door, promising Wedge that he would return very soon. He stepped outside and took a deep breath. The morning was cool and misty.

Last night, Coral had been too troubled to sleep, or even to make love. She was losing confidence in her treatment. Of the eight people who had sickened so far this summer, three had recovered, two had died, and the three still sick were not responding as well as Coral had hoped.

One of these was Feathergrass. A year and two seasons ago he had come to Loop Lake, a war deserter on his way to Midcoast, where he had hoped to sign on for an overseas voyage. Rockdream regretted talking him out of this. Oh yes, they had a new way of life at Loop Lake. No dragon would ever attack them. What good was that if there was no sure cure for swamp sickness?

"I need to find Coral," Rockdream said to everyone who tried to say anything else to him.

He went to the new isolation huts and found Salmon sitting on the platform of the one where Feathergrass was. She said that Coral was inside but in deep trance, trying to guide the mariner's spirit toward life.

"I wanted to tell her myself, but Wedge has the sickness," Rockdream said. "Restlessness, high fever, and he wet the bed."

Salmon jumped off the platform and hugged Rockdream, her body heaving with slow sobs. She composed herself and said, "Let me get some goldroot tea. We have plenty brewed up. How much does he weigh? The dose should be in proportion to that. It may be hard to get him to swallow the stuff. I know how he is about tastes he does not like, and not much tastes worse." She climbed back onto the platform and went inside. Rockdream heard Coral scream, "What?" and Salmon telling her to calm herself.

Coral was a pretty woman in her twenty-fifth year, but the woman who jumped off the platform looked twice that age, and defeated by the sorrow of her life. "I am sorry. I am losing myself," she said, trembling in Rockdream's arms. "This is too much. Where can I find the strength to go on? How can you be so calm?"

"One of us must be calm," Rockdream said.

"I just worked through a powerful vision for Feathergrass. I think I pulled him up, but it took so much out of me. And now Wedge is sick? Swamp sickness is more—more deadly to children. We have to move him, to keep him away from Ripple. I fear we will not have enough goldroot." Coral broke down into tears again.

"Grow your roots back into the Nameless Mother," Salmon said from the doorway, her voice deep and booming. "Take a deep breath."

Coral laughed through her tears and took several deep breaths. "Mommy is very scared," she said, as if she were at Wedge's side talking to him. "You want to live, and I want to heal you, and I will."

Salmon went back inside the hut. When she came back out onto the platform, she said, "Feathergrass understands your distress. He says he would react the same way, or more so."

"I need some of the goldroot," said Coral.

"I was getting it for you. Here," said Salmon, handing her down a small pot of tea.

"I could go to the mountains and bring back more," Rockdream suggested.

"You are the village master," Salmon reminded him.

"And how could you leave while Wedge is sick?" asked Coral. "But someone will have to go."

"Someone else," Rockdream agreed. "I just thought—well, I will do whatever I can to help."

"Just be understanding. I know I have not been much of a wife lately."

"Of course I understand. You are a warrior going to battle every day."

When they climbed onto the platform of their hut and went inside, after a moment's pause, Wedge started screaming. Coral sat down on the straw bed, right on the wet place, moved over, picked him up, and held him. He was very hot.

"Calm down," she said, half to the child, half to herself, for her heart was beating very fast. "Breathe."

"Hurts!"

"I know it hurts, but breathe. It will feel better if you breathe. Let me give you some medicine." She made her voice as soothing as she could. "Just pour half an inch into a cup," she told Rockdream, who did this and handed her the cup. "Drink this."

"Too hot," Wedge said, then made a sound of disgust at the taste. "No." He pushed Coral's arm away from his face with more strength than she expected, spilling some of the tea. She set down the cup.

"Wedge, remember last year when Salmon and Bloodroot went away for a long time?"

"No."

"They had to go all the way back to the mountains to get this special tea, which people like you who have swamp sickness must drink. I know it tastes bad, but if you spill even one more drop of it, I will be very angry."

"I am not swamp sick," Wedge said. "I am not."

"Mommy is a witch, and she can see the sickness in you. You must drink the tea."

"Maybe you could mix it with berry sweets," suggested Rockdream.

"Would you like that better?" Coral asked, but then she said, "No, I cannot let you drink berry sweets now. You must stay calm, and berry sweets would make you want to run and jump and play. I know how you are."

"Please?"

"No," said Coral. "Rockdream, sit with him a moment, while I mix something else." She took one of the small clay jars off the high shelf, held it in her hands while breathing deeply, then set it on the hewn workbench and pried off the lid. With the handle of a small spoon, she touched the surface of the brown syrup, stirred this tiny amount into the pot of goldroot tea, then poured a half inch of the mixture into the cup. "This might make it taste a little better," she said. "You can either swallow this one spoonful at a time, or you can drink it all at once and be done with it."

"Do I have to?"

"Do you want the spoon or the cup? If you take the cup, we can wash out the taste with water that much quicker," said Rockdream.

"The cup," he said, and closed his eyes and took a quick swallow of tea. "Yugg! How much more?"

"Not much. Drink again," said Coral.

"All right. Blehh!"

"Very good. Here. Have some water," Rockdream said, handing the child another cup. This he drank eagerly.

About ten minutes later, Coral made him drink a half-cup of the same tea, but now he was less resistant, and shortly after he swallowed this, he was sound asleep.

"Sleepflower?" asked Rockdream.

"A little bit," said Coral. "I had to do it. If exertion between fevers is bad for a patient, what would tantrums during a fever do? Maybe this is why the disease is so bad for children. We should move him to the old isolation hut."

"That one? But it is so far from the village."

"It is the only one not in use."

"But someone will have to stay with him all the time."

"I intend to," said Coral.

"Are all three of us moving there, or just you and Wedge?"

"You can visit us, but for your own protection, you should stay here."

"Just now, we worked together well," said Rockdream. "Why make this harder than it has to be?"

"Please be understanding about this," said Coral. "If I made an exception for you, every husband would insist on staying with his sick wife, every wife with her sick husband, and the whole village would become infected. Something like that likely happened to Sharp Bend, and to some of the boats. This will not last forever."

Coral carried Wedge to the old isolation hut while he was asleep, and Rockdream and Salmon brought Coral's clothes, books, and medicines.

79.

Coral was deep in meditative trance.

"Mommy! Mommy! I have something to show you!"

Wedge was running. Her patient was trying to show her what he needed to be healed, or maybe her son was playing a game with her. Where were they? It looked like the Rose Garden of Newport. This was strange. Did Wedge remember the Rose Garden from when he was an infant at her breast? His spirit might remember anything.

She was chasing him through the park from statue to statue, when she noticed that the statue of Fire the Warrior looked different. The details that Spiral the Sculptor had not lived to finish were all there. Coral had thought that the statue of Fire was more powerful, more expressive of a warrior's nature, for being rough and unfinished, but now she saw that this was not so, for the completed statue was perfect.

"Mommy, come here!" Wedge said insistently.

"Of course, the statue is perfect," said the voice of Coral's mother, Moonwort. "Spiral had time to finish it here. In fact, all eight statues are here."

"Mother, where am I?" Coral asked.

"Where do you think you are? I am dead. Wedge is dying. This garden is perfect, not only the statues, but the rose trees, the lilacs, the lawn. The plants have no dead leaves, no leaves chewed by insects. The caterpillars here live on light."

"I hear your voice but I do not see you," said Coral.

"Mother, where am I?" asked an older boy's voice. Wedge was as tall as Coral, and except for his curly hair, he looked very much like Rockdream.

"This is the Rose Garden," said Coral. "You were going to show me what I need to do to heal you. This is the place where I used to meditate with the goddesses and gods, when you were an infant, and before you were born. Can one of them help you?"

"Mother, I am dying," he said.

"He wants to stay here," said Moonwort's voice.

"If you are here, show yourself to me," said Coral.

The woman who faced her looked very much like Coral herself, except for the gray streaks in her hair. "The first thing I did when I realized I was dead was get rid of the flab and wrinkles," said Moonwort. "I decided I like the gray hair. Wedge seems to want to be older."

"Well, you can get older if you stay alive," Coral told him. He was shorter now, maybe a year or two older than his real age.

"Mom, is there a cure for swamp sickness?"

"I do not know anything about it," said Moonwort.

"Can you lead me to the one who does know?" asked Coral.

"You know where the statue of Cloud the Wizard is. Ask him."

"Mommy, come here!" said Wedge.

He was getting younger and younger as he ran, and by the time Coral caught up with him, he was a crawling infant. They were on the lawn of the statue, not of Cloud the Wizard, but of the Nameless Mother, one of the statues which Spiral the Sculptor had not even started.

The statue showed a mature woman, wearing a soft, flowing robe, open in front to expose her breasts, swollen with milk. Unlike most statues and statuettes of the Nameless Mother, which show her veiled or masked because her face is too bright to be seen, this statue had a face—Coral's face.

Wedge was a wordless, crying baby. Instinctively, Coral picked him up, unlaced her bodice, and held him to her breast.

"You have seen my face, and it is your own," said the goddess. "Feel the sickness with your own body, and look inside yourself for the power that will help."

"I am frightened, Mother."

Was that Wedge's voice, or her own?

80.

"What are you doing?" asked Rockdream's voice. He sounded disturbed, almost angry.

Coral found it difficult to speak aloud. She shook her head and opened her eyes to the stinking dimness of the isolation hut, the blinding sunlight through the opened door. She was naked, and holding a swaddled four-year-old to her breast.

"I must remember what the goddess said," she said slowly, and mumbled, "Feel the sickness with your own body, and look inside yourself for the power that will help."

"Bloody death! You have the sickness," said Rockdream.

"Give me a minute to shake off my trance. I was in a deep trance."

"You are delirious. You think Wedge is a baby, and you are trying to nurse him. You weaned him last year."

"I can explain," she said, but Rockdream felt her forehead.

"You are hot," he said.

"I know that. I am moving healing energy through my body into his. Feel *his* forehead. His fever is less than it was this morning."

"His fever comes and goes, as does his strength, or it would, if you did not keep him doped all the time with sleepflower. Now you have the sickness yourself. People always deny it at first."

"If I had the sickness, I would either feel very cold, or else be sweating heavily. Even in this stinking hot hut, I would be bundled up."

"Why are you naked? I could have been Mother Cedar, or almost anyone else."

"No one comes here but you and Salmon, and it is easier to deepen my trance when my body is unrestrained, at least on days as hot as this. It worked. I was so deep that I did not feel the hut shake when you came up the ladder."

"You stay here. I will send Salmon to examine you."

She placed Wedge gently on the bed, and opened the door. "Rockdream, Rockdream, husband, wait. Talk to me. You promised you would be understanding."

"Coral, you *were* nursing him." By the sunlight on the porch, it was easy to see the drops of milk on her nipples.

"I guess I was," she said, surprised.

"Do you know what you are doing?"

"I—I was nursing Wedge in a trance vision, and talking to the Nameless Mother about how to heal him."

"And did she tell you to bring the sickness into your own body, and summon the power that will help? Coral, that is black sorcery."

"What she said was, '*Feel* the sickness with your own body, and *look inside* yourself for the power that will help,' which is not the same."

"You are quibbling."

"You are accusing me of black sorcery."

"I do not mean to accuse you, but rather to warn you," Rock-dream said.

"If so, you are warning me about dangers I understand much better than you."

"Well, make certain that this spirit is indeed the real Nameless Mother, before—"

"I will challenge her before I follow her advice. But filling my breasts with milk is certainly a magic suggesting her power."

81.

"You must know my husband's concern," Coral said.

"Then touch me," said the goddess. "Ask the young girl inside yourself whether or not I am Mother of All."

Coral found herself sitting on the goddess's lap, feeling her strong, gentle hands on her back and knees. "Mother," she said hesitantly, "my child is very sick."

"You are a witch. You have the power that will help inside yourself. Summon it."

"But that is—"

"Black sorcery? Child, the only demon you have inside yourself is your own fear."

A young wizard ran through the streets of a city, while people chased him, throwing stones. He funneled his fear and rage into a curse of scales and fire, ignoring the fast bloody pain of the stones that struck him, ignoring even the moment of his death. For timeless time, he was shadow and twisting fire.

Coral knew that she had been this man, in a previous life many centuries before. "Did I make a dragon destroy that city?" she asked.

"A dragon did destroy that city, and your name was long remembered for your curse," said the goddess. "The people who had known the handsome young wizard, whose chanting and harping and skill with herbs had healed many illnesses, but who had been falsely accused of black sorcery because he had seduced one woman too many, now told stories of the ugly, twisted man who had made himself seem handsome with a glimmer, who had used black sorcery to gain wealth and power by creating and healing a plague, and whose last curse had brought a dragon to the city."

"You mean *I* was the Starmoon of Starmoon's curse?"

"You were the real wizard behind that legend."

Coral stood in the charred ruins, surrounded by ghosts. "I was arrogant and ambitious, and I became evil. I am very sorry," she told them. "I will never do that again. I am a very different kind of person now."

"Are you?" asked a harsh voice. "Your enemies at Sharp Bend are dead—the two priests, the first mate, the others. Villagers there mutter about *the witch's* curse, not daring to name you *Coral.*"

"That cannot be! That is a lie! I made no curse."

"You did not curse, but you desired their deaths."

"I did not. I felt angry, nothing more."

"Are you sure?" asked the voice.

"Why will you not believe me?" pleaded Coral.

"Do you believe yourself?" asked the Nameless Mother.

"I am confused. All I want to do is bring my son back to life and health. He led me to you, and you told me to look inside myself for power, but what I find are reasons why I should not have it. Mother, I must do something *now*. Wedge is dying!"

82.

Suddenly Coral was very angry, and out of trance. She examined Wedge, who was barely breathing, and very hot. "I think I know what to do," she whispered to herself. The fever was hottest when the infection was worst, which was his body's way of fighting back, but if he became too hot, he would die, and he was too hot. Maybe she could break the fever, if she also gave him a poison to kill the infection. This was delicate and dangerous, but what else could she do?

She put on her sandals, and after a moment's thought, her shortest leather dress, though she did not bother to lace the bodice, then jumped off the platform and ran to the lakeshore. The fairladies were no longer blooming, but their late summer leaves were rich with toxins. Offering a prayer of gratitude to whatever had jolted her out of trance, she squatted down and picked a few small leaves. After hurrying back to the hut, she mashed them between two cobbles, and put them into a bowl of cold boiled water. She pulled the covers off Wedge, and wiped his forehead and chest with cool water. When he began trembling, she covered him with just one blanket. She took a spoonful of water from the fairlady mixture, mixed it with another container of water, then put a spoonful of the second mixture into a cup, and filled this with water from the kettle.

"Wedge, wake up," Coral said, pulling him into a sitting position. He gasped, shuddered, and opened his eyes. "Drink. It is just warm water." At this dilution, the fairlady would have little taste. She had to help him hold the cup, but he had no trouble swallowing.

"I am cold," he said. "Wrap me up."

"You are too hot. I have to cool you down just little bit, then I can wrap you up again."

After fifteen minutes, Wedge broke into a sweat, which Coral washed off; then she wrapped him. She watched his light patterns with her trance-eye, and told him a new story, about how, long ago and west of the sea, a young wizard named Starmoon became bad.

83.

Breaking Wedge's fever and giving him fairlady made his condition less stable. His fever no longer rose and fell in a regular cycle, but could become dangerously high at any time, and each time this happened, Coral gave him willow bark, and more fairlady. Some nights she had to wake every two hours to check his condition.

Rockdream was trying to be understanding, but Wedge did seem worse than before, and if Coral had found a treatment that would keep him alive, it did not seem to be curing him. Every few nights, Coral would manage to spend an hour or two in bed with Rockdream, and they would try to forget everything but the love they felt for each other, and the warmth of skin against skin.

Another week passed, and another. Limpet caught the sickness, and then Hod, and Coral left their treatment entirely to Salmon and Mother Cedar.

On the night of the last full moon of summer, Wedge had another high fever at dusk. Again Coral gave him willow bark, fairlady, and sleepflower, varying the dosages slightly, hoping for more lasting results. Only when Wedge was out of immediate danger and asleep did Coral allow herself to break down into tears.

She went outside, to a certain place on the beach, and checked the moon's position. It was too early for what she now had in mind, for she did not want to risk being discovered in the middle of her ceremony, but she sat there awhile, to make sure she felt comfortable with the spot. River lizards stayed in the water at night, but leopards and drakeys were possible dangers. Having her bow and quiver within reach would be sensible, but any weapon would defeat the purpose of the spell. She would have to be completely vulnerable, completely open to whatever came to her. She emptied her mind of thoughts, and watched the moon move.

When she judged it was late enough, she returned to the hut and checked Wedge. He was sound asleep, and breathing steadily. He would probably be all right until dawn.

Then Coral made herself a strong peppermint tea to stay awake, and added just enough sleepflower to make the spirit world visible to her waking eyes. She had never before tried anything like this, but Feathergrass's story of the vision-inducing sleepflower tea served in the sailors' bars of Lizard River gave her the idea.

The full moon was moving toward the west. Coral drank the tea and walked back to the beach. She sat cross-legged facing the moon and the water, and began chanting softly:

> I open my eyes to see,
> I open my ears to hear,
> I open my heart to feel
> the spirits known to me,
> the spirits not known to me.
> Hear me!
> I need help to heal my child.
> I summon the power that will help.

The moon, the stars, the lake, the willows, the reeds, the stones, the mud—all were vibrant patterns of light, shimmering, changing, alive. Coral breathed exhilaration. Opening her heart to deep joy also opened it to deep pain, but this was better than numbness and fear.

If you are in the east,
Where life begins, I summon you.
Help me heal my child.

If you are in the south.
where life is fullest, I summon you.
Help me heal my people.

If you are in the west,
where life ends, I summon you.
Help me heal my world.

If you are in the north,
where life awaits rebirth, I summon you.
Help me heal myself.

This invocation reminded Coral of Drakey, of Glowfly, of Cicada. Did they live? Did their loved ones? Brief visions of battles between goblins and humans shimmered above the lake's surface. Were these old battles, or was the war still being fought? Tears rolled down Coral's face while she continued chanting:

So many humans have died.
So many goblins have died.
The sorrow and fear of those
who live is beyond measure.
I do not know what to do.
I summon the power—

Feathered wings stroked the night air. The condor landed on the sand bar less than ten feet from Coral. The moonlight darkened his feathers, paled his leathery head and hooked beak, and made the pupils of his staring eyes swollen and black.

Coral had seen a live condor this close once before, when Glowfly had helped her journey to the center of the world of her heart to find her totem spirit. "Sometimes the spirit brings the real animal," Glowfly had explained. And the Nameless Mother had told Coral to look inside herself for the power that will help, but instead she had summoned it.

"Father Condor," she whispered.

I will help you heal Wedge, he said. His speech was no sequence of words, but a complete idea received by her mind all at once. She knew now that she had been giving Wedge the best herbs, but not at the best time. She knew that with Father Condor's guidance and power, she might make him well in a few days. *And then you must change your life*, he said. *I will also help you do this*.

84.

Rockdream walked south along the lakeshore, carrying a small bundle of cooked drakey meat, and more oddly, its claws, finger and toe bones, and two wing ribs. Coral wanted to make something from these, which she would show to him when she was finished. She was quite annoyed at his unvoiced suspicions, and said that she would kill a drakey herself if he would not bring her these bones. Her ability to hear his thoughts seemed greater than before, and proportionately more annoying. He would give her the bones, but enough was enough. If he was her husband, and she knew so much about his private thoughts, it was only fair that she tell him something about hers.

Coral was standing on the porch of the isolation hut, wearing the much-patched green muslin dress he had bought for her many years before. "Please calm yourself, husband," she said.

"You are doing it already," he said, unable to control his irritation. "You hear everything I think and feel, but tell me next to nothing about what you think and feel, except that my suspicions annoy you. Tell me something to ease my suspicions." He took a deep breath, and released it with a snort. "How is Wedge?"

"He is asleep with a fever, but a low one, and maybe the last. Yesterday afternoon after you left, he actually helped me clean the hut. As for your suspicions, I might be more willing to talk to you if I did not have to fear your reaction. Suppose I did summon the power that will help, and suppose that is why Wedge is getting better, and why I can hear your thoughts so clearly. What then? How would you react?"

After a moment of stone-faced silence, Rockdream asked, "What price must you pay for this help?"

"There is nothing to fear or be angry about," Coral said. "Nothing bad has happened to me. I am still the same woman you have loved and lived with these past eight years. Will you calm yourself and listen to me? Your spirit fangcat is fierce when you feel frightened."

"My spirit fangcat?" Rockdream asked.

"You have felt the Great Mother Cat inside yourself," Coral replied. "Remember our very first night together, when we danced the summer solstice in the Rose Garden, how you compared our movements to a cat and a bird? And remember when we left the city, when we were climbing the trail from the mammoth valley to the pass, how you knew the fangcat would not attack us?"

Rockdream sighed impatiently. "What does this have to do with my question? You have not told me what price you must pay the power you summoned, you always talk circles around what I want to know, and I have had enough!"

When Coral made no response, Rockdream's anger lessened, for its intensity had surprised him. In a moment he would accept his anger and it would become worse. Before that moment came, Coral spoke: "Husband, a condor soars in circles before touching down. This is just the way of condors. Father Condor is my spirit beast. He is the power who is helping me. His price is that we must change our lives. We must become goblins. I must be a goblin shamaness, and you must be a goblin chief."

"Coral, what do you mean?"

She sat down on the edge of the platform, and gestured for him to come closer. "We cannot continue living here. You know this. You agree. And going to another city as bonded slaves is at best a temporary answer. Sooner or later a dragon will come to that city and make us refugees all over again, or kill us. But if we say we are goblins, and we know our spirit beasts, and we live the goblin way, which is not so different from how we live here, then we *are* goblins, near enough, and we can live on Goblin Plain."

"I doubt that any goblin would see it that way."

"Drakey does, and he can persuade the others. Think about it. At the peace talk when he said, 'We welcome goblins here,' he looked right at us. The thought behind his words was, *If you choose to be goblins, you are welcome*. I missed it then. He reminded us that his people had welcomed the Elk Coast people. He wanted us to remember that we are people from the Elk Coast. He wanted me to remember Glowfly's story of Raven the Shamaness, who saved her people from dragon attack. My own dreams could have been as clear as Raven's, but I was afraid, for Lord Herring had made that stupid law against foretelling the city's destruction. Drakey wanted us to remember that he had taught us some things about being goblins, and wanted us to know that he was willing to teach us more."

"Maybe he was willing then," said Rockdream. "Maybe if we had gone to the goblins when Canticle exiled us from his keep, they would have welcomed us. But now? The notion seems absurd. Is Drakey even still alive? Is Beartooth? Is Glowfly?"

"Drakey and Glowfly are both still alive. They are bitter. Persuading them to accept us will not be easy, but with the help of our spirit beasts, we can do it."

"All right," said Rockdream. "Suppose we do this, and now you are a goblin shamaness, and I am a goblin warrior—"

"A goblin chief," corrected Coral.

"Of what people?"

"Of the people of Loop Lake who come with us."

Rockdream sighed. "If I assume that things will go the best possible way, I might imagine Beartooth and Drakey accepting you and me as people of Beartooth's Camp. I cannot imagine them letting us set up our own camp, and even if they did, Strong Bull would object."

"I have dreamed that you are a chief," Coral said firmly. "I have even dreamed that Feathergrass will live in our camp, and Strong Bull will sit an honest peace circle that includes him."

"Maybe we can negotiate a truce with the dragon Riversong while we are at it," said Rockdream.

"When you are strong in the spirit, you can do what you dream," Coral replied. "I have dreamed a way for you and I and our people to become goblins."

"I believe Goblin Plain is at war with the survivors of Newport. I refuse to join that war on either side."

"We do not have to," said Coral. "Only Strong Bull's Camp, and one or two others, are still at war with the humans. The others withdrew from that war last year. Our camp will be like those. We can help end the war. Our camp can welcome any humans who are willing to change their lives and become goblins, and warn away any others."

"I do not know what to say," said Rockdream. "You have dreamed something very unlikely, yet you speak as though the accomplishment will be simple and easy."

"Not simple, not easy, but certain, if and only if we let Father Condor and Mother Fangcat guide us to do and say exactly the best things at exactly the best times," said Coral. "Now, the dye Cedar made for her new robes will work well enough on leather for the messengers' vests. We must arrive at Beartooth's Camp while Drakey is there. I will dream the best time, once Wedge is well enough to travel. It will be soon. Let me show you something. I was going to wait till I made the necklace, but—" She went inside.

She came out wearing a leather dress very much like one of Glowfly's—the skirt was far above her knees, and the top was a tightly fitted vest, sleeveless and scoop-necked. But what surprised Rockdream most of all was how natural and confident she looked.

"This moment feels like the memory of something important that has already happened," said Rockdream. "You do look very much like a goblin woman."

"I am a goblin woman."

"I am not so sure I can become a goblin man. When we were at Beartooth's Camp, the goblin way came much more naturally to you—"

"Not at all," said Coral. "I had as much trouble spinning flatbread as you had flipping a spear-thrower. But I remember you sitting with Sees Far and Gray Lizard, learning to make bone arrowheads by watching them make spearheads, and now, how is everyone at Loop Lake tipping their arrows?"

"Well—"

"And I also remember you explaining the goblin warrior's way of life quite articulately on several occasions."

"All right," Rockdream said. "I will do what a goblin warrior would do. I will pray for a vision, and wait four days, and if no vision comes, I will make the best decision I can. But one thing I know for certain. I want to live with you. This separation has not been good for us."

"Yes, husband, yes!" Coral said, jumping off the platform to hug him. "Go get your things and bring them here."

85.

On the evening of the fourth day following, Rockdream called everyone in the village to a special meeting, where he and Coral presented Coral's plan. Only Ironweed and Birdwade spoke strongly in favor of it.

Ironweed said, "When I was Fairwind the Merchant's bookkeeper, I spoke several times with Strong Bull, Drakey, and Beartooth. I know them well enough to think they would listen respectfully to Rockdream and Coral. From the goblin viewpoint, Coral's proposal is valid. Before Strong Bull became high chief, it was not unknown for camps to war with each other as bitterly as the Goblin River camps did with Canticle's Keep. Warriors who disagreed about going to war or who had friends on both sides would move to a nonparticipating camp. Some even withdrew from a war in progress. Those of you who left Canticle's army to come here have done the same thing. We as a people are not at war with Goblin Plain. If we became goblins, we might be invited to settle there. I must say I never expected to be anything but a bookkeeper, but here I am, a hunter and fishcatcher. Why not a goblin?"

"I would rather die of swamp sickness," someone said.

"A wish granted easily enough," Rockdream muttered.

Feathergrass said, "It is much too late for humans and goblins to trust each other under any circumstances."

Birdwade listed all the times that Coral's wisdom had saved or improved her life. "I do not think her wisdom is failing now. She is brave, for there is some chance that she will be killed, but she is not foolish. She is taking every precaution. If she succeeds, we will have a wonderful opportunity."

Salmon said, "We can wear goblin clothes, and imitate their way of life as well as we understand it, but we will still be humans. And if we imitate goblins only because we think we have no other choices but swamp sickness or slavery, will Drakey and Beartooth and Strong Bull accept us as people like themselves? Certainly we can learn things from goblins, or elves, or pooks, and use this knowledge to enrich our lives. But our lives are human lives. We cannot change that."

Mother Cedar made a long speech against "letting our spirits sink into the animal realm."

Rockdream said, "I know this is blasphemy, but I think that our gods and goddesses have failed us. I cannot believe that they wanted everyone in Newport to die miserable deaths, nor can I believe that they have contrived these sorrows to test our spirits. But if not, they have done little to help us. But when I feel the strength of Great Mother Fangcat inside myself, I know I can do things. The strength is mine, and I can use it."

Coral said, "I say that the Nameless Mother helped me find Father Condor. All spirit beasts are, in fact, her children, as are solid beasts, and goblins, and humans. This sounds like nonsense if you envision her as a human woman with her breasts exposed, but that is just one way of seeing her. Look around you—" Coral spread her arms wide, and looked at all the others. "Everything you see is the Nameless Mother's body, for she is this entire world, and even the dragon Riversong is one of her children. Just because I envision her spirit in human form does not mean that by her nature she must favor humans over her other children. Whether I am human or goblin, I am still one of her children."

86.

Coral, Rockdream, and Wedge traveled by day through the swamp, moving mostly southeast, though their trail twisted around countless bogs. Only so late in the summer, when the water was lowest, was foot travel in this direction even possible. Sometimes Coral would make them stop for a good portion of an hour, or change direction, to avoid hunters, homesteads, or villages she said she perceived. They were wearing human clothes, and hiding was likely unnecessary, but she wanted the practice. Considering the number of ripe berry batches and delicious tubers she found, it was surprising that they encountered no human gatherers, and no larger animals but one family of swamp deer. They did not hunt, but depended on a small pack of provisions, and what they found on the way. Sometimes Coral knew what kind of food they would find in advance. The nights were warm, and they slept on dry ground without shelter or fire. Rockdream had to admit that of all their journeys through the swamp, this one was by far the easiest. Even Wedge had few complaints.

At midmorning of the fifth day, they stopped at the edge of the marsh, where Coral said they must wait for a sign.

"What kind of sign?" Wedge whispered.

"I will know when I see it," Coral replied. "My spirit beast is a condor. Let us watch all the large birds, and see what they have to tell me."

The only large birds in sight were white cranes and egrets, and a few blue herons at several distant pools, but these did nothing unusual and came nowhere near them. Rockdream said nothing, but thought to himself that Coral was becoming more and more like a witch or shamaness from an old story, guided by impulses that made little sense but somehow led to good results.

"A shamaness dreams while she is awake," whispered Coral. "These dreams are most powerful of all."

At that moment, a raven cawed and took flight, circling over the marsh's edge and flapping back under the trees. They turned to watch it go in the direction they had come from.

"Let us make camp in the bronzeberry patch," Coral said. "We must travel by night, and cross the Goblin River before dawn. This land is open, and we cannot risk being seen by anyone."

"If you want to reach the Goblin River before dawn, we will have to leave here well before sunset," said Rockdream.

"All right," said Coral.

They had some trouble making Wedge take a nap, even though they lay down with him, but before long, the heat of the day made all three of them drowsy, and they did not wake until the shadows were long. Hurriedly they changed into their goblin messengers' clothes and set off across the marsh. Twilight deepened to stars, and the pale sky river curved above them. Somehow Coral found a dry path through the darkness.

The stars became dimmer with the moonrise, a frowning crescent bright enough to make them feel uncomfortably exposed. When they reached the low ridge between the marsh and the river, much less prominent here than at Canticle's Keep, Coral made them crawl, lest they be seen in silhouette against the sky. A bit below this, they sat up to scan the landscape. Pale grass with scattered blotches of trees and brush stretched toward the distant river. No fires or other obvious signs of either goblins or humans could be seen, but Coral looked things over thoroughly with her trance-eye before standing up, and again before choosing a route.

"Do not say anything, either of you," Coral whispered. "I will hear your thoughts, if you need to call anything to my attention."

Wedge was drowsy and awkward, so Rockdream carried him. Mile by mile they neared the river; then quite suddenly they were standing on the bank, looking at the spread of pale gravel, the dark shining water, the wisps of mist that veiled the other side.

"If it is too deep to ford here, we will swim," Coral whispered, and jumped lightly onto the gravel. Rockdream climbed down carrying Wedge, then woke him gently and sat him on his shoulders, on top of his pack. "I think the current is slow enough for us to swim with our packs," Coral whispered. They stepped quietly like herons into the cool water. When it was hip-high on Coral, she began swimming smoothly with frog kicks. Rockdream made sure Wedge was clinging tight, then did the same. The pack at first helped buoy him up, but by the time he reached the other side it was heavy. "Climb the bank, keep moving," Coral whispered. "That will warm us."

The sky brightened toward dawn, but they did not look for a place to hide. They were goblin messengers dressed in red, going to Beartooth's Camp. On this side of the river, Coral could see the lines of light on the ground as clearly as the streets of a city. Sometimes the patterns would shift, and she changed direction to follow what she saw, and Rockdream followed her, carrying Wedge.

A few miles after sunrise, they stopped to eat a meager meal, and spread the contents of their packs on the ground to dry. Wedge, who was better rested than his parents, was first to notice the multitude of scattered bones.

"Do not touch them!" Coral said quietly but urgently. "These are bones of people." She trembled while she knelt beside a crushed skull. She stretched her hands close to it, closed her eyes, and relaxed into trance. "This was the battle I used to dream about, the one where you were killed," she said, opening her eyes to look at Rockdream. "It happened two summers ago."

"The massacre of Beadback's Camp," Rockdream said quietly. "I would not have fought such a battle under any circumstances."

"Those dreams were partly prophecy but mostly fear," said Coral. "I feared what you might do as a warrior, much as you more recently feared what I might do as a witch."

"I am sorry," said Rockdream.

"So am I. I would like our camp to do a ceremony for those who died here. Many of their spirits are still lost in the black cloud of battle."

They rested on the edge of the battlefield till their things were dry, then repacked them and resumed walking. But after a few more miles they realized they were too tired to continue, and stopped in the shade of a big oak. "We can take turns sitting watch and sleeping, then go on a bit, then rest again," Rockdream suggested to Coral, for they were in the open, and Wedge was unlikely to sleep through the day.

While Coral and Wedge slept, Rockdream watched a distant herd of aurochs moving toward the Blue River, a speckled hawk swooping down at something in the grass, an orange butterfly's erratic flight, and a treeworm lowering itself on a silk thread. Then he woke Coral with a kiss and took his own turn asleep. She and Wedge were playing a quiet game with bits of twig when he woke again.

Now it was late afternoon. They ate the last of their provisions and resumed walking. At sunset they were walking around patchy brush. Some hours after dark, Rockdream saw a flicker of red light toward the river.

"I see it," Coral said quietly. "I think that is Beartooth's Camp. But the spirit path is leading me toward a power place first. Maybe—maybe you need to dream something before we go to the camp."

Looming ahead was a big, spreading tree, which was not as close and much bigger than it appeared at first—the redbark where years ago Coral had journeyed in trance to the center of the world of her heart.

"Here," she said. She wrapped Wedge in a blanket and laid him beside her. She and Rockdream sat with their backs against the trunk and watched the moonrise. "You can be asleep, or in trance, or awake, whatever feels best, and you will dream your true dream," Coral said.

Wedge was still asleep, and Coral asleep or in trance, when Rockdream woke to footsteps, and a sound like a purring cat, but deeper. By the twilight of a coming dawn, he saw her, a huge female fangcat less than twenty feet away and stepping closer, ever so slowly, while staring into Rockdream's eyes.

"I hope you are my spirit beast," he said in a low voice. A shimmer of light around her sleek fur suggested this, but she looked very real, very dangerous. "I am not a shaman, but a warrior, a hunter like yourself. I do not know how to speak to you."

You must learn.

"Coral, did you say that, or—?"

"No," she whispered. "You really heard her voice."

When you speak, you will know what to say. Remember how you feel now. This feeling will help you find me.

The fangcat was gone. Rockdream thought he glimpsed her, running in the distance, but he could not be sure.

"You will know what to say to Beartooth and Drakey," Coral said. "I can do much of the talking, but you must speak first."

The sun rose, a brilliant red like their vests, revealing a thin curl of smoke coming from a cluster of tiny conical tents. They woke Wedge and began walking toward this camp.

12

DANCING THE DREAM

87.

Beartooth's goblins were eating breakfast in the center of camp when one of the scouts came running back. "The humans Rock-dream and Coral are coming with my partner," he said. "They want to talk to Drakey about something. They are dressed as goblin messengers. I think their concerns are personal. Their young son is with them. They said their totems are Mother Fangcat and Father Condor."

Glowfly's surprise quickly became recognition of an important moment, though she did not know yet what this moment would mean. She had never before seen Drakey look so surprised, but his surprise changed to bitterness and regret. "I will talk to them, even though they have come much too late."

"What do you think they want?" asked Beartooth.

"We will know soon enough," the old shaman replied.

Glowfly boldly walked around the cookfire to the chief and the high shaman. "I want to talk to them also. I want to hear what they say to you," she told Drakey.

Beartooth frowned and grunted.

"Talk to them near the fire," Gray Lizard suggested. "Then we all can hear and speak."

A number of warriors, and the shamaness Cicada, made murmurs of assent.

"No," said Drakey. "That would make a hard thing much harder." He stared at Glowfly, and she stared back. "Glowfly may make it less hard. She knows something."

Glowfly did not know what she knew, but recognized climbing through the door into Drakey's tent as another important moment. She arranged the mats into seating for four, hesitated, then made a fifth seat and took her place. After several minutes, Drakey came in and took his place on the seat farthest from the entrance, followed by Coral and her little boy, then Rockdream.

"I know what you want, but you are years too late," Drakey said quietly. "When Canticle rejected you, then was the time for you to join us. We might have stopped the war. But you were afraid and ran away." The high shaman stared at Coral, waiting for her reply. Glowfly looked at Coral also, but looked away when she sensed Coral's discomfort.

"If you must hate someone, hate first the general who led his army against your people for no fair cause, and then hate the lieutenants and warriors of that army," Coral said. "Can you hate all those people and still have enough hate left over for me, a woman who considers herself your friend? You are an elder, a leader of many people. You think of life the big way. I was, and I still am, a young woman with a small child who is used to thinking of life the small way. Yes, I was afraid. I dreamed many times that my husband would die in battle here. I had no hope that Strong Bull and Canticle could make peace."

"Now you come here because you fear your family will die of disease," Drakey said. "Canticle's people had the same reason."

"I came here because Father Condor gave me a vision," Coral replied. "He showed me a way to help my family and friends that might also help the people of Goblin Plain." Carefully Coral and Rockdream explained what being goblins meant to them, and what a camp of goblins who were formerly human might mean for Goblin Plain.

"What you propose is much like the vision I had before I brought you to this camp," Drakey said. "I still had hope that it might come true when I invited you to the peace talk. But you went back to the swamp and the war began. Your own vision came too late. I might sit peace with you, and Beartooth might, and

Sundance might, but not unless Strong Bull also sits peace with you."

"I understand," said Rockdream. "Can you arrange for Coral and me to talk to Strong Bull?"

Drakey made a gesture of negation. "Strong Bull went to Big Claw's Camp to help them choose a new chief. He may even be leading a force of warriors into the thickets of the Emerald Hills to pursue the humans who killed Big Claw. I do not think he will want to hear you."

Glowfly, who had been praying silently to Father Otter for inspiration, now spoke. "Before Big Claw died, he was the only other chief who sat the broken peace circle who was still alive. Strong Bull must know that he himself is next. But sitting peace with Rockdream and making this vision real might be enough to stop the curse."

Drakey said, "Did Strong Bull break the safe passage agreement because someone prophesied an unlikely attack from Upriver? If so, he must certainly fear the peace circle curse. But maybe he did it just because he hates humans. A strong hatred would explain everything he has done. If he feared the peace circle curse, would he go to battle at every opportunity?"

"He must prove to himself that he does not fear the curse," said Glowfly. "He is high chief. The war is his responsibility. He alone understands why it must continue. His hatred may be the biggest reason. But no matter how many battles he fights, his hatred will not be purged. Even Canticle's death made no difference. This is the curse of the broken peace circle. Strong Bull will die in a battle both petty and unnecessary. But the new high chief will be a very different kind of man. But Strong Bull's spirit knows these things. If we offer him peace with Rockdream as a way to end the curse, he will find a reason to be interested."

Drakey said, "To end the curse, the new circle must include someone from each side who sat the broken circle."

"There is someone at Loop Lake who did so," Coral said. "I have dreamed that he will sit a true peace with Strong Bull and live as a goblin in our camp."

Glowfly felt a sudden deep pain in her spirit. "Who is he?" she asked.

"Feathergrass the Mariner," said Coral.

Glowfly's mouth went dry. "He killed my husband," she said.

"Quick One is dead?" said Coral. "Oh no, no! I am so sorry."

"Feathergrass did not kill Quick One," said Glowfly. "Quick

One died in the retreat from the first siege, stupidly, going back into battle with a bad wound just to prove how fierce he was. Feathergrass killed Condor, my chief, my true love, in single combat while leading a platoon to massacre our camp."

Coral shuddered and sobbed.

"Why are you crying tears for my grief?" Glowfly demanded.

"Because you are my friend," Coral replied.

"Is Feathergrass also your friend?"

"There are many parts of his spirit that he will not let me touch," Coral said. "He deeply regrets participating in the war. He especially regrets that night. He would rather go to Midcoast and sail away, but he will come to Goblin Plain and live as a goblin of Rockdream's Camp if in some way that will help."

"Are you sure you can speak for him this way?" Rockdream asked.

"I have dreamed this," said Coral.

Glowfly felt her lips quivering, felt the tears swelling in her eyes. "I understand," she said. "If I want Strong Bull to act against his hatred, I must be willing to act against my own."

"Ah," said Drakey. "Maybe I was wrong. Maybe they are not too late. Let us go outside and talk to Beartooth and Gray Lizard and the others and hear what they think."

"Good," said the little boy. "I want to eat."

"What do you say, Wedge?" asked Coral.

"Can I please have some food?"

Drakey looked at the child. "Are your teeth strong? Goblins almost never eat stew. This morning we have fried mammoth bits and flatbread. The mammoth bits are hard to chew but really greasy. They taste good. Mmm. Shall we go out?"

88.

Glowfly went out first, and quickly found Little Ant, who wanted to know what was happening. "You will find out soon. I want you to do two things. First, make a plate of food for the little boy and give it to him. Then get Henna and Jay out of the tent. They must meet these people. Tell Henna they are also goblins from Newport. Just do it."

Glowfly moved back towards Drakey, Rockdream, and Coral just as Drakey finished saying something to Beartooth.

"Ha! Hey, yo. Ha!" Beartooth called out. "Rockdream and

Coral have told Drakey their vision. He wants the rest of us to hear it."

Conversation stilled to silence or whispers. Little Ant brought the food for Wedge.

Rockdream said, "This vision came first to my wife, Coral. She prayed for a vision to help her heal our son, who was very ill with swamp sickness. She was sitting on the lakeshore, staring at the full moon, and chanting. Before the war, while we were guests at your camp, Coral made a vision quest to find her totem. When she woke from her trance, a live condor was perched close to her, on a branch of the big redbark. This time, the condor landed on the beach and spoke in her mind. He told her how to heal Wedge. She followed his instructions, and soon the child became well. He told her we must change our lives. We must now be goblins. We must start a camp on Goblin Plain."

While Rockdream spoke, Glowfly studied him carefully. His wispy beard was gone; his shaved chin was as smooth as a goblin man's. His phrasing was much like a warrior's. Usually when humans tried to mimic goblin speech, their sentences became too short, and they overemphasized the stressed falling tone given to important words at the end of a phrase.

When he finished, Glowfly could tell that the warriors and women at the fire were not sure how to react. Ah, there was Little Ant bringing Henna and baby Jay. Henna's reaction was sudden wonder: *These are people like me!*

Coral spoke: "If I say I am a goblin shamaness who was once a human witch, how can you know this is true? Maybe I am only pretending. I can say it would be good for you to welcome my family and friends to make camp on Goblin Plain, but maybe it would not be so good. I must share my vision with you, so that we may all know whether it is true. Will you dance my dream? Will you dance all the way to the center of the world of the vision Father Condor showed to me?"

"We will dance," said Chief Beartooth. "Who will drum?"

"I will drum," Glowfly said immediately.

"I will drum also," said Cicada.

After a few moments of silence, Henna said quietly, "I would like to drum."

Coral turned to see who had spoken, and was very surprised to see a woman whose skin was paler than her own, whose fox-red hair was brushed over her ears. Before this, Henna had only drummed for dances that were more celebration than ceremony, but it seemed right for her to drum this dance.

"Get the drums," Beartooth said. "Bring the fire. Drakey will mark the center of the dancing ground." Beartooth might have had the dance in the center of camp. Having Drakey choose a special site showed that he considered the dance important.

"You and Coral should eat something to give yourselves strength," Drakey told Rockdream. "This could be a long dance."

Cicada and Glowfly both got their big drums. Glowfly's drum was stretched on a storage barrel—salvage from one of the human boats attacked by Strong Bull and Quagga. It came to Beartooth's Camp as part of a gift exchange. For this dance, the drum's history had symbolic importance. Glowfly gave Henna her best small drum to use.

Drakey chose a spot, and the warriors cleared a circle for the fire. Once this was lit, Drakey offered a prayer to the four directions.

Henna looked at Glowfly and Cicada, then began tapping a walking beat on the small drum, with occasionally doubled or missing offbeats. When the warriors and women, including Rockdream and Coral, began pacing the dance in a double circle, Glowfly began a long, deep, subtle roll like wind or waves. Cicada answered with a similar roll. They did this again and again, sometimes loudly enough to overwhelm Henna's beat, sometimes softly. This was a rhythm made by the women of the Elk Coast goblins when these people were first welcomed to Goblin Plain, a rhythm to preserve the memory of the Great Sea for their grandchildren's grandchildren.

Rockdream, Coral, and Wedge also came from the Elk Coast. In Coral's vision they were goblins. Was this vision true? Should they be welcomed to live as people of Grass, River, Wind? This was the dance.

Some of the dancers were already trembling as they paced. Drakey's eyes were closed, his face raised to the sky. Coral looked ecstatic. On the other hand, Beartooth, Rockdream, and many others were still just pacing the dance. Glowfly found herself slipping into trance each time she played a long roll. At first she resisted this, but then she let herself enjoy it. It was like diving into the river and swimming underwater as far as she could before surfacing. She tried actually holding her breath to enhance the effect. This was the playful strength of Father Otter.

Overhead, a lone condor was circling. This might be an omen

if it did anything unusual. Little Ant saw it and shouted, "Yiyiyi! Yiyiyi!" as did a few other women. Now, what was that girl doing dancing? She was supposed to be watching children.

Glowfly played another roll and looked at Rockdream. He was starting to slip into trance, starting to feel the presence of his totem fangcat. Now most of the dancers showed signs of such contact.

Cicada played a very long roll, beginning softly, becoming louder, fading slowly, becoming louder again, softer, rumbling into deep thunder, and stopping with an abrupt slap. Henna, startled, stopped drumming two beats later, and the dancers faltered. Glowfly stared at Cicada, wondering why she had stopped.

Something close made a screeching, howling roar. There in the open, less than fifty feet from the dance circle, stood a huge female fangcat, as heavy as three strong men and far more powerful. Her breasts were pendulous with milk.

No one moved. The warriors in the dance were unarmed, for this was not a war dance. The few who stood guard did nothing, for the cat was likely an omen. What ordinary fangcat, especially a nursing mother, would approach a goblin camp in the noon sun, much less stand tall and roar at a dance circle of more than a hundred? Surely she was possessed by a spirit.

"The balance must be restored," Drakey said firmly.

The fangcat slowly turned her head and fixed her eyes on the high shaman.

"The balance will be restored. I will see to it," he said.

The fangcat looked briefly at Rockdream. Some of the goblins nearest to her said afterwards that she purred for a moment, but others just as close did not hear this. Then the cat turned and walked away. She would not have been afraid even if all the warriors had been armed. Everyone stood still and watched till she was gone.

Then Drakey had Glowfly and Cicada send a smoke message that was relayed up the Goblin River to Strong Bull at Big Claw's Camp, telling him to meet Drakey at Beartooth's Camp as soon as possible.

89.

No reply was seen that afternoon, nor all the next day, but Drakey was sure that Strong Bull would come, and Rockdream and Coral were satisfied with this.

By evening of their second day in camp, they were sharing jokes with people they had known before.

"These people are funny goblins," said Sees Far. "Rockdream hunts with a bow and arrow. He has to or his camp will starve. Imagine him hunting an auroch with spears. When he flips the spear thrower, the spear wobbles sideways and slaps the auroch on the nose. The auroch becomes indignant."

"No," said another warrior. "The spear flips backwards over his head and stabs him in the rump. The auroch doubles over from laughter."

"Then Rockdream stabs him to death with his thrusting spear," suggested a third warrior. "So he could use real goblin weapons after all."

"No," said Rockdream. "It would take me forever to master flinging a spear to hit myself in the rump."

Glowfly's mother, Antelope, offered equally funny exaggerations of Coral's lack of skill at making flatbread.

"I may shoot arrows better than I cook, but I will not be the only woman in our camp," said Coral. "Come visit us and we will offer you the best flatbread you ever had."

90.

Strong Bull came at dusk on the day of the new moon, the third evening after the dance. Only five other warriors and the shaman Split Hoof accompanied him. These warriors were young, fierce men, intensely loyal to Strong Bull. They had joined his camp after being rejected by their own chiefs for taking part in the attack on the human boat camp that betrayed the safe passage agreement. They had fought in all of Strong Bull's subsequent battles. Strong Bull knew that Drakey and Beartooth opposed this war. But was bringing so few of these warriors with him to Beartooth's Camp a gesture of conciliation or arrogance?

It was not because they were the only survivors of the battle in the Emerald Hills. Their tale was of victory, indeed of massacre. They had trailed the humans through the lush, tangled thickets of the wet forest and surprised them with a deadly volley of throwing spears.

"You should have seen us. You would not have seen us," Strong Bull boasted. "Our warpaint was like sun and shadow. We stuck bracken ferns in our hair. We were scattered. They were in a line on the path they were making. They did not have a chance."

But Strong Bull got no applause of howls and foot-stamping from the warriors of this camp for any part of his story.

Drakey said, "I have not spoken to you since your betrayal of the safe passage agreement. A year and most of two seasons have passed. Six chiefs have died since then, and many warriors. For what? You are still fighting humans now, humans who otherwise would have gone to Upriver last year. Do you really believe that you can kill them all?"

"We did this time," said the high chief.

"I doubt that," said the high shaman. "I know that your forces did not kill as many humans on the boats as you like to claim. I have dreamed this. The humans who made it to Upriver are angry because you denied them honorable defeat. Each time a few more humans slip away with a new tale of battle, they all become angrier. Maybe they even know how Canticle died, a captive in single combat with you, fighting sword to spear with his unskilled arm. I do not think they can return to make war. But the sword you gave Canticle to use was not his own. Where is Canticle's sword? The prophecy about your death could come true if a few strong and clever warriors returned from Upriver with Canticle's sword to surprise and kill you."

"You twist the combat into something dishonorable," said one of Strong Bull's young warriors. "Strong Bull also fought with his unskilled arm. I saw this myself."

"I did not hear it that way," said Drakey. "The humans in Upriver might not hear it that way either."

"I do not fear my death," Strong Bull said firmly. But he did fear something, which Glowfly was trying to perceive while he spoke. "I will fight and kill until I am sure myself that the humans cannot return to make war."

"You are afraid to be wrong," Glowfly said.

"Ah," said Drakey.

Strong Bull was silent.

Drakey said, "With your heart closed, you made a false peace. You fought a trickster's war. You were not satisfied when the humans abandoned their keep. You should have stopped fighting then. You were not satisfied with Canticle's death. You continued fighting. The more you fight, the harder it is to stop. You think you know enough that there is nothing you must learn. But the spirits will teach you, in life or in death. This is your fear."

"What did they tell you to teach me?" Strong Bull asked.

"That goblins and humans are the same inside. A human who

makes a vision quest will find his totem. If this human is important to the spirits, the real animal will come. If this human lives the life of the spirit that we live, then he is a goblin, and should be welcome to live on Goblin Plain. Two such goblins brought this vision to this camp. We danced the dream. It is true. Great Mother Cat brought a solid fangcat to the dance circle to tell us so. You must sit peace with these people. Their small example will end the war. Perhaps no such war will ever be fought again."

Strong Bull grunted. "Who are these people?"

"They are here," said Drakey.

Rockdream and Coral, who had been sitting with Antelope, Little Ant, and Sees Far's family, stood and raised their hands in greeting. They no longer wore red, but were dressed like everyone else. Coral's necklace was made of drakey bones. Wedge also stood and raised his hand.

"They are my friends," said Drakey.

After hesitating, Henna stood and raised her hand. She was fast becoming friends with Coral. Glowfly was sure that Henna would move to their camp. She would miss her.

Drakey continued, "The curse of the broken peace circle may be ended by sitting a new circle that includes people from both sides who sat the broken one, and people from both sides who refused to do so. One of Rockdream's people sat the broken circle. By sitting a real peace with them, you can end the curse."

"How many people follow you?" Strong Bull asked Rockdream.

"Maybe ten others. Of course, I hope more will join us."

Strong Bull laughed. "And for this that curse is broken? Very well, Chief Rockdream, I will sit peace with you and your people."

"What if they become a camp of several hundred?" asked one of Strong Bull's warriors.

The high chief's response reminded Glowfly of the way her father, Screaming Spear, used to set limiting conditions after being persuaded to grant permission. "Most camps now have forty tents or a few more. Yours must never have more than twenty."

"I accept this," Rockdream said.

"Your hunting ground is between the Blue and Goblin Rivers, no more than a half-day's walk from the meeting place of these rivers. Your fishing water is the Blue River. When you leave your hunting ground, you must wear the red of messengers. You must live the life of the spirit."

"They will live the life of the spirit as given to them in the vision," Drakey interrupted. "No captive animals, no walled houses, no farms. Gift exchange must be open-hearted. But they will use the weapons they know how to use for hunting, and the women who are hunters will continue to hunt."

"You should not object to this," Glowfly said. "You yourself have used human weapons in battle. I have saved a whole camp by acting as a warrior when the men refused to believe my vision."

Strong Bull would never admit it, even to himself, but he was a little afraid of Glowfly. She had to be careful what she did and said around him lest they become enemies. This gave her voice more power when she did speak out.

"You have all danced the vision. This is how it is." Strong Bull was making the statement and asking the question at the same time, for he knew the truth but did not quite accept it.

"This is how it is," said Chief Beartooth. "This is what the spirits want us to do."

91.

At dawn on the day of the fall equinox, long rolls of thunder and dark clouds spreading from the west announced the first rain in more than a month. Salmon was on the platform of her hut, with Feathergrass.

"Coral and Rockdream are coming back today," she said, a statement she would repeat in every conversation she had that morning. "It always rains the day they return."

"What kind of news do you think they will bring?" Feathergrass asked. He had dreamed something disturbing, which he hoped Salmon would have patience to discuss, but this idea disturbed him more.

"I do not know, because I do not think I want to know," she replied.

"I feel the same way."

"Look, if you do not want to go with them to play at being goblins, do not go. I am Coral's best friend, and I am not going, at least not until I am convinced she can make this crazy notion work. Someone has to stay here, just to make sure that she and those who go with her will be welcome to return."

"I must go," Feathergrass said. "Loon tells me I must sit the new peace circle. If I stay here or try to go anywhere else, I will die, and the visions I had in my sickness will go on forever, and there will be nothing else. Gods and goddesses, I had a bad night! This thunder! I was lying on a bed in the settlement surrounded by priests and priestesses who were trying to take Loon away from me. I must have told you that story. It was after I was captured and released by Strong Bull. I was supposed to persuade Canticle to accept the Upriver resettlement offer. Do you remember? Well, in my dream this morning they were not priests, but demons. Their faces were like river lizards."

Salmon laughed. "River lizards dressed as priests? Oh, that is funny. It may not have seemed funny while you were dreaming it, but think about it for a moment."

"When I realized for what they were, they kept saying that I was dead, and now they would have me forever. I could not move."

"Feathergrass, the spirit world is not like that, not unless you want it to be like that. Even when you are dead, you can change what you experience. If you practice changing your dreams, death will seem less fearsome."

"But Mother Cedar says—"

"Oh, what does Mother Cedar not say?" Salmon interrupted. "Atone for the wrongs you have done? Choose an appropriate penance or you will suffer for a much longer time? Well, what did she tell you to do? I am sure it was not to become a goblin."

"She suggested I become a priest."

"Oh, bloody death! Well, your dream this morning warned you against that, by showing you the true nature of the clergy."

"Salmon!"

She laughed.

"I know becoming a priest is useless," Feathergrass said. "I knew several priests at the settlement who felt as tortured and twisted as I feel now."

"Let me help you do something about those dreams," Salmon urged him. But when he realized that this involved entering trance and confronting the demons, he became too frightened to enter trance, despite Salmon's assurance that she would be in the vision with him, to help him fight them.

"Thank you for trying to help," he said, and jumped off the platform into the rain.

By this time, all the villagers had carried in everything they did not want to get wet, and were back inside their huts with bowls of breakfast stew. Even Birdwade and Holdfast, who had been tending the cookfire, had gone in. Feathergrass tipped the lid of the big cauldron and sniffed. He was not hungry, but ladled a small serving into his cup anyway. Climbing onto the platform of his own hut, he sat down in his wet clothes and stared at the rain.

It stopped a few hours later, and shortly after that, Coral, Rockdream, and Wedge returned, just as Salmon had predicted. Almost immediately the village had another meeting. Despite Strong Bull's alleged acceptance of Rockdream as a Goblin Plain chief, everyone said more or less the same thing they had said before. Ironweed and Stonewater thought becoming goblins was a good idea; Birdwade's family would follow wherever Rockdream and Coral led them; and other opinions varied from sympathetic to denouncing.

The strongest argument against their plan was Strong Bull's consistent dishonesty: the broken peace circle, the false safe passage agreements.

"Yes, we are taking a chance," Rockdream admitted. "But those people were human leaders. They did not know their totems. They certainly were not acknowledged by a physical manifestation of the Great Mother Cat while doing a spirit dance."

"Why make so much of a fangcat's stupid mistake?" someone said.

Feathergrass said, "I think this time Strong Bull will keep his agreement. If he and I are the two people from the broken peace who must sit the new peace that the spirits are trying to put together, well, maybe I know how he feels. Maybe he has dreams like mine that frighten him awake in the dark night. Maybe he knows what his death will be like. Maybe he is afraid to go to sleep. All right, he is stronger than I am, and less sensitive, but his deeds were worse than mine, so it balances out."

This sounded less persuasive than Feathergrass had hoped. He just was not good at speaking to a group when his feelings were strong. But Coral appreciated his attempt. For a moment, she looked at him with such empathy and love that she seemed more beautiful than any other woman he had ever seen.

"I cannot argue with your dream," he muttered.

The meeting went on. It ended. The ones who were going to become goblins crowded into Rockdream and Coral's hut for instructions about what to bring along, how to retailor their leather clothes to goblin specifications, and so on.

When this was over, Coral had a long, private talk with Feathergrass about Henna and Glowfly. Henna was alive, and considering joining their camp. She had recovered from the spear wound, though she was slightly lame, and had a year-old daughter named Jay, by her goblin husband, Lizard Toes.

Feathergrass could not imagine how Henna had come to love this man who had claimed her as a captive wife while she lay unconscious and while Strong Bull was killing her human husband, Keg, and her friend Scoff. And Lizard Toes had gotten Henna pregnant while she was still barely able to walk, and living in the midst of war. But she loved him as much as she had loved Keg. Lizard Toes was killed in battle the night Feathergrass's platoon tried to massacre Condor's Camp. Somehow Henna's spirit beast had helped her keep her mind and heart.

Glowfly was a shamaness of Beartooth's Camp who would be part of the peace circle. She was Coral's friend, and Henna's closest friend. During the war she had been Chief Condor's wife.

"Oh, bloody death!" said Feathergrass. "Does she know?"

"Yes," Coral said. "She will not forgive you for the deed, but she wants to sit peace with you."

"Strong Bull killed my wife. I killed Glowfly's husband. Now we all sit peace together."

"Do not do it just because you fear spiritual punishment," said Coral. "Find a reason that comes from your strength."

92.

Day after day of their journey through the swamp, Coral urged Feathergrass to let her guide him on a vision quest. Birdwade and Holdfast told him what a wonderful experience it was. Even Ironweed— Could anyone imagine a man so unimaginative, so unchanged by all the things he had experienced, as Ironweed the Bookkeeper? Yes, he had become a hunter and fishcatcher in a village in the swamp, but his mind still approached any problem, even the question of whether to become one of Rockdream's goblins, as a tally of income and expenses. That is, until now. Now he was babbling on and on about his vision of being a fierce fangcat in the shimmering starlit spirit world.

"Maybe the others enjoyed the vision quest, but I am not ready," Feathergrass told Coral. "I—I am too frightened of what I may find."

While the others set up camp, he and Coral were sitting together on a log, looking east across the marsh. The pale gibbous moon seemed to brighten as the sky dimmed through twilight toward night. A white egret made a strange cry as it flapped to a landing in the reeds.

"Maybe your totem is something like that bird," Coral said.

"I never dream of flying," he said. "If my totem were a bird, I think I would sometimes dream of flying."

"What are your best dreams about?" she asked.

"I have no good dreams. For the past several nights I have not dreamed at all. I like it that way. Why should I want to stir things up again?"

"To end the numbness and make yourself feel alive again. Ah, yes, it hurts, but you must do it." Was Coral imitating Loon's accent, or was that really Loon's voice? "Come with me, come, we have someplace to go." Coral and Loon were both short, slender women with curly hair. In the moonlight, the woman in a short goblin dress who jumped off the log could have been either of them.

She took his hand. "Do you see where we must go? Do you see the path?" Her voice was Loon's.

Something on the ground was reflecting the moonlight. It was not water, for it made no splash when he tapped it with his foot. "Step lightly," she said. After a while, it looked as though the glittery path he was walking on was a few inches above the path of dried mud between the reeds. Now they were standing on shimmering light above the tops of the reeds.

"All right, you got me into a vision," Feathergrass said.

"Where else could we meet?" asked Loon. "You are alive, I am dead. You married another wife and now she is dead too, but still you look for me. Ah, such love!" She circled into his arms, stood on tiptoes, and kissed him slowly, deeply, vibrantly. "See what you have been missing for fear? But we have someplace to go. This spirit plain is much bigger and flatter than any place on the curved solid world. It touches that world wherever you are and goes to the sky place and beyond."

Hand in hand they walked the path of light, higher and higher over the marsh, higher and higher over the spreading grassland and dark rivers of Goblin Plain.

"If you stop looking down and look around, maybe you can start to see this world," Loon told him.

This was the shimmering star plain, surrounded by vague, dark mountains. Here the spirit beasts lived. First to come were the wolves, always restless, always curious. Feathergrass was not one of their children. Then he and Loon met a herd of great elk browsing through the grass. They welcomed Loon, who was a daughter of their mighty antlered chief, and told her that her husband's people lived in the forested foothills of the mountains. This was a long journey.

But time is timeless on the star plain, and soon Loon and Feathergrass were coming near the forest. A huge mother bear with twin cubs, all shaggy and shadowy, came out of the dark trees.

Suddenly Feathergrass found himself drawing his sword to parry Chief Condor's thrusting spear. Condor jerked back on the spear to hook the sword. Feathergrass lunged forward, Condor knocked him down, Feathergrass rolled aside and jumped to his feet. They circled each other. Feathergrass said something. He noticed the spirit bear inside Condor.

Now this Great Mother Bear loomed over Feathergrass. Would she punish him in some terrible way for killing one of her children? She stared at him for a moment more, then grunted, turned aside, and led her two cubs away. These cubs were bigger than any bear Feathergrass had ever seen in the solid world.

Now Feathergrass and Loon entered the forest. Once they were inside, it looked no darker than the open plain. Those who can see, can see whatever there is, in the spirit world.

The unicorn appeared first as a vibrant patch of light, a liquid movement shaping a horned, three-toed horse, the grace of a unicorn from the solid world transmuted to dream. When Feathergrass embraced the unicorn's head and touched the horn, he fell into a deeper trance vision, which he could not afterwards remember.

Feathergrass woke from chill to find himself slumped forward, still sitting on the log. Coral was gone; his bedding was neatly folded where she had been sitting. From his vision he understood that this was a power place, a spot where the spirit plain touched the solid world. Coral had brought him here and talked to him about his dreams, and his beloved Loon's spirit had come to him and guided him through the vision. Now, did Coral think he should sleep here, or had she just brought his bedding so that he could find it easily?

"I have seen my vision," he told himself.

He carried his bedding back to camp and went to sleep.

93.

At noon on the day of the first full moon of fall, by human reckoning the 193rd day of the 202nd year, High Shaman Drakey drew a circle of chalk dust on the cleared ground, just inside a circle of fourteen other goblins, eight of them formerly humans of Newport. At Feathergrass's suggestion, the two groups making peace were not clustered on opposite sides of the circle, but thoroughly mixed. The sky was also like this, with shifting patches of gray cloud and clear blue. It was pleasantly cool. Nearby to the east was a particularly beautiful oak tree. A quarter mile to the south was the Blue River. The poles and mammoth hides for three tents lay on the ground with many packs and bundles. Here the apprentice shamaness Little Ant was playing a quiet game with the three children, Ripple, Wedge, and Jay.

Drakey did not have the people step over the chalk circle, as Sees Patterns had done, but left a small gap, which they entered in file as if climbing through the doorway of a tent. Then Drakey finished drawing the circle, told them to be seated, and took his place between Stonewater and Chief Skyrock.

"This is good," Drakey said. "I think all we need to do is speak around the circle, your name and one other sentence. I am High Shaman Drakey. I pray that this vision continues to come true in the best possible way."

"I am Stonewater. I thank you for welcoming me to live in this beautiful place."

"I am Feathergrass. This time—this time will be better."

"I am Chief Sundance. I welcome you to the life of the spirit."

"I am High Chief Strong Bull. I am here at the will of the guardian spirits of this land."

"I am Birdwade. I—I feel really happy."

"I am the shamaness Coral. May we all dream the true dream together."

"I am Chief Beartooth. I welcome your people to Grass, River, Wind."

"I am Ironweed. I feel renewed."

"I am Rockdream—Chief Rockdream. I have come home."

"I am the shamaness Glowfly. May our camps dance together next summer on the Scared Ground."

"I am the shaman Split Hoof. I thank those who have brought their experience and wisdom to this circle."

"I am Holdfast. I am open to this new life."

"I am Henna. I am thinking both the small way and the big way."

"I am Chief Skyrock. I also welcome this new camp."

Now they clasped hands and closed their eyes. The vision was the river of light that flows forever, hand to hand, heart to heart, binding these people to the new peace.

94.

Rockdream's Camp started out with more people than Loop Lake Village had started with, but for the first few months it did not grow, and supporting such a small group here was harder. At Loop Lake they had hunted deer, pigs, and occasionally drakeys. Here the only animals of comparable size were the antelopes, which were hard to stalk or surprise, and incredibly fast.

To hunt bigger game such as aurochs or quagga, at least six had to go out, leaving only Holdfast to guard Birdwade and the children. One time when they did this, a cranky old bull mammoth came to camp. Birdwade grabbed Jay; Ripple ran with her, and Holdfast grabbed Wedge and ran in a different direction. Fortunately, the mammoth neither chased them nor trampled the camp, but merely browsed a while on the oak tree. The frustrating truth was, even their whole camp together could not have killed or driven away this mammoth without taking great risk.

The only efficient way to kill small game such as hares was to trap them, but the camp would not do this, for it was against the law of the spirit. Once in a while, either Coral or Feathergrass would manage to stun or kill one with a thrown rock.

Most of the time they ate fish. But their diet was more balanced than it had been in the swamp, for here they had the wild grain, which Birdwade made into the most delicious flatbread.

About once a month, High Shaman Drakey came to camp. The first time, a few weeks after the peace circle, he taught Coral some ceremonies and dances to do for the spirits of Beadback's people, on the night of the next full moon. Each time after that, he taught her more things to do, appropriate to the coming moon.

Glowfly came once to visit, accompanied by Gray Lizard and another warrior. She also taught Coral some things, and told them all an old story about the ice people.

Gorge's Camp, which was across the river, midway between their own camp and Beartooth's, sent a messenger named Tusk, with a pouch of opal and turquoise pebbles from a gully in the Gray Hills, to open a gift exchange. When Tusk ate his first loaf of Birdwade's flatbread, he said, "You must find something to give our camp, soon. I want to come back here to eat some more of these."

The people of Rockdream's Camp considered and discussed what might be an appropriate exchange gift. Then one day their hunters shot at two antelopes, and by luck downed them both. While feasting on one, they smoked the other. The next day, Ironweed, Stonewater, and Feathergrass packed the smoked meat to a place across the river from Gorge's Camp. They got the attention of Gorge's scouts, who got a canoe and ferried them across the swollen river. The goblins of Gorge's Camp were delighted with this gift. Antelope was a delicacy, hard for anyone to kill.

"We had better give you a big canoe," said Gorge. "Next time you can fill it with gifts for us."

He did not really expect this. In the gift exchange, it was traditional to make up a selfish reason for a generous gift.

Rockdream's people used this canoe, on days when the winter's flood subsided, to fish in the current where the big ones swam. One day while Rockdream, Holdfast, and Henna were out fishing, they saw a small human sailboat tacking against the current toward them.

Its captain and crew of five were quite surprised to encounter three apparent goblins who turned out to be people from Newport. "We thought we would try our luck sailing for Upriver now," said the captain. "Most of the goblin warriors should be hunting far from the river, and might be less likely to get us. But this current is a struggle."

"It gets worse farther upstream," said Henna. "I do not think you will be able to run the pass."

These people were from Lieutenant Hardtack's Village, founded soon after the betrayal of the safe passage agreement. They had each caught swamp sickness there last summer, and they knew that catching it a second time was always fatal.

Rockdream explained the peace agreement between his people and Strong Bull and Drakey. "What we are doing, you can do," he said. "You can make the vision quest. You can become goblins."

"No, thank you," said the captain. "I trust my luck sailing this swollen river more than I would ever trust another one of Strong Bull's agreements. He may kill us, but at least he will not make fools of us first."

But their luck with the swollen river was bad. Two days later, a storm swept them back downstream, sails furled, sailors struggling to keep the boat from spinning broadside to the flood.

Birdwade and Coral, working under the cookfire awning, saw them pass, but there was nothing anyone could do.

This same flood brought the log which became Rockdream's Camp's first totem pole. Drakey told Coral how to make the carving, by painting fat on the places to be hollowed out, soaking the rest of the wood with water, carefully setting the fat afire, putting the fire out, and scraping out the ashes. Father Condor's wings were carved separately, then notched and pegged in. Then they colored the pole with paints made from bonewhite, charcoal, and red and yellow ochre.

Most of the people of camp were working on this, one cloudy afternoon, when Swanfeather and Flatfish showed up, bringing exciting news from Loop Lake. They had rowed their skiff through the channels and pools of the backwater and marsh, carried it over the rise to the Goblin River, and nearly swamped it rowing across the flood.

"Salmon sent us here to see how it is," said Swanfeather. "She is no longer village master. Her—um—disagreements with Mother Cedar about certain things have made her unpopular, that is, with the newer villagers who came from the war, who outnumber us now. Maybe we will all come here and become goblins."

"That would be wonderful," said Coral.

"The ceremonies we do are spiritually fulfilling," said Birdwade. "You will be happy here."

Swanfeather and Flatfish stayed for several days, went on guided visions to meet their totem beasts, joined a successful auroch hunt that gave the camp a plentiful supply of meat to smoke, then went back to the swamp.

They returned less than a month later, when the midwinter moon was a thin evening crescent. With them came Salmon, Bloodroot, Limpet, Hod, Frond, and Threadleaf. Rather than delay to build canoes, they had walked, which meant detouring far to the north of a direct route.

They had passed near Canticle's dirt-block fortress, abandoned two springs ago and now a ruin slowly melting in the rain.

The goblins of Skyrock's Camp had welcomed them, for they were now dressed like Rockdream's people, and Bloodroot and Salmon wore messenger's red. The travelers spent one night there, and the next morning were ferried across the Goblin River.

"I found my totem the night we spent at Skyrock's Camp," said Salmon. "I am a daughter of Great Mother Wolf. She told me—

Let me explain that I was bleeding two weeks before, when Swanfeather and Flatfish came back with the news. I felt so glad. I did not want to wait another month, but gave Bloodroot my pouch of freedomwort right then. What Mother Wolf told me is that we have already done it. We should have a child sometime next fall."

"That—that is wonderful," said Rockdream. "I mean, I am glad that you have such confidence in my peace."

"But you were expecting me to be the mighty hunter you knew at Loop Lake, and here I am, about to be complaining of morning sickness, stumbling on my feet, and burdened with a baby after that," Salmon said. "Listen, chief, I am as tough as you, or more so. I cannot promise that my pregnancy will never keep me from hunting, but I intend to do my share."

"Must I apologize for my unvoiced thoughts?" Rockdream asked.

"Yes, if you must think them so loudly."

"Oh, stop it, you two!" Coral said. "Give my husband credit for the thought he did voice. It really is wonderful that you have so much confidence in our peace. How many Newport women living anywhere have dared to conceive a child in the three years since the city fell? The only one I know of is Henna, who was living with Lizard Toes at Condor's Camp."

"I am no longer a Newport woman, but a woman of Grass, River, Wind," Henna corrected. "But not many goblin women have had children either. I was a captive wife. I did what my husband chose. But I am so glad that he wanted to have a child."

"I cannot imagine being forced to have a child," said Salmon.

"The custom of taking a captive wife from your enemies' camp is a way of making peace for the future that depends on having children," Henna explained. "Indeed, because Lizard Toes, who lost his family in the massacre of Beadback's Camp, did so, there is now a true child of that camp living here. There are far fewer children of Beadback's Camp left alive than children of Newport. Jay is utterly precious, for she is both. She may even be a reason why Strong Bull made and honors this peace with us."

They all looked at the toddler girl. Ripple was arguing with Wedge about a game they were trying to play with her. Jay decided that she was more interested in her mother, and ran to her.

Salmon said, "I missed having Wedge and Ripple around, more than anyone else. This surprised me, for I never played with them much. But now I look forward so much to having a child of my own."

"So do I," Bloodroot remarked.

Henna was pulling down the top of her dress to free a breast for Jay to nurse. "You will be happy," she said.

APPENDIX ONE

CHRONOLOGY

Year
1. Turtleport, first human settlement east of the sea, founded by Windsong the Mariner and her people, political exiles from the Middle Kingdom.
10. Coveport founded by a group of monotheists, religious exiles from the Middle Kingdom.
14. Settlement of the Two Rivers Valley begins. Some trouble with goblins.
22. Midcoast founded.
23. Southport founded, by commercial interests from the Middle Kingdom.
28. Death of Windsong.
30. First Goblin War begins. Many goblin peoples unite to oppose the spread of the humans.
33. Isle of Hod pirates trouble Southport and Turtleport.
38. After eight years of war and many deaths on both sides, five goblin high chiefs and many chiefs sit the peace circle with the human Lords of Coveport, Midcoast, and Turtle-

port, and many keepholders and village masters. All lands of the Two Rivers Valley, and all lands west of the Foggy Mountains within a hundred miles of the Turtle River Delta, are to be human, and all other lands of the region are to remain goblin. Goblins from the Elk Coast north of Turtleport move to Goblin Plain, and goblins from the Two Rivers Valley move to the Moon Valley, or else east of the Silver Mountains.

44. Bracken, a dragonbound wizard on the Isle of Hod, kills his dragon to gain great power, but the storm he creates devastates Hod Town.

50. Rockport founded.

57. Auroch, a dragonbound witch living in a remote forest near the headwaters of the Bigfish River, is killed by neighboring villagers, but her dragon, Mugwort, escapes.

62. Mugwort attacks and destroys Turtleport. The survivors move to the Two Rivers Valley.

66. The Human War begins, Valley monotheists opposed to Turtleport orthodox.

70. A group of priests and priestesses from both Churches reach a compromise. The monotheists' Lord of Light and Darkness is said to be embodied in the eight gods and goddesses of the Holy Family. The one is worshiped through the eight, and the eight through the one.

71. A private army raised by Baron Whitethorn, a younger son of the Lord of Midcoast, supposedly to attack Mugwort, instead founds a city at the mouth of the Moon River, thus breaking the Great Peace Circle.

72. Whitethorn wins the Moon Valley War: few goblins survive.

107. Human traders build a camp east of the Silver Mountains, with goblin permission, but when this quickly grows to become the city of Upriver, the goblins become alarmed.

117. Blue River Goblins attack Upriver.

120. Humans found several keeps in the Dragonstone Mountain Country to prevent these goblins from joining the war. The warrior Wentletrap, an exile from Rockport, joins the Upriver army. A brilliant tactician, he is soon appointed general by Lord Starkweather.

123. Pip the Elf persuades the Blue River Goblins to sue for peace. She and Wentletrap muster a private army, kill the dragon Mugwort, and found Newport.

124. Wentletrap and Pip's daughter Blackberry born.
137. About this time Drakey is born.
139. The dragon Redmoon destroys and occupies Southport.
141. Herring born, son of Blackberry and her husband Stock, one of Wentletrap's original warriors.
144. Wentletrap and Pip leave Newport to journey to the country of the elves, but do not return. Stock becomes second Lord of Newport.
149. A female dragon tries to attack Newport and is killed.
155. About this time Screaming Spear is born.
160. Oakspear born, first child of Baron Herring.
162. Pelican born.
164. Fledgeling born.
165. Swordfern born. About this time Strong Bull is born.
168. Crossing, son of Pod, born in Midcoast.
169. Drill born. Canticle born in Midcoast, child of bonded servants.
170. About this time Beartooth and Condor are born.
171. Lupine born, youngest child of Baron Herring.
173. Pod becomes ninth Lord of Midcoast. Canticle's mother dies. His father, Drydock, whose bond is ended, takes him to Newport, a city without bonded servitude. During the voyage, Drydock carefully studies what the mariners do and how they speak, and learns enough to bluff his way into a job as sailor on a Newport riverboat. He boards little Canticle with a storyteller.
175. Birdwade born.
176. Feathergrass and Bloodroot born.
177. Canticle qualifies to become a squire at Newport Castle. Coral born.
178. Rockdream, Salmon, and Ironweed born.
179. Lord Stock's Comet. Swanfeather born.
180. Lord Stock dies. Herring becomes third Lord of Newport. Fledgeling passes her warrior's test at Loop Lake.
181. Battles in the Dragonstone Mountain Country. Glowfly born.
182. The dragon Riversong destroys and occupies Moonport.
183. Lord Pod deposed. His son Crossing, though only 14, becomes tenth Lord of Midcoast.
185. Canticle passes his warrior's test with high distinction.
188. Strong Bull, a young and mighty warrior, becomes High Chief of Goblin Plain by winning a trial defined by the

council of shamans. He ends the petty battles between camps and begins an assertive diplomacy with the human Lords of Newport and Upriver.

189. Feathergrass, dissatisfied with the prospect of life as a herder, becomes a cabin boy aboard a riverboat. Coral studies with the old wizard Treeworm and briefly becomes his lover.

190. Marten born, son of Baron Drill.

191. Canticle wins his first grand prize for swordplay in the Newport spring tournament.

192. Feathergrass becomes a mariner and voyages across the sea to the Middle Kingdom and Godsfavor.

193. Canticle becomes a tower lieutenant; Fledgeling is one of his warriors. Strong Bull negotiates a fishing rights agreement with Lord Herring, which many Newport fishcatchers disregard.

194. Rockdream and Salmon pass their warrior's tests. Rockdream lives in Canticle's Tower, becomes Coral's lover. Human sailors and goblin warriors engage in skirmishes over turtle hunting. Salmon becomes a boat guard and marries Bloodroot. Feathergrass marries Loon in Prosperity, a city of Godsfavor. The new agreement between Newport and Goblin Plain ends the Turtle Crisis.

195. Rockdream marries Coral, becomes a guard at Eastgate. Feathergrass and Loon voyage together to Lizard River, a city of Jade Forest. Birdwade's daughter Ripple born that winter.

196. Chief Screaming Spear tries to close his camp to human traders. Beartooth, who opposes this, challenges him for the leadership and wins. Feathergrass and Loon voyage back to Godsfavor. Their ship is swept off course by a storm and attacked by Cape Horn pirates.

197. Feathergrass and Loon voyage across the sea to Newport, where she becomes a favorite at Lord Herring's court. Coral becomes pregnant. At the end of winter, she and Rockdream journey with High Shaman Drakey to Goblin Plain.

198. They spend two weeks at Beartooth's Camp, then return to Newport. Wedge born that summer. Lord Herring's Comet followed by a hard winter.

199. *Spring.* The dragon Riversong besieges and destroys Newport, killing Lord Herring, most of his family, and most of the population. Rockdream and Salmon desert.

General Canticle evacuates the city. Rockdream's people and Daffodil's crew build Sharp Bend Village. *Summer.* Rockdream's people move to Loop Lake. Swamp sickness kills many boat people. Drill tries to establish a settlement at the First Cataract. *Fall.* Canticle's army builds a dirt-block keep. Strong Bull protests. Feathergrass marries Fledgeling. *Winter.* Truce negotiations culminate in a peace circle. Arch and Coldspray meet Lord Crossing of Midcoast.

200. *Spring.* The auroch hunt, the Wolf Dance, the sick woman. Arch and Coldspray detained in Bridgetown. Strong Bull attempts a siege of Canticle's Keep. Battle of Beadback's Camp. *Summer.* A drought minimizes swamp sickness. Mother Cedar comes to Loop Lake. Arch and Coldspray meet Lord Blackwood of Upriver. The mammoth hunt. Arch and Coldspray captured by warriors of Strong Bull's Camp. What happened to Foam's platoon. Battle of Charging Elk's Camp. Glowfly's spirit warning. Condor's people dance the storm. *Fall.* Henna becomes pregnant. Holdfast and Birdwade. Canticle's army moves against Quagga's Camp. Fledgeling's platoon and Hooked Beak. Strong Bull attacks the Winter Boat Camp. *Winter.* Drill retreats to the backwater. The *Great Stag's* unusual crew. Battle of Condor's Camp. Feathergrass deserts. The long siege. Birdwade and Holdfast move to Driftwood's Village.

201. *Spring.* Splash's swamp sickness. Breaking of the safe passage agreement. Hardtack's Village founded. Human raiders attack Beartooth's Camp. Strike and Wolfkiller at the mouth of the Goblin River. *Summer.* Strike and Wolfkiller move up the Blue River. Henna's daughter Jay born. Twelve get swamp sickness at Loop Lake; seven die. Graywall and Canticle move up the Blue River. *Fall.* Salmon and Bloodroot in the Foggy Mountains. Coral and Salmon visit Driftwood's Village. Birdwade and Holdfast return to Loop Lake.

202. *Summer.* Eleven people at Loop Lake get swamp sickness, including Feathergrass and Wedge. Coral summons the Power That Will Help. Meeting with Strong Bull at Beartooth's Camp. *Fall.* New peace circle. Start of Rockdream's Camp. *Winter.* The sailboat and the totem pole. Salmon's group joins Rockdream's Camp.

APPENDIX TWO

THEOLOGY

1.

The Lord of Light and Darkness is the god of the monotheists. In this heresy's original form, God is an artist, who created the universe with his mind and hands like a sculptor, and then breathed life into it. In the traditional view, the universe is not a creation but a growth, and the deities of the Holy Family are parts of this growth. In the reformed view, the Lord of Light and Darkness is the spirit who gives life to the universe's growth.

These are the goddesses and gods of the Holy Family, their attributes, their globes, and how they correspond to the positions in Lady Bluestar's card-reading:

The Nameless Mother, the world, the significator.

Sky the Father, the sun, the source.

Wind the Hunter, first daughter, the moon, the goal.

Fire the Warrior, second daughter, red planet, the obstacle.

Lake the Lover, third daughter, brighter twilight planet, the helper.

Thunder the King, first son, big planet, the fate.

Cloud the Wizard or Messenger, second son, dimmer twilight planet, the chance.

Mountain the Priest, third son, slow planet, the meaning.

2.

Totem beasts are guardian spirits of the land and the people and animals who live there. They preserve the balance. Each person has a totem inside. A powerful shaman may be adopted by a second totem, or by even more. The danger is that the shaman will lose himself and become the tool of the spirits. This can also happen to a shamaness.

These are some totem beasts: Great Mother Wolf, whose people drove away the ice spirits. Great Father Elk, who stands guard. Great Father Condor, who sees everything. Great Mother Raven, who talks about everything. Great Mother Bear, who is powerful and unpredictable. Great Mother Fangcat, another warrior. Great Father Otter and Great Father Weasel, both tricksters. Great Father Unicorn, who sometimes runs and sometimes fights.

On Goblin Plain, Mother Mammoth, Mother Auroch, Father Quagga, and Father Antelope are spirit beasts who seldom become totems, because the goblins are always hunting and eating their people.

INDEX OF NAMES

With the following exceptions, places mentioned in the text may be found on the map.

Rockport, Coveport, and Bigfish are cities of the Two Rivers Valley north of Midcoast. The Dragonstone Mountains are north of Upriver. Places west of the sea include these countries (and their cities): Four Lakes Kingdom, Middle Kingdom (Great Rock), Jade Forest (Lizard River), Cape Horn, and Godsfavor (Prosperity).

The following list briefly identifies every character named in the text:

AGATE, human woman, ruling Lady of Coveport.

ANTELOPE, goblin woman of Beartooth's Camp, Screaming Spear's wife, Glowfly's mother.

ARCH, human man, warrior and diplomat serving General Canticle.

BAND, 2nd c. human man, weaponmaker who made Lord Herring's sword.

BEADBACK, goblin man, chief of a Blue River camp, sat the broken peace circle.

BEARTOOTH, goblin man, chief of a Blue River camp, Cicada's husband.

BIG CLAW, goblin man, chief of a Goblin River camp, sat the broken peace circle.

BIG ONE TUSK, bull mammoth of a herd near Charging Elk's Camp.

BIG TOAD, goblin boy, Screaming Spear's son, Glowfly's brother.

BIRDWADE, human woman of Loop Lake, former baker, Ripple's mother.

BLACKBERRY, 2nd c. woman, daughter of Wentletrap and Pip, Stock's wife, Herring's mother.

BLACKWOOD, human man, fourth Lord of Upriver.

BLOODROOT, human man of Loop Lake, sailor, Salmon's husband.

BLOODSTORM, human man, hunting group leader at Canticle's Keep.

BLUESTAR, human woman, Lady of Midcoast, Crossing's wife.

BOLD, goblin man, warrior of Charging Elk's Camp.

BONEDANCE, goblin man, chief of a Blue River camp.

BOTTOM, human man, warrior of Canticle's Keep, joins Fledgeling's hunting group.

BRAMBLE, human boy, son of Henna and Keg, died of swamp sickness.

BRIGHT OWL, goblin man, warrior of Mammoth's Camp, afterwards chief.

BRINE, human man, priest of Driftwood's Village.

BROWN FOX, goblin man, Screaming Spear's son, Glowfly's brother.

CANTICLE, human man, general of Newport, founder of Canticle's Keep, sat the broken peace circle.

CAPSTONE, human man, hunting group leader at Canticle's Keep.

CEDAR, human woman, priestess who comes to Loop Lake.

CHARGING ELK, goblin man, chief of a Goblin River camp, sat the broken peace circle.

CICADA, goblin woman, shamaness, Beartooth's wife, Glowfly's teacher.

COLDROCK, human man, former dockhand, hunter at Canticle's Keep, Harmony's husband.

COLDSPRAY, human man, warrior and diplomat serving General Canticle.

COLD WINTER, goblin man, chief of a Goblin River camp, sat the broken peace circle.

COMFREY, human man, hunter in Fledgeling's group.

CONCH, human man, lieutenant serving Lord Drill, sat the broken peace circle.

CONDOR, goblin man, chief of a Goblin River Camp, Picks Herbs' husband, afterwards Glowfly's husband, sat the broken peace circle.

CORAL, human woman of Loop Lake, witch and hunter, Rockdream's wife.

COWARD. Lord Coward is Strong Bull's name for Lord Drill.

CRABCLAW, human man, sailor aboard Frogsong's *Great Stag*.

CREVICE, human man, warrior of Canticle's Keep, joins Fledgeling's hunting group.

CROSSING, human man, tenth Lord of Midcoast, Bluestar's husband.

DAFFODIL, human woman, riverboat captain, Sharp Bend village master, died from a festering wound.

DEAD CENTER, human man, forward dragon gunner aboard the *Golden Turtle*.

DRAKEY, goblin man, High Shaman of Goblin Plain.

DRIFTWOOD, human man, former merchant, master of a Spirit Swamp village.

DRILL, human man, Lord of the Newport exiles, Herring's son, sat the broken peace circle.

DRYDOCK, human man, former bonded servant, Canticle's father.

DRYMOSS, human woman, hunter in Fledgeling's group, Jib's wife.

ELKHORN, goblin man, warrior of Strong Bull's Camp.

ENDIVE, human woman, cook at Canticle's Keep.

ENEMIES RUN, goblin man, warrior of Charging Elk's Camp.

FAIRWIND, human man, merchant of Newport, killed by Riversong.

FEATHERGRASS, human man, former mariner, warrior at Canticle's Keep, Fledgeling's husband, sat the broken peace circle.

FERNBANK, human woman, priestess of Newport.

FLATFISH, human man of Loop Lake, fishcatcher, Swanfeather's husband.

FLEDGELING, human woman, lieutenant at Canticle's Keep, Feathergrass's wife, sat the broken peace circle.

FOAM, human man, lieutenant at Canticle's Keep, sat the broken peace circle.

FORWARD, human man, hunter at Canticle's Keep, son of Coldrock and Harmony.

FROGSONG, human woman, captain of the *Great Stag*, a fishing boat.

FROND, human woman of Loop Lake, Hod's wife.

GAPING WOUND, goblin man, chief of a Bear River camp, sat the broken peace circle.

GILL, human woman, hunter in Fledgeling's group.

GLOWFLY, goblin woman, shamaness from Beartooth's Camp, Quick One's wife, afterwards Condor's wife.

GORGE, goblin man, chief of a Blue River camp.

GRAY LIZARD, goblin man, warrior of Beartooth's Camp.

GRAYWALL, human man, lieutenant at Canticle's Keep, sat the broken peace circle.

GRAY WOLF, goblin man, Strong Bull's father, killed by Fledgeling.

GREASEBURN, human woman, Lord Crossing's private guard.

GREENSWORD, human man, hunter of Driftwood's Village.

GREENWAVE, human woman, rear dragon-gunner aboard the *Golden Turtle*.

HARDTACK, human man, lieutenant at Canticle's Keep.

HARMONY, human woman, weaver, hunter at Canticle's Keep, Coldrock's wife.

HAWTHORN, human man, hunter in Fledgeling's group.

HEAVY DEW, goblin woman, shamaness of Condor's Camp.

HEMSTITCH, human woman, hunter in Fledgeling's group, Scoff's wife.

HENNA, human woman, hunter in Fledgeling's group, Keg's wife.

HERRING, human man, third Lord of Newport, killed by Riversong. He was father of Oakspear, Pelican, Swordfern, Drill, and Lupine.

HIDDEN POOL, goblin woman from Beadback's Camp at Condor's Camp, Lizard Toes' sister.

HOD, human man of Loop Lake, Frond's husband.

HOLDFAST, human man of Driftwood's Village.

HOOKED BEAK, goblin man, chief of a Goblin River camp, sat the broken peace circle.

HOT WOLF, goblin man, warrior of Charging Elk's Camp.

HUNGRY SNAKE, goblin man, warrior of Gorge's Camp.

HUNTING STAR, goblin man, warrior of Charging Elk's Camp.

IRIS, human woman, warrior of Canticle's Keep.

IRONWEED, human man of Loop Lake, formerly Fairwind's bookkeeper, Stonewater's husband.

JASMINE, human woman, priestess and healer at Canticle's Keep.

JAY, half-human, half-goblin girl, daughter of Henna and Lizard Toes.

JETTY, human woman, warrior of Newport, commander of half the Citizens' Army during the retreat.

JIB, human man, hunter in Fledgeling's group, Drymoss's husband.

KEG, human man, hunter in Fledgeling's group, Henna's husband.

LAUREL, human woman, fishing boat captain.

LEAST OWL, goblin man, chief of a Goblin River camp.

LIMPET, human woman of Loop Lake.

LITTLE ANT, goblin girl of Condor's Camp, becomes Glowfly's apprentice.

LIZARD TOES, goblin man, warrior from Beadback's Camp at Condor's Camp.

LONG FLOOD, goblin man, old warrior at Beartooth's Camp.

LONG HOWL, goblin man, chief of a Goblin River camp, sat the broken peace circle.

LOON, human woman, minstrel from Four Lakes Kingdom, Feathergrass's first wife, killed by Riversong.

LUPINE, human woman, Herring's daughter, killed by Riversong.

MAGPIE, human woman of Loop Lake.

MALLOW, human woman, old priestess serving Lord Drill.

MAMMOTH, goblin man, chief of a Blue River camp, sat the broken peace circle.

MARTEN, human boy, Lord Drill's son.

MOONWORT, human woman, witch of Newport, Coral's mother, killed by Riversong.

NETTLE, human woman, hunter in Bloodstorm's group, Splash's wife.

OAKSPEAR, human man, Herring's son, killed by Riversong.

PACKTAIL, human boy, lookout aboard the *Golden Turtle*.

PELICAN, human man, Herring's son, killed by Riversong.

PETREL, human man, acting high priest of Canticle's Keep.

PICKS HERBS, goblin woman, shamaness, Condor's wife.

PIP, early 2nd c. elf woman, Wentletrap's wife.

POACH, human woman, hunter in Fledgeling's group.

QUAGGA, goblin man, chief of a Blue River camp.

QUICK ONE, goblin man, warrior of Beartooth's Camp, Glowfly's husband.

QUIET CAT, goblin man, chief of a Goblin River camp, sat the broken peace circle.

RAVEN, pre-1st c. goblin woman, shamaness of an Elk Coast camp.

REDBARK, goblin man, warrior of Big Claw's Camp, afterwards chief.

REDSPEAR, goblin man, chief of a Bear River camp, sat the broken peace circle.

REEDFLOWER, human woman, riverboat captain in Fledgeling's fleet.

RIPPLE, human girl of Loop Lake, Birdwade's daughter.

RIVERSONG, male dragon, destroyer of Moonport and Newport.

ROCKDREAM, human man of Loop Lake, warrior and hunter, Coral's husband.

SALMON, human woman of Loop Lake, witch and hunter, Bloodroot's wife.

SCOFF, human man, hunter in Fledgeling's group, Hemstitch's husband.

SCREAMING SPEAR, goblin man, former chief of Beartooth's Camp, Antelope's husband, Glowfly's father.

SCUPPIE, human woman, riverboat captain in Fledgeling's fleet.

SEABRAND, human man, riverboat captain in Fledgeling's fleet.

SEES FAR, goblin man, warrior of Beartooth's Camp.

SEES PATTERNS, goblin man, shaman of Strong Bull's Camp, led the broken peace circle.

SHIVER, human man, riverboat captain in Fledgeling's fleet.

SKYROCK, goblin man, warrior, Charging Elk's brother and successor.

SNOWFLAKE, white mare lost by Capstone's hunting group.

SONNET, human woman, warrior of Foam's platoon.

SPINCLOUD, goblin man, warrior of Whitemouth's Camp, afterwards chief.

SPIRAL, 2nd c. human woman, sculptor of the statues in the Newport Rose Garden.

SPLASH, human man, hunter in Bloodstorm's group, Nettle's husband.

SPLIT HOOF, goblin man, shaman of Mammoth's Camp, afterwards of Strong Bull's Camp.

STAR BEAR, goblin man, shaman of Condor's Camp.

STARKWEATHER, early 2nd c. human man, first Lord of Upriver.

STARMOON, human man, legendary wizard west of the sea.

STEPSTONE, human woman, new midpriestess at Sharp Bend.

STOCK, 2nd c. human man, second Lord of Newport, Blackberry's husband, Herring's father.

STONEWATER, human woman of Loop Lake, formerly Fairwind's house servant, Ironweed's wife.

STRIKE, human man, lieutenant at Canticle's Keep, sat the broken peace circle.

STRONG BULL, goblin man, High Chief of Goblin Plain and chief of a Blue River camp, sat the broken peace circle.

SUNDANCE, goblin man, warrior of Condor's Camp, afterwards chief.

SWANFEATHER, human woman of Loop Lake, warrior, Flatfish's wife.

SWORDFERN, human man, Herring's son, killed by Riversong.

SWORDNOTCH, human man, lieutenant at Canticle's Keep, sat the broken peace circle.

TERRAPIN, human man, captain of the *Golden Turtle*.

THORNBUSH, human woman, warrior and hunter who comes to Loop Lake.

THREADLEAF, human man of Loop Lake.

TREEWORM, human man, old wizard of Newport, Coral's teacher.

TUSK, goblin man, warrior of Gorge's Camp.

WALKING TOAD, goblin man, warrior and scout of Condor's Camp.

WAVE, human woman of Sharp Bend, Wren's mother, died of swamp sickness.

WEDGE, human boy of Loop Lake, son of Rockdream and Coral.

WENTLETRAP, early 2nd c. human man, first Lord of Newport, Pip's husband.

WETROCK, human man, riverboat captain in Fledgeling's fleet.

WHITEMOUTH, goblin man, chief of a Blue River camp, sat the broken peace circle.

WHITESTONE, human man, storyteller and diplomat of Canticle's Keep.

WHITETHORN, late 1st c. human man, first Lord of Moonport.

WINDSONG, early 1st c. human woman, mariner, founded Turtleport.

WOLFKILLER, human man, lieutenant at Canticle's Keep.

WOLF WOMAN, a name of respect given to Glowfly by Strong Bull.

WOMAN. Lieutenant Woman is Strong Bull's name for Fledgeling.

WREN, human woman of Sharp Bend, Holdfast's wife, died of swamp sickness.